CRUEL PROVOCATIONS

Cruel Provocations

D. Harrigon

Contents

Was the earth made to preserve
a few covetous, proud men to live at ease;
or was it made to preserve all her children?

Gerard Winstanly 1849

1

A Sickness of Revenge

"Are you heading out, my dear?"

"Yes, Mother."

"Where are you going?"

"I'm going to kill some soldiers, Mother."

"Oh. Well. Have a nice time, dear."

Sadness dulled the edge of Therasia's simmering fury. Her mother was never quite right again after the stroke. Physically, she'd recovered remarkably well thanks to Thera's ministrations. However, mother's long, dark curls frizzed more than flowed, streaked with grey. Her working hands showed more strength than softness. But she stood straight and true in her simple dress and apron, awake before the sun, kneading bread at the counter of her large, rustic kitchen. Thera was proud that she helped her mother recover from something so often fatal or debilitating. That was the catalyst for Thera to commit herself to the medical profession. She sought the Mountain Monks, south of

Lorda, qualified as a surgeon and returned to her little village a few years ago.

But there was still something wrong with Mother. Inside, Therasia felt that this was her mama. Definitely. She was warm and loving, hard-working and forgiving. Strict without being cruel. She always seemed to say exactly what Therasia needed to hear, like she was an extension of Thera's own subconscious. Despite that, Mother sometimes didn't seem to understand all that happened in the world. If the morning went badly this might be the last time Thera ever saw her. Heavy heart pounding out a rhythm of fury, Thera pulled back her determined chin, crossed the kitchen and gave her mother a quick hug, a peck on the cheek. Mother returned the gesture with gentle grace.

"Ah, but you're so skinny! Have you had breakfast? You must eat, Thera! Here, take this." She smiled and handed Thera a chill, stone bottle. "For when you're done. You always get thirsty."

Yes. This was exactly what she would need for later. If she survived.

"Thank you, Mama," she said and tucked the small bottle into the square, leather pouch hanging from her waistband.

Thera crossed to the back door and slipped out into the rear garden. The dark sky held a faint tint of faded orange, promising dawn. Heading down the stone path, the grass brushed all the way up to her knees. Father would be out with his scythe soon. Now the sun shone it was time to make hay. But there would be no rolling in the barn for Thera this year. Not after what the soldiers did.

Beyond the stone wall at the rear, the apple orchard sprawled. The low trees melted into a tangled mass in the indistinct light. Only the scent revealed their nature, crisp and sweet on the cool air. Early-ripening apples beginning to turn. And in other fields, all over the village, grapefruit and cucumbers, broccoli and beets. Therein lay the problem. As late spring faded into summer the city of Tolosa came to negotiate the early harvest. They sent soldiers to guard their strongbox and officers to hammer out a deal.

The city and their hammers.

"Thera!" her father called, emerging to ambush her from the back shed. A candlestick with three stems lit the workshop behind him. A small light and warmth in the pale dawn.

"Ai! Not now, Father!" she said, extending her long stride towards the orchard. He may be the village head man but he was still a farmer and rose early. Especially now, with so much work to do. She expected him to be out in the fields but something needed attention in the workshop.

"Where are you going at this hour?" he called.

"To do my job."

"Someone is ill?" He emerged further into the grass, a wood-chisel in one hand, a look of genuine concern on his face.

"My other job."

"Oh. Have a care! Do not upset the soldiers!"

Thera rounded on him. Her anger rose to burn all thoughts of caution from her mind.

"You ask that of me? Four dead at the hands of those thugs! Kerchiefs up to mask their faces. And you ask me that?"

"Ah, now. I have sent a letter. The commandant, he will visit this afternoon!"

"Then I will give you something to talk about!" She turned, stalking apace and headed for the small, wooden gate in the low, dry-stone wall.

"Thera! No! You must-"

Something stirred. A flicker of that other thing, that strangeness living inside her. She turned a glare upon the local head man. "Do not speak again!"

Her father recoiled, blowing and blustering. He said nothing, either through fear or because the inkling of a spell slipped out and silenced him.

Crossing into the orchard, Thera headed out. From the ordered rows of the apple trees she paced into the chaos of the broad coppice that backed her small village, coating the hill behind, shading the village stream that fed the little settlement. Shadows still lay heavy under the canopy. That suited her mood.

Veering towards her prepared trap, Therasia let her threads flow into the world. She found all manner of little animal friends to help her. Some, not so small. She gathered the birds, the spiders, her buzzing jar already tied to her waist. The mad wolf required less subtle nudging but it ran as she herded.

Smaller branches lay scattered among the twigs on the floor of the coppice. She gathered straighter sections and expertly cracked them to form sharp stakes. Heavy, hard wood. They stirred bloody intent as she wrapped strips of rag around to form the handles. Good for murder. Metal would not flow into that ... other realm.

Therasia marched the long way around to her pyre.

The sun had yet to clear the hills but the day already started warming by the time Thera reached her wood piles. It took all of yesterday to properly clear the grass and debris, gather enough fuel for these long, low bonfires. The wood was dry. It would blaze hot and quick. A few fresh leaves on top would generate a bank of smoke far too broad and close to the soldiers' encampment for comfort. There was but one open patch of land between her lure and the gathering of canvas that contained the city-folk. Thera had a spot picked out in that dry, dusty meadow.

The fire caught, quick and fierce. The crackling blaze matched Thera's own mind. She tossed greenery onto the heap, waited to stamp out a few, stray embers, then stalked into her chosen position. The harsh smell of smoke lingered in her nostrils.

She wondered what they would send. A lone scout would be hardly worth the effort. If the scout failed to return, however, they might send numbers of a size that Thera could use to make a statement.

The sun rose.

Strange sounds echoed from behind the ridge, where the track below the hill ended.

A distant thumping began.

It was a squad of twelve supporting two walkers. Boots crunched across the dry hillside accompanied by the loud grating stamp of the iron beasts as they made one step for every three of their support. The buzz from the lightning jars crackled faintly under it all.

This was the first time Therasia experienced these mechanical monstrosities. She felt the weight of each step.

The soldiers glanced at her, standing stark on the dry, rocky meadow.

Breathing even, Thera focused on being part of the world.

The soldiers sang as they marched, women carrying the melody while the men bore the bass:

"A! Ca ira, ca ira, ca ira! (Oh, it'll be fine, it'll be fine, it'll be fine!

"(When the King comes home in peace again!

"(Oh, it'll be fine, it'll be fine, it'll be fine!

"(The mutineers cannot perforce maintain!)"

They sang of drinking to the return of their "King" who was absent since the last great war nearly a century ago. The promise of his return was something the cities used to hold power over those within.

If only they knew...

The soldiers looked, saw her, and dismissed her, like the grass, flowers and weeds dotting the dry slope. She wore a yellow top and green britches. Natural colours like daffodils, marigolds and buttercups. The mask of tree bark helped as did the vines woven through her belt and over one shoulder. Also, none of them concentrated. It was easy to flick their minds away. They sang, comforted in their companionship. Unafraid. Un-alert.

Therasia would make them afraid.

The walkers stamped behind them.

Surprisingly small. Barely wider than Thera could reach, a little over twice her height. The backwards knees on their four legs accentuated their beast-like appearance. Each leg moved, one at a time, in some strange parody of a living thing. They seemed to crouch, traversing the uneven pasturage like dark bugs in a slow scurry. It was the hellish gun, mounted on top, that settled dread over the land. Six barrels that blasted shattering shells into crowds. Death en-masse. The machines' bodies were nought but armoured tubs with three dragoons inside to pilot them and operate those dread cannon. Brass accents glinted against the galvanised steel.

This was a kill squad. A worrying quantity of men and machinery that sent cold into the pit of her stomach to fight with the fire. Her palms sweated at the sight of them but her rage burned too deep for fear to gain purchase. She wanted revenge and cared not if it cost her own life.

Besides, she had a buzzing jar.

The metal beasts lumbered along.

The marching soldiers wore no jackets in deference to the season's heat. Some even rolled the baggy sleeves of their shirts. They retained their long waistcoats in vivid blue with gold piping and hats with brims folded up such that they could carry their muskets on either shoulder. Metal buttons shone bright and polished.

She couldn't take them all. However, she could do some damage. She'd prepared for a fight. This might be too much. They were so desperate to intimidate that they sent two metal monsters and twelve soldiers to investigate what might turn out to be a charcoal burner working an early load.

The woman stood alone in the dry, open meadow. The metal beasts stamped closer and closer.

The foot-soldiers clustered in three groups of four. One group marched behind each stamping monster, carrying their new, three-barrel muskets. Nought but a quick flick of the wrist between each shot. Worrisome in their own right. The last fire-team trailed behind them all. Command and squad support. This group lurked at the back, hiding the adjutant, a signaller, a medic ... and a fusilier with his long, rifled musket.

That's what she feared the most. That sharp-shooter. One single click, from further than she could affect, and it was all over.

Perhaps she should kill him first?

Gathering her resolve Therasia leaned into the else-where, folding away from solid into ... the other. Time slowed. The air became thick about her. She swept up to the troops. Some of them were mid-step, boots hanging in the air, drifting towards the dirt. Some of them laughed, mouths distorted, chests caught mid-pulse, collapsing in strange, slow distortions. One of them spat and the spittle pushed torpidly through her lips. Therasia dragged her feet, kicking up a storm of dust, leisurely trickling skyward from the hillside. One circle around the command team and she dropped the effort, coming back to the same space as the real, both her stakes plunged deep into the fusilier's back, leaning there as she caught her breath.

The dust rose.

Soldiers heard the snap and crack that was the real speed of her dragging in the soil. They glanced about but didn't register what happened. The command team kept walking, confused at the swirl of grit rising around them. The fusilier tried to breathe but coughed loudly. He softened, weakening. As he let his rifle fall, Therasia caught it deftly and aimed, one handed, at the signaller. The first call of alarm came from one of the other fire teams. "FEY!!" Ah. They'd seen her. Therasia flicked the contact on the underside of the rifle. Lightning flashed between the two strange cylinders projecting in a "V" from the back of the barrel. It flashed from the bottom of one to the other, through the barrel, through the powder inside, igniting, exploding. The weapon's kick surprised Therasia such that she dropped the awkward weight. The heavy, lead ball flew wide from the musket, shattering glass tubes on the back of the signaller's large lightning-speaker. Close enough.

Sparks flew. Dust rose.

Planting her feet, the half-fey grabbed both stakes and lifted the dying fusilier. She threw him off at the adjudant. A shot rang out, inaccurate through the dust-screen. Another. Something buzzed past.

A woman screamed, "Hold fire!" Others: "Don't shoot us!" "Hold Fire! Fix bayonets!" That was the shorter caporal. A woman.

Another shot. More orders screamed. By this time, the dying fusilier flattened the officer in charge. Therasia followed up, plunging a stake into the side of her neck just above her officer's pin. The tip cracked into her spine. The officer stared at Therasia in surprised pain, convulsing, dying. Thera felt hot blood slap the side of her hand. Her heart stirred but she had no use for sympathy.

Time to move.

Her plan was ambitious and would likely kill her.

Therasia felt the bloodlust pumping. Probably because of the thread she kept towards that wolf down by the stream, shrouded in mists at the bottom of the slope. Rage demanded she take them all. The medic cowered. The signaller curled up on the ground screaming in panic. Dust rose, starting to dissipate.

She leaned into the elsewhere, folding, thrusting with both legs. She threw a dozen threads out to the starlings she'd brought from the coppice, wings flapping slowly through the air. Another dozen threads.

The city-folke climbed into their metal monsters using steps on the side of the legs. Therasia flung herself at one.

Instead of only using her jump she pulled with her arms against the threads, using the motion to tuck the stakes into their belt-loops. The birds above dipped and adjusted. She used much less strength to cover the distance and was able to aim precisely with one foot.

Then the elsewhere began to shift and flow in a most unnatural way.

It was dangerous to attack the walkers from behind. That's where they kept their lightning jars. She started to lose track of her extremities. The unnatural confinement of the lightning distorted the other world. She fled the horror of it and folded back to the space that had weight and smell.

Fortunately, she was past the nearest group of soldiers. They stared back at the decimated command squad. The walker hid her from the other group on the ground. Momentum carried her. She landed and grabbed at the handhold. Her other hand pulled the knot on the clay jar at her waist.

The walker stopped at the first call, buzzing and crackling, as three dragoons scrambled about inside getting the gun ready. Therasia was able to balance on the single foothold, jump to the one at the front. The pilot yelled something into the body but hadn't closed down the grill. She tossed the jar inside. As it shattered she threw all her threads to the arctic hornets. "Fear! Defend! Kill!" Two dozen angry buzzings grew louder than the lightning jar.

The screams grew louder still.

Hanging off the monster for a moment Therasia caught her breath. The effort drained her but she was young, strong and in the mood to misbehave.

Stakes out.

The fire-teams stared at the remains of the command squad in confusion, rifles up, all peering into the hazy cloud of dust. Then the screams from the walker attracted their attention.

Filling her lungs, Therasia dropped just as the team below her glanced up. She landed beside one fantassin with both pointed, wooden daggers sinking into her back. Kicking up, she knocked a barrel away, extracting her weapons now slick with blood up to the wrappings. The caporal was out of reach, raising her weapon. The last squad member was on the wrong side of the monster's supporting limbs, sprinting around.

A shot fired from the kicked musket, going high. That soldier swung the bayonet down, a desperate slash. The blade locked into the weapon's spine in the middle of the three barrels. Not fast but heavy. Its metal blade sang, wicked sharp. Steel. Therasia threw herself back and away from the slashing edge. She thumped into the monster's leg.

An underhand flick took that one through the liver.

The caporal adjusted her aim. Therasia threw a stake at her but the woman was quick. She jerked herself back, under the flying, wooden spike, eyeballed her shot and fired before she hit the ground. The lead slug shattered against the walker's leg. Shrapnel scraped along Therasia's side. The hot metal caused her to flinch. Blood. The other squad closed in, guns up. She had no weapons left.

Time to go.

The caporal recovered. She grabbed at her rifle and flicked the next barrel around to the lightning pegs at the top. Therasia looked towards the stream at the bottom of the hill, leaned strongly in that direction, and folded. She sprang the other way. The rifle fired. A horrific, hollow boom echoed within the elsewhere. The shot screamed out, unbelievably swift, tearing at the unreal. It flew past Therasia before she'd taken two steps. So fast.

Before she'd taken three, the effort began to tell. Pain screamed from the scrape at her side. Three folds in a row was beyond most witches. Mostly beyond Therasia. She did not have enough breath. The log was close. Too close? Would they see her? She released the thread holding the wolf in place and rushed danger at it. Her trajectory cut perilously close to the caporal. Air could not move into her lungs fast enough. Her muscles began to burn. She flicked her feet onwards using her arms to haul on the birds, keeping her step light and hidden.

Desperate to reach the log, Thera leapt, allowing herself to fall through the fade. The landing might not be pleasant. Grimly, she held onto the fold until she'd almost settled onto the ground, tucked behind her cover, pulling on starlings at the very last moment to soften her crash. As the real crunched back upon her, she slammed into the rocky dust.

Everything hit.

Everything hurt.

Three jumps. Too much noise? Far enough away? Therasia lay panting, small lights dancing in her vision, a desperate hope that her plan would work.

This was always the case. She pushed. She strained. She tried harder than everyone else. No wonder she was so thin. No generous milkmaid's bosom for her. Arms like sticks, legs almost shapeless. No matter how much she ate.

Soldiers yelled, shooting in panic at the landscape. None at her. Confusion reigned.

The log lifted at one end. Therasia painfully shuffled along with her shoulder-blades until she could peer underneath that gap. The soldiers stared streamward. Excellent. She felt the panic of the wolf as it bolted. Would it run into the trees? Would they miss it?

"There! She flees!" cried one.

Everyone looked. Therasia sighed and took the opportunity to scatter the guarding spiders from her mother's stone bottle of creamed fruit she'd hidden under the log. She needed something in her stomach.

"By the stream!" called another. "Hammer and sparks! She turned herself into a wolf!"

Poor pup. She'd wrapped a yellow scarf around its neck and forequarters. An off-cut from old Saliesa's green skirt around the hindquarters completed the look. Yellow and green like her outfit.

Shots cracked out but none of them were snipers. The three-barrelled carbines didn't have the range of the longer, rifled, fusilier's musket.

Therasia gulped the creamy juice through her mask, savouring the silky texture of her mother's old recipe.

The sudden, horrific BOOM! of the walker's six-barrelled long-gun worried the air, causing Therasia to spill. She wiped at the mess and peered under. The huge, steel bullet shrieked towards the running wolf but ditched well short. It struck a stone and shattered into fragments of shrapnel, as was its design. The stench of gunpowder filled the air. The next barrel flicked round on the monster's cannon, aim adjusted. Thera watched the operation of the cannon with interest. A fascinating collection of levers to spin, lock and fire.

BOOM!

Poor, poor little wolf. Rabid, vicious sheep-killer and good riddance. Two birds with one stone. But she couldn't help feeling sympathy.

"All after! All after!" someone called. The soldiers ran obliquely, trained not to get into the line of fire from the cannon. Even the remaining monster crackled and whirred into motion stomping down the slope. Its gun boomed again. So fast.

But one stayed. The caporal who dodged under Therasia's stake. Thera's escape ran close to the woman and the woman felt it. Felt hat flopping about, the last soldier looked everywhere, confused but trusting her gut.

"Wait!" she called to her comrades. Her voice rang surprisingly round and sonorous. "That's just a dog! It's…"

The caporal came from some high-born house. Perhaps one fallen low. Or the woman rebelled against her parents and- Therasia stamped on that ant-trail of thought. This woman was the enemy. Prey for the hunter. Twisting her gaze all about, the caporal even looked behind where her eyes fell on the log. She squinted, puzzled, and flicked the last barrel of her gun around.

Smoke and grime. That was the worst.

Therasia cautiously gulped the last of the drink. The richness of it, her body urgently needed. There was plenty of meat down there. The fusilier hadn't even finished dying. Fresh. But that was the wolf talking. Maybe. Blood still dripped from the scrape along her side. The low shrubbery was a short sprint away. She would die if she tried it.

Yells and shots came from the soldiers running the wrong way. Screams no longer sounded from the remaining walker. Only the low buzz of the arctic hornets. Even if anyone was still alive inside the monster they were swollen, paralysed, and unable to breathe. Death would come soon enough. The caporal stared at the droning behemoth. She turned and charged at the log, bayonet extended, a low roar of deep fury building from her.

Therasia timed it as best she could.

With what little remained of her strength the half-fey flicked the stone bottle at the soldier, catching her on the side of the head. Therasia rolled to her feet. Crack! The gun fired. Therasia's heart leapt into her throat. The shot went wide. A spray of dust.

Thera staggered up. The caporal had a rifle, so her attacks were obvious. Therasia could attack with anything. She backed into a stance. At full strength she could have folded forward, reached into the woman's chest, and pulled out her heart. Exhaustion swam her senses. She'd have to do it the slow, dangerous way.

The caporal screamed, leaping the log. Her landing made her position predictable. That gave Therasia her window.

A flick of the foot swept the gun aside. Therasia continued the turn, lashing out with a hearty slap, which the soldier ducked, catching her footing. This woman was fast. Fey blood? Or a natural fighter? More likely Therasia was slow without her threads to draw strength and speed.

Spinning and spinning, Therasia stepped in with her turn, back to her enemy, wrapping an arm around the gun as the caporal tried to bring it up. She back-heeled the soldier in the shin, as a distraction, and slid the bayonet free.

Now she had a knife.

The caporal flicked the contact. The rifle didn't fire but a sudden jolt ran through Therasia. She sprang away with a cry of alarm. Lightning shock. Nice trick.

The caporal sliced at her. Therasia had the blade so the attack swept past harmlessly. Therasia slashed in return. She lacked strength. The knife didn't sever the soldier's arm. It opened a wide gash down from the elbow. The woman screeched in pain and staggered back, toppling over the log to the ground, clutching her wound.

Therasia picked up the fallen gun and stood for a moment, staring at the caporal. Only her writhing boots were visible over the top of the log. The uniformed woman dragged them down and peered over, furious in her fear. The half-fey had no strength left for the kill. Turning, she limped for the brush at the forest's edge. Rage still burned but exhaustion weighed her down with its dizzying grip.

The other soldiers yelled and distantly shot their loads into the stream at the bottom of the hill. The living walker avoided the boggy ground, buzzing and clanking around up the slope, firing down into brush and damp. All too remote and noisy for this scrap to have caught their attention.

The treeline embraced her. Glancing back, Therasia saw the medic cautiously edging forward to attend the wounded caporal. The soldier glared over the log with raging passions at the retreating half-fey. Thera could see in the soldier's eyes the sickness of revenge in her heart.

2

Misery to Feed Upon

A ghost haunted Commandant Warren. A strange, ethereal thing he could not see nor hear. He felt it as he stumbled across the hillside next to the walker that was now a coffin for his dragoons. A fey killed them with bees. Who could have imagined such cruelty?

"Commandant! I have the survivors."

Paxton, his lieutenant, approached. Hard everywhere that Warren was soft. The commandant admired the lieutenant for his proper, military manner. Not an original thought in his balding head but a man with discipline and loyalty was hard to find among conniving officers.

"Yes. The survivors," said Warren. A small cluster of uniforms stood at the edge of the field. "Excellent. Ah, just, er, give me a moment, Lieutenant. I need to, er," Warren searched desperately for some excuse to be alone with that other presence. "I need to examine the field. Studying an enemy is, ah, important for defeating them."

"Indeed, sir. These twisted creatures have no honour or discipline. They ambush and-"

"Yes. Thank you, Paxton. I shall walk the field and glean what I may. Please keep the rest of the troops at a distance."

"Yes, Commandant!" Paxton clicked his heels, nodded, and turned back to the waiting soldiers. That was how it should be. He, Commandant Warren, the man in charge, giving orders. His subordinates instantly obeying. Two dozen men and women stood in attendance. Dragoons to check the broken walker. His personal guard. The ragged group of survivors. All at waiting for his commands. That was right and proper.

The ghost ruined everything. It turned him into its slave. It was his soft nature that brought this downfall. Some leaders had no sympathy for the soldiers under their command. Warren felt the loss of his men deeply. That thing fed upon these emotions. What it gave in return was an ecstasy so profound, so beyond any experience, that Warren would do anything for the tiniest sliver.

Warren turned and moved under the walker, sheltering, hiding. The sun burned in the sky with not a trace of cloud to sully its glorious showing. It lacked but an hour of mid-day and it was already unseasonably warm. The dead scattered across the meadow washed the scene in a distinct odour.

Well, he'd brought wagons and strong-stomached soldiers for them.

Death and blood all about. He strode some distance into the field. It was so hard to find a moment to himself where he could indulge this new shame. Warren stared at the carnage and allowed himself wisps of fear, anger, sorrow. This failure would reflect so poorly on his record that he would suffer permanent demotion, humiliation, the loss of everything he worked so hard to build. He felt such things so deeply. Much more than any other officer. There was also bloodlust. The need to crush such a thing that could worry his career in this manner.

The presence pressed against him, sipping these emotions, delicately sampling, washing him with the ecstasy it radiated as it fed. Warren felt his knees trembling in vital euphoria. He swayed in rapturous delight.

The wash of ecstasy faded. The presence moved on. But was it really present? Did it really touch him? Those were the vital questions Warren long sought to answer.

Hands shaking, he found himself unsatisfied. Another jolt. He needed more and more. More fear of failure, more desperation to advance his station. Fervently, Warren searched about for some way to stir himself again.

That woman. Sprawled and bloodied on the ground. Yes. She would make him feel things. He marched with great determination to the decimated command team. The fusilier pinned the lieutenant. The woman had bled out in anguish, neck shattered and torn. Unable to move. He allowed a deep horror of sorrow to overwhelm him at the loss of ... whatever-her-name-was. For this he received the touch. If it was that.

He floated on an intoxication of rhapsody.

Warren did not understand the nature of the thing that attached itself to him. Or even if it was attached. Perhaps, the cruelty was the point. What he did know, and wished fervently that he did not know, was what happened when this thing drank deeper emotions from him. His reward. Each touch of the other was glorious. It filled him with velvet-electric shivers.

Joy absolute caused him to lose all sense of time.

Afterwards, well, one might expect to suffer after such immeasurable joy. The pain left him twisted, cramping, almost paralysed. His breath threatened to tear into a ragged panting. It required great effort to keep his composure, keep his secret, keep his feet underneath him. Later, he would soak in a tub and recall every agonizing bliss, drifting in the memory of sensations that satisfied him more than any woman's caress.

He collapsed to a crouch, pretending to study a bloodstain.

Once he'd regained a degree of composure, settled from the ecstasy and agony, Warren rose and absently brushed the dirt from his knees.

One more? No. He must not lose himself to this new pleasure. He still had discipline.

Back to work then.

"Right, Paxton," he called, approaching the group of waiting soldiers. "The survivors."

"Caporal Adelaide Lelaing." Paxton indicated each in turn. "Sergent Francois d'Foix and, and Fantassin, ah, LaBion, sir. Awaiting at your pleasure."

"Good. Yes. Thank you, Lieutenant."

Warren noted the signaller's bottom lip was already beginning to tremble. Food for the beast, that one. Two other survivors stood beside. A simple but enthusiastic fantassin. Best of all, a wounded caporal who bled her hatred into the air.

Churning passions like that were a thing his unseen companion savoured as a fine, sipping brandy. Emotions from others it could sample. Delicately, unnoticed, from a space outside the survivors, leaving only the tiniest grain of pain. Like swallowing something sharp into one's soul.

They should be grateful he spared them the knowledge of the agony he experienced. Perhaps, like him, they would find the moments of soaring rhapsody more than adequate compensation.

"You have the smoke from Valencia?" he asked.

Lieutenant Paxton waved an underling over. From the soldier's satchel he gingerly pulled a glass jar sealed with waxed paper.

"Valencia said this was not her most potent concoction, sir, but it should suffice to clear out the insects. Also useful if you're having trouble with rats."

"The driver's grill is open," said Warren. "Toss it in through there." The lieutenant stepped deliberately towards the walker. "Careful not to miss. Whatever Valencia says, her poisons are deadly. You could wipe us out instead of those damned bees."

"Hornets, sir," said the caporal.

"Excuse me?" This woman dared interrupt him?

"They're arctic hornets, sir. The venom in their sting is particularly potent. See that one perched on the opening? You can tell from the white fur on their bodies instead of the yellow and black. That's how they get their name. They're also bigger th- b- er, sorry, Commandant."

Warren shook his head and called to the lieutenant, "Just throw the damned jar."

"Ah, Lieutenant, if I may?" the caporal interjected. This woman was not afraid to overstep her mark. He'd seen this before from young nobles. They were used to being heard in their household. It made them insolent of rank. "If you climb up the leg you should be able to reach the grill easily. Just drop it in. I think that's how the fey did it."

That did, indeed, seem less dangerous than throwing from the ground.

"Huh. You may be incapable of minding your rank, Caporal," said Warren. "But you do make sense."

Warren nodded to his lieutenant who was grateful for the caporal's suggestion. Paxton climbed up and easily flicked the jar inside. It shattered in an initial impact. The pieces tinkled onto the floor. He jumped down swiftly, scurrying away, not gasping a breath until he was well clear.

The buzzing inside grew louder and suddenly louder still. The bees, hornets, flew from the walker in panic. They whirred about seeking escape from the poison within themselves. The ghost would welcome the tiny panic of those soon to join it. For as much as Warren could discern its location, it seemed reluctant to go near the walker with its lightning jar at the back. Warren had noted this distaste for technology in the thing before and devised a little experiment he wished to run. But that was for later.

The dying hornets should keep it happy for a while.

Part of him wished otherwise. He wanted that contact. Desired it above all reason. Even if it might kill him.

Distractions. Yes, the caporal in front of him was most distracting. Fair-haired and subtle of feature. Full lips that snarled well. Beautiful even in anger.

"Caporal. You fought this witch-thing?"

"Aye, Commandant," the woman replied, gesturing to her arm in its sling.

"Man or woman?"

"Hard to say, sir. It was thin as these fey tend to be. I think it was a tree spirit. Its face was wood. Vines grew about its torso. The feet seemed, well, covered in dirt and dust, but it felt like hard bark when it kicked me in the shin."

"Then took your gun."

"Had to damn-near hack my arm off to do it but yes, sir." She looked puzzled. "I didn't think such things interested them."

"Tree spirit, eh? There are different types?"

"Aye, sir, as I've observed."

"Well, you are observant enough to tell the difference between a bee and a hornet. I suppose I should listen. What makes you such an expert?"

"My family had a small estate outside Albiga, sir. Within the circle. I know something of farming. We kept quail and python for meat, peach and cherries for eau-de-vie and liqueurs. I would visit villages outside the wastelands, with my father, to net new quail and look for breeding strains of the fruit trees. Also, our farmhands were mostly displaced country folk. They told country-farmer's tales."

"Had? Had a small estate?"

"The bone disease ate both my parents, my sister. To ensure my position, they sold the land before they died. We kept an apartment in Tolosa which my father used on his business trips. I inherited that but my stipend was not enough to buy a full commission. I joined anyway. I shall bring glory back to our family name."

"And buy back your farm?"

"No, sir. The land is now slum housing and the manor is a works for the clay pits. Woad is Albiga's main business. Blue-clay, along with a copper mine near the wastes."

"You mine in the wastes? That is forbidden! We do not breach those dusty circles of death that confine the cities except to cross them as quickly as we are able. Those that linger are seldom heard from again. Albiga defies the rule of the council in this manner?"

"Near the waste, Commandant. I said, near the waste. I believe the miners were forbidden from pursuing a promising vein of copper that led out and under. I'm not sure if the fey rule beneath the land as well as above it but, in any case, that is on the other side of the city and not our family's purview. We farm. Our workshops supply, I mean, we supplied, ah, the snake skin. Belts and boots and, well. The workshops are converted now. As is the house. I prefer to remember it as it was. And I am determined to retire in a good position, retain my name to pass down to my children."

"And that name would be...?"

"Lelaing, sir."

"Oh! Yes. The lieutenant did say. One of the ten original houses from the north, yes? Sad about the great flooding. Those cursed ancient gods raising the seas. But now you're a farmer at heart. Tell me, do you feel an affinity with these people?"

Fury flashed into her eyes but she answered steadily. "No. Four of my squad and three of your dragoons are dead at the hands of that horror. My lieutenant- She-" Adelaide gestured to the pinned officer. "No, sir. I have no affinity for those who would commit such a slaughter."

"Good. Good. Yes. They are despicable. It is a shame we didn't win the last war. A hundred years ago the new powder-guns widely replaced bows. Any fantassin could spray death with little training or skill. Faster than a fey could move. You might have thought that would be enough."

"Indeed, sir."

She was attentive upon his word. Quite right. Warren relished the opportunity to demonstrate his knowledge.

"And those smaller cannon. On light carts? The old barrow-guns? They could move faster and into deeper places than the regular artillery, challenging the woodland hideaways. I studied the last war while I came up through the academy. Read the original reports. Not just the history books. We could have taken it all but there were droughts, plagues, causing shortages of food, deaths in the cities. Dreadful business. Stunted our advancements."

"Some say the fey caused those," Lelaing replied.

"Please don't parrot that superstitious nonsense, Lelaing. They're not that powerful."

"They are powerful enough to burn those circles of death around each city. Barren bands two miles wide, a few miles outside the walls of every large city, where nothing can ever grow."

"Well, that's the old magic. It took every witch combined, I'm sure, to spend everything they had on each one. A show of desperation not strength. But the officials at the time fell for it." Warren shook his head. All those bad decisions made centuries ago. He stared out over the rolling hills. Mostly forest and grassland. All criminally underutilised. "We're supposed to farm the land inside the circles to feed the cities. Like that was ever going to be enough. The house and gardens on my estate take up most of my allocated land. What's left barely feeds my town-house and the staff of my farms."

Adelaide nodded. He suspected she was agreeing with him out of politeness, deference to rank. He leaned closer to impress upon her the import of his words.

"This uneasy peace, brokered by politicians, will never hold," he said. "Barely a hundred years and every decade brings a new cycle of skirmishes. Now, we have these walkers that can move our new, six-barrelled cannons into the most awkward terrain, well protected from ambush. This will show them our will. Our determination. You attribute vast powers and god-like abilities to these fey. They are small, individual creatures. Their only strength is their viciousness. Never doubt for a moment they would tear your, well," he gestured to the bandaged gash, "hack your limbs off and feed you to their wolves."

"Dere were a wolf, soir!" said the fantassin in a thick, gutter-rat accent, eager to join the conversation. He wanted attention from his betters. Well, people who had better teeth than he. "We done chased it 'cross the stream!"

"You fell for its tricks, LaBion," the caporal chided. She stepped over to straighten the commoner's collar. Stepping away from him but that was surely just a coincidence. "That dog was a decoy. It wanted you in that burn so it could slip away. They have water-spirits to drown unwary fools like you."

"Be dat true?"

"Aye, LaBion," said the caporal. "Never cross the streams. Except at a ford. You could go under and sink forever."

"Well, it be dead now, dat dere wolf. Deader than a dead man's hand what's been cut off."

The commandant and caporal exchanged a glance.

"Thank you, Fantassin," said Warren. "Now, Caporal. You are one of the few to have fought a fey and lived. I must hear the story sometime. It's a shame that arm will have you removed from the guard. If you can't handle a rifle you can't fight."

He watched the emotions rage behind the woman's eyes. All her hopes and dreams dashed. To her credit, she kept it in check. Warren felt dirty. Such cruel provocations kept his unseen companion close about him, gave it misery to feed upon. The presence drifted back over. It was done with the ... hornets.

"The wound will heal, Commandant," the caporal replied. "And I can still help in the fight."

"How will you do that? Spit at them? You glare most angrily but it will take more than that to make our claim on these lands."

"The bottle, there, on the ground, sir. That thing threw it at me, made me miss my shot. These peasants mark their stoneware when they make them. A house stamp. We did the same on our family's farm. We can find who feeds this beast, leaving it such treats."

"Well! Caporal! You are a rare creature, yourself." Warren gestured. "Fantassin. Bring me that bottle."

"Aye, soir!"

"Remind me. What is your full name, Caporal, that I might mention you in my dispatches?"

"Adelaide, Commandant." The woman broadened with delicious pride. "Caporal Adelaide Lelaing."

"Very well, Lelaing. Stow this bottle of yours. I am to travel to the village and meet the head man, La Granger, this afternoon. You shall accompany me. We can show him your arm, the human cost of his demon dealings. Mayhap we'll find something of the people aiding these cursed pixies."

The presence pressed close about him threatening a touch. It was almost like it wanted something. He needed to reach out to it, found his arm half lifted, but there was no physical direction in which he could make contact.

"Commandant?" Lieutenant Paxton enquired, curious at the raised arm.

"The, ah, the radio operator. What's his name? Bring him."

"d'Foix, Sir. At once."

The presence eased back. A relief and disappointment. The fantassin, LaBion, returned with the bottle held between two fingers like he'd picked up a turd. It was sticky from spilled contents but he seemed more repulsed at the idea of handling something touched by a fey. At least he'd flicked off most of the ants.

"That red rag you keep in your pocket for wiping your face, LaBion," Caporal Lelaing gestured. "Wrap it in that and hand it to me."

"Me wiper, Cap?"

"Aye, man! And quick about it," she ordered, with a slight nod in Warren's direction. The fantassin glanced at the commandant. He fished out a strip of cloth, greatly prized in spite of its grubby, faded appearance. A remembrance of a loved one, perhaps? Making the sign of the hammer, he thumped a fist onto one side of his breast then another. As if Thor himself would protect a lowly soldier. The church may have the general populace in its thrall but men of intelligence gave little heed to such petty rituals.

"You two." Warren caught their attention mid exchange. "Check out that walker. See if those hornets trouble it no more. Then get the dragoons in there. I want to know if it can make it down to the wagons under its own spark. The oxen can wheel it back to camp."

"Yes, sir."

"Aye, soir!"

That was another thing he wanted to raise with the local head man. The dreadful camp.

The only land allowed them was a broken meadow. Angled and rough. A trickle of a stream, barely a rill, ran along the bottom, inadequate for a company. And he, the commandant, slept in a cursed tent. On a narrow cot he could never get level. The village donated no building to the officers. These farmers showed precious little respect for his rank or the amount of guns he had at his command.

Paxton brought the radio operator.

"Thank you, Lieutenant. Watch these woods. The fey have a nasty habit of leaving curses and hexes upon places they have visited. They even ambush the medics when they come to aid the wounded. Foul things." His man nodded curtly, taking up a position. That should provide a sufficient excuse for what was about to happen. Warren reached a friendly arm to the signalman, patting him on the shoulder. "Walk with me, Sparky."

"My name is d'Foix, Commandant. Sergent Francois d'Foix."

Warren grimaced, turning his face away as he led the unfortunate across the site of the skirmish. He hated knowing their names. It was always more difficult when he knew their names.

"Take your time, Sparky. Breathe and focus inward." Warren closed his eyes, wishing to see as little of the coming horror as possible. "Tell me what you need."

The radio operator hesitated. A strange demeanour surfaced through his eyes. He said, "d'Foix, sir. My- Foix." The man seemed to feel the need to assert who he was even as that understanding drowned within The Presence. Hesitation and fear faded from the man's voice as the ghost consumed him. "F... Fo... Foix. My... F... F... *Fooooool*!"

Warren shifted uncomfortably as the voice became ... something else. He glanced back to the others. Distant and busy enough, paying this interrogation little mind. From the corner of one eye he caught the sparky's expression of searing rapture mixed with a posture of euphoric pain.

"Foolish thing!" the possessed soldier chided him. "Wh... Why waste time? Here nothing. Wave... Wave come soon!"

"Did you provoke those men? Did you make them attack that those villagers? Did you? Were you so hungry for suffering?"

"...creature... Other creatures hurt, humiliated. Such rich and vibrant experiences. We cannot feel such things else. Not in the sun, not under the earth. Not in the simple hungers and terrors of the beasts. Only humans suffer so. We will feed much after the wave!"

Uncertainty still lingered in Warren's mind. The thing may not have provoked the men to attack the villagers on their way back from harvesting mushrooms in the woods. But it enjoyed the result. Unfortunate that they were near an escarpment, that the woman chose to jump after the men were killed. And now more of his men were dead. Another intended result? Did the thing plan ahead and create these chains of suffering, revenge? Or was it an opportunistic feeder? Did it enter and twist the minds of men? Or just enjoy the results of man's own twisted nature?

How much of Warren's mind was still his own?

That was the big question. Did the presence that haunted him control him? Did this ghost have a broader goal in mind? The thing had precious little understanding of human speech or concepts. Most of these it seemed to borrow from the possessed.

He pressed the issue. "You talk of this flood, rush, again. What is it? A wave, now? Is that because the sparky was from a coastal town? You suggested this visit, this location. What brought us here? What is coming soon?"

"Spray here. Flecks."

Warren sighed in frustration. The presence might remember he asked it a question, eventually. In the meantime it would ramble in broken, disjointed thoughts.

"Spray? A fey?"

"Death."

"Yes. Many died-"

"Death, this fey."

"Kill it? You want us to kill it? First, we have to hunt the cursed thing down."

"Death! This speck on the wave. Death!"

"Death to whom? Our entire army? A single fey could never-"

"Wave! When wave come there will be ... signal. I follow. Triangulate signal. Like radio. You ... follow."

The radio operator began to collapse under the engulfing sensations, knees weakening, hands vague and out of control.

Triangulation. Definitely a concept stolen from the mind of a radio operator. "We don't have to wait for this wave. We can beat the brush in which it hides!" said Warren ardently. "These peasants, they have no respect for my rank or the precarious nature of their position. I could wipe out that whole village with two rollers and half a company! That would flush it out!"

"Not one. More. Must find speck, Death, on wave."

"If there's more than one we'll flush them all out and slaughter the lot! Every dirt scratcher in this lost village and all the fey besides! You remember the mines? How we met? We drove those paupers into the open wastes. They worked that old silver mine day after day. You slaughtered them. You fed. I saw what you did. I felt you, tasted the ecstasy that you can bring. You felt me. I led you out of those wastes. You are free because of me!"

"You ... much silver for promotion. I allowed your mine. Knew your greed. Killed witnesses to your crime."

"We both benefited. Don't you want to feel that energy again? The kind of energy that you said gave you strength to break your bonds? I can lead you to so many glorious massacres!"

"F... Fooooooolish mortal! Must secure food before ... many kill."

"We can bring in others to farm these lands! The debtor's prisons overflow with-"

"War!" the other said. Blood started to sweat from the sparky's face, tears of red dripping from his eyes. "No small fight! Need food for war! Many, many fight! Fight everyone! Consume! All are food for the war!"

The peasants would be its food. But what was this war? Was that its broader goal? Peace reigned in these lands for nearly a century. At the end of the last war, with the help of the fey, the peasants threw out the lords and took control of the land. They burned rings of wasteland around the cities and larger towns, from the giant-ruled Eastern Mountains all the way to the Western Sea!

Now the cities cowered behind desolation.

The unruly serfs ruled the land.

Not only did they control the food but the flow of trade between the cities. These unworthy bumpkins strangled the machinery of the nobles with their demands for equality. As if they could ever be equal to those of noble blood.

The king set out into the world, quested to seek help from the gods, supernatural aid of his own. Well. That was the official story. No one believed that. No one expected him to come back.

Wars and sorties into the countryside continued for nearly a decade. All failed. Even these latest skirmishes stuttered in the deeper lands like this awful village. Clumsy things that scratched in the mud should not stifle the ambitions of conquerors! There should be war! Conquest! Glory! His city, Tolosa, could rule it all!

Might this ghost deliver on such a promise? He could barely imagine the sensations his Presence could drink from a battlefield of thousands. The screams of the dying would be edged with delight. The sensations such a sight could stir in him, win or lose. That was something the ethereal beast would reward. A magnificent remuneration for his soft nature.

He might very well die of elation.

"If you insist, we shall leave these wasted lives. They'll help us conquer all the known world. From the Lands of Gold to the Leviathan Sea! From the Arctic Wastes to the Chrysalis Deserts. There shall be war! We will–"

"*Foooooooood!*" the thing expunged, breath fading, presence slipping away. The radio operator returned for one last, gurgling scream of shivering pain, blood flowing from his flesh inside and out.

The others reacted. That caporal, Lelaing, rushed over, awkwardly drawing her sabre with her off hand. Warren jerked out his pistol and waved it around, feigning confusion.

"Fey!" he called. "Fey here, here!" His guard rushed up. The walker whirred and crackled half a step. Bloated bodies lay beside the machine but the dragoons had it working. "Back!" he cried in something approximating distress. "Form up around the walker!" But the thrice-cursed caporal kept running, that over-eager fantassin with her. She caught sight of the body.

"Ha!" she exclaimed. "A curse!"

"Look!" Warren cried, to disguise the fact he was trying to hide the body's appearance. "Look what it did! Just like my lover, Esmeralda, at the Forest of Domanialle!" After she had learned of the ghost that haunted him. "A curse! A hex! Or it yet lingers and blasts us with spells! Guard yourselves lest it suck the life from you!"

The fantassin squealed and looked about in panic, thumping each side of his chest, a rude knife from his boot his only weapon.

The caporal seemed less inclined to panic. "Calm yourself, LaBion!" she chided the lowest rank present. "If the fey were here more of us would be dead. This is but a curse, likely laid when it attacked, meant to scare us long after. Some Sarramauca trick." The woman kept glancing at him. By scolding the fantassin she avoided calling her commandant foolish.

"Or the wicked thing watches us from these woods," he rejoined, continuing to play his weary part, "and attacks with its conjurations!"

"An' why it not kill you, soir?" asked the simpleton. Damned awkward question.

"Best not linger and find out," said Warren. "You there! Dragoon!"

"Aye, sir!" answered half a man poking out from the top hatch.

"Can this walker make it back to camp?"

"Some way, Commandant! The stench of death in here is overwhelming and I ain't so sure these masks will save us from Valencia's poison. The jar has a crackle. We can, at least, get it off this cursed hillside and onto an ox wagon!"

"Then do so! The rest of you be vigilant! Paxton?"

"Here, Commandant!"

"Get the bodies on the wagons, hornet-stung, staked, and cursed alike. I want them all burned by sundown. Proper ceremony but we can't have this panicking the men."

"It will be done, sir."

"Come, Lelaing. Let us descend swiftly. This field is lost to us. We must prepare to invade the living room of La Granger and gain there what territory we may."

3

Death Lies That Way

The gun was killing her. Therasia shifted her grip on the weapon and continued the determined, exhausted march to her house.

She felt numb after her battle except for the scratch along her ribs. The rage lingered. She buried the pain in a cold, cold place. It flickered at her in defiance like the noonday sunlight flickered at her through the dappling trees.

This entire coppice was rich with smells of wood and earth and flower. The town's stream ran through here before plunging down the steep slope past the market square.

Perhaps, one day, she would stand in the market and let all in the village see and understand her. But none of the fey-touched ever did that. The villagers enjoyed their protection but they were uncomfortable with the nature of their safeguard. To them she was their local barber-surgeon. That position was useful for gathering all the gossip and insights that made her real job easier. I was also pleasant to play at being a real person. With friends. A quiet, normal life.

Stars forbid that anyone should see her staggering through the woods, covered in blood, and lugging a triple-barrelled rifle.

She approached the village from the back so as not to traipse her current state through the main street. The gun crackled faintly now, barely discernible.

Therasia could not resist playing with that strangeness, like a tongue that couldn't help sampling a bitten cheek. She leaned into the elsewhere, slightly, almost as if she leaned against it. Even that tiny amount of lightning, all that remained in the little jars at the stock of the gun, caused distortions and confusions. It threatened to return her to the real with her thumbs on backwards, like the fey of folktales. She hated her fascination with the thing as much as she hated those who brought it into her world.

The back orchard opened before her. The house lay on the other side. A generous, well-built structure of two-toned brick and bright red tiles. She lingered in the trees, catching her breath before-

"What are you doing?"

"La! Little Kat! You startled me."

Katrienne. The fey-touched child stood so still she blended with the landscape. Darkness settled over Therasia's heart. This one contained a monster. It stuttered on the edge of the world. More so than Therasia at that age. Insanely feral, Kat would make a good fighter if she lived. Now, though, the village must not become aware of how far this thing-that-used-to-be-a-child strayed from human concepts of innocence.

"You stink of blood and death," said the little creature. "Can I have a taste?"

"No, Kitty-Kat." Therasia crouched down as one does when talking to a child. "You should try to eat human food."

"But my mama is all scared of me now that I can do witch things. She makes the food bad deliberate. I don't go home often. Did your mama try to scare you out the house when they found out you was fey?"

"My mama had a stroke," said Therasia. Talking openly about her life and nature was a luxury. She revelled in it even though her conversational companion was yet to develop adult empathy. "But that was a few years after and wasn't my fault. It took me a while to work out that it wasn't my fault, something that happened because I was different. Her brain tore open. I actually saved her. My father never forgave me."

"For her brain ripping or saving her?"

Therasia smiled. "Both, I think." She tried to rise. A dizzy spell took her to an unexpected tree where she propped while the world stopped spinning.

"You is sick. If'n you die and I eats you, do I get your spirit?"

"No, Little Kat. That's not how eating, or spirits, work. And I'm not sick." Therasia pushed at the tree but it took a couple of tries to get her unsteady legs under her. She felt like a new calf trying to walk for the first time. "I'm just a bit dizzy. I wearied myself this morning. Then, instead of resting, I spent the whole walk back playing with this thing."

She hefted the gun. "Once I get some food, somewhere to sit for a moment-"

"That thing makes my bones itch."

Thera smiled. "Mine too."

The girl's revulsion scrunched her face. "We should smash it."

"Yes. I want to keep this one, though. For experiments. It's almost like ... I feel as though I could speak with the lightning. If only I could talk fast enough. You shouldn't do that. The lightning is dangerous. You should smash any soldier guns you find."

"All of them?"

"Indeed all! Guns are very bad."

"Why?"

"Good question. Guns are a tool. In the right hands they are as useful as any other tool. Like the way old Broquesh uses that flintlock shotgun of his to keep the rabbits off his carrots."

"And makes him some nice pies."

"Yes! His rabbit pies are excellent. But guns make it too easy for a coward to kill and still think themselves brave. Also, I've seen people get addicted to the easy power they are able to wield over life and death. Even the death of a rabbit. So you smash all the soldier's guns you find. First making sure that you won't get caught."

"Oh! I is real careful!" said the little beast. "I put rocks under the comm'dant's bed-legs every night so as he don't sleep straight. He hates that. No one in the camp ever sees me, to or fro. I sneaks so good."

"Wow! That's excellent! Have you been working on the fold like I showed you?"

"Yeah, but that's all weird. I-" Kat turned and looked at the orchard. "Boys," it said. "Boys with sticks and stones."

Therasia rubbed the creature's back. A group of young boys, eight or ten years, crept into the orchard, giggling and hushing each other. William the tanner's kid and his little gang. Up to no good. "You remember not to touch anyone from the village, Little Kat?"

Katrienne looked up with a grumpy, disappointed face. "...yeah... I 'member."

"Well then. Let's play a game," said Therasia, desperate to reach the safety of her house. Points of light danced in her vision even as she breathed. "Show me how well you can sneak me across this field with no-one noticing."

"I can throw stones better 'an any of them," said Kat. "We was playing and I done knocked a bird straight out the sky and it were never nothing they could throw so high."

"Did you help them get the bird so they could cook it into a nice pie?"

"Nah. Fox done got it."

"...and did you help the fox to get it...?"

Katrienne shared a guilty grin then nodded, embarrassed.

"Remember to try and help the village, Little Kat. No matter what is burning inside you."

The two of them made it to the house unseen. The boys were more interested in checking out the trees for early apples. Trying to knock down the one or two they found with their sticks and stones. They were cooking apples. Inedible. Maybe the boys wanted to try their hand at making cider. Alcohol poisoning would bring them to her surgery soon enough. She could reprimand them there.

Speaking of which. A quick sweep of the residence with her threads found no one waiting in her surgery. She sighed with relief. Her father was in the study, Mother at the sink. She always knew where Mother was.

She entered through the kitchen. Shining copper pots and beautifully finished earthenware stood on neatly stacked shelves. Drying herbs hung from the roof. The stone floor was spotlessly clean. Mother stood in front of the deep, porcelain sink. Unnaturally still, staring out of the window, lost in thought.

"Mother," Therasia called gently. "Mother...?"

The woman did not respond. Her hands strained in a half-fulfilled gesture. Therasia's threads hummed a warning. Something swirled around her mother, barely peeking into this world. She sighed, dropped the gun onto the large table with a clatter and clunk, then sank into a plain, wooden chair. Fatigue pushed at her senses. If she was going to deal with something from that other place, she'd take a rest first and stars burn the end. Thera hefted the water pitcher from the middle of the table, lifted the covering cloth and drank copiously from the side of the red-glazed jug.

"I think you is sick," said Katrienne.

"Ahhhhhh. Good water. If you're hungry, Little Kat, there is a nice ham in the pantry and a dish of butter, probably a fresh loaf, too."

The little creature scurried away in search of sustenance. This human body needed ongoing maintenance. Eating. Shitting. And other pleasures currently too painful to think on. Maybe there was some cheese.

Therasia was going to need a knife.

Reluctantly she rose. Even with that short rest her legs were stiff. She shuffled like an old woman towards the sink. In spite of the cost to her health and sanity she followed the threads tied to her mother, seeking to dislodge-

"It will be you," something said, using her mother's mouth. "Come the akelarre, you will be named strongest. The crisis is upon us. The strongest must be in charge."

The contact from the fey buzzed along Therasia's threads, pouring into her. Without those threads to relieve the energy, that fey presence would consume the possessed. The spoken words seemed like only the shallowest echo of the full message. The akelarre, the meeting of the local witches, would take place on harvest morrow. Less than a week. The fey chosen her to lead? That seemed insane.

"I can barely stand," she said. "Why are you calling me the strongest?"

"Three movements. And yet you live. This thing lives. You walked home flirting with our world and that abomination."

"Katrienne is not-"

"The thing that screams in the fey."

"The gun? ...yes. It is like a scream. But not one without meaning, I think. There is almost a language to it. Some sort of sense, at least."

"Danger! Death lies that way! The crisis! That you can feel the scream is strength. That you are alive is strength. You will lead the gathering! Hello, my dear, I didn't hear you come in."

Mother casually put an arm around Therasia's shoulders in a passing hug before she went back to the washing in the sink. "If you're hungry there's some fresh ham in the pantry. Oh, what am I saying? You're always hungry." She laughed and flicked a little soapy water at her daughter.

Therasia flinched and smiled, eyes sad. She was grateful to have her mother in her life. Sometimes she almost seemed like her old self. The kind and loving figure Therasia always remembered.

Therasia's very core thrummed from the power she'd received via her threads. Without those threads her mother would have died from the fey-touch, broken and bloodied. She'd seen it before. When one of these creatures, in its purest form, visited a human it brought horrors not of this world.

"I put cheese on your plate," said the little beast, startling them both.

"La! Little Kat! What have you there?"

"Oh, hello Katrienne," said Mother. "Have you come for a visit?"

"Hello, Madame Garonne. You was busy so we not want to bother you. I made plates."

Sure enough, the sneaky little creature held two plates with ham, fresh rolls, and cherry tomatoes. Cheese on the one for Thera. Where did it even get the tomatoes? The early crop had only just ripened.

Therasia smiled, buzzing with energy, still reeling and puzzling out what the visitor had to say. "Mother," she said, "there's some washing out on the line. Why don't you grab a basket and see if there's anything ready to bring in."

Mother blinked as if she didn't know where she was, or anything about this strange young woman standing before her. Therasia brushed away her uncertainty with a few, gentle threads, feeling the scars that still existed in her mother's mind. She fed her love and certainty.

Mother hugged her.

Something deep inside Therasia let go. This was her hearth and her centre. When everything seemed ugly, when all her work brought death and suffering, she always had this. Someone who simply loved her. Mother rubbed her back and smiled. Then she wandered over to collect the basket, drying her hands on her apron before she went into the garden, humming a merry tune.

Therasia washed blood and dirt from her hands and strode back to the table, ignoring the damp from mother's hug on the back of her ruined longshirt. Kat seemed disappointed at her new strength and vigour. They sat. Katrienne climbed onto a chair. Tall enough now that she could see over the tabletop without cushions or books to sit upon. Therasia tore open her chunk of bread, liberally dropped ham inside, wolfing down the rest, barely chewing. She picked the stem off a tomato and threw it into her mouth mid-chew.

"Do you have the knife there, Little Kat?" she asked.

"What you mean?"

"I need to spread some butter on my roll. May I please borrow the knife you used to cut the ham and cheese?"

The little beast thought about this for a moment. Then she reluctantly fished the sharp, curved kitchen blade from her skirt.

"Thank you, Little Kat," said Therasia. She continued with great delicacy, chewing half a mouthful. "You remember what I told you about helping the people of the village? That you must always be thinking of ways to help?"

The terrifying creature grew a grumpy expression. It shifted uncomfortably on its chair. Therasia smeared a generous amount of butter into her torn bread, casually, as if it were a passing conversation.

"It's like those boys in the orchard, out back. They know they can steal an apple or two. But they can't take all the apples in the orchard." She swallowed half her mouthful. "Because then everyone would hate them and run them out of town. They know that. So there's no need to bother them. No need at all. When we, us special folke, see people being evil, and the hunger is upon us, it is tempting..." Therasia swallowed the rest. She stared into the middle distance remembering her own broken childhood, feeling her own hunger. "It can be so very, very tempting to think that we have found an excuse to ... be ourselves, to stretch and flow and feast. But that would ruin it for everyone. The whole village would know and hate us for being so strong. We need to be able to live here. It's okay for people to be scared of us. The fey-touched. But not so much as they want to get rid of us."

Therasia took another mouthful as she waited. She popped in a second tomato. So good. Little Kat's face emerged from behind her veil of hair with tears glistening on her cheeks.

"My mama don't want me no more. My papa don't even look at me." she sobbed a breath. "You don't think I'm a 'bom-nate?"

"No, child. You are not an abomination. You just get a bit confused sometimes."

"Can," she sniffed and stuttered a gasp, "can I come live here with you, Aunty G? Will you be my mama?"

Therasia's heart caught in her chest. Ah, she thought. That's why the little creature sought her out today. Poor thing. It made Thera hungry. "Tell you what, Kitty-Kat," she said through her food. "You finish your meal while I go wash up. I'm going to take this knife with me. And the gun. When I come back down, I'll go with you to your house and-"

The back door opened. Mother entered looking confused. "I thought I had some washing on, outside," she said. "Oh! I hope you haven't eaten all the ham!"

"Oh, no, Madame Garonne. I left heaps," said Kat.

Mother laughed. "Ah. Thank you. So very kind, my sweet."

Therasia rose and hefted the gun onto one shoulder. "You stay and chat with Mother, Kitty. Be polite. Then I'll come and have a word with your parents."

She rose, dumped her plate into the sink, and gave her mother a brief hug in passing. Laughter was her reward.

Not all her fey work was born from anger. Often she helped spread joy and love. Today, though. Today was a day of fire. Her mind still burned with emotion. It needed some way to escape. She would have to be careful not to do anything foolish but it was long past time she had a word with Kitty's parents. Thera strode into the hall and began climbing the stairs. Her father came out of the front study.

"Not now, Papa," she said. "Today, I am very busy."

He huffed through his beard and brushed back what remained of his hair.

"Ah, girl. Look at the state of you."

She looked down at the front of her long-shirt. Only patches of original yellow showed through the stains. "I'm fine, Papa. None of it's my blood."

He huffed again. Therasia recognised one of his moods. He was determined to be angry about something. It gave him the illusion he was still the master of all he surveyed.

"And what do you mean by bringing a thing like that into my house?" he demanded, gesturing to the gun. "Do you know who's coming here this afternoon? Practically now?"

"The Commandant. You told me, Papa. I tried to get home earlier but today," she gestured to her shirt, "today was difficult."

"Difficult? I am trying to prevent this mechanised company from sweeping our village from the map and you slaughter half the soldiers on a whim!"

"Not on a whim. Never on a whim."

"Not on the best day, either! Did you even think of talking to me about this? I am still your father, you know!"

Therasia stepped heavily down the staircase until her head was level with the old man, one step higher. "You were my father, once. And in many ways you still are. It is convenient and comforting for me to continue playing the role of your daughter. But do not think, because of that, you still have any proprietary over me." She gently caressed his face. "I love you. I am grateful for all that you have given. All the patience you have displayed with my unusual upbringing. But I am not yours any longer. Not Daddy's little girl. You talk with these soldiers all you like. I will do the unpleasant and necessary things. That is the burden of my kind." She leaned in to kiss him but the despair behind his eyes pulled him away.

"You stink of blood," he said.

"Best I go change then."

Steadier legs carried her up the stairs while she wolfed down the last of her food. Cool, blue walls with warm artworks greeted her as she entered her modest room. The patterned, down-filled covers of subtle purples and crimsons on her bed whispered of promised rest. She had miles to go before she slept.

The gun slipped into the back of her closet, the secret, sliding compartment. The knife she tossed onto her dresser. Once she'd stripped, she rubbed off the dried gore from her ricochet wound. She lied to father. Some of it was her blood. But he'd only fret even more. It started bleeding again so she smeared some salve onto it and set her threads to work, healing.

With a damp sea-sponge she rid herself of blood and lingering traces. Leifa liked the sponge. Much nicer than a rag, she would say. Leifa used to like the sponge. Leifa was gone. Therasia felt the weight of that upon her. Leifa's face rose in her mind. A cheeky smile, her tongue making a lascivious gesture. Therasia held the rim of her enamelled basin and brought her breathing back under control.

She'd killed enough soldiers but vengeance was a raging sickness that could never be sated. This commandant who came to bother them this afternoon. From him Thera would glean whether this response was sufficient to have an effect in the camp. If not–

Ah. No. Little Katrienne required her attention now.

Patting herself down with a pescémal, Thera breathed, calming and focusing. She should dress. A sulphured linen over the gash to keep it clean. A bandage around to stop the wound from staining her fresh clothes. The wound would be gone in a couple of days, without even the faintest scar, but only if it didn't become infected.

Therasia threw on her blue longshirt, a heavier fabric that would hide the bandage underneath. It matched well with her light, tan knee-britches. She tied a beautiful, red scarf made from chrysalis silk about her waist as a sash, hanging a many-pocketed pouch from it. A short vest over her chest eliminated the need for a bandeau. The embroidery's colour blended well with the scarf.

The pointed ankle-boots.

Sadly, she'd have to burn the yellow and green outfit. There was no way to clean that much blood. She bought new outfits at such a rate that Melissa, the local seamstress, could barely keep up.

Energy from the fey-touch still lingered. That and a brief rest in the kitchen. Some food in her belly. Therasia felt ready to walk out into the world.

Katrienne giggled and ran all about the cobbled main street of Arros. The beast lingered overlong in hidey-holes along the arcade and generally tried to delay meeting her parents. The little monster even lingered with Ignace, the connerierre, as he rolled his manure wagon far enough up an alley to collect some dog shit. Therasia bumped into him sometimes as both their jobs necessitated them taking the back-street. She waved him a greeting and called Little Kat to heel. The street was not busy today. Most were out in the fields tending the crops. Various bugs and creeping things took advantage of spring's fresh, abundant food source.

Flowers decorated most of the houses and shops. The buttercross was vivid with summer blossoms from yester-day's market. Spray from the fountain inside kept the flower displays moist and vibrant for a few days.

The Dourbie family lived in a narrow house two doors down from the blacksmith. Therasia made a point of drop-ping by the forge to chat with the smith. Never mind how uncomfortable the metal made her feel. Kat hung from her shirt and kept pulling. Therasia laughed and apologised, making excuses about getting the child home in time for lunch. The villagers knew to keep iron on their doors and windows to deter the hungry fey. As long as Therasia did not make her discomfort obvious none would suspect her true nature. She even touched the metal on occasion, just to fool people about how little it bothered her.

Therasia stood before the solid, bright door for a moment, settling herself. Katrienne was very quiet and still, leaning against her. Therasia knocked. Using the iron knocker. Madame Dourbie answered, wiping her hands on a cloth. Her happy greeting froze on her young face.

"Good aftern..." the woman forced herself to continue with a brittle civility. "Why, Katrienne! We wondered where you'd gone. It's after lunch, you know?"

"She found her way to our kitchen. We fed her already."

"So kind of you!"

"Do you mind if I come in, Madame Dourbie?"

There was only the slightest hesitation. Therasia had a reputation around town. "Of course, Thera, my dear. Please, please!"

The house was barely wide enough for a staircase in the hallway and a small parlour beside. The kitchen occupied the whole of the back. One storey of bedrooms and facilities above. An attic and cold cellar. It was clean, modestly decorated, but Therasia immediately recognised poison in the air. Little bits of iron. Everywhere.

"La. Monsieur Dourbie, how are you?"

The young man stirred in his parlour chair, a look of small fear creeping upon his face. Not yet thirty. A herb-collector and woodsman. He tended towards laziness. Therasia seethed at the idea of a wasted life. Home in the middle of a fine, clear afternoon when he should be out, cutting or picking. An axe lurked behind the door. Therasia was tempted to use it.

"Little Kat," she said. "Why don't you go up to your room for a moment?"

"...mmmkay." The beast clattered meekly up the stairs.

Taking a long step into the parlour, Therasia reached and hauled the lazy woodsman from his padded chair. Back in the hallway, she hooked Madame around the throat and dragged them both to the kitchen, kicking the door shut behind.

The young woman inherited this house as the last surviving member of her family. There was nothing suspicious about their deaths but the lazy woodcutter had his hands on her soon after, marrying and moving in to a cosy dwelling. He didn't even have the vigour to sleep around. Both seemed content to coast through their small lives.

She sat them down. Hard. For all her admonishments to Little Kat about not harming the villagers, the fey-hunger conspired with her rage to undermine her restraint. Though they were not the cause of her rage nor did they deserve sympathy.

"As a woodsman, doubtless you know a lot of beautiful little places to picnic and seduce a young girl," Therasia began. "Pleasant spots with flowers and views of the distant mountains. Fucking in the woods is how the Kindly Ones found you, blessed your child."

"They ain't kind!" Madame cried. "You can't tell me that little monster is kind! It ate a rat! Ate it whole!"

"What were you trying to feed her? Something filled with iron filings stolen from the blacksmith? If you show her kindness, as my mother did, she will reflect it. Tell me, young woman who has never had to work for anything in her life, was the extra demand upon your ample time too much for you to bear?"

"She kept us up, night after night!"

"Most children do."

"We didn't know what to do with it!" Monsieur whined.

"Few people who have children ever know. You only had to ask." Therasia stepped back and reached onto the door lintel. "But you begged for help from the wrong place, didn't you?" She pulled down a small, hidden, iron symbol. It was shaped like a stylised hammer. "Things have skewed from honesty in this village for too long. Why would you place your trust in something so ridiculous as this city religion? You thought this would rid you of all your burdens? Did you so desperately desire to go back to your lazy lives of fucking in the bushes?" Thera felt too much of her anger. She took a breath and focussed in on the real issue. "Who told you these would protect you from the likes of me? Whoever sold them to you lied. Who is selling these?" Neither answered nor looked her in the eye. "Well, that's information you'll share later. Tell me, Madame, was there ever a time when you loved your daughter?"

"Don't you talk to me about my daughter! I loved that little babe with every fibre of my being before it ... turned! She weren't my little baby no more!"

"That happens with all children." Thera thought of the look in her father's eyes. "Quicker than parents can imagine."

"What would you know of being a mother? You're just a, a *thing* yourself!"

Therasia placed a hand around each of their throats and leaned in. "I know a mother's love. I am loved more deeply than either of you can imagine."

"Don't think you can do anything to us!" the woodsman wheezed. "We know who you are! We'll tell everyone if you try anything with us!"

"You have never had courage, little man," said Therasia. "Don't pretend to any now. Neither of you will remember this day." She began to work her threads into them. They wore iron trinkets around their necks, under their clothes, doubtless also in the shape of hammers. That made invading them a chore but she was proving a point. Mostly to herself. "You did love your daughter, Madame. But you, Monsieur, you have never truly loved anything or anyone. I will have to take hers, dig down and find it, a mother's lost love, and then split it between the two of you."

It took but a moment. The longest moment of either of these two, worthless lives.

Therasia rested on a chair afterwards, drinking some cream she'd found in the pantry, dipping a biscuit into it and munching grimly. No wonder she never got fat. Constantly working. She kept her mind numb from all the assaults of her inner world. The soldiers and Leifa, her mother and father, now some wandering tinker selling religious trinkets in her territory. All these things would plague her mind later but, for now, she dipped and crunched.

Katrienne stood in the doorway and curse the little beast but she was so good at sneaking that Therasia didn't even know how long she'd been there. As soon as Monsieur and Madame Dourbie became aware of their daughter they burst into tears, rushing over to hug the child. Hopefully, people wouldn't gossip too much at these extreme, emotional outbursts. Their senses would calm as they adjusted. Kitty seemed most surprised but didn't mind at all, hugging her parents right back. Therasia smiled at the Monsieur.

"Woodsman," she said. "Why don't you spend your afternoon gathering up all the little bits of iron you've hidden around the house? I'm sure the blacksmith would be grateful for them. He could melt them down into something useful. Let's start with the pendants you and your wife are wearing. Give them to me." They both did so. She tucked them into her pouch. She could use them to track their sisters.

Therasia squatted down next to what remained of the child clinging to its mother's skirts with a sullen, desperate happiness.

"And you, little Kitty Kat," she said, "do not abuse this surfeit of love for your own devious purposes." She tickled the monster so it wouldn't close off to her words. "You might become the talk of the town. Remember what I said about blending in? Finding your place? Acting normal?"

"What's a suffit?"

"Surfeit. It means, a lot. Your parents might love you a little too much until they settle. You have to help them, like you should help all the village."

"So. They're, like, my first task? Are you giving me my first task as ... as one of you?"

"Aye, Little Kat. I suppose I am."

The thing grinned like she'd been given a whole box of sweets. Rising, Thera bid the family farewell. It was an appalling thing she'd done. Yet the rage lingered. Would anything ever be enough? She took care not to let rage rule her hunger. It was exhausting. She was tired of hating. The beastly child might need a little help with her first task. Therasia could manage that. If it meant not having to hunt down Kitty-Kat and kill her, or banish her to the woods with the rest of the murmecks, the broken ones, it was worth it.

As she emerged into the glaring, afternoon sun, a rattle of intrusion drew her attention to the bottom of the street. She frowned and allowed her vision to press in. Two palanquins approached along the northern road. A figure sat in each. The commandant himself rode at the fore in full dress uniform, come to visit her father. The other had curtains drawn. Those wafted in the breeze enough to reveal a woman, again in uniform but with something in her demeanour. She sat like a broken bird, a forlorn air about her that awoke the doctor and healer within Therasia. There was something else in the air. Something that flowed. Some strange presence, like light glistening in too much dust.

4

Sadness Buried Deep

Adelaide was going to lose the arm. She couldn't make a fist, barely felt it when she touched anything with her swollen fingers. Tears mixed with the sweat on her face. Swaying back and forth in the palanquin. The fever tickled at her mind, letting her know the rot had begun.

She did her best to remain focused, calm. Panic would only accelerate things. Perhaps Valencia, with all her chemicals, might have something. If she lost the arm her life would be over. The sun, the deep knife wound, the blood loss, and the effort spent today, all these things conspired to burn her where she sat.

Adel would not show weakness. That was detrimental at the best of times. Unforgivable in front of her commandant. Fears blew about her, despair feeding on her soul like some living thing.

Now they were in the village.

She'd lost track of time. That was a sure sign of fever descending.

Blossoms hung in baskets from the fine, clean houses and overflowed from window boxes. This looked like part of High Town in the city or some wealthy estate outside the walls, only the street was a damned sight cleaner. She could hardly credit this as some dirt-scratchers hovels. Cobblestones rose up to meet the bearer's steps. That would hurt a lot more than a dirt road when she fainted.

The commandant called to stop. Adel thanked every star in the sky, the hammer, the anvil and the twist of snakeskin she kept in her sash.

She sat sweltering. The sling cut into her shoulder. Fortunately, protocol dictated she not emerge before the commandant. He had to wait for the bearers to form into a guard. That took a relieving moment.

The men snuck the opportunity to refresh themselves from water skins hanging on the back of the palanquins, eyeing their surroundings anxiously. Adel took a similar opportunity to sip from her flask, a watered-down eau-de-vie, to fortify her for the walk up the hill.

She lingered on the edge of consciousness where she felt the fever as an actual presence, tormenting her, enjoying her suffering.

Eventually, she had to emerge. She did so in proper military fashion, standing almost steadily to attention as she swept her hat onto her head. With the wrong hand because of her injury. The sword hung awkwardly on the wrong side. She should be able to draw it more easily than on the hill, back when that horrific curse struck the poor signaller.

Marching carefully over to the commandant she stopped on his left, two steps behind. They all marched up the hill. Four of the honour guard formed the corners of a protective square around the two officers. The other four fell in behind. Alert. Watchful.

The village seemed terrified by their presence. All shutters closed. Not a soul intruded on the cobbled street.

Except for one girl. More a young lady, lithe and graceful, dark hair piled up on her head, revealing a beautiful, long neck. She skipped merrily up to the marching soldiers with an amused smile tugging at her lips.

Adel was utterly captivated by this tall, lively woman in her fine long-shirt and rough, embroidered vest. Was that a silk sash at her waist? Adel could not afford such a thing and yet this peasant sported one as day wear? The girl's britches ended just below the knees. From there, all the way down to her short, pointed ankle-boots, her slender legs were scandalously bare. Dark olive skin shone in the sun.

Adel forced her attention away. The woman did not seem to notice.

"La. Commandant!" The soldiers halted and turned to the young woman. She ignored them. "Welcome to Arros!"

The commandant smiled at the woman uncomfortably. "Thank you, Mam'selle. I'm afraid we do not have time for pleasantries."

"Of course, no. You have an appointment with my father, La Granger."

"Ah," said the commandant. "I was not aware there was a daughter. Are you to be our escort?"

"Not officially. I was visiting my friend, the smith, at the forge there." The woman smirked mischievously. "Although I may have been visiting him at this particular hour. Come, come. You look foolish marching down the middle of the street in the heat of midday! Everyone else is indoors, hiding from the sun. See? The shutters are all closed against the glare. Please, walk under the arcade. La! You will find the shade much more comfortable."

"Thank you, but I think the street might be safer."

The woman stood at her full height, taller than Adel, as tall as the commandant and able to look him straight in the eye. "Commandant Jev Warren. Such an action insults the villagers. You imply that they are so impolite as to do violence to a guest of La Granger."

"It is not the villagers that worry me."

"La! You will find no fey here, Commandant! We may rely on the Kindly Ones for our protection but we name them in irony. The village is well aware of their feral nature. There is iron protecting every dwelling. You are safer from them here even than in your camp. Besides, I think the lady is feeling the sun already, or her injury bothers her, perhaps? You have been rude not to introduce us. Come along."

The woman slipped past the guard and hooked Adel's good arm like they were the best of friends. They walked over to the shaded arcade that ran the length of the village's main street, contiguous but changing styles as it ran under each different building.

The coolness was an instant blessing. That spirit of despair seemed to flutter away from Adel at the graceful woman's touch. That made Adel like her even more.

The bemused soldiers looked askance at the commandant. He waved them back.

"Form the men up behind us, Paxton," he said. "Proceed in an orderly fashion. Stay vigilant." The commandant joined them. He smiled with rigid civility at the presumptuous woman, removing his hat, bowing and indicating Adel. "Myself you seem to know. This is Caporal Adelaide Lelaing."

"A melodic name! I am Therasia Garonne. You may call me Thera and I will call you Adel. We shall be sisters."

As the young woman patted her arm, Adel smiled uncomfortably. She was still unable to say anything though her little bird in its hairy nest was singing with hungry insistence.

"I am curious," the commandant said as they continued their ascent. "Does the iron really keep the fey out of the village?" He peered about as if he'd lost something. Adel could see a small iron mark above the door of a nearby house in the shape of a flower.

"As much as anything. I have some new pendants if you would like one?"

Thera fished into her pouch, a large, square thing of many compartments. Adel fought with the ideas raised by the woman's fingers questing inside. The mademoiselle brought out a pair of stylised iron hammers on leather thongs, typical charms sold by agents of the church. It surprised her to see such things in a village like this.

"You can wear it or just carry it about your person. Then, when you meet a fey, you pull it out and press it up against them!" She touched the charm with deliberate clumsiness, her face twisting into an expression of exaggerated pain. "Ayi! And the fey will scream and flee as they are burned by its holy power! Although, I'm told an old nail effects much the same result. Here, you keep this one," she said and tucked the metal charm into Adel's waistcoat pocket.

"So metal repels them?"

"Iron does. It helps if it's magnetised. We also leave out gifts for them. You passed many little shrines at the edges of the fields?"

"Ah. Yes. We have an item that was left out for your fey, perhaps. Can you tell us something about it? Caporal?" He gestured to Adel's other pocket.

"Oh. Your arm. Allow me," said Thera. Her long fingers lifted the flap on Adel's waistcoat pocket and slipped inside, rummaging about.

Adel's little bird wished those adept fingers would rummage inside other things. She stopped dead in her tracks, unable to breathe in this woman's presence. Adel cursed her weak nature that she could not dismiss such abhorrent, unnatural thoughts.

"A bottle?" said Thera, pulling it out. "La. It's one of ours."

"Yours?" asked the commandant. He turned and continued up the street, posing the question in a casual manner that fooled no-one.

"Yes. Look. This is our house mark, here. We have a clay oven in the works next to The Grange. There are a couple of other people who make stoneware in the village but ours is the best! My father gets the clay in from the pits at Boussens. We make most of the piping around the village for the water and waste."

"You have sewers here?"

"Oh, yes. And running water, too. We tap the local stream, before it enters the village, while it's still fresh. Some goes for house use, some for the sewers. There's an excellent plumber in Murel, the next village over. This bottle is old. We changed the house stamp a few years ago when I came back from the Mountain Monks and set up as village surgeon. There's a striped pole in this quarter now."

"Can you tell where it comes from?"

"I'm sure this has been around Arros a dozen times. We make things to last. Each owner would get the best use out of it they can." Thera sniffed the opening. "You washed it but a scent lingers. It had milk or cream. Going sour. That sweet aroma before the rot sets in. Or, perhaps, the sweetened milk that the fey like."

"The fey have preferences?" The commandant was determined to push the matter. Adel could see that Thera was well aware of this and playing with him. She cursed her misfortune. The bottle meant nothing. Her contribution to this day was a failure. Her hand was about to rot off. Adel's stature would shrink in the world and none would remember the name Lelaing.

"People leave small gifts out for the fey," Thera replied. "If milk is getting old, or was out in the sun, people will sweeten it with juice or honey and leave it for the fey to find. They'll eat anything offered as long as there's enough sugar in it. Set some around your camp. Maybe they won't bother you any more."

"Really?"

Thera laughed. A deep, rich sound like a carillon of bells rung by the happiest campanologists in the world. "No. You stink of the city and they want you gone. Ah! Here, here! Have a seat, sister. Commandant. I think this is what was in your bottle."

The woman skipped into a small residence near where the street opened up into some sort of agora. A bench sat outside the entrance.

Commandant Warren glanced about, seeming agitated by this interruption of his planned march. He sat reluctantly and only then did Adel gratefully follow suit.

The agora was broad and clean, taking advantage of a curve in the stream that ran down the other side of the village in a shallow gully. A strange, covered fountain stood at one corner under the shade of a huge, old tree. There were flowers.

The land dropped away opposite, granting a sweeping view of the summer landscape. Hillsides browned as crops ripened in the sun. Rich green forests rambled abundant. Fields filled the valley floor. In the distance, blue mountains rose so high they yet displayed caps of snow. Such a beautiful place. Adel felt ease drifting over her. Also a sadness that these people were her enemies.

"Saliesa? Ah! Sal." Thera spoke to the old woman inside, using some local dialect. The old lady accepted the bottle and opened an evaporator. Such devices usually graced only the best houses in Tolosa. Here an old shop-keep had one on her counter. A wooden cabinet with a trickle of water down the iron back. The dampness evaporated, keeping the inside of the insulated cupboard cool. Wrinkled old hands drew out two cold bottles. Thera dropped a few coins onto the table and returned.

"Commandant?" Thera asked offering him a bottle.

"No, thank you."

"La. Your loss. Adel, you must drink some. It will do you the world of good. Here. Allow me." She used a fingernail to punch through the waxed paper tied around the top as a seal. "It has egg whites, cream, sugar, fruit juice. In Saleisa's native tongue it's called morir sonando, which means to die dreaming." Adel reluctantly accepted the bottle. It was roughly the same size and shape as the one she'd recovered. The drink was very silky, chilled with ice. It went down like a cool caress. Ah, there was her hairy bird singing again.

"Would the old lady know who purchased that bottle?" the commandant asked.

"Oh, half the village buys from Sal. Even some of the itinerant workers come in for the harvest. I doubt she could even remember everyone who came to her in the last two days. Tell me, Commandant, where did you find it?"

"The creature who, ahem, who killed my men threw it at me." In her eagerness to answer Adel spilt a little of the drink down her chin. This was the first time she'd spoken to the beautiful Thera. Every word was clumsy, like her tongue was twice its size. She had to clear her throat after half a phrase. Now her face was a mess. Adel felt like an utter bumpkin and couldn't look the young woman in the eyes as she dabbed her chin with her sleeve. "H- Hit me in the head. Made me miss my shot."

"Smoke and fire! Tell me it is not true! You fought a faery and lived? That is amazing! Come, sister, you must tell me all about it. Was the creature hideous and covered in thorns?"

"I- There-" Adel felt her jaw seizing up. She wished the arcade would collapse suddenly and bury them all to save her from this horror of clumsiness. She covered her social failings by coughing and taking a long draught of the refreshing drink. Such a wonderful taste.

"Dreadful business," Thera continued, straightening. "Come along sister, we can chat later while the men wave their penises at each other."

Adel almost choked on her drink at the crudity. The woman was like a whirlwind, a true force of nature. Even the commandant smiled. Adel rose slowly but was steadier now than she'd felt in a while. Her arm ached less since this woman arrived. The rest and cool drink soothed her tormented soul.

The commandant rose. They continued.

"Dreadful is barely adequate," Adel said, confidence returning with each invigorated step. She felt as though she was supported by a dozen small threads, easing her actions. "Seven troopers slaughtered without meaning or provocation."

"Without provocation? No," said Thera. "It was because of the massacre at the escarpment."

"What? I didn't kill anyone!" Adel glanced at the commandant. He who avoided her gaze.

A strange look passed over Thera's face. Underneath the mischievousness Adel caught a hint of something brittle, shaking. "Maybe not, my sister," said Thera. "The story is all over the village. Did you not know? Four soldiers attacked a group of villagers at the edge of the high fields. A friend of mine called Liefa. She and her companions were picking mushrooms. They killed the men and chased the girls over a low cliff. Not low enough. I believe my father sent you a letter, Commandant. But you did not present the men for punishment. The fey dislike injustice more than anything. Or they like the excuse it gives them. They can be, sometimes, less than accurate in the extremes of their rage." This with a look at Adel's arm. "But the deaths of your men are on your own head."

"There were no accurate reports of the event," said the commandant uncomfortably.

"From your own men? I'm sure there were not."

"I found the matter not worth pursuing, young lady."

"You should not talk that way about a friend of mine who is dead because of your people," said Thera. Her voice resonated in the village square. Gone was the playful shrew. The pain underneath showed through. "There is nowhere to hide here, Monsieur. This village is not your army, your city. There is no general malaise of wilful ignorance. No automatic deference to authority where none would dare question your decision. You will have to learn to deal with your failures in leadership if you wish to leave with any of your men alive." To his credit Commandant Warren did not rise to this bait. Adel wanted to interject on his behalf but she still processed the fact that the commandant did not even mention this business to the rest of the camp. "La! Adel! But you are dripping all over your uniform! Oh, the house is here; the house is right here. You must let me have a look at your gash."

Adel flushed, embarrassed even further. "The wound has only opened a little. It's not serious."

"Do not tell me what is serious. I trained with the Mountain Monks, you know." Thera pulled a small, white kerchief from her pouch and used it to catch the drips. "My surgery is at the back."

They approached the gates of a walled grange. A most pleasant seat. Broad in the main house with several works buildings scattered in the courtyard at the front. Blossoms graced every facade. Even the utilitarian sheds.

It reminded her of the better, architect-designed houses in the estates around Tolosa. Everything about this village seemed too clean and well-made for a bunch of peasants. Adel could not reconcile the ideas in her head with the finely built dwellings about her, full of flowers and a shaded arcade. Half the windows in the city were paper or cloth. Here every opening glittered with finest glass, those that she could see on the shaded sides of the buildings. No few of these houses displayed stained-glass panes in their main window, under the arcade, coloured and pictorial. Gorgeous.

Thera led them down the tree-lined walkway. When they reached the door she turned to the soldiers behind. "Paxton, was that not your name?"

"Lieutenant Paxton," the old soldier replied stiffly. Adel wondered if he knew about the business with the villagers.

Thera looked confused. "Is this not the badge for adjudant?"

"We are a support unit for Walkers," the commandant explained. "Thus we all assume dragoon rankings. You should address him as Lieutenant."

"Dragoon. From Dragon. A thing that stamps around and breathes fire. Appropriate. Well, Lieutenant Paxton, you and your men might be more comfortable in the long shed over there. A table is set up for the workers' lunches." Thera leaned in, conspiratorially whispering. "And there is a tun of cold beer in the evaporator. Help yourselves."

"Sir?"

The commandant nodded a dismissive approval. "That will be fine, Paxton."

Thera bustled in through the wide front door calling, "Papa! I have brought your visitors! One of them is leaking!"

The interior was a rich mixture of tasteful, blue walls and polished wood. This was not the dwelling of peasants.

A stunning painting of the razing of Ciney hung opposite the stair. A war fought over cows. Oddly fitting.

An older, handsome gentleman emerged from one of the front rooms. Neatly dressed, he spoke with gruff disapproval through a thick, sable beard, silvered with age. "Thera! Where did you run off to? I told you I am expecting... Ah. Commandant! Huh. Welcome, Monsieur. Please, please. Come into my study. And your companion."

"No, Papa," said Thera. "She leaks, see? She fought a faery this morning and survived! She is going to tell me all about it while I attend her injuries."

The old man glowered. "Fought a... Well. If you do not mind, Commandant? For all her impertinence, my daughter is a fine seamstress."

"Seamstress? Ha!" The daughter feigned offence at her father's cruel banter.

"It is of no consequence," said the commandant.

Adel wished her superior would not be so dismissive. These people played with him, pushing and grabbing, seeing how much they could get away with. Perhaps he had some other agenda. The commandant kept looking around as if he'd lost something. It seemed to unsettle him. However, he moved with confidence into the study. Adel was but a pawn in this cavalier game. She did not have the knowledge or experience to bring deeper strategies to bear.

"Wonderful!" said Thera. "I shall send Mother with some refreshments for you." She led Adel down the corridor, calling out, "Mama! The guests have arrived! See if Papa has left any good wine in the cellar!"

A striking woman, clearly Thera's mother, emerged, a slight air of vagueness about her. "Do you have a patient, my dear?"

"Yes, but I shall take care of her. Papa has a guest and will require refreshments. You should go and see what victuals might pique the commandant's interests."

"Oh, yes. Yes, of course." The woman wandered past, straightening her clothing.

"She seems lost in her own house," Adel commented and immediately regretted saying such a thing out loud. "I'm so sorry. I- I forgot myself for a moment."

Thera looked at her. There was another pause in the performance of mischievous shrew. She spoke quietly from a sadness buried deep. "A stroke. Over ten years ago. She never fully recovered. We all look after her. I had to grow up quickly, take on many duties about the house. My father rallied well but it made him over-protective. La! Enough! I want to hear more about this fey attack! Come through to the surgery."

Adel followed the woman down a broad corridor, past the room from which her mother emerged. A well-appointed kitchen from the brief glimpse available. There were staff, other men and women, busy inside. Probably preparing the worker's lunches.

Between the exposed, wooden pillars along the hallway, more paintings hung. Mostly pastoral scenes, but a portrait or two. Even the ceiling displayed plaster roses and cornices, tastefully blended in with the rest of the décor.

Adel was silent, nodding absent admiration at the art-works. She pretended to compose her thoughts in a mind awash with raging emotions. This sudden burst of honesty from the peasant promised things she dared not entertain. Thera opened a door at the end of the corridor and ushered Adel into a small vestibule.

"Straight through, go on, on," said Thera, indicating the door at the other end of the short corridor.

A sideboard and collection of smocks furnished one wall. Chairs lined the wall opposite. Adel walked with deliberate steadiness to the door and through into a lighter room, furnished plainly but comfortably. A chaise, table, chairs, cupboards of equipment. It rivalled the best surgeries in the city for cleanliness and facilities. The fresh green made for soothing wallpaper. She stood and caught her breath, glancing back to see what delayed her doctor.

Thera bent over, undoing the ties at the knees of her britches. She looked up and smiled, amused. "On the far wall, to the left, there is a sink. Grab yourself a chair and rest your arm inside. You can bleed to your heart's content. I must change. If I get any more blood on my good clothes Mother will kill me!"

Once seated Adel began working one-handed at the copious buttons down the front of her waistcoat. Eventually she was able to slide out of it. There were stains on her best brocade that she'd worn to impress La Granger. Ruined, now. There were three more buttons at the wrist of her shirt. She cautiously undid these and rolled up the sleeve.

Red soaked through much of the bandage's length. At the deeper part of the cut, near her elbow, blood leaked in small drips. She could feel the tingle of infection all up her arm.

Misery told her that the rot had set in too far and she would die even if they removed it. Despair contributed that, without the arm, she might as well die. A tiny flutter of hope lingered at the back of her mind. She hoped that the infection was not serious. That the wound was simply fresh. The tingling wasn't even a disease. Above all, she wished that this village quack would somehow prove to be a worker of marvels beyond reason.

The woman strode into the room wearing a rough-spun smock and, apparently, nothing else. Her long legs flicked her across the room to an armoire, bare feet pattering on the wooden floorboards. She collected various accoutrements to her profession.

The smock ended far above her knees. The utter shock of sudden sensuality quickened Adel's pulse. The rich tones of the surgeon's dark skin matched the deep black of her hair. They gave a solidity to her slight limbs.

Lights danced across Adel's vision. Abruptly, the woman was beside her, clattering her gatherings onto the wooden draining board at the side of the sink. Adel realised she was staring only when the angle hid the woman's graceful legs from view.

"Don't be shocked," said Thera, aware of her gaze. "It's just us girls. Now, let us unwrap this unwanted present." She leaned in from behind and used a small, flint angle to cut through the linen, unwinding it only a few turns before she stopped and said, "Ah, no, this will not work." Moving around to the front, she cupped Adel's arm along the length of hers and began feeding it back through the sleeve. "Can you pull it out?"

Adel nodded mutely. Words! Words! She had magnificent words. Studied, poetic words. What happened to them all? The woman untucked Adel's shirt, hauling one side up on top of her shoulder, leaving her arm free. The cool air over her skin was almost more than Adel could stand. She covered her shiver by wincing in pain at a slight movement of her gash.

"Oh, so sorry," said Thera. "My, my! You wear a wide bandeau across your chest." She peeked under Adel's shirt, her eyebrows rising in appreciation. "A magnificent bosom! Ah! I am so jealous! I waited years for my tits to grow. I'm still waiting." Adel's other arm wandered vaguely across her torso, seeking to cover some aspect of her exposed self.

Thera ignored all of that and rapidly unwound the bandage, sneering in disgust. "La! Who did your stitches? A shoemaker? Oh, that will not do at all! No, no. This would leave a clumsy scar. O! so ugly. You would also lose much use from your hand. We have better ways to fix such things these days." She tossed the flint and pulled a small pair of wooden tweezers from a pocket on her smock. Skilfully, she undid all the work done by Valencia, the camp medic. "We should numb this," she muttered. "And I need more light."

The woman moved behind Adel and stabbed her in the shoulder with a bone needle which ended in a rubber bulb. She squeezed and something went into Adel's arm. The needle came out and a bubble of blood emerged diluted by some tincture, which Thera wiped away. She pressed a sulphured square against it and said, "Here, hold this," before she flicked about the room, opening shutters in spite of the day's heat. Warmth and fresh air wafted in, smelling faintly of apples.

Adel sat. She felt powerless in the presence of this confident woman, who shuffled a couple of full-length mirrors into position. She angled and twisted them to reflect a harsh glare at Adel. The soldier shielded her eyes with her off hand. Peeking through her fingers, she tried to catch a glimpse of those beautiful legs that flashed about the room. The small square of cloth stayed stuck to her shoulder so she let it be.

Suddenly the woman was before her, then behind her. Adel became aware that she could no longer feel her arm. Instinctively, she tried to flex her hand. Thera spotted the action and slapped her on the shoulder in admonishment. "Be still!" It was all too much for Adel to bear. She wanted to rise and confront this flitting thing, grab the woman and pin her down, then... NO! No. Not that. She flinched as Thera began cleaning the wound, pouring water from a clay pitcher and dabbing at it with a sulphured cloth. Everything was sterile and sanitary in here. Adel felt ashamed for making it all so dirty. She housed a filthy soul that no amount of scrubbing would ever cleanse.

"Now," said Thera, "this will hurt. A lot. The muscles will be numb but we will be dealing directly with the nerves." She walked around in front of Adel with a strange copper tube in one hand and a wooden spoon in the other. "I'll need you to bite down on this spoon. And then I will use my new toy." She waved the copper tube. "The inside is silvered. This little prism at the top will reflect the light down inside, right into the cut. Sorry it's so bright in here. Just close your eyes. The numbing agent should prevent you from moving your arm. I'll strap it to the chair. However, I will be prodding around deep which will fire your instinct to flinch. I'll use my fine tweezers to insert these. Voilà!" She fished out a little, glass bottle containing small, brown things. They looked like tiny, thorned branches, barely wider than a hair and about twice the length of an eyelash. "These are made from hard gelatin. They will hold the muscle together for three or four days while it heals, help the nerves to align, then they'll dissolve. Bite down hard when it hurts." Thera leaned in with a maddening twinkle in her splendid, dark eyes. "And I don't mind a bit of moaning."

There followed an unmeasured period of alternating blinding agony and stolen glimpses of this exquisite woman. She moved so close to her that Adel could study each strong feature in perfect detail. Even her ears were salacious. The smock swung forward enough that she could see the woman wore no wrappings about her own chest.

Adel's teeth ground into the handle of the spoon.

There was a moment when Thera reached out with one long leg to hook a stool and drag it over to kneel on. That exposed so much of her sensuous limb that Adel wondered if the woman even wore lower wrappings. There followed an extended agony which Adel bore with a sense of guilty castigation. Her eyes began leaking tears long before it was over and she couldn't stop. The spoon became loose in her mouth. She didn't have the strength to gather it.

Eventually it ended. Thera stared down at her tear-stained face with a strange expression. She pulled the spoon free leaving an emptiness in Adel's mouth that desperately needed filling. Adel felt red-eyed, runny-nosed and disgusting.

"Ahhh, my brave soldier. You are arousing my sympathies," said Thera. She wiped Adel's face with a fresh, damp kerchief. "That is a bad thing for a, er, a surgeon like myself. We must always remain hard and practical. Never allow anything soft into our lives. It is the same for a soldier, no?"

"I- Er, yes. In some ways." Adel's voice was still thick from her emotional release.

"These little strips with glue will hold the wound closed well enough. I will prepare a couple of twists of cloth soaked in a dilution of that numbing agent. A little ungent in the mix to drive away any infection. One on each side of the wound, bandaged in tight, will press it closed and keep it clean. You won't be able to move your fingers for the next day or so, but don't panic. Once the numbness wears off, the pain will set in. Bear it as best you can. Come and see me in, say, a three-day? I'll need to check it's healing properly. Clear of infection. Drink this." The woman handed her the second bottle of morir sonando then movoed away to prepare her twists. "Come now! You promised me stories of battles with faeries! Was it dreadfully frightening?"

Adel drank a long draft and wiped at her face, sniffing. "Frightening enough. Sorry, could you move that mirror? It's so bright." Thera did so. "Thank you. The fight is not something I wish to talk about."

"Perfectly understandable. Tell me more about you. Where did you grow up?"

"Actually, on a farm outside Albiga, in a house much like this. Perhaps a little grander. An estate in the fertile lands within those circles of devastation left by the last war. We bred snakes and grew cherries."

"Snakes and cherries? What a wonderful combination! How on earth were they used?"

Having found her voice, Adel talked at length about the happier moments of her childhood. The woman listened with interest.

Once dressed and dressed, they both headed back to the study to rejoin her superior. Arm bandaged and slung, Adel found the commandant sat across from La Granger. They both sipped a liqueur, heads bent over some tafl game, chatting convivially.

The four of them ate a small supper and sported over a four player game of Tafl-Up. One of Adel's favourites as a child. She liked stacking the pieces into the tallest-possible towers regardless of their tactical efficacy. Thera was remarkably unprovocative in her behaviour. She played well and made many shorter stacks which could stay mobile. Her father won through good defensive play but Adel felt Thera may have aided that.

They parted with no ill feeling. Walking back down the hill the commandant did not speak until they were already at the palanquins. He said, "You appear to be doing much better after that woman's administrations."

"Indeed, sir. We might consider sending more of our surgeons to study with the Mountain Monks. I think there is much they could learn."

"Believe me we have tried. The monks are famously picky when selecting their students. They abhor military families. War. Do you feel you developed a relationship with this ... surgeon?"

"I'm not sure what you mean by relationship. She did ask me to visit again in a few days to check up on the wound."

"Excellent," said the commandant, musing deeply. He stared at the air next to Adel, seeing something that pleased him. "Excellent. She told me much without even realising. It was amusing to be provoked by a child. La Granger seemed mostly concerned over his village. They are oblivious to my true purpose. Even the girl. We might well be able to exploit that. You should further develop your relationship with her."

Adel's heart leapt in her chest. Immediately she felt a crushing weight of guilt feeding upon that longing. She answered calmly enough, "If you insist, Commandant."

5

Fear Underneath

Would Therasia have to slaughter everyone in this clearing? The half-fey rested under a tree and contemplated the possibility of a massacre.

Many travellers passed through seeking to dig out what coin they could. The countryside contained wealth. The wanderers often vanished with their caravans before consequences arrived or familiarity brought declining income. Most offered entertainment on varying scales.

Of the official troupes, the orchestra was Therasia's favourite with its compositions new and old. As a child she listened to the latest symphonies at the Boussens' amphitheatre. One day she would travel to the city to see the full orchestra. That sometimes contained over a hundred musicians in a great hall. The touring orchestras usually had thirty or forty players attracting folkes from villages all over.

Many of the craftsmen in the cities also travelled in circuits round. They sold everything, from furniture to jewellery, of varying quality. Most of these had a permanent home in the cities like the orchestras, operas and ballet companies that toured.

Troupes of actors and bands of more rustic musicians also stopped in local fields. Then there were the travelling fetes with all kinds of colourful games designed to separate villagers from their coin. These were homeless companies made up of those who yearned for adventure or wished to leave their homes for various reasons.

They were sometimes less than trustworthy.

All paid lip-service to the fey. Those that lingered in the cities also paid lip-service to the hammer and anvil. The church, like the cities themselves, felt they deserved every ounce of respect the countryside offered to the fey and all the wealth besides.

While trinkets and wards against her kind were common, few travellers would ever traffic church-wares in the villages. Thanks to what remained of Katrienne's parents she knew which group currently dared that trespass in fey lands. Kitty-Kat's mother bought their trinkets from a wandering troupe.

This troupe. In the dell below.

How many would she kill?

They danced for themselves, fire-lit in the evening. Therasia eyed them with a weary hunger. The fey-half in her revelled at the opportunity to feed. Since the visit of the beautiful, wounded soldier her human side grew cautious at the idea. Not all of them were evil. Most didn't even understand what was happening.

What was happening?

Festival time. First harvest. Villages reaped the early crops, slaughtered the fat, spring lambs. Wagons grew full. Oxen strained at their yokes ready to transport the early produce to the cities. Nominally, this is what brought the likes of Commandant Warren and his troops to the village. Soldiers protected the payment out and food returning. Examined the produce. Negotiated this year's prices.

Thera could smell deception on the commandant. He stank of lies. A man of his rank, capable of commanding an entire regiment, on a "trip to see the countryside" as he'd put it over their game of Tafl-Up a few days ago.

Unlikely.

He had some ominous purpose. Something followed him around. That pale smear she'd seen behind the palanquin. That strange pressure swirling around Adel. Something that vanished the moment she touched the woman. What was that thing of less substance than smoke and mists that fled the touch of her threads?

She would bring this up at the akelarre. A question for the true fey when they crossed over at the witches' gathering. She would catechize the one who visited their little cabal. It was a complex idea to structure. The fey were notoriously difficult to interrogate. Their minds, if they had such things, worked in ways she had trouble comprehending. It was more like having a conversation with oneself when half asleep and still dreaming. Even as "the strongest" it would require forethought. She suspected it might be something made by Adel. If the soldier was touched with fey blood it might cause her emotions to manifest externally.

That didn't feel right.

It was more.

More than some stray thought or after-image of the battle. More than Adel's pain and uncertainty given form.

Pits and fires! Therasia should have killed that woman on the battlefield! She had no time for regrets, second guesses and other emotions the woman stirred. Her actions had to be absolute. Instead, she was preparing tinctures to accelerate the proliferative stage of healing in a wound she inflicted!

Adel should be calling soon. A three-day had almost passed. The soldier sent no note to say how she was doing after Thera was kind enough to seal that cut. She'd left threads working in it but refused to follow them and track her new patient. It felt wrong. Aiya! Such a thing! Wrong to spy on an enemy? Not an enemy. Adel. Adel of the strong arms. Those thicker limbs might take a while to heal. Perhaps she was just busy- NO! No. None of that.

Therasia had work to do.

Songs and a merriment floated up from the camp. The troupe, hidden between villages, danced for themselves this evening. A perfect opportunity. Four travellers sat in two pairs across from each other. A row of percussion instruments rang between them. Some nice, bass drums with other shakers and stretched skins. Flutes carried the wild tune with something stringed and strummed giving structure.

A large fire burned in the centre. Later on men would prove themselves by jumping over it. Seven, no, eight women. Three older, seated, clapping and laughing. The presence of older women was a good sign. It meant a more established troupe not some flighty collection of ruffians. Unless these were old ruffians, tricksters and thieves. Five younger women danced with as many men. A grey-haired man sat in an actual chair, sipping on a flascon, a couple of other elderly men on cushions beside him.

She could slaughter the lot of them.

Was that the best solution? Were all of them involved in the trade of lies? Who deserved death and who should live? Why did it fall to her to decide such things? The idea of exterminating this troupe was tiring. Especially after walking all this way. They camped in between, in lands not belonging to any village. Thus they avoided scrutiny from the fey-touched.

Thera watched them dance and play and clap and sway. Filled with joy.

She was forever the harbinger of misery, the bringer of sorrows, so the larger joy could continue.

Was it the old woman? That strapping young lad? Well, she had a piece of theatre of her own designed to catch the conscience of these iron-peddlers.

Therasia faded into a thicket and stripped. She smeared herself with mud to break up the lines of her body. Reaching into the fey she pulled down her wooden mask, wrapping vines about her torso, leaves like scales of armour. Vines hung like a skirt about her waist. Her stakes she tucked in at the back, above her seat, concealed. The boots she left on as there was likely to be an extended chase. It was safer than going barefoot. Technology had its uses. She pulled more vines stored in the fey and lashed her boots tightly.

Though Thera regretted the necessity of her visit she gathered her sense of duty. With an old bag over one shoulder, containing her theatre, she slipped up to the merry troupe.

Her threads felt about the camp. The centrepiece was a covered wagon with a bed. Space enough that it also served as storage during transport. They had no oxen so all had to push the wagon by hand. Arduous work. As was finding a place off the road level enough to lodge the vehicle, wheels wedged. Tents made for the majority of dwellings. Low things requiring less of the heavy, waxed canvas. They formed a circle about the fire. Within that the wanderers danced and celebrated being alive.

That tent.

The little iron hammers tucked under the pillow in a lump of impenetrability. The tent with iron nails in the endposts; with a line of iron trinkets down the centre-rope. Most of the tents contained iron. None who scavenged a living off the land wanted the fey to come visit. There were deer and boar in these woods. However, it was easier to steal a sheep such as the one shared among the revellers, ribs and haunches, bones scattered into and near the fire. That rabid wolf she'd dressed up for the soldiers to shoot was not the only reason livestock went missing from her village.

That tent.

With the iron-bound box at the back. It held many bits of metal. Coins Bits of trinkets. Wood and leather. A density of papers. Maybe free-passage dispensations from the churches at the smaller towns or letters from a loved one.

That tent.

Therasia worked her way closer and closer. She needed to save her energy for later. She kept to the real and used the trees, brush and the distractions of a girl dancing with carelessly-tied laces about her shirt-front.

The music shifted in rhythm. Young men began stripping their shirts, eyeing the fire for a good launch point, a shorter distance and safe landing, chanting:

"The life of a person, throw it on the fire!
"The life of an insect, throw it on the fire!

"This dark life, in all eternity,

"Is just the dream of a frenzied soul!"

Therasia flowed under the flap at the back of the tent. She lit her candle with a flint struck in time to the music to hide the noise. It burned dimly. She propped it onto a lever over the bowl and slid back out.

Yelling "Quelle follie!" one of the men dove over the blaze, tucking into a roll as he landed. "Oh!" called the crowd and, "Oh la vache!" Cows jump surprisingly high.

Allowing the music to take control of her Therasia edged into the circle of dancers. Another youth sprang over the flames, splitting his legs in a display of athleticism, before arching his back and reaching for safe ground. More cheers and exclamations followed. Amid the applause Therasia leapt over the fire. Somersaulting twice, she landed lightly at the feet of the grey-hair and the table of scraps before him.

Someone screamed.

Without missing a beat the half-fey lifted the near-empty jug of wine. Swaying to what remained of the music Thera tipped back her head to pour it down. Gasps and uncertainty reigned but the flute player kept up their flowing tune with the help of a single drum.

"Welcome!" the old man called from his chair. "Welcome spirit of the woods! Share our food! Drink our wine! Dance! As all should dance!"

The base drums gathered back underneath. The strings thumped out their chords. The old women clapped and cheered. Therasia frolicked with passion, completely absorbed by the rhythmic melody. For a few, precious moments she lost herself in the measure, forgetting all her duties.

She delighted in the enjoyment she brought to these people once they'd recovered from their shock. Others danced and jumped with her. Thera jumped them higher than they ever jumped in their lives. They screamed and laughed with delight.

Not everyone enjoyed her dance. In a few there was fear underneath the wonderment. That might just be wisdom from folkes who knew the nature of her kind. These she tagged with threads.

Releasing her legs Thera kicked high in the air, cartwheeling, curling over, pulsing her spine in sensuous twists and curves, arms floating in graceful counterpoints. The melody rose. She leapt the fire again, spinning flatly over the blaze, higher than any human could fly. Landing away from

That Tent. Her threads around the candle told her the time approached. She danced and revelled.

At the appropriate time, she flung herself high over the flames, relishing the chance to move, spin and turn, flipping and flailing in a balletic display. Shouts of delight sounded from the crowd. It was so good to display herself before others. No children in this group. Highly unusual. Suspicious, even.

As she landed next to That Tent Therasia allowed her limbs to flick into twisted positions, legs tangled, bent at the waist and spine tortured. She froze, curled up, unleashing a hollow scream of agony. Her threads carried the sound to resonate in the air.

Everything stopped.

Rising to her full height she extended an arm towards That Tent and unleashed a growl that might deafen a wolf. Trees shook at the sound.

The diminished candle no longer balanced the counterweight. It fell, plunging into the dish of oil. That swished into flame, outlining the little chest inside the tent. It spilt and flashed and danced the most horrific light into the back of the canvas. The fire crackled and grew with alarming rapidity. It needed immediate attention. Stray fires usually prompted swift action in a small camp such as this. That impulse strained at the nerves of everyone present. None moved.

Confusion, confusion, confusion all around. Except That shirtless youth. And him. That skinny one. Also, the girl with the loose blouse.

"We're rumbled!" cried one guilty stripling. "Pierre! Run!"

"Shut it, Hallik," said the other, eyeing the burning tent and the money it contained. The more prescient Hallik briefly halted his retreat, wondering at his partner's bravery. Or perhaps Pierre was a city boy and unfamiliar with the consequences of displeasing the fey. There was something about his accent as he cried, "Hammers protect me!" and edged towards the burning canvas.

She rounded on them, crooked finger extended. "The heavens cannot shield you from me, peddlers of lies!" The fire curled away from her as she spoke. Threads shook the air, amplifying her decree of calamity. Hallik bolted into the trees pulling at his friend, Pierre, who half followed. Footsteps measured and sinister she paced around the fire towards the elders.

How much did they know of this?

"And why should we not grub for that we can gets?" yelled the loose woman, interrupting her intent. "We deserves more 'an this! I willn't be sleepin' in no tent all me life! I shall 'ave down in me pillows and sheets o' silk!"

"Chevrette!" the half-fled Pierre called to the woman, reaching from a stone-cast away, steps to and fro with indecision. Young love.

"What you deserve, young lady, I cannot say," Therasia replied.

"I can! I says as I should be livin' high with oxtail lunched, paint on me face. An' why should I not?"

Truth, the woman was just as vapid and self-centred as many of high-born blood. Indeed, this Chevrette snatched up a quarterstaff, brandishing it clumsily, so was braver. Therasia contemptuously turned her focus back to the grey-hair on his chair.

Any human deserved the best that humanity had to offer. There were many plays of misplaced children swapped at birth, to show that souls should gravitate to their natural position. But there were far, far too many trapped in lowly places who deserved a higher life. In the country the fey saw to it that few had more than anyone who worked hard for their living and respected their fellow villagers.

"It was no accident of birth that made this company," she said to the grey-hair. Her eyes bored into the old man's soul but addressed the camp at large. "No children here. This is a gathered gang. Forest-lurkers of misdeeds. Not some family of the road. A once great troupe diminished and picking up strays. The old teaching the young their wicked ways. Where did each of you fall that you slithered down and sank to this?"

"You ain't better 'an me!" the loose woman screamed and swung her staff. Therasia didn't even look. She casually swatted at the blow. For a brief moment she connected to the rocks under the earth. The heavy pole shattered like a twig against her hand. The camp gasped. Chevrette sat down in surprise, shaking her hands in pain.

Thera's eyes bore into the grey-hair on his chair.

Behind her the half-fled Pierre slinked back to his tent. He tore at the canvas, trying to beat out the flames with the part not burning. He served only to fan the fire. wooOOOSH! A great billow. He collapsed onto the dirt, slapping his clothes and hair. Therasia ignored this comedy of desperation and missing eyebrows. Her focus remained on the leech who set himself above these leeches.

The head man pleaded with shaking lips. "O! Ancient spirit!"

"I am not old or ethereal," said Thera.

"Oh, Kindly One!"

"I am not kind."

"...ai-ya... Dread creature of fates!"

"That I am."

"Ai! I beg mercy for my clan! Our worthless souls bear no ill-will to your kind. Whatever transgressions-"

"LIAR!" The word shook the world. The fire gutted and flared. She leaned in, one hand on his shoulder the other wrapped around his throat. "You know what transgressions. The leader takes a moiety from every scam committed by their gang. Tell me, grey-hair, how much was your cut?"

Therasia saw the truth of her guess in his eyes.

"I take a trifle from all! I do not plan or soil my hands! Are you not the same? If a thief leaves you milk and honey, do you not take it?"

"No. We do not take stolen milk. Our souls are not for sale. Unlike yours."

Anger flared in his old eyes a habit of violence behind. "And if we have not the luck of your kind to have a whole forest to plunder, what of it?" He slipped a blade from its sheath up his sleeve, a short thing of concealment and sudden pain. As if a fey would not notice the presence of iron.

"You may take what you like from the forest, as may all. But no more than your due," said Thera. "Instead you steal sheep and other things from the villages."

"We tax those who reject us! We take only our cut and cut those who would spit on us!"

"You take what you're too lazy to earn. Hunt. Work. Don't steal."

"Bah! You're just a girl in a mask!" His shoulder tensed as he readied his strike. "I feeds this whole clan and you'll not stop me!"

Therasia lifted his head off. She tossed it over her shoulder onto the fire, leaving the body to fountain and spurt as it collapsed. His little, steel knife she pulled and peered at, then licked the blade in contempt. That also went to the fire. She turned with deliberate fury to Chevrette and her comically-clumsy lover.

To his credit Pierre had rescued the iron-bound box from the flaming tent, wrapped in a wool blanket, juggling the heat of it. Chevrette backed in confusion rather than fear.

"Chev!" the youth called, tugging at her sleeve. "Chev! Come on!"

It was only when she saw that Pierre held the box containing their wealth that Chevrette picked up her feet. She trotted away, following the desperate flight of the youth into the trees. They headed for the road, open meadows, away from the deep woods. Wise in their amazement.

The rest stared with contrition, outrage and betrayal at the fleeing young fools. Some sobbed and wailed at the twitching, spurting grey-hair. Therasia doubted any of these knew of this amulet-selling business. Pickers at the edge of society, parasites on the work of others. Occasional thugs. Maybe they suspected. Their ignorance was wilful but ignoring small misdemeanours, like boys stealing apples from an orchard, is what passed for justice today.

Perhaps they all deserved to be in noble houses, in soft beds. There were those in the cities who did no work, merely leeching off the land they owned. These poor creatures owned so little. Their greed was now tempered by this lesson.

In her righteous teenage years she would have torn them all to pieces. Left their bones in and around the fire like their stolen mutton. One alive to spread the tale. For now she reserved her wrath for those in guilty flight.

Thera was glad she wore her boots.

Hands reached for her, pleading, accusing. She leapt back over the fire, folding as she hit the peak. She pulled at the trees, gliding down, away from the blaze.

Every face in the camp was a frozen picture of sorrow. Every eye a reflection of horror. Every gesture a sculpture of anguish. No more music and merriment tonight. Because of her.

She fell through the other, curling around a trunk. Pulling on its branches softened her landing. She waited a few moments before fading back to the real.

The screams at her vanishing, the wails of fear and sadness, greeted her return. She would have to slip away in the real. Therasia was already exhausted. Or she was tired of leaving misery in her wake.

The camp would be gone by morning. They would bury the old man, or throw him on the fire with his head, load the wagon and flee.

What rich and interesting lives they might lead.

Circling back around to the thicket Therasia washed off the worst of the blood. The water from the rill felt fresh and cool. She collected her clothes and trotted down the thread she'd stuck into the girl. Chevrette. A type of mushroom, if her botany served. She ran in the real, a steady jog, with an uncanny ability to miss every tripping root or patch of slick leaves.

It wasn't long before she heard something, clunk, clunk, from up ahead. They had not even cleared the woods, exhaustion having overcome desperation.

Both young men were still shirtless from their fire-jumping. Chevrette fussed over Pierre's hands, doubtless burnt from carrying his prize. A few paces away the boy Hallik struck at the fire-blackened box with a heavy stone, clunk, clunk, trying to get in without the abandoned key. The scene stank of charcoal and sweat.

Burned Pierre kept an anxious watch about the night-shadowed trees. That made it awkward for Therasia to slink her way close. Which was fine. She needed a moment to catch her breath. The lid eventually cracked on one side. Hallik ripped the blackened wood away, pushing a hand within. That provided distraction enough. As the gang an-gled to see what prize remained, Therasia flitted from cover to cover with leaps and runs no human could manage.

"The bags are barely warm, mon enclume!" said Hallik. "I think everything's alright!" This one spoke with a better accent. Some village boy hounded from home or run off to find a life of adventure.

"What about the pamphlets, Hallik?" asked Burned Pierre, in an educated, city voice.

"Your little hammer trinkets is fine. Ah! And so is this!" He pulled something from the box. "Forget the damned pamphlets."

"I will not! These people deserve to hear the truth about the hammer and the anvil! How Thor struck the land and drowned the wicked empire!" He thumped a fist onto one side of his chest, then the other. Thera could never remem-ber which side to hit first, or if it mattered. "I came here to spread that truth and burn these fey tricksters from the land! Not to grub for coins!"

A believer. Maybe she should kill him first.

"Yeah, it's alright for you, mon enclume," said Hallik, fussing with the thing he'd pulled out. He was probably try-ing to untie the coin-purse after the leather dried in the fire. Her threads felt only metal. No shape. His back was to Therasia so she could not see. "You got a place back at your church." A priest, then, this burned stripling. Come from the city to poison her lands with his lies. Hallik continued. "I just left the only people that ever took me in. They ain't gonna want me back after this if nary a one of them yet lives."

"Were yer coin, there?" Chevrette asked, ignoring both their dramatic crises. Practical girl. "How much?"

Therasia tucked her clothing onto the branch of a wide tree, hard up against the trunk. Stakes out.

"Stars, Chev! Why is it always money with you? That's all you ever-"

Folding halfway through Hallik's admonishment made for a humorous counterpoint. He looked comical with his arm bent in some awkward chide, eyes half closed, mouth twisting into a sneer. This was a little game she liked to play. Freezing their faces in the most ridiculous moments. She came back to the real after a short arc, ending with both her stakes plunged into the back of the young priest. She rested, gathering her strength after her second fold of the night.

"Spit on my prick!" Hallik exclaimed.

Chevrette looked at him like he was a crazy person and turned back to her lover, only then realising his thin frame was so narrow that both of Therasia's stakes punched out the front of his chest. Mushroom girl screamed, scrabbling away, kicking with her legs to shuffle her bum across the forest floor.

Hallik fussed even more urgently. What was he fiddling with? The answer to that came with a snap and click as he locked the frizzen into place and pulled back the hammer of a small, flintlock pistol. Her threads didn't detect the old-fashioned device amid all the metal. He snatched up the box and pointed the gun at her, surging to his feet.

His mouth worked at some unthought threat or plea. Half-formed, staccato sounds escaped.

Therasia ignored him. These were ancient guns. En-masse they might bother her kind but the flint had to spark the pan before igniting the powder in the barrel. By which time Therasia would have already folded. A brief fold. She didn't have the energy for anything else.

A thought crossed Hallik's face. An evil thought that left a manic grin. He swung the pistol at Chevrette and fired.

Therasia shifted into the fey, driving herself at the girl, reaching to push her out of the bullet's path. She misjudged and bounded into the air, pushing off her legs too strongly. The pan flashed as she left the ground. She'd barely extended before the bullet burst from the barrel in a flare of burning powder. She might not reach Chevrette in time.

Wait.

Why was she doing this? Wasn't she going to kill the girl, anyway? It was instinct. Her instinct to protect. That impulse had her folding a third time, straining every part of her being for a woman who'd recently tried to cave in Therasia's head with a big stick.

The heavy, lead ball screamed in the fey. It would be safer to fly over the girl and let the bullet take its course. But she could not. It was not in her nature. She aimed a stake at. No. Both her stakes were still stuck in the poisonous priest. Sweet boy. Already dead. Falling slowly.

As the bullet neared Chevrette's torso Thera curled her fingers around the woman's shoulder. Too little, too late. Even with her best effort she barely moved her. The bullet punched into Chevrette's lower ribs, scraped around the side and stuck between two. It would have shot her through the heart so that was a win. Therasia came back to the solid, almost deafened by the tearing fey. She landed hard in a crouch, hands slamming into the soil.

The boy, Hallik, didn't even wait to see if he'd hit. His footsteps pounded away, heading for the open road. Towards Casaeres, she figured, that being the nearest town with a church.

It took a moment before Therasia had the strength to rise. Chevrette made small sounds of agony at each breath. Therasia staggered to her feet, ignoring this whimpering as best she could.

All pretence and anger fled Chevrette's face. She looked from a place of pure vulnerability and asked, "Why he crump me?" Therasia crouched down, trying to examine the wound past Chevrette's flapping hand. "They was fightin' o'er me love."

"Deluded child. The priest was only interested in his religion. Hallik's infatuation with you never matured only faded."

"I ain't even tussled neither enough. Ahhhh! Split-prick, half-faced, dung-eater!" Therasia rammed two fingers into the hole, gripped the lead ball hard enough to dent it and ripped it from the wound in one blinding motion. Chevrette screamed, clutching her side. "You's killin' me! Raggity dish-cloth!"

"I have just saved your life, girl," she said, waving the bullet in front of her.

"You're a potato with the face of a guinea-pig!"

Therasia staggered upright, exhausted. "Oh, bind your own sides, harridan."

"Aaiii! Fils a putain!"

With a measured pace the half-fey reached the wide tree that hid her bundle. She retrieved it and sank to the ground, leaning against the trunk, out of sight of the still wailing and cursing ingrate. She released the thread on Hallik. Let him run. Let him spread the story of what happens when liars attempt to poison fey lands. Tomatoes and a small block of cheese from her bundle did little to sate her hunger, for all that there was blood on her fingers to sauce them. It did give her enough energy to rise and slip away from the sobbing mushroom girl. She headed back into the woods to a chill stream. There she could wash off this new coat of dirt and blood. Packing away her mask and vines, she lay in the flow and rubbed herself vigorously.

The young priest was the one infecting her village and doubtless others about. She'd dealt with him sure and hard. Everything else this evening was a disaster brought on by soft decisions. There were those quick and well who should, by every measure, be feeding worms.

Was this maturity on her behalf, wisdom even? Or weakness?

She felt the rage lurking inside, the constant pain that tugged in her heart since the loss of her lover. Run off a cliff by four, masked soldiers. She'd killed twice that many in revenge but the sadness, the loss of her love, still pulled at her.

Now this new, woman soldier infected her soul. A soldier she'd tried to kill, whose wound she'd tended and seen the pain and bravery in the woman's eyes. She shut herself off from every impulse that it produced. But that made her too soft.

Tomorrow, she would spend time with her parents and work on her centre. Father, in spite of his domineering behaviour, offered a degree of solidity and safety in her life. And mother always loved her. They might do some baking together, like when she was small. Both she and her mother enjoyed making things and getting messy. So childish but so much fun.

Would that be enough to make up for the misery she fed into the world?

The water was too cold to allow her to ponder such things. She rushed from the stream, shivering but cleaner. Thera dried and dressed. There would be more than enough time to torture herself with second guessing on the long and weary walk back to her village. Back to her hearth. Back to her home.

6

A Lure of Suffering

Commandant Jev Warren woke from another bad sleep. His bed shifted again in the night, creating little rest.

The tent was cool, the blanket coarse, the cot under him no substitute for a proper four-poster. Too narrow and, of late, he had none to share it.

He didn't think to bring anything more substantial. The idea that he would sleep under canvas every night never occurred to him. In his mind he would arrive and be made a guest in the best house, with accommodations for his servants. His personal chef and ordonnance was technically an aspirant. He had her promoted to an officer of warrant so she was due the proper deference. They received no damned deference at all.

"Nicole!" he called. Knees. Always the knees in this damp air by the stream.

Footsteps sounded on the gravelled path outside his tent. A squelch in the puddle. Dampness everywhere. The tent flaps parted.

"Commandant."

Nicole was another of those very efficient people. Clipped hair, short fingernails and a serious frown permanently affixed to her ageing face. Her uniform was always impeccable. Warren needed that type around him. His ideas were often scattershot and over-large. He needed people who could break things down into manageable chunks. People who could get things done. Those were the kind of officers he sought. They were often overlooked by others of senior rank as being too bossy or forward. "Too clever by half" as General Loftus used to say. Nicole could pull actionable meaning out of his most outlandish concepts. She needed only the smallest prodding to keep her in line.

"How's that sword of mine coming along?" he asked.

"Delivered last night. I've put it with your exercise gear for the morning." Nicole indicated a pile on the canvas, folding chair at the foot of his bed.

"Excellent. Yes. Excellent. Give me a ... a moment and I shall-" He waved a hand at the bundle. "Then I'll call you for breakfast."

"Yes, Commandant." Nicole nodded efficiently and left.

The bed shifted as he tried to rise. Why was it so hard to keep it level? He put boards under the legs but they still refused to stay flat. He could order a larger bed made. That was not something he felt would sit well with the other soldiers. They seemed to admire the fact he slept with them, eating the same food, suffering the same discomforts. He heard mutterings about camp. Other officers had thought themselves so much above the men but ol' Jev was one of them.

Utter nonsense.

His breakfast was quail's eggs and fresh madeleines. His mattress stuffed cotton. His waxed tent, large and with its own attached facilities. If he could only get the damned bed to stay level he could even enjoy this glamorously rustic adventure.

He needed the absolute loyalty of these men. So let them think he suffered as they did. Them and their flea-ridden bracken under plain canvas, with their twice-stewed cuisine. They had no idea why an entire company occupied this damp field. Warren needed them to follow him without question. To fight when told. Even against the most terrifying enemies imaginable.

War.

Yes. That was his companion's ultimate goal. To drive all the lands into war and endless suffering. To feast upon peasant souls.

Meanwhile, he could take proper possession of the lands. The prisons and workhouses were overflowing. Workers aplenty that he could control. Reaping all the benefits without having to deal with these bumpkins demanding payment. And then on and on, over all the lands. An endless war. Endless suffering. Endless power for him! Perhaps the king had returned in him! And if he could control that thing, that spirit of ecstasy, with wires and lightnings, he could master all the spirits!

The canvas stirred in a direction that had nothing to do with the wind. The strange presence that haunted his waking hours might at least have the courtesy to provide him with a pleasant sleep. Perhaps it enjoyed his suffering and drank from his nightmares.

It certainly enjoyed provoking more extreme emotions about the camp. He had trouble enough keeping the various factions and cliques within the company in check. This mystical thing stirred matters for its own pleasures. Unease sparked at the slightest pique. Was this hungry presence that haunted him involved in that business with the escarpment?

If only those idiots from the fusiliers had kept their pricks in their pantaloons. Instead they had to stamp their arrival at this village. Hunt down some poor local girls. Damned snipers. Thought they were more important than everyone else because of their fancy guns. Now the whole company buzzed with fear.

Seven dead. There were barely a hundred in the whole camp, not counting the baggage. Seven was a sizeable amount of soldiers to lose. Especially considering that three of them were dragoons, killed inside one of their special, new, metal walkers.

The damned things were supposed to be a terror to all that beheld them. They'd proven devastating in skirmishes with the Rhenosian cities. One of these mystical fey-kin, just one, and all that bravado, all the confidence these walkers brought? Gone. Yesterday he heard people use words like "deathtrap" and "liability". Their greatest weapons rendered low by a bunch of wasps.

Hornets.

Where was that damned woman? She made him feel better. Her aspect was most pleasing. Even the memory of her full lips was enough to make him wish he could linger in bed a while. Her eyes of deepest blue. That pale skin and bright hair. So rare this far south. Furthermore, with her arm in a sling, Adelaide Lelaing was eager to make herself useful in other ways. If nothing else she was good food for the beast with her deep rage and passion to succeed.

He rose and headed for his morning ablutions. Cold water. That would help. "Nicole!" he called again. Sometimes his ordonnance did not answer but now she knew he was about. She would begin his breakfast.

He drew his morning exercises from his fencing instructor's insistence on stretching and warming up before exertions. A worthwhile habit. His poor sleep position brought a stiffness to his left side but with a few bends and twists it melted away.

The new sword felt good to swing. A hidden wire ran up his sleeve, leading to a small socket on his belt where he could plug in one of the sparkers from the pistols. A nasty shock to any opponent. Now it appeared to be something that might prove even more effective against these fey.

Where the hell was Adel? Again, his thoughts circled around to her. These damned canvas tents didn't offer enough privacy to relieve some stress. He couldn't keep sending for her every time something came up, at every urge. He could play no favourites. Not now. Not when he was so close to his goal. He would be the first to capture a fey. Magnets, iron and lightning. Each aspect worked on his imagination. A visit to the sails would be the best way to start his day.

He finished his exercises with a few good, brutal slashes, enjoying the speed and power of his trained arm. He imagined La Granger's shocked expression as he carved the man in half. And struck the head off that smug daughter of his. The presence sipped at his fury. That small contact threatened to overwhelm his thoughts. He was addicted to it. A few moments served to bring his mind back. Zap that thing and all of its kind, all those like it that the creature sought to release from the circles around the city. Imagine a horde of such creatures subjugated to his command! The sword, yes, felt good in his hand.

He longed to plug it in, take a swipe at his ethereal companion. But that was part of the problem. He didn't know if it was really there or just a pressure on his mind, a distant attention that made him think it present. Bringing it to an absolute and predictable physical location. That was his next test.

After washing and dressing in a fresh shirt Warren sat at his private table. The soldiers ate in a collective canteen. His aspirant brought in his breakfast accompanied by the inevitable lieutenant.

"Paxton," he greeted the man. "What is on the docket for today? Thank you, Nicole. Smells delicious." He sampled the eggs, scrambled with milk and cream, seasoned with chopped parsley. There were fresh tomatoes, an early crop, purchased from the village. "Excellent!" Nicole nodded and returned to her side tent.

His lieutenant read from notes. "The sails are performing most unusually, sir. Too little charge or too much. The details elude me. And Cheryl has finished your ... outfit."

"Ah! Good, good! I shall be able to walk about as a common worker out with his friends. It is ... oh, very good madeleines, Lieutenant. You must try one. Yes. Important to my work. We should visit the lightning mill first. Any further sightings or encounters with these mystical forest demons?"

"Nothing, sir. Though the men have taken to carrying iron about themselves, thumping their chests every five minutes. I'm not sure how some little trinket is going to be more effective than their iron guns, the which can shoot the cursed things if they appear."

"Might be best not to open fire on one if they spot it," said Warren. "We, er, don't want to antagonise them. Look what kind of curse they left on the lands with what happened to, um, that poor signaller."

"d'Foix, sir."

"Yes, yes. Him. The last thing we need is some sort of concentrated spell running rampant through the camp."

"I feel, if you'll forgive me Commandant, that if such a thing were possible they would have done it already."

"That is the problem with these things, Paxton. We don't know what is possible for them. I don't think they'll kill us all. They want us to pay the farmers as much as the farmers want payment. While we hold that up our sleeves then tit-for-tat admonishments are all we should expect."

"Further to that, Commandant, I've managed to narrow down some suspects. There is a small gang in the fusiliers who always make sure they dip their wicks when they arrive in a new town. They've been known to be ... less than patient about it. Perhaps they continued that tradition?"

Warren knew damned well exactly who was responsible. It was information he kept to himself. This half-hearted investigation was a way of not punishing some of his best troops.

"A few in the dragoons match that description, as well. These villagers should expect no less if they are unable to provide proper doxies to take care of such matters."

Warren felt frustrated in that regard himself. Since the death of his current lover he had to take his relief where he could get it. It was unfortunate that Esmeralda discovered too much about his unseen companion. Her death was necessary but it left him with an uncomfortable itch.

"And speaking of that," Warren continued, "have none of the local travellers offered any such service to the camp?"

"I think the nearby fringe-dwellers are intimidated by the sheer size of the camp. The payments for this village usually warrant only a squad. Eight guns plus support. Regular soldiers. The armour, well, the locals find it overwhelming. So we have no prostitutes. The men grow irritable. There are some unpleasant suggestions circulating around the more frustrated men. A few of the female soldiers are single."

"That we will have to stop. We can't have our own soldiers not feeling safe because of our own soldiers."

"There are those that say they did not volunteer into the army to be celibate."

"Huh. Make sure the women of rank have organised appropriate measures in their section of the camp. Don't let any of the girls walk around unsupervised."

"I believe they have already taken some measures. Perhaps if you made mention in your next address to the camp?"

"Hopefully my next address will be to give them something to kill. That'll help discharge some tension. I'm confident nothing will happen until then. Do have a madeleine. I'm not going to finish them all. Almonds this morning."

The lieutenant took a polite taste. "Indeed, Commandant. Almonds."

Breakfast over there was only the matter of a lot of fussy buttons on his waistcoat, further ablutions and finding his damned hat. Then Commandant Warren walked out into the camp.

He remembered to keep a stern but benevolent mien. He was to become the ruler of all. It would help not to be painted as a tyrant like so many history cast in poor light.

The workings of the army unfolded before him. It was a town in miniature. Laundry hung behind tents as if strung across alleys. People gossiped around the water barrel as if it were a fountain in a square. The sounds of hammering, carving and all manner of small industries filled the field. People made, broke and repaired things.

They all needed feeding. There lay the core of this undertaking. The amount of food consumed by a hundred hungry men was more than the village could provide and still meet their quota. And women. Men and women. And more in the baggage. The soldiers hunted the woods extensively but not too deeply. After The Incident the commandant was strict about not stealing local livestock. His colonel, Craon, warned against it before he came. Now he understood the seriousness of such a ridiculous restriction.

He was afraid.

Damn it all, but this fey attack had put the fear of reprisal into everyone.

For all her uncomfortable misconceptions of the larger politics La Granger's daughter was right. He could not expect to force his way in the world outside the towns as he did within.

That was the other thing that drove him. His dominion should spread over all without restriction by circles of blasted wastes. These were all the king's lands. And he was an officer of the king.

He had ideas about that.

The ghostly presence that haunted him faded back as he approached the sails. Warren's heart leapt when he noticed this. The thing came and went much as it pleased but he'd begun to spot a pattern in its absences this year. Its absence now all but confirmed it. His unseen companion was some sort of fey! Or, at least, something that ran by the same rules. The lightning master should be able to contrive-

"Commandant!" Smoke and grime! It was the chief medic Valencia. The woman wove her way through the camp towards him. She used three gestures for every two that were necessary. They called her Pas de Trois. A fussy, flighty creature but with a cunning mind underneath. And a nasty habit of asking awkward questions. "Commandant Warren!"

He stopped and turned with great patience. "Caporal Valencia. A good morning to you!"

The woman used to be an officer. Lauded as one of the finest surgeons in the army. With an unhealthy interest in chemistry. She was demoted because of her tendency to experiment on prisoners. And, on one notable occasion, the soldiers under her command.

"No! It is most not a good morning! A good morning would be one where my ideas were not appropriated! Stolen! Taken out of all meaning and context!"

"Dear lady, please, please! Do take a moment to compose yourself. Er. Lieutenant Paxton can hear your concerns while I deal with a matter at the sails." His subordinate blanched at the idea of having to interact with a hysterical Valencia.

"Unacceptable! I have petitioned. I have asked as nicely as I can. This is beyond! The greatest advancement in agriculture is at our fingertips. At every turn I am brushed off! Dismissed! My work has value! Significance!"

"Caporal. It has been five minutes and you have yet to convey what it is that upsets you so. Please. Compose yourself. Better still, compose a short letter. Take as many attempts as you wish to communicate whatever-"

"No, no, no! I must be heard."

"Madame, I am hearing you but I am not hearing any sense."

"The wasps, Commandant! The wasps!"

"Arctic hornets I think you'll find. You can tell from the white fur-"

"I haven't seen their fur! I have seen nor heard not a single thing about them! That is but a small part of the problem. I have no idea how effective my compound proved or what lingering effects, if any, remained in the walker."

"The mechanic's lot is near the sails. Shall we proceed in that direction? The dragoons repairing the walker wore their masks as suggested. I understand the walker was cleaned of gore and powders. They tested it thoroughly with no ill effects on the crew."

"Ah! Now that, Commandant, that is interesting!" She started off towards the sails. Warren was forced into a brisk pace in order to catch up. Fortunately he'd stretched this morning. "Do you know what they used to clean the inside?" Valencia continued. "That could be most helpful if I need to locate a neutralising agent."

"I believe it was something quite strong," he replied. "The bodies inside had already begun to smell when we arrived an hour later. The heat. Wood and leather tend to absorb liquids. Despite their metal shells their insides contain an abundance of both. Perhaps these are questions more suitable for the mechanics. I shall introduce you."

"Thank you, Commandant! Most generous. Now, the wasps all died, you said. Roughly how long did that take?"

Warren rolled his eyes. Then he remembered that his unseen companion snuffed the life from the wasps - hornets, dammit! - so it might be her powders did not work at all. That could prove awkward. "I'm not sure if they died or if they were just incapacitated. I certainly did not see any of them rise again before we left. Did you, Paxton?"

"No, Commandant."

"Ah! Lieutenant!" She rounded on her next victim with the hunger of a rabid wolf. "It was you who tossed the jar into the beast, was it not?"

"Lieutenant," Warren interrupted. "If you could introduce Valencia to the mechanics after you've answered her, that would be most helpful."

"Indeed, Commandant... This way, Caporal."

"Thank you, Lieutenant" said the woman. "Now. How quickly would you say the gaseous effects began to take hold?"

Warren watched the two of them head down the slope to where the wagons, rollers and walkers lined up, protected in tents even larger than his. He let out a sigh of relief. The woman was very useful but she never stopped. She could only be distracted or diverted like a river, constant in its flow.

The skin-sails rose before him in a field that crackled with new possibilities. The camp's oxen ravaged the meadow in the distance. They didn't like coming too close to the sails. No one did. The lightning fields always stood a fair distance from the main camp. Few people liked to visit for long without covering themselves in leather insulating-suits.

"The eels are wriggling a bit more than they should, this morning," said the maîtres foudre, without formalities.

"And how much, Master of Lightning, should the skins from monstrous eels, hunted from the depths of the Leviathan Sea, strung up from high poles to draw lightning from the air, wriggle of a morning?"

"Less than this, Commandant. For days now the skins have been telling me that a deep disturbance is building. I expected a storm but that doesn't smell right. The air is too dry. Far as I can roam, long as I can see, the clouds are high and fine."

"We had a little rain the other day."

"Not enough, sir! And the air still buzzes. We draw far more than we need!"

"Then we should increase the frequency of our training."

The lightning master stared at him oddly. The man was trying to communicate something. Warren already suspected what.

His unseen companion spoke of a wave coming soon with flecks of spray upon it. One of them being death. This confirmed Warren's theory. These festivals, these summer revelries the peasants celebrated, coincided with fey rituals. His strange companion, being some form of fey itself, could sense the coming wave. It wanted to be here for whatever incomprehensible design excited the thing.

Warren was more than willing to attach his secret plans to this expedition. The extra wiring did not interest his ghost. That frightful, ecstatic presence did not attend his long talks with the maîtres foudre. Now the person in camp who knew most about these esoteric forces confirmed that something was building in the air.

He just had to find out where. Preferably before that ethereal thing. He was not sure it would approve of his plans.

"I was the obvious choice," he said.

Out loud.

"Beg pardon, sir?"

"What? Oh, er, I was-"

"Commandant!" a runner interrupted him, charging up with some urgency. Saved by a common soldier.

"What is it, Fantassin?" he asked, glancing back down the slope to the camp. A commotion drew a crowd. A shrill woman's voice reached him. Nine curses on the lot of them! Was someone confronting the fusiliers about their misadventure? Even Paxton hadn't uncovered who it was though it was only a matter of time.

"Some strange vagrant harpy is screeching and raising a fuss, sir. No one can make heads nor tails of her speech. Walked right into camp, she did. Keeps screaming for, if you'll forgive me, sir, "the toff in charge" and won't let no one touch her."

"Has anyone tried to touch her?"

"We's all too afraid, sir, after that speech what you made about not interfering none with the local girls."

"Very wise. If you'll excuse me, Master of Lightning, I must settle his uproar. Expect my return. I wish to understand more of what you're trying to say. Lead on, Fantassin."

"Aye, sir, though the fuss ain't hard to miss."

Warren hastened back to the tents. He could feel the maîtres foudre scowl at his back. "Paxton!" he called. The man emerged from the mechanics lot, drawn by the now rambunctious nature of the campsite. The commandant waved for his underling to follow.

A woman in patched clothing staggered about inside a circle of soldiers. Wild-haired and wailing she clutched her side. Some of the men stared with unkind intent like dogs circling a wounded deer. Much as it might relieve some tension in the camp to allow these hounds their feast Warren regarded this as a fine test of his power over the soldiers.

"Stand back!" he called. "This is not a form of entertainment! Back, I said!" He could feel it. The respect and obedience of his underlings. To have a crowd this large, lustful and curious, part at his word. A tangible thrill! Ah. There came his unseen companion to feed upon his pride and the woman's tribulations. "Two stay as guard. You and you. The rest, be about your business!"

The crowd dispersed. Some with great reluctance. The huddled wretch held one hand against her ribs in a gesture of pain. The rags beneath were dark with blood. She created a strangely hypnotic sight. Odd chimes tinkled from her iron amulets as she twisted like a stabbed snake. She had a charm bracelet of anvils. Other trinkets hung from strings about her waist. They also dangled in clusters from a crown around her headscarf. Her hair exploded from that like dark smoke from a grenade. Her face might be comely if it was not filthy and sneered into pain.

"Dyin' I is! Oh, good noble! Grovel 'n' more grovelling! Stars 'n' thistle 'n' all under the earth what shines! That molly trip done for me! Oh, it grieves me something awful! Great noble! Good and gracious mighty sovereign o' lands! Help a sorry wretch."

This was a test. Warren felt uncomfortable with this screeching intrusion in the middle of his camp. Deal too harshly with the parasite and he'd lose too much respect from the women in the camp. That included all his remaining drivers. Why women had a talent for moving those machines about he never understood. The respect was hard won. He lived here not in some house while they shivered. He shivered with them. To make this business private, end it efficiently, he crouched. The woman looked at him with hope. She cringed and then began sawing the air with one arm.

"Yer smoke is suppin' me soul! Me charms are nought!"

It sounded like nonsense but Warren quickly tried to distract the listeners. His ghostly presence found the woman a delicate buffet of turmoil. But it was here! The woman seemed to think it was physically here! Did it have to be present to feed? Could he confine it to a location with a lure of suffering? Ah, but first he must contain this woman.

"Whoever has wronged you, Mademoiselle, the army is not in the business of settling local grievances. This is a matter you should take up with La Granger or whoever it is that supervises your gypsy business."

"Dead! Oh! All dead! On the fire with his head!" There followed a tirade of mixed curses, pleading, something about dancing. Buried under all the nonsense sat half a phrase that quickened Warren's pulse. "Belenus bitch! ...nor kindly nor spirit..."

He rose casually. "Paxton. Is there someone about the camp, one of the women, who might act as an interpreter? Someone with a rustic background?"

"Beggin' yer pardon there, soir!" said one of the fantassin who'd remained as guard. "But that'll be Cap'ral Lelaing, soir."

Warren feigned a grimace. "Her again." He exchanged a knowing look with Paxton. "People will talk." His second suppressed a twitch of humour. "Very well. I caught something in that rant that might be of interest. It's, er, La Bain, isn't it?"

"LaBion, soir!" the man broadened with pride. "An' thank you for remembrancing me!"

"Hard to forget." The smell if nothing else. "Beat about the camp until you flush out Lelaing."

"I just saw her at the mechanic's lot," said Paxton. "She's trying to learn how to work as a support in the recovered walker. We have a shortage of dragoons after that incident. It's something she thinks she can do one-handed."

"I can think of- Er, yes. Commendable initiative. I may have to promote her. LaBion, fetch her to the medical tent. We shall bring this lady there ourselves."

"The medic, Valencia, is with the mechanics as well, Fantassin," said Paxton. "Fetch her also."

The gypsy-drop refused all aid, shied from every touch. They goaded her with gestures towards Valencia's workshop. It doubled as a medical facility. She sank onto a cot in evident pain and stared with small, fearful looks about the tent. It was mostly reed-woven cabinets. Lightweight field furniture. The few instruments on the canvas, folding table seemed to strike terror into her pagan heart.

Warren heard Valencia approaching long before she arrived so incessant was the woman's chatter. Both LaBion and Lelaing entered with postures of weary politeness. Valencia followed.

The medic waved them all away with exclamations of necessary privacy. Warren was of half a mind to take affront but indicated that they should leave the medic to work in peace.

They all stood in a small group near the tent. Screeches and counter admonishments warred inside. Warren dismissed the two fantassins he'd retained as guards. Paxton and Lelaing should be enough to subdue the wounded woman if she proved difficult.

He deliberately did not pay attention to Lelaing. Her beauty was like a weight determined to draw his contemplation. Worse now that it was over two weeks since his last relief. But Lelaing was no camp concubine. She was a lady of birth. Worth courting for that reason alone. His children might carry a title.

Warren chatted with Paxton about some minor logistical matters. The tent grew quiet. He felt a relief of pressure that indicated his unseen companion wandered away from the medical facilities. That was a sign that some form of sedative may have been administered. If only he could see that ghost. Torture. That might attract it, get the ethereal thing to a real place where he could try some experiments of his own.

Valencia bustled out and called for Lelaing. "Not you!" she said, indicating Warren. Caporal Lelaing grimaced an apology and followed Valencia into the tent.

The commandant's patience started to fray. He was about to thrust impatiently through the flaps when the caporal poked her head out and waved him inside.

"Commandant," Lelaing greeted him. "I believe this woman may have something of interest." She gestured to a canvas chair. Lelaing sat on the bed next to a remarkably transformed gypsy. The woman was clean and relaxed. Her eyes betrayed some chemical assistance to her current placid state. She lay under a fresh sheet in a white shirt. Her hair spread out, combed.

"Well, I have wasted a valuable morning. Let us hope so."

Lelaing introduced the woman. "This is Chevrette. As far as I can tell she is a traveller from a deep line of travellers. She used to be a ... girl."

The woman wailed from her bed, "Trug bangtail, I was. Poor little me."

"A, er, cheap girl as I understand the slang. I'm not sure if she was paid less or considered herself worth more-"

"If she's a doxy there is plenty of work to be had around the camp. She could earn a deal of coin." Cleaned up the woman was attractive. More than handsome enough for that purpose.

"Yer as wants somethin' special, great noble? I has me some tricks! I e'en scrubs meself out when ya comes a visitin' such as yer ain't getting' all them other men's slops all o'er yer prick."

"Delightful. Thank you. Lelaing, you were saying?"

"Indeed, sir. Well. She fell in love with some village boy named Harrik, might be Hallis, and they ran away to a town together. There may have been a theft of some money; it's not clear. Their coin ran out. They returned as a guide for some young church missionary. He sold trinkets to the locals to protect them from the fey."

"Like those that La Granger's daughter gave us?"

"Therasia, sir? Yes. She probably brought them from this woman's boyfriend."

"I'm surprised a gypsy would sell such things to villagers considering the possible consequences."

"It may be the priest was her boyfriend at this point. I'm not sure if she switched or if she thought of both as her boyfriend-"

"The details of her relationships are of little concern."

"Sorry, sir. Well. It appears that, last night, a fey attacked her camp."

"For selling trinkets."

"Probably. From the description it might be the one who attacked me on the hillside. It's difficult to sort out the details. Before the drugs took hold she was hysterical. Afterwards she grew ... a little vague. I think the camp was wiped out. She managed to escape with Harrik, Harris, Hallik, whatever his name, but the fey caught up. It's unclear. She tends to wander into a string of curses. Her boyfriend, Hallik at this point, tried to shoot the fey but it tricked him into shooting her instead. After that she mumbles about being alone and left for dead and in pain. And tortured, somehow. I don't know what happened to the young priest. Val says she definitely has a bullet wound on her side but there's no bullet in there."

"A fascinating story. I'm not really sure how it helps us."

"She has an offer, sir."

"Maybe we could have started with that."

"Sorry, sir. I wanted you to understand the validity of the offer."

The woman herself suddenly spoke up, words slurred by drugs and her own incomprehensible accent. "Give yer all o' the fey! Me baba shows me all the old dells, all the deep grotts and hollys."

"What is this nonsense, Lelaing?"

"She comes from an old family of travellers. They lurk between villages, stealing not too much from two or three about then moving on. They do some dancing in the summer–"

"Again, off the point."

"Sorry, sir. But the travellers know which areas of the woods to avoid. Areas haunted by, she used the colloquial term, murmecks. We know them as tasloi, Deep woods spirits. Utterly feral. She knows these local woods well. "All the deep grottoes and hollows" is a common expression for places where fey linger. I think she can tell us where the fey will gather. More importantly, they will gather on Festive Morrow. The day after the village's cardinal harvest festival."

Warren's heart raced. "La Granger has invited us to the local Spring Harvest gathering. And then, the night after that, the fey gather. How interesting." Where and when. He tried to keep a leash on the rampant emotions flooding through him. The presence was not about. It hadn't heard this. It might be able to glean his purpose at some later point. The less buzz about camp the better. Feigned indifference would be his best defence.

"We will, of course, have to confirm this story of hers. Lelaing, I have ordered a set of commoner's clothes from that northern seamstress. The one who does such an excellent job with the shirts, leathers and so forth."

"Cheryl?"

"Ah. You know everyone, of course."

"She's adjusting some leathers for me. I'm attempting-"

"Yes, yes. The walkers require dragoons. As she has your measurements it would be a simple matter for her to, er, a pair of those short pantaloons they wear and a long-shirt. For you. We can clean and add another patch to this woman's outfit. Head out into the woods as locals taking a stroll. A chance to test the worth of those charms from La Granger's daughter. This afternoon, if possible."

"Commandant," Valencia interrupted, "She will not be able to move for several days."

"Oh, come now, my dear medic. She made it this far. I'm sure there's a shot of something you could give her that would get her moving sooner."

Valencia perked up at the idea but then frowned in all seriousness. "Tomorrow morning, at the earliest."

"Very well..."

7

Infected by Evil

Caporal Adelaide Lelaing woke from another night of bad sleep. Her arm ached to the bone. Weeks remained before it would be fully healed. At least she could feel it. And all her fingers. No rot or lasting damage thanks to that woman. That made things better.

Instantly, a vision of her saviour poured through her soul. Therasia. La Granger's daughter. The wash of sensations that aroused threatened to make her late for Warren's big day.

Shifting on her bracken she adjusted the pack she used for a pillow. Her long underwear and woven socks kept the fleas off most of her body. She scratched about her neck and hair. The nights drew in with enough chill that it was yet cold enough to wear such things as she slept. They would be out of here before the nights grew too warm. Even so, it was time to smoke the bracken again. She could use some of Valencia's stinky incense and smoke the inside of her tent.

Clearing out the fleas on the regular was half the trick of camping.

Writhing, stretching, she warmed her muscles. That allowed her to sit upright and begin the process of waking. The long, low tent provided her with that much headroom. Her apartment in the city had four bedrooms. Her proper bed was a layered cotton mattress in a grand frame, tall posts carved with rustic themes. Goose down for her pillows.

But she rattled about the place since she'd moved in. The empty rooms felt lonely. It was her father's apartment from when he came to the city for business. Filled with guests. Constantly busy.

Adel refused to engage help. Her meagre stipend could stretch to minimal staff. A cook and a maid. However, the idea of people serving her, fussing over her every desire, felt like an unnecessary intrusion on her tormented life. Filthy creature that she was, Adel deserved no servants waiting on her hand and foot.

The morning held a little dew on the outside of her tent. Adel flicked the inside but couldn't get the drops to collect and run off. She liked to do that of a morning. Watch the light scatter and dance from the droplets as they ran down the canvas.

Most mornings she rose in her room and then made her way down to the kitchen. She'd grill some fish and eat it with bread or eggs, walk to the barracks. This created a sense of disconnection from her fellow soldiers. Many lived at their homes when the company was in the city but there was an extra edge of closeness created by those who shared the barracks sleeping quarters.

Shuffling into her pantaloons and shirts Adel edged down the bracken mattress. The women's tents fastened from the inside to discourage unwanted visits. The knots proved difficult though she had some use from her injured hand.

It healed remarkably quickly. Valencia inspected it and was much impressed. The medic even suspected some fey spell. The village surgeon was definitely a woman of science, not sorcery, but she had Adel's heart under a powerful enchantment.

Emerging, Adel headed out to begin her morning ablutions, awake before much of the camp roused. The air was cold. Mist from the stream still lingered. The hot spring sun would soon rise and burn that away. Adel felt the chill and damp as a righteous discomfort created for her alone. It was a shame the rest of the camp had to suffer this punishment meant only for one of her foul nature. She scrubbed thoroughly with cold water. It wasn't cold enough. Her thoughts still strayed. If she ever saw that beautiful, young woman again she would die at the very sight of her.

Thera.

Ayi.

She scrubbed harder.

Efigenia accosted her as she returned from the slit trenches.

"Hey, Cap. We still on for tonight?"

"Morning, Sergeant Chef," Adel replied as one of the men passed on the way to relieve himself. She waited until he was out of earshot and spoke quietly. "Have we had any confirmation about Cheryl's rumours?"

"Hardly rumours. She heard them herself. I've got a few trustworthy girls together."

"Right. Well. I am to spend the morning appeasing Jev the Great, then I am to accompany him to this peasant harvest festival."

"An entire day with the commandant? People will talk."

"People are already talking. That is what people do, incessantly, about everything, regardless of whether there is any accuracy to their prattle or not."

"And is there anything to these rumours? Capturing a Commandant would be quite the trick for you. I hear he is very well seated. A mansion with orchards, in town, across the river. And an estate outside the walls."

"It is not- Well, that would be untrue. I have considered it an excellent match and something that would regain my noble title. However, one must also consider the man himself who I find mildly repellent."

Talking about such matters only brought her a painful reminder that Adel was not like other women. Her thoughts strayed in unholy directions. Even as she tried to pretend to enjoy such talk an image of that beauteous surgeon ran through her mind. An angle as she leaned over Adel, revealing a length of sensuous leg, the hint of her small breasts through her smock. Effie was talking.

"Only mildly? I'd marry up that far for mostly repellent. You have to admit there is an energy about him. And, at least, a comely face."

"Also a habit of exercise that will keep him trim as he ages." This was something she'd heard other women say was important but the entire idea of sleeping with a man repelled her. It was hard to fake these conversations, even if they allowed her to keep her vile essence hidden.

"You will have a chance this evening to see how well he ... dances."

Effie put enough sauce on that last word that Adel felt it might be a cue to laugh in some lascivious manner. She smiled in duty to social custom.

If she was to take a husband, as society demanded, she should at least burden herself with someone who could dance. Her repugnant soul felt the need to punish her foul nature with the most hideous and uncharitable brute she could find. Warren was far from that. His interest might distract him away from too much ... dancing. Perhaps she could come away with the payments, twice a year, and find herself some village doxie to do a little dancing of her own.

"Indeed," said Adelaide. "I am looking forward to dancing a little myself. I will make some excuse and leave early. My arm growing painful. Valencia has agreed to meet up in the woods. I'll have a location for her after this morning's jaunt."

"She seems weird keen to try out some of her anaesthetic draft. Gives me the creeps. Is what they say about her true?"

"I doubt it. It's the men that say it."

Effie nodded sagely. "Still gives me the creeps. Something's broken in her." She glanced behind Adel. "O, put a stick up yer arse; here's Warren's favourite lapdog."

"And I thought I was his favourite," said Adel, straightening her posture. Effie smiled. Adel turned to greet the perpetually grumpy officer. "Bonjour Lieutenant Paxton. Is Warren ready for our outing?"

"Caporal." He nodded to Efigenia. "Sergeant-Chef. The commandant wants you to report to the quartermaster for additional kit."

"Ah. The peasant's garb. I'm sure the deception will prove extremely effective if we run into any locals."

Paxton frowned. He did not approve of women being insolent. Adelaide suspected he did not approve of women in general. Did someone break his heart when he was young? Or was he just an asshole?

"Be quick about it," Paxton commanded. "Warren wants to be away before the sun clears the hills."

Just an asshole.

Adel kept her sleeved woollens under the long-shirt against the morning's chill. The scratch made a poor substitute for the suffering of cold. Her thoughts ran constantly hot. Such a chill would be suitable punishment for someone of her squalid tendencies. She'd be no use to anyone if she caught the flu, however, so she had to make do with the uncomfortable garments as punishment. Warren didn't bother. He wore the peasant shirt in all its rustic glory. The laces at the chest he left loose, showing the hair on his chest.

He even wrapped his feet in tied leathers. Adel wore properly made shoes. So did most of the locals.

"Ah! Lelaing!" He greeted her without ceremony as she entered his tent. "Do you have a satchel of some description? I have one of my own but I need to take more maps and instruments than will fit."

"Not on me, sir, but I'm sure I can uncover one on our way out of camp."

"Excellent. I like a soldier who can show initiative. I spent much of yesterday afternoon with the local maps. There's a full company of rifles to the north. Capitaine Alden can come up along the river. That idiot's mobile artillery would be very useful in helping to create the net." Alden was famously incompetent but well enough connected that he only ever suffered promotions for his failures. "Once we have a better idea of the location I'll compose a brief missive. The other company commanders will be ready to move tomorrow night."

"Will we need that much firepower?"

"We are hunting fey in their own lands. It's not a matter of firepower. We must ensure they cannot escape. Everyone thinks the metal beasts are the army's most dangerous new invention. But no. A subtle mind, like mine, a clever mind, can do far more damage by coordinating attacks with these new lightning-casters. Radios. Fascinating things."

"It is, indeed, amazing how much they can communicate with a few rhythmic beeps."

"Quite! Yes! I'm glad we are so much of the same mind! And don't we look quite the pair! We might start a fashion in the city!"

Adel gave him a non-committal smile. Warren stared at her outfit, using the excuse to stare at her figure. He seemed disappointed that she had her laces tied primly up to her chin. Adel wanted to show off the lace trimming on the collar Cheryl included. He turned to regard the sunrise as it flared over the hill.

"Excellent," he said. "Looks like it will be another bright day. Let us be on our way. I have some brief business at the lightning fields so we'll leave camp via those."

In spite of his outward bluster Warren seemed unsettled. Over the last week bags grew under his eyes. His hair, this morning, spiked in an uncombed mess. An affectation? The locals were usually much neater about their appearance.

"Are you well, sir?" Adel asked.

"I'm fine. Fine. A little flushed from my morning workout. Cramps. Bad sleep. The leg of my bed sunk into a damp patch from some spilled water. The damned thing never lies straight. I keep hearing this child laughing in my dreams. And excitement. Yes. Flush with excitement."

Adel regarded him curiously.

His thoughts were more scattershot than usual this morning. That was his common mode of operation. He spouted ideas, randomly and prolifically, to such an extent that any time someone did something on their own initiative, he could claim to be the progenitor. His memory was sharp enough that he could remind his superiors of that time he mentioned ... whatever was done.

Adelaide pitied whoever had to read his frequent, wordy dispatches at the barracks in Tolosa. One positive thing about the lightning casters. They encouraged brevity in communication.

Adel pulled at the skirt. It hung well enough but it would be awkward for traipsing through the forest. She hated this deception. This elaborate game of dressing up and sneaking out of camp via the lightning fields. It was childish. Warren had some purpose, some plan to attack the fey with his walkers. Why? She did not know.

His energy this morning bordered on insanity. Laughing children in his dreams? Why did he subject himself to such abominable conditions? He could commission a house in the village. She assumed that's what he went to see the headman about the other day. But he stayed with the camp and desperately curried camaraderie. The soldiers would attack where he wanted. They were soldiers. But why did he want this attack at all? Was it cruelty? A desire to destroy all truces? What did this little man want from the world?

Paxton arrived with the much-recovered doxy. "Your charge, Caporal," he said with a faint smile of sadism. The young woman walked tentatively, still feeling her injury.

This could be an excuse to visit Therasia. Bring her another soul that needed healing. That idea fired her heart and washed all thought from her mind. Paxton stood staring at her.

"Thank you, Lieutenant," she said automatically. Thanking him for what?

The ragged woman stared at Adel in a way that made her uncomfortable. "Yer has the eyes of a girl what's in love," said the woman. "Dreaming of yer sweets, is it? Or just feeling yer moule all itchin' as yer dreams o' somersaults?"

"I'm trying to think where I can get a satchel at short notice," said Adel. The young woman cleaned up well. Dressed in more of Warren's idea of standard peasant attire, with her hair tied back by a scarf, she could almost pass as a villager.

"Ain't never heard no one call it that 'afore."

"No, I need to get a bag for... Never mind."

She accosted a young recruit and instructed him to empty the dispatch satchel from Adjudant-Chef Nicole's tent and bring it to her. Immediately. You had to add the imperative or nothing would ever get done on time. One thing she'd learned on her slow climb up the ranks. Swearing at them was also useful.

The lightning fields lay in the opposite direction to the forest. The gypsy did not like the idea of approaching the crackling sails. Adel dragged her closer. Difficult with one arm. She held the woman at the edge of the waving sails of eel-skins. Warren had a brief chat with the lightning master. The commandant glanced about himself. He seemed to be looking for something and failed to find it. This seemed to satisfy him immeasurably.

They circled back into the trees. The woods grew more tangled. The gypsy led them by winding routes amidst the impeding foliage. Warren paused regularly to plot their exact position. The route ran convoluted but in a general direction, north and east. The trees grew widely spaced and not that substantial. The underbrush blocked their path more than any growth of wood. It would be pleasant place for a stroll were it not infected by evil. With a little work they could get the ox-wagons for the walkers through here. Warren marked a possible road. Adel made some small suggestions that might steer them around damper patches of ground.

All the while they kept their eyes on the trees and shadows. Looking for lurking ambush.

They journeyed deep. The trunks and underbrush grew thicker. Warren was confident of driving the rollers through at some pace to catch this hunted coven. He crested a small rise and began to make more notes. Adelaide was almost impressed. He had an excellent eye for cartography.

"I believe we have arrived, sir," she said.

Warren looked up from his map and the roots threatening to trip his feet. They were on the lip of a wide, stony hollow. A gully retreated back into a low cliff, tangled with briar thistle, sporting a brilliant display of white flowers. A large tree grew at one side of the hollow. It was a pleasant spot with plenty of room for fey to dance and revel in whatever manner suited their kind.

"The wretch seems terrified enough," he said, gesturing to their cowering guide. "It might well be the place. Or she's feigning and wishes to go no further. Remember what I said, Wench. You will get a sizeable bonus in coin if your information proves to be accurate. But only after the festival morrow."

The woman hunched silently.

"I believe she has led us true," said Adel.

"And why is that, Adelaide- er, Caporal."

"The silver nightshade. There in that gully."

"Silver...? The white flowers? What about them?" asked Warren, wandering over to get a closer look.

"Ah, if you'll forgive me, sir. Best not get too close. Take a sharp look at the middle of the flowers."

"Hm. Some of them are ... sort of furry."

"That would be the arse end of an arctic hornet, sir. They favour white flowers for gathering their nectar. These nightshades bloom twice a year. Enough to feed the nest. They are highly toxic but the hornets strip out the toxins as they gather the nectar. It's stored in their stinger sacks. That's why their sting is so dangerous. White fur on their abdomens makes it almost impossible for the passing birds to see them while they're doing this."

"Hornets gathering nectar? They don't make honey, do they?"

"Some rare breeds of hornet, sir. These do. And build nests in the ground. If you look, there, in the lee of the shallow cliff. That crack is the opening of the nest. The honey has a sharper flavour. Quite the delicacy but prized more because of the difficulty in gathering it than because of the taste. Unlike bees, they don't respond to smoking. It's a bitch to get rid of nest."

"Speaking from experience?"

"Not personal experience but one of the other farms at Albiga had a nest move in. A number of their workers died during a harvest. In the end they burned the field containing the tree where the hornets nested. It was the only way to get rid of them. Fortunately, arctic hornets are very rare. I don't think I've ever seen a nest that wasn't immediately destroyed. I think this is where the fey who ambushed us gathered the hornets she threw into the walker."

Warren peered around the dell. A deep satisfaction swelled his chest. He glanced at his map. "Huh. Well, then. Valencia's smoke dealt with them well enough last time. We'll make sure to bring some on our sojourn. Let us regroup at camp and plan an ambush of our own."

Adelaide nodded and noted where he stored the map. She would need that if she was to get back here. Tonight. After the dance.

8

Ominous Nature

"**Y**ou is dancing clumsy on purpose, ain't you?"

"La! Little Kat!" Therasia sunk down onto a patch of grass next to the small monster who tapped her tiny feet to the rhythm of the drum cart. "Now, now. Don't give away all my secrets."

"But you can dance so much better. I's seen it," said Katrienne, her face scrunched up in annoyance. "You would be having more fun if'n you danced proper."

"I'll dance proper tomorrow night. I don't want everyone in the village to see. You know all about not being seen," Therasia reached out, "don't you little rascal?" She tickled the thing-that-looked-like-a-child while music swam about the field.

Ignace, the connerierre, had his shit-wagon scrubbed for the festival. Today he was the most important man in town. He sat on a special stool next to his inverted wain. One foot kicked the base in a lively cadence with his special, heavy clog. That produced a skilled, underlying pulse to the night.

His hands added counterpoints and sophistication with two weighted sticks. They chimed off the iron-bounded wheels and rang the axle.

Flutes played over the top, giving the night specific songs and dances. A caller cued a group of merrymakers on their moves. Others revelled freely in smaller groups, often with their own tambourines and shakers.

The connerierre's young son struck the tailgate almost in time. The hinged unit jangled as well as thumped. The child was getting the feel for a beat. He'd get tired before long and Therasia would take a turn shaking things up.

The shit-wagon was the best-maintained vehicle in the village. The soap and oils almost covered the smell.

She'd danced and enjoyed herself, ignoring the lines and leaping as much as she could without giving anything away. Tired, she'd wandered from the crowd only to be surprised by the ticklish Katrienne. The monster laughed and squirmed under her quick fingers, a look of unexpected innocence in her eyes.

"Why don't you go have some fun, Little Kat?" Therasia suggested. "I'm sure you'd like to join in a dance."

The creature looked at the crowd with an eager gleam but her step was hesitant. She turned back to Therasia. "Can I ... can I dance proper?"

Therasia laughed. "Dance nicely. But if you do jump a bit high tonight, people won't mind. They'll say the fey have come and lifted everyone's spirits. I'll jump a few other people so they won't be wrong."

"I has to act all grown up now my mamma is a child. It's not fair what you did. I hate having to be the 'sponsib one.'"

"Well, tonight you have no responsibilities. Say the word..."

"Responsibs..."

"Responsibilities"

"Responsbilties."

"Very close! Well done! Tonight you have none of those. So have a little fun."

"You wants to have fun with that soldier lady what has pretty yellow hair."

"...that's... Just go about..."

"You been looking at her all night. Even when you's not looking at her, you's still looking at her."

"Never you mind that. Go on, now."

"But she's here with the comm'dant. So you can't dance with her. Is she and the comm'dant going to get married, now? Is that why they's dancing together? Like Arrienne and Guillaume? They danced at the festival last year and they is married. Why do you want to dance with another girl?"

"Sometimes girls want to ... dance with other girls."

"Is that something I have to do?"

"Not if you don't want to, Little Kat. It's not a fey thing. It's a me thing."

"You used to dance with Liefa. She ain't here. She brings her lyre and plays it. She's really good."

"Liefa's not here anymore. She won't be playing for us again. I have other people I can ... dance..."

"That's what being dead means, isn't it? No more playing. No more dancing."

Therasia had to swallow an unexpected lump in her throat. "Yes, my sweet. That's what it means."

"If you dance with the soldier lady is she going to die?"

"Stars, I hope not! Half the countryside would be in peril if that was the case. Go on your way, Katrienne! Enjoy the music! Dance! As all should dance!"

Little Kat skipped merrily into the throng swaying and giggling. Old Saliesa took the child by the hand and danced the line with her.

Therasia found herself not looking at Adelaide again. Damn the woman. She was smitten. It was something that she had to get out of her system. A good ... dance would do it. A lively trénis or a delicate, twirling walzer. Therasia was not happy about the idea of spending time with the enemy. Especially one who drifted so easily around her guard, like perfume from a field of flowers stealing over a hedgerow to delight a country lane.

Ai. Definitely smitten.

A figure rushed at her. Thera snapped out of her reverie, reaching for a stake, before stopping herself at the sight of Depe. The broad girl was breathless, as well she might be if she'd hurried all the way over from Murel, the village she haunted. The girl hugged her and began speaking before they'd even separated.

"News of an ominous nature. Movement from the company north of Boussens. That makes a total of a hundred and fifty guns coming this way," she said.

"And it's nice to see you, too, my child. How are you settling into your village now that dear old Bethanea has gone West?"

"Ha!" The young girl smiled briefly though it never reached her eyes. "Sorry. I'm fine. I don't look much like I've come for the dancing, do I? I should have thought that through."

"Ah, you'll get the hang of it, keeping cool under pressure. You are still so young. Nearly two years younger than I. A child. Practically a baby."

"Watch it, old woman."

Therasia laughed. "Don't worry. We'll pass it off as some medical emergency. What troubles you?"

"I am ... worried to be honest," said Depe. "There are also reports of another platoon under that bastard Alden on the river."

"Alden? Capitaine Alden? Wasn't he demoted after Foustain Forrest? None of his men escaped with their lives."

"He escaped with his officers and camp baggage. Tolosa promptly gave him an artillery division. Fifty men, now sailing up the Garunna. They have those heavy, six-barrelled guns on wheels. No messengers have run between but they seem to be converging. I'm not sure how."

"Indeed. Their signallers can talk over great distances with these buzzing lightning-boxes. They wish to disrupt our revels tomorrow night. They may have a location. That Jev Warren- No! Don't look. I think he has somehow tamed a minor spirit. He may have help. There's also a woman in the camp. The caporal dancing the line. She might have some fey blood or he may be a twisted fey himself."

"Men cannot be fey! It drives them insane!"

"Oh, there are hedge-workers, stealers of breath, and faery-friends aplenty with penises. There are some who are not burned by their inheritance, if it is far enough back in their lineage. Usually limited to a simple trick or two. Also, those like Pausette."

"Ah, yes. Of course."

"More likely it is a strong resurgence in him from a grandmother long past. He, himself, is not a monstrosity but something drives him. I've yet to discover what."

"Have the camp doxies no clues?"

"No. The commandant has been clever enough to keep the doxies away from the camps. It's a shame. I miss them and their earthy gossip. That has led to ... an unfortunate expenditure of energy by some of the soldiers, for which I made them pay."

"Oh. The Escarpment. Leifa was one of your ... friends. Leaned your way."

"A special friend."

"Ah. Is that why you keep looking at that lady soldier? Well, nothing gets you over the last one like the next one."

"I'm not- There-" Thera had to take a moment to compose herself. Depe meant nothing wicked in her observations; she was just annoyingly accurate. Stars! Did half the village know? "The soldier was in the group that I attacked. That injury to her arm is one I gave her."

"Really? Then healed it yourself?"

"While she stared at me in a very unsubtle but highly repressed manner."

"Oh ho! Well you should definitely... I'm sorry. This is affecting you more than I thought. Please, let us return to matters of business. Have you no idea what might be happening. And when?"

Thera was grateful for the change of subject, though that was also something that worried her. "Sadly, without the whores, we're practically blind. I'm amazed he manages to keep his men loyal without giving them some way to vent."

Depe frowned, radiating concern. "We should call off the akelarre. I shall-"

"No! No. Sit down. Sit! I have some queries for our faery habitué concerning spirits and the lightning jars. It will name me Strongest. They told me. My first act as leader will be to ask some very awkward questions."

"You will be Highest? Is that why you don't wish to cancel? You're putting all of us in danger so you can-"

"Careful, child! There are larger things at stake than our local coven. They spoke of a crisis. Death. These new lightning-speakers may be more dreadful than we have realised. Their stamping machines can speak to each other, even during a battle, and act in ways we will find difficult to counter. This is a test. It must fail. Their lightning will... But if I can... I don't know." Therasia leaned in close to Depe. "I feel, it's almost like I can hear the lightning talk. Like I could understand it if only... Ah! I need to spend more time with it but that will likely be my destruction. The habitué might know. I have so many questions."

Depe leaned away, looking worried at the earnest nature of Thera's words. "And how will you ask them if we're all dead?"

"We won't be dead. They will. We'll end the meeting as soon as it starts. Gather again at another festival, somewhere, for our actual talks. There are plenty of festivals in the villages at this time of year. Once they fail, we can pick them apart over the next few days. Make them flee in terror." Therasia rose, peering with casual intensity around the dance, calculating. "Stay here. I must find an excuse to leave the revels early. An injury in your village. Some old woman at your festival has broken a leg." Thera glanced at the dancing Adel. "There's one source of information I can ... probe. After that, you and I, well... Commandant Warren will want to bring his own company in for the kill. The other groups of soldiers will likely be used for corralling. We'll see how well they fare against the murmecks."

"Stars above! You mean to call upon them?"

"We. We will call upon them."

"I will not! There is no power on this earth or under it that could compel me to get anywhere near those savage horrors!"

"I'll bring you some of my mother's morir sonando."

"Okay, done."

Thera's eyes narrowed in amusement. "Stay here. Jump some of the dancers. Katrienne will likely come and say hello. Don't do anything to provoke it. The child is still adjusting. And, most importantly, whatever you do, under no circumstances should you even think of- oh, the dance has ended. I must go speak to the soldiers."

She skipped away as Depe muttered "...bitch..." under a smile. Therasia allowed half a dance into her step. She tried to keep her demeanour light. The playful shrew was the character she'd established with the soldiers. Her heavy heart and anxious mind worked against this. Any breaks in character she could explain away with the medical emergency.

Six soldiers gathered in a cluster at the edge of the dance, drinking, chatting. Left alone by the locals. How rude. They were invited. In past years the leader of every squad was always invited. Many of them came and they were welcome. Six was a lot, though. It enabled the soldiers to cluster and intimidated some of the villagers. There was some token mingling. They'd danced a line and a circle, drank and fed. Adel looked a little flushed. By wine or exertion, it was hard to tell.

"Greetings, good people of the city!" she said with more bon-vivant than she felt.

"Ah! Mam'selle!" said Commandant Warren with a slight slur. "Allow me to introduce you. This is my ordonnance, Aspirant Chef Nicole d'Avinhon; her husband, Caporal Elias Camden; Engineer Gustave Arden with his wife Simone. She's a camp seamstress. Myself and Adelellel, dellell, Caporal Lelaing you already know. This Therasia Garonne, La Granger's daughter. Also, by all evidence, an accomplishush s-surgeon. Oh. Too much wine."

"Bon soir a vous!" Therasia greeted them. "And it is, indeed, as a surgeon that I come to visit you. My sister! You have been most remiss in not visiting me to check up on my work!"

Adel smiled to cover her awkwardness and responded jovially. "Do forgive me, sister. I have been kept insanely busy!"

"Ah! But I told you to rest! La!" She turned to the others of the group. "Patients always seem to know better than their doctors!" The company chuckled politely. "May I borrow my charge, Commandant? I will not have the opportunity to check her injury for a few days."

"You should come to the camp," said the commandant. "We have another poor soul, injured by the fey, if her story is to be believed. Shot in the side by her enchanted boyfriend."

Thera's blood ran cold. The mushroom girl with the loose blouse. A daughter of travellers by her speech. She would know areas to avoid. And areas of interest to the soldiers. They could well have the location of the akelarre. "Perhaps when I return," she said, calmly enough, reaching for Adel.

"But it is a dance!" said Adel.

"Which you may rejoin once I have examined you. I am called away, unfortunately. A foolish woman in the next village has lost control of her hand-cart, full of good meat for their festival. It rolled back over her leg. I must go fix the bone. I fear it will keep me occupied for most of tonight, preparing, setting and tending. I may stay overnight. Before that, I must fetch some things from my surgery. Which is an excellent opportunity to drag you there. With your permission, Commandant?"

"By all means, Mam'selle," said the commandant. "I am eager to learn for myself the effica-cecy of your..." he waved a vague hand, "min'strations. Adel. On your way."

"Well, sir. If you insist."

"...yes, yes, yes..."

Therasia smiled merrily to the group, "À plus!", linked arms with Adel and hauled her away. They headed across the common to the bottom of the village. Adel felt very stiff, as if she were cautious of violating some sort of military protocol. Doubtless the commandant lectured his troops strictly about their behaviour. He obviously failed to understand the point of a festival.

"I am curious," Adel said, without looking at Thera. "Why do you keep such a fertile field, so near the village, unploughed? Shouldn't you be growing crops here? I can feel the ground is softer and ripe for planting. I'm enough of a farmer that I can tell just by walking on this good earth."

Thera's heart pulled in her chest. A girl of nature trapped in the city. This soldier was a captivating damsel who deserved some release.

"Ah, but then, my sister, where would we dance?" she replied. "In some rocky, distant meadow?"

"I suppose it would be handier if it started raining. Does it rain often? In summer?"

"Not nearly enough. Or far too much. Farmers are seldom happy with the amount of rain."

"Indeed! My father never tired of talking about the weather."

"Most rural communities live by it. Crops. They want to know when to plant, when to reap, if it will all die in a drought. When the snows will come. We use this field in the winter to graze animals we bring in for slaughter on the Yule. The hedgerows, there, are abundant with mistletoe."

"Isn't that poisonous?"

"Some varieties but this is a milder strain. The squirrels love it. We scatter hay as well. Sometimes the snows will reach us all the way from the mountains. It's best to have somewhere we can gather the livestock. They shit all over the field making it more fertile."

Adel laughed. The sound was a thrill that pierced Thera to her core. "Yes, of course. We had to buy our fertiliser. Snakes and quails don't shit that much."

Thera laughed in turn.

"You are enjoying the festival?" she asked. "How does it compare to your grand, city affairs, with orchestras, gowns and fireworks?"

"I have to admit I prefer the dancing here. There is something wild about it. The summer balls are more formal affairs involving intrigues and fan signals. Dowagers scrutinise everything in the glare of the electric lights. I prefer this looser business in the dark."

"Oh, we have our dowagers and coy signals. I would be fascinated to see all the glitter and glamour of your great halls, with the gilded walls and sculptured gardens."

"And the fireworks!"

"Oh, I have seen fireworks. It was noisy but quite the spectacle. They floated a barge out onto the Garunna, the river that lends its name to my family, outside Carbona."

"My family name may receive a boost. Lately, the commandant has shown me some favour. It would be quite the match."

"Would you not lose your name to his?"

"Such barbaric practices are not followed in the cities. Family and lineage are important. A husband would take the wife's family name if, as in this case, their family is of an historical lineage. We honour nobility in the cities. I have an obligation to my pedigree."

As Adel spoke her eyes shone with remembered glory. Thera could not help but smile at the way she used the commandant's casual attentions as a bright shield to hide her dark desires. Leaning against the shorter woman Thera could feel the trembling determination to deny her passions. Adel smelled of wine, dancing and weakening resolve. Thera decided to provoke the girl, get her spirits racing.

"Whereas we have no respect for people who think they can own everything."

"We do own everything. The king owns all this land, the entire country. You are his stewards."

"La! Let us not be serious," said Therasia. "I will play a little game with you, my noble soldier. Do you want to play a game?"

"It is the season for such frivolous things."

"Certainly. In this game, today I give you all the money in the world-"

"All of it! How splendid!"

"Indeed, every coin and shaving. However, I will own all the land in the world. What do you think will happen tomorrow?"

"Ah. Tomorrow... I do not wish to think on tomorrow."

"That's as it may be. But I'll tell you. Tomorrow, you will have to give me all the money in the world."

"What? All of it?"

"Oui! Every shaving. You will have nowhere to sleep, nothing to eat, nothing to build with. Because I own all the land. You cannot have one person own all the land. That leads only to ... well, you have seen the horrors of poverty that money imposes. You lie to yourselves that you somehow earned every livre you have. That every peasant is somehow unworthy. But no. You own the land. That is all. Here, no-one owns the land. La Granger estimates what must be dedicated to farming, trees for building and furniture, clay for pottery, so on. Then we sell the food, the chairs, the pitchers. No one gets anything unless they work. Even my father. Even me."

"Well, you have fewer people. The cities are heaving. And more are born every day. What do you give to someone you've never met when they show up with a bowl? Is it even their bowl? Perhaps they stole it. People need managing or there will be chaos. And all deserve to be fed. Money is a token in earnest of work performed."

"Or it is stolen. Or hoarded from overcharging. Or... But if you used the land within the circles efficiently, you could feed everyone without even bothering us at all. Instead you waste it on inefficiencies, like cherries for brandy and snakes for the rich."

"Ah, but you have never been to a city, country girl. Nor even a large town, I fear. You simply do not understand how many people there are. Tens of thousands. You know every-one in the village by name-"

"I am a surgeon so I also know half the people in the sur-rounding villages."

"And in the city there are ten times that many and more. Not all of them can get work. We only need so many black-smiths, so there are those with a talent for metal-work who starve. Is it not the same here? There are more people than there is work, even in the harvest. They lurk at the edges of your society. We have a gypsy girl in camp, right now, who wishes for more than a life of, er, dancing and sleeping in a wagon. People in the city lurk at the edges of our society, the same as yours. Our edges are within the walls."

"We should use the phrase, 'traveller'. Gypsy is not a po-lite term."

"Oh, I had no idea. I'm so sorry. But yes. Determined not to be a traveller, all her life."

"But does she deserve it?"

"Ha! Well. And do the rich deserve to be rich? Everyone deserves to be fed but now we get to deeper matters. How pleasant to be able to converse about such things. Usually I find no-one prepared to talk with me deeply. They are usu-ally too cautious because of my beauty or noble rank."

"Most people are too busy making a living or pursuing their own personal desires. Deep is reserved for summer camp fires and languid nights."

Adel flushed with an idea that added a slight tremble to her breath. "Perhaps... This may be something you and I can... If you wish for further discussions I would be delighted to be able to accommodate, during my time here..."

Therasia smiled. "Yes. Indeed yes. Your company is surpassingly agreeable. I find myself most pleasantly challenged by your ideas. We should meet regularly. For conversation. Our meetings should certainly continue beyond what is necessary for medical purposes. Speaking of which, how is your arm?"

"It is good. Ahem. Good. Yes. The pain was troublesome, at first, but now I can even make a fist. After only three days! I feared I might lose it but it seems to have healed well."

"It will take a few weeks to regain full strength. You must REST! Ai! The amount of times I tell patients to rest and heal but they rush out half-fixed. It hurts my surgical sensibilities. Do not worry about losing the arm. It'll be fine as long as you rest it. You have nothing to fear while I tend to you."

Adel snorted. "Mam'selle. I confess I do, indeed, feel safe in your expert hands."

They walked into the village, swapping inanities. The mild weather this pleasant evening. The bad food in the soldier's camp. The fact that the stream running down one side of the village was unusually high for this time of year. Thera reminisced about a patient and related the mild story about a finger cut that turned septic.

Thera could feel Adel soften as they walked. By the time they reached the village square she could see that Adel was aware of how much her facade crumbled. The soldier stopped to rebuild her defences and admire the buttercross.

"I find myself surprised by the architectural acumen displayed in such a distant village," said Adel.

"You think of us as simpletons and peasants. We do not. We enjoy beauty in architecture, painting, music. People."

"To be sure! And... What ... what is that thing with the fountain inside?"

Thera smiled and danced over to the open, pillared dome. A hint of the festival's rhythm still reached them. She used it to create a beguiling performance.

"This," she made an exaggerated gesture of presentation, "is the famous Arros Buttercross! On market days we divert the stream, up there. The water trickles over the dome, down the outside, these channels in the pillars, la! Evaporating to keep the butter and other dairy products cool on summer days. And on stormy days, the roof keeps the rain off the cheese. A wonder of technology!"

Thera bowed deeply. She straightened to see Adel giggling like a child, framed by the fading light against the arcade. The sight quickened Thera's pulse. She found herself also uncontrollably merry. Some small, sane aspect of her soul frowned disapprovingly as she skipped back over to the woman. Long ago, she'd learned to ignore that part of herself.

It was close inside the house though the surgery was cooler. The sounds of the festival faded almost completely. Thera warmed at the thought that she would soon be drumming out her own rhythms on taut skin.

She could feel her mother asleep, upstairs. She always kept a thread connected there. Her hearth. Her home. With her condition, Mother was no longer able to tolerate the festivals. Thera sent her sweet dreams. Papa was at the dance and would not return until late.

As they entered the surgery Adel's knees began to soften. The woman became solidly determined to regain her composure. She stopped in the doorway. Thera had to squeeze past, enjoying the contact that made her companion even stiffer.

"Sit, sit," Thera said, gesturing to the chaise.

Adel took a steadying breath and marched to the seat. Thera quickened about the room, lighting few enough candles to cast but a warm glow over the soldier's beautiful, pale skin. The woman was a fulsome sight. So handsome in her uniform.

"Your waistcoat, my dear," said Thera, opening an armoire to collect a few, token items. "You know the drill."

"Is that really necessary? The arm feels fine. I'm sure it's ... fine."

"And which of us is the trained surgeon?"

"Sorry. Yes. Of course."

Thera watched sidelong as Adel tried to undo the buttons casually. She had to stop and gather herself before she reached the bottom. The waistcoat clunked to the floor. The pockets sounded heavy with something. Probably a flask of that eau-de-vie she'd smelled on Adel's breath when they first met. The buttons at the shirt-cuff Thera undid herself. She slid the arm back through and pulled Adel's shirt up over her shoulder, taking care to spare the woman's blushes. No need to rush.

The bandage unwound, revealing dirt and grease rubbed in. The woman liked to sweat and get messy. Thera had threads working at the injury. Weak, at that great distance to the camp and with the distortions from the metal and lightning. Even so, it healed well.

"This has healed well," she said. "You must have some fey blood in you. It is said they can heal any injury without a trace. This, however, will leave a scar. Faint but something you can show off to your soldier friends. No sign of any impurity."

"Are you sure? It feels somewhat impure."

Thera smiled. "I'll add a compress with some disinfectant before I bandage it up." She gently pressed her fingers into the muscle, enjoying the touch more than she should. "Slowly, very slowly, move your fingers for me."

"Is another bandage necessary? I was hoping to be ... more active by now. Tomorrow at least. Or, or the next day."

"No, no. Make a soft fist. Good. I'm afraid you will still have to rest for a lot longer. It takes weeks for something like this to heal. Even with my expert touch. Frustrating for a woman of action like yourself. Certainly, do nothing to strain the wound so soon after removing the twists. For a week."

Well. They planned their attack for tomorrow. Thera was almost glad to have her suspicions confirmed. She had to keep her woman out of the fracas at all costs. Her heart pained to think of this soldier going anywhere near a battle likely to be so one-sided.

"I insist," Thera continued. "A week, at least, with no strain of any kind. I'm sure you can make yourself useful enough about the camp."

Adel looked disappointed. She nodded softly. "Well. If you insist."

Thera smiled in return. "I do," she said, one hand rising to cradle Adel's cheek. "I would be most disappointed if something untoward should happen to you. In spite of my better judgement and all the rules of being a ... good surgeon, I have found myself thinking fondly of you since our last appointment."

Adels breath quickened but her eyes became evasive. She gently pushed Thera's hand away. "Please do not say such things while I am in such an indecent state of undress."

"What state of undress would you prefer?"

Adel sat for three, four trembling breaths without answering. A longing poured from her eyes. Indecision made her increasingly agitated. "Please, Mam'selle. I am not ... not that sort of woman."

In reply, Thera pulled Adel's shirt off the rest of the way, pushed her down onto the chaise, and ravished her.

9

Punishment Profound

Stumbling along a narrow path out of the village Adel felt ecstatic and mournful, cleansed and filthy, violated and liberated. She wanted to scream but she didn't know why. In pain, in joy, in anger.

The night air was warm against her face thanks to a thin covering of cloud that trapped the heat below. Again, her hand felt numb, lifeless, like a dead, bloated fish inside the sling hanging from her shoulder. She wished for numbness all over. No feelings. The turmoil brought on by the act itself paled in comparison to the realisation of how deeply she felt for Therasia. The luminous, filthy, graceful surgeon of her soul. A swarm of feelings infested her. Inside she raged and laughed, bathed in ecstatic memories and then fled from them into shame.

She couldn't move. That was the embarrassing part. That woman started her firm, gentle stirrings. Adel froze. Unable to understand or accept what was happening. So embarrassing. Thera laughed at that, looked straight into her soul, took Adel's hand and-

Adel jerked into motion, fleeing the memory as much as she ran back towards the camp. She was running. Her legs felt wobbly, her knees trembled at what happened, but somehow she could still run and run and-

Crack! Her foot hit a rock in the meadow behind the village.

Down she went.

Adel tucked and rolled on instinct. The rough, dry ground hit her shoulder, scraped across her back and she was up on one knee, ready for... Ready for what? She wanted to rise, head back to camp, start the plan. Instead she knelt, panting, in a patch of grass. Her eyes stared, not at the landscape, but back to the dim shadows of the surgery. Shadows that moved and surged and moaned. It was just kissing and awkward groping. The same as she'd experienced with a few boys, in quiet corners of the farm, well out of her father's sight. Trying to prove to herself she was normal. Why did this thrill her so much more?

"Why is you staring at them wheat fields?"

"Ah! Oh, my. Hello, child. Ah! I remember you. Katrienne, isn't it? You were at the dance?"

"You 'membered my name! You is called Ladder-aide, I think. Is that right?"

"Adelaide."

"Oh, that's even prettier! I was dancing. I jump real high. Everyone was impress and said the fey was come visit. Other people was jumping too. Not just me. Real

high. Then my papa didn't stop me having a sip of the nice wine. I got a bit sleepy so came home. I danced real good, though."

"I'm sorry I missed that. Shouldn't you be in bed now?"

"I was coming back to my house, with some other kids, but then I saw you leaving the big house and going the wrong way. You is going the wrong way. I can take you back to the right way."

"That would be most kind of you but I am actually heading back to camp." Adel rose. She brushed vaguely at her knees and the side she'd rolled along. Awkward with one arm in a sling. "I fell over."

"Yes," said the child, her expression deadly serious. "I saw. It was very funny."

Adel laughed at ... everything. It was all so ridiculous. On a summer's night, in a southern meadow, after a lively ... dance, a child came to her rescue while the moon struggled through the cloud. Still her knees felt uncertain.

"I want to head down," Adel said. "Down is where the stream lies. I can follow that back to camp."

"Why not just take the road? The road goes right by the camp."

"Well, Katrienne, I have my reasons for avoiding the road. I shall take the stream."

The girl looked up at her, frowning with the precious intensity that only the young could achieve. "You'll get ate. Wolves hang out down by the river, waiting as for animals to come drink. Everyone says you soldiers is bad. I should let you get ate or smash your head in with a rock, myself.

But Aunty G likes you and I like Aunty G so I won't smash your head in or let you get ate."

Adel reached out with the only hand that worked and squeezed the child's shoulder. She said, with all the sincerity she could muster, "Thank you, Katrienne. I am very grateful."

The child smiled and led her across the meadow to a small cairn of rocks. She added a stone to the pile as one should. Katrienne pointed into the distance.

"See that other lump thing down there? That's another pile of rocks. Add rocks to them piles as when you pass so they stays, even in winter. You can see the path. Look."

"Ah, yes! Excellent."

"Go left at that next pile of rocks. You should be heading towards the camp but, like, above the stream, with no wolves to munch on you. They's too lazy to climb a hill."

"I thank you again and, oh. We are quite some way from the village. Will you be able to get back?"

The child looked at her strangely. "I's not the one in trouble in these fields at night. You really should watch out for wolves."

"A good rule in general. But, tonight, we have a plan. And if we can pull it off the wolves will need to watch out for us."

Katrienne giggled. "You talk funny. I can see why she likes you." Then the girl skipped away towards the distant candlelight peeking from one or two of the village windows.

Thera liked her. The very idea was repulsively wonderful. It was so much more than a filthy pervert like her deserved. Tears stung her eyes and she almost, almost lost control to weep openly.

Stars above! She'd only met the woman a few days ago. Had all of two conversations and twice as many nights of longing. This sudden physicality between them left her undone.

Adel gathered herself with deep steadying breaths. She watched the small figure of the child carefully pick her way over the rock-borne treachery of the field. Adel turned and marched down the little track, furiously trying to calm her mind.

She wanted to stick her fingers in her ears and sing loudly. However, the voices were inside her head so it wouldn't help. And she needed to be quiet.

Thera had stuck her fingers in- NO! no. None of that. She had work to do.

The woods beckoned. They were deceptively open, with beautiful, pale poplars and aspen. These were the production groves on the edge of the forest proper. The village planted them in straight lines with space in between and harvested after a few years, on a rotation. Deeper in, the pale trunks still prevailed though they were much covered in moss. In the forest proper aspen formed dense, ghostly clusters. The terrain roiled in broken hills, gorges, cliffs and abutments. Heavy thickets of fir trees pushed against open spaces. The undergrowth gathered densely. These ancient, untouched woods nurtured fey horrors in their hearts.

Fortunately, Adel had a map.

She pulled it from the deep pocket of her waistcoat, awkward with the fresh numbness in her injured arm. Slings and compresses and needles. A wound she had yet to avenge. She almost dropped the heavy, flat box of the compass. Juggling it in one hand, she trapped it against her leg. Then she got a better grip and opened the latch with her teeth.

Her waistcoat had clunked onto the surgery floor. Adel worried that Thera might ask what was inside. Neither the surgeon nor her own commandant paid any attention to what she carried in her coat. Both proved they were more interested the body it clothed. The distraction of her beauty was often annoying but this time proved useful.

Wonder of wonders, Warren marked the track on the map! This was the signature of good cartography. Not just the main roads but the walking trails, small ponds and lines of cliffs. The deeper forest was a blank area with the odd wiggle of trees to indicate its nature. Recent markings now covered the area from the commandant's surveying. Whatever else he was, the man knew how to plot out a map. Adel aligned everything carefully, noted landmarks and took a bearing. This track should lead her well enough. At the treeline she'd have to take another bearing and follow her compass into the woods as best she could.

She found herself humming a merry old tune she'd heard at the festival. Filth and shame seemed to be fading.

The ... sex ... left a pleasant- She had sex with another woman. As shameful as it was, the idea drew warmth and wonder into her soul. No more nights of desperate imaginings. She knew. That's what it was like.

Fun.

She giggled as she folded the map. Thera had not been remotely ashamed of what she was doing and happy to help. She'd teased and played. Allowed Adel her panicking and denial. Persuaded her with hugs and sensual pressures in all the right places.

Perhaps she could come here with the Autumn Harvest payment. This was a messy business that she could leave behind when she entered Tolosa. She would pray at the church, with all its strictures and admonishments against such things. Perversion, the church called it. For every hammer an anvil. She could even marry the commandant. Twice a year, she'd slip away to the country with the early and late harvest payments. Here she could ring out a merry little tune with another, like-minded anvil.

Her musing carried her further into the woods than she'd intended. Adel stopped, backed up and took another bearing where there was enough moonlight to see the map. She only had a few matches for light. She sighted a peculiar tree, twin trunks split low, then wound her way through the under brush towards it. Upon arrival, she used her compass to sight a particular, distinct rock in line with her bearing. Then she took whatever convoluted path the woods offered to that point. Thus she tracked a true line through the woods to the meeting point.

Valencia paced, rustling the forest floor in her anxiety.

"You look like you had a roll in the hay," the medic said, before she even offered a hello.

"I- There was dancing. And wine. And these wonderful, little pastries with preserves and fresh cream."

"I'm glad you enjoyed your ... dancing."

"Don't say it like that!"

"Did Warren mind you leaving after only one ... dance?"

"He doesn't know yet. I went with the surgeon, La Granger's daughter, to check my arm. I left from there. I'll give him some excuse in the morning about needing rest. If we're successful he'll be too distracted to question the matter."

"I've half a mind to hack some bit off my own arm so I can pay her a visit and compare techniques," said Valencia. "Gossip about the camp has it that La Granger's daughter is a great beauty."

"Indeed. Yes. I have seldom met a woman more blessed of features and grace."

"Dancing with the surgeon, then, were you?"

"Women should not dance with other women," said Adel, with a perfectly straight face. She was surprised to find that she agreed with the sentiment in spite of the night's activities. If she had the slightest chance she damned well intended to go and do it again. It was wrong. Absolutely. But only for other people who might not possess her sense of moral restraint.

The camp medic laughed at her. "Ha. Don't be so innocent. Women dance with women, men dance with men-"

"Men dance with other men? I've heard that but how does it even work?"

"They stick their pricks up each other's bum holes."

Adel's eyebrows climbed in astonishment. "Well, that's..."

"Ah, enough about dancing. Especially if I'm not getting any. It's making my crotch all itchy. Now it's time for work. I brought a square of sacking and ball of twine, like you asked."

"Good. Good," said Adel, bringing herself back to the task at hand. "...and... Oh, gloves and hood? The dragoons were stung on their hands and faces because they didn't have their gloves on or masks up. The driver wasn't even wearing his insulating jacket as it was so hot inside. He died first, I think."

"Oh. Interesting. That's very interesting. I should make a note of that. How quickly would you say he died? Was he stung a lot? Ten times? Twenty? The commandant burned the bodies before I could examine them. As someone who was there-"

"Val! I was fighting for my life against a terrifying creature of mists and magics. For the last time, I made no particular observations of the hornets. Other than to avoid them. I only saw the bodies long after they'd died, when we pulled them from the walker."

"This could be very important work! Anything you recall-"

"Nothing, Val. Please. Did you bring the gloves?"

"Yes, yes. Cheryl has a full suit of the leather. Should be cool enough to wear it."

"Cheryl's coming? You told her? Val, the less people-"

"She's a capable girl! She might surprise you."

"She's a seamstress, not a soldier!"

Cheryl stepped into the small clearing, a bundle tied and slung over one shoulder. "I'm ze one who uncovered ze wolves in our midsts," she said, her northern accent distinct in the warm, empty woods. "I 'eard zem through ze walls of zeir tent whispering about 'ow the farm girls disappointed zem. Who zey would pick next. Me! Zey said my name! And yours, Adel. And girls from ze village including your surgeon friend. We are not safe with zem unrestrained."

"Cheryl, my dear, we're not going to restrain them. We're going to kill them."

She spat. "Pah! Either is good!"

"Besides," said Val, "we need Cheryl. Who did you think was going to do this? Your arm's in a sling and I'm not going near those damned wasps."

"Hornets," Adel corrected her automatically. "It's a risk having so many people involved."

"Bah!" Cheryl gestured dismissively. "You may as well ask why Val is 'ere if she has nothing to contribute." She turned a sneer on Val. "Why in ze seven 'ells are you 'ere? Come to watch? You want to make some notes about ze wasps and zeir stings as zey kill me?"

"Val has-" Adel began but the camp medic waved her away and stepped forward.

"I am sure most of you think of me as some sort of mad clown," said Val. "A figure for ridicule. You may be surprised that once I retained a respected position. I was respected. Highly. Liked, even. And yes, I followed my passion for formulae and alchemy. At every opportunity my superiors tried to take my concoctions and twist them, make them... I once refined a fume so concentrated that it would put any soldier, in any state of injury, into a slumber so deep. Ah! We could operate on them without them moving, twitching, screaming. It was flammable. They tried to turn it into the burning gas you may have encountered. The one that burns so quickly it does no real damage to an enemy, nor sets anything ablaze, but not fast enough to be a useful explosive. Failures they tried to blame on me. And one particular, respected capitaine... You see, I required special letters and dispensations to acquire my chemicals, perform my experiments. He wished to trade them for favours of the body. When I refused a gang of soldiers under his command... It was to persuade me to comply. Even after that... Never. I still refused. Later, a few months later, when I was able to function with some normality, except that, sometimes, I can't stop talking, running sentences together. My mind-" Val paused and slowed her breathing. "Yes. What you've heard is true. It was a few months later that I conducted a special experiment with my chloroform, en-masse, on those pigs who violated me. Then I tried some other, more personal, experiments. I made many interesting anatomical discoveries in the process."

Adel coughed. She'd never heard such a coherent version of the story before. Val was reluctant to talk about her fall from grace. She said, "Val has earned her place, Cheryl. Most of the girls involved in this have ... earned their place."

"Et vous?"

"I have been fortunate enough to avoid that particular cliché."

"Ah, very well. Let us get on with zis."

"Very well, indeed. Just let me get a bearing."

They trudged towards the clearing. Val kept up a steady stream of chatter about the various types of vegetation they saw. She mentioned the properties of some night-flowering bushes and vines. This loquaciousness faded to silence as they pushed in and Val began to tire. The exertions of the day took their toll on Adel. She could not exercise regularly with her injury. Now, this very active evening. For all that she mostly lay transfixed in ecstasy, the surgeon's attentions did send her pulse racing, her breath heaving in her chest. That and the dancing wore her out. She paused at the crest of a small rise and caught her breath. The others stopped with her.

"We must be heading up that large hill," Adel commented. "My legs ache like a pulled tooth."

"Ze cool breeze carries some rich, earthy scent," said Cheryl. "Perhaps it is an enchantment from ze fey to ward us from zeir lands."

"Either that or her knees are trembling because she had a tumble at the festival," said Val.

"Zoot! Who with?"

"With no-one!" said Adel. "There was dancing. And wine. I'm not used to these country jigs. There was a great deal of jumping. A sort of competition to see who can jump the highest."

"Did ze com'dant jump very 'igh?"

"...high enough." She and the commandant were gossip about the camp. That could help to deflect any gossip that might emerge about her and ... Ai! That woman was in her head as deeply as her fingers had- "Let's press on! It's over this ridge, if memory serves."

Memory did. Adel saw the cracked hillside through the trees. The wide clearing left by the shallow topsoil. She crouched and slipped up closer. That really started her legs aching. The low, thin clouds began to sliver washing the dell with drifts of clean moonlight. She beckoned the others closer.

"Zis is a pleasant spot," said Cheryl.

"Yes. It looks like a cave collapsed, deep down, breaking up the topsoil. The ground cover has come back, bushes, weeds. The water flow sunk again, leaving this. It is doubtless digging out a new cave beneath us as we speak. The hornet nest is over there. Can you see? Against the lee of that cliff." She pointed out to Cheryl. "Roughly in line with that poplar. The thin, white tree."

"Alors! I will 'ave to cross ze whole clearing!"

"We'll cover you from here. I can shoot well enough with my left hand. I've been practising." She glanced at Valencia who stared back in blank horror. "Val... You, you did remember to bring a pistol for me?" Val bit her lip and shook her head. Adel sighed. "There are wolves, Val. This girl on the hill, from the dance, warned me about them."

"'Ow many girls did you dance with?"

"She was five! Maybe eight. If that. A child. I- Well. Let us hope the wolves are asleep. Along with all the fey. Look. Let's not make ourselves overly concerned. You're a seamstress aren't you, Cheryl?"

"Overly concerned? We don't even 'ave a gun! We creep up on ze fey's favourite dancing dell and we don't even 'ave a gun!"

"I have a delightful hammer charm Thera gave me," said Adel. "You can borrow that. Now, the bag."

"Forget ze cursed bag! I am not going out zere without... Ai!"

"Keep talking this loudly and the fey will come to us. Right. This flat piece of sacking is basically your hornet purse. You're going to weave the twine around the top like it's a drawstring. Throw the sacking over the nest, let them get all agitated so they come out and fill it, jerk the drawstring tight. Voilà. A bag of hornets."

"You are insane."

"If you're not going to do it, I will. Also, we're running out of time."

Cheryl's face twisted in disdain. "Ai! You soldiers are crazier zan ze wasps."

Both Adel and Val said, perfectly together, "Hornets."

"Whatever. I refuse. I will not do zis."

Dressed in full dragoon leathers Cheryl edged out into the clearing. She glared back. Adel waved her on, impatiently. With a frustrated whisper of curses the northern seamstress crept across the dell. She reached within a couple of arm-lengths and sized up the twined sacking for a throw. A stray hornet, some sort of night-watch for the nest, buzzed about her. Cheryl waved at it vigorously which only made it buzz louder. That seemed to stir the next layer of defences. Cheryl was too focused on the one near her to notice the ground shift, distinct in the moonlight.

"Throw the damned bag!" Adel whispered as softly as she could shout. "Throw it!"

Cheryl looked back, then at the nest, let out a little scream, and flung the sack-cloth in panic. It landed well enough. Cheryl began a funny dance of her own, with a couple more hornets buzzing about her. She slapped at herself a few times, half reached for the strings, rose, waving at her face in fearful flapping. With a drawn-out yell of quiet determination she snatched for the draw strings and yanked them. The bag began to close but mostly it dragged along the ground towards her. Cheryl jerked the strings in snatches. Finally she trapped the leading edge of the bag with one foot. She yanked the drawstrings with both hands, sealing the hornet purse. She then bolted back to where Adel waited, flailing about herself with her free hand. A couple of white spots chased her through the pale clearing. More than a couple.

"Er... Up." said Adel. "Get up, up, Val. Move. Move! Down the slope!"

Val saw the trailing hornets and snatched up her bag, scrambling out of the way.

"Get zem off me! Get zem off!" called Cheryl as she lumbered over the crest in her awkward leathers, following them down. At the base of the slope they paused. Adel drew the map from her pocket and used it to swat at suspicious areas of Cheryl's outfit. After a moment or two they realised the only buzzing came from the sack purse.

"It's okay," said Adel. "I think you're clean. You may have to keep holding the sack closed while we head back."

"I need to get zis leather off. Ze pants if nothing else. Too 'eavy for walking."

"Oh, give me the left glove. You keep the right. We can take turns carrying the purse."

"Ah! Excellent! A good 'ead on your shoulders."

"Yes. The commandant said something about me and head but I'm not sure that's what he meant."

The girls laughed and packed away their kit for the return journey. They swatted an occasional stray that came to investigate their buzzing bag.

They walked three-quarters of the way back to camp. In a cluster of aspen, surrounded by thickets of briar, four fusiliers and half a dozen women waited as they approached.

"Password," one of the women demanded.

"I honestly can't remember," said Adel. "Can either of you?"

"Nope."

"Zere was a password?"

Adel looked down at the nervous young recruit. As kindly as possible she said, "Who else, in all the seven hells, is going to be coming out of the woods with a sack full of hornets?"

The woman shifted her grip on her rifle and said, "Identify yourselves or, or come no farther!"

"I am ze daemon rabbit of Eastre's long-lost cousin," said Cheryl helpfully.

Efigenia stepped up. "Hey Adel. Gate inspection. What's in your bag?"

Adel smiled. "Why don't you come and take a real close look, Effie?" They both laughed. The fantassin relaxed. "Any trouble?" Adel asked.

"Pfft. The big one didn't go down even after two mugs of Val's beer."

"Two mugs?" said Val, surprised. "How big is he, exactly? Which one? Oh, I must get some measurements." The medic fussed into the thicket, fishing into her bag.

"It's fine," said Effie. "He was real woozy. Three of us beat him unconscious. We lured them away for a private party, served them the spiked beer. Then we all ambushed them."

"How did you convince them to come with you?"

"We laughed at their jokes."

"Ha! That'll do it." Adel looked about. "No one saw? No one followed?"

"Caporal. You insult your superior by suggesting I could not plan such–"

"Ah! You bitches! You star-cursed spawn of whores!"

Val skipped back from her measurements as the big one awoke and tried his bonds.

"–such a simple operation. Yes, connard!" Effie said, turning to the fusilier. "I am the daughter of a whore. My whore mother taught me to read and write well enough to get into the army. And after three years I passed the exams for the Non-Commissioned Officers. I paid them a healthy sum my mother earned fucking a bunch of nobles. Et voilà!" She gestured to her piping. "So you should address me as Sergent-Chef when I shoot you in the balls."

Adel grabbed the camp medic. "Val, you'd better help Cheryl get that suit on. This is going to deteriorate rapidly."

The big man growled low. "Where have you brought us? Is that Cody? Cody! Why is... Oh, you fucking bitches! Are you siding with the fucking faeries, now?"

"You chased a bunch of villagers over a cliff, bastard. We lost seven because you couldn't keep your powder dry. Did you think nothing bad was going to happen because of that? How did you think it was going to end?"

"I fuck who I want and stars burn the end!" the big man growled. "You can take your slimy, fish-stinking slits and–"

Effie punched him in the face. He shut up more from surprise than pain. He came back three-fold furious, staggering to his feet, pulling at his bonds with strong, determined arms. The women backed in fear, instinctively. He tore one hand free of his restraints and reached out for Effie.

Adel shot him through the chest.

Without a bracing hand the gun kicked. She was close enough that her shot went true. He coughed in furious surprise and turned a brutal stare on Adel. His first attempt at breathing made him hunch in pain. He stood for a moment, waiting for a brief respite to gather himself. He never managed to get a proper breath as he sank to his knees, eyes becoming vague.

"Effie," Adel said. "Get your rifle. You two, grab that Cody. Get him up where I'm standing." She cradled the rifle in her sling and slapped her hand against her thigh for attention. She spoke quietly but strongly, like someone used to giving orders. "Quickly! Now! Now! They will have heard that back at camp. The others need to be shot within a minute. Move! You, grab his left arm, you on the right. Let's go!"

One of the girls sat down in shock and removed herself from usefulness. Was it Yasmine? Was that her name? Yvette, that was it. Adel made a note to visit her later and give the youngster some reassurance.

This was only the second time Adel had ever killed someone.

The first was when her unit put down a pauper's uprising in the warehouse area of Tolosa. People demanded work. A group decided that, if there was no work, they'd put masks over their faces and kill a bunch of honest labourers until there was work. Her squad cornered eight or ten ragged men wielding clubs and knives. She threw up, after.

The lieutenant sat her down the next day and, well. The lieutenant was dead now. Kill by some fey thing that drove a stake into her neck.

Effie was a disciplined and experienced soldier. She shot her man through the liver in quick order before he'd even woken up.

The last two stirred as the ladies hauled them into position. Neither fully woke before they died. One of the girls went and threw up. Adel ordered that evidence dug into the ground.

"Dig! Dig! Use your bayonets. We've got less than five minutes," she told the others. "They will take a while to organise a patrol, find this place. Effie, take those two girls. Sprint back. Enter the camp from the officers' tents so they won't notice us all missing or returning together."

Effie grabbed her bayonet and looked sternly at Adel. "You do know that I out-rank you?"

"Shut up and get moving," Adel replied, with a smiling attempt at humour, the which failed in the grim reality of the scene.

The three moved off at a pace.

"Val, you get to your medical tent. You've done all you can. Ready Cheryl?"

"What- I don't... What do I 'ave to do?"

"Um. Right. You should- Val! Go!"

"Ai. I go, I go," said Val and walked away without a backwards glance.

"Right. Cheryl. Hold the bag open, up against all of their faces. Give it a shake to make sure the hornets are angry and will sting. Visit each face quickly, or the hornets will run out of stings. A couple on the hands if we have time. Are you up for this? I can get one of the soldiers-"

"Non, non. Je suis fort. I can do zis"

"Can... Can you do it now?"

"Zoot! Alors!"

To her credit the seamstress even managed to briefly check the faces of each soldier after she'd visited them. The big one flinched and half stirred, still alive, bleeding out slowly.

Cheryl opened the sacking wide, face down to the soil. She cleared the area before flipping it over with one of the drawstrings. The furious, white blobs of the arctic hornets buzzed up, agitated. They kept in a small cluster, robbed of any landmarks so far from their nest. Cheryl pulled the sacking clear and they didn't follow. Adel stamped on a stray caught in one of the folds before picking it up.

"Very good," she said. "You've all done very well." The last three girls stared at the bodies with mixed expressions. "You kept good discipline. Remember to keep up that discipline. Never, ever, under any circumstances, speak of what happened. We've told you what rumours to spread, what to say. Stick to that. If you feel a desperate need to talk about this confide in myself or Sergent-Chef Efigenia. Only when we are alone and you've double checked no one is listening. We'll always be happy to lend you our time. Sneak back in via the latrines once they send the patrol. Two at a time.

You can practice your discipline of silence by not talking at all on the way back to camp. If you notice one of the others talking, stop them. Keep discipline. Keep your mouths shut. That will keep us all safe."

Adel had no one to talk to. Something happened to her this evening of a far greater importance than this. Something that deeply affected her place in the world. She was besotted and overwhelmed by feelings for a woman. She acted upon them. She remembered the hot damp taste of the other. She had held and hugged and writhed.

Then ... come here and done this.

And was successful. She'd transgressed in ways that she was told over and over would lead to eternal suffering. Punishment profound. Only now, having succeeded in tonight's endeavours, did she realise she'd fully expected to fail. The gods should birch her for such lasciviousness and how much she'd enjoyed it. Equally true for murder.

Perhaps she could talk to Val? The medic was a woman of broader understanding.

Were there others the same as her? Soldiers often exchanged crude jokes between the women and men. She dared not take those at face value.

The girls saluted her and moved off. She heaved a sigh of longing and frustration and then went to help Cheryl. The seamstress was mostly out of the leathers. Adel tried to helped her with the heavy trousers but got in the way as she bundled them up.

"Let me do zis! I can manage."

"Okay, okay. You can take your sweet time getting back into the camp. Drop those off at the mechanicals on your way in. They are my leathers, fitted for me, so they'll be expecting them."

"Yes, I know. It was I who made ze adjustments."

"Right! Yes. Of course. Thank you. Don't get drawn into the fuss about camp. No-one is going to expect a response from the baggage. That's soldier's work."

"I made a good choice to be a seamstress. My 'eart could not take so much of zis soldier work. Et vous?"

"My heart is acclimating to my chosen trade." She stared back down the road. "I'll get right out of the way, back along the road, and wait for things to die down. I can wander in when I like. I don't want to get shot by mistake."

"I meant, 'ow are you feeling, after all zis?"

"What?"

"Now zat you got revenge for your arm. Done, no?"

"Half done. I didn't do this for my arm. There is a girl in the village who is much sorrowed at the loss of her friend. This is my gift to her. Tomorrow is for my arm. Tomorrow, I get to kill some fey."

10

Unearthly Torment

Pausette arrived first. Therasia watched from her secluded tree branch without bothering to awaken. This was Pau's first akelarre without her senior. She was overly eager, bouncing into the clearing with nervous, excited energy. She reminded Thera of a kitten out exploring the world. A certain feline grace hovered around the young woman. If she could own her nature, Pausette would become a great witch. Now, she still enjoyed playing with her prey more than she enjoyed killing it. She was also one of that rare breed of witches born with a penis, often misidentified as males at birth. A useful reminder to the rest of the coven that the world was full of variation and nothing in it could be easily defined with simple labels. Pau balanced her oil lantern on a natural shelf in the cliff, adjusting the reflective dish to cast light into the clearing.

The moon struggled with streaking clouds. It felt like a storm. Therasia could not remember the last time it rained at an akelarre.

Thera allowed herself to drift, dozing, neither asleep nor awake. After a solid supper of fresh fruit, buttered bread and some cured beef, she needed to rest and gather her strength. Last night was busy with little sleep. Then a fretful day. She visited the minds of some small, burrowing creatures snoozing in their nests and matched the rhythm of her thoughts with theirs. After a few minutes her threads woke her again.

Ragonde shuffled into the dell, leaning heavily on her stick. Ragonde of the Root. Rags the Twisted. An old foot injury that became infected. A foolish mistake that left her wiser than most. She was the most archetypical of the coven. Rags lived in a genuine cottage in the woods where she brewed her herbals and accepted clients. She played the reclusive midwife well enough but Rags was viciously protective of her dominion. Tucking her lantern into the roots of a tree, Rags directed its light into the dell.

Selika the Traveller strode in next. She broke no abbreviations of her name. Her dark skin gleamed. She wore traditional Eastern attire of crop and trous. Many crystals glittered from the fabric and the black dome of her hair. This was an established woman who danced hypnotically and played a fife of floating melodies. She ran the famous Enfents du Sud-Est, the travelling troupe that popularised the works of ancient writers from the Chrysalis Deserts and the far eastern shores of the Backwards Sea. They wintered in Lorda, rehearsing. The rest of the year they travelled all over the region. Even playing regularly in Tolosa.

If only all the travellers could be less like Mushroom Girl and more like Selika. That encounter with Chantrelle and her two lovers still twisted Therasia's mind. Decisions always had consequences. Thera brooded over that night but the past could not be altered and the future was yet to happen.

This was something she learned from one of Selika's plays.

It was truly an honour to be blessed by the actor at an akelarre. She brought with her a beautiful young girl, younger than Katrienne, who shone even darker. Selika commanded the glade as she entered. Therasia suspected her presence was not a coincidence. Selika's lantern was a gleaming wonder of silvered metal and clearest glass. She placed it deliberately on a stone outcrop directly underneath Therasia.

Rude Jacinte and pleasant Laurette wandered in shortly after. Old Jacinte was not dead yet, though young Laurette now performed most of her duties. The old woman did not wish to relinquish her dominion. Peaceful retirement did not interest her. While the younger woman would never be good enough in her eyes, Laurette already surpassed Jacinte in many areas. Laurette was an especially accomplished fighter with a creative flair for brutality. She also made the most wonderful pastries with some secret honey flavouring, the which recipe no-one was ever able to wheedle out of her. They both placed lanterns into the increasingly luminous halo.

Platée was a woman blissfully unaware of her own hideousness. She gleefully marched into the group and greeted the circle joyfully. Her vivacious nature lifted everyone she met. All were glad to see her. Platitudes, embracing and dancing accompanied the woman everywhere she went.

On her third husband, now, she had seven girls to look after. That made for some small neglect in her dominion. Others happily rallied to cover her duties. She buried four sons. All of them tragically burned out trying to contain even the tiniest, latent threads of their inherited power.

Platée and Selika were particular friends. They greeted with laughter and hung upon each other like long-lost lovers, squealing and hugging. She brought but a small candle. Selika lit it from her shining lantern and placed it proudly beside.

Therasia descended, drawing surprise from some. Pau began dancing, humming her own accompaniment. Rags pulled a rhythm stick from her pack and tapped it against her cane. It felt like the beginnings of a lively evening. Thera lit her lantern from Platée's candle and placed it on a farther edge, bringing light to a darker area.

She circulated, waiting patiently.

Arnalta finally arrived. Thera's beauty was long and graceful. Arna's was wide and flowing. She'd failed to prevent the slaughter of her parents and several villagers at the hands of some well-armed bandits. A group of soldiers gone rogue. She sustained fatal injuries herself. One of Thera's first duties as fey was to snatch her from the shores of death and put her back together. This knack for healing lent

Thera her recommendation to the Mountain Monks. Before she left, Thera helped in the revenge and rescue. They should be close but Arna carried a sadness none could reconcile. It kept her distant. She smashed every gun she ever saw. While many sought to console her, for beauty's sake as much as kindness, the woman was already dead inside. This made her harsh in her judgements. She placed a simple lantern into the circle, opening two of its four doors to let some light shine out.

Subconsciously, the women began to flare the lights. Threads amplified and reflected, setting shapes dancing across the dell. The witches matched these with brief gambols of their own. They would begin with discussion, stories, songs. Eventually, conversation would die away completely. Dancing would be the only form of communication.

But not tonight.

A sound intruded upon the clearing. A faint weeping with a slithering, dragging accompaniment. It grew closer and closer. The dancing stuttered at the sounds of quiet misery. Stillness settled as everyone looked down the path. Little Katrienne dragged a soldier into their midsts.

"Tell me, Little Kat," said Thera, echoing her voice to bring a chill to the clearing. "What present have you brought us, wrapped in colourful blue?"

"Is a scout or look-out. Not a very good one. He can't sneak nearly so good as me."

"What's wrong with him?" asked the graceful Pau with genuine concern, half a step forward.

"He's very silly," said Kat. "He tried to hurt me, so as I had to break his arms. Then he tried running away, so I broke his legs. Now he just makes little crying sounds like a big baby."

"Oh, I see," said Pau, stepping back.

Blood trickled from scrapes and scratches on his back and legs, left as Katrienne dragged him here. Also an eye closed, blackened, from when he learned to shut up and do as he was told.

"He's going to do more than whimper," said Thera. "He's going to tell us what festivities Commandant Warren has planned for us this evening."

The soldier stared about in bewilderment and pain, gasping his last breaths. "You... You're just a bunch of girls..." he snivelled. Dark Arna outright laughed and danced closer. Pau backed further, still of a mind to let others do the real work.

"Soldiers coming, are they?" Arna inquired.

"Aye," the scout answered, already broken.

"Let me guess," said Thera. "A hundred and fifty from the north. An entire company." Some of the witches gasped at this news. The soldier nodded, dumbfounded. "Another fifty from the south-east, carrying artillery. Some of those big, six-barrelled guns."

"Cap'n Alden were delayed," said the scout. "We just got word. The jetty where he were unloadin' done collapsed under the weight of his weapons."

"You're welcome," said Laurette, half a glance at old Jacinte.

"Ha. Good work. He'll still bring his soldiers. And there's Warren's company from the south-west with their walkers. I can already feel them rolling their way through the trees."

Rags rapped her stick twice for attention. "Perhaps he can tell us," she said, "what happened to Depe, Marie and ... the other girls. We are four lights missing."

"Caila and Kalantha are the names you cannot remember. Do not fret for them," said Thera. "They guide the murmecks."

Everyone leaned back.

"No!" said old Jacinte. "Say not that you have invoked those terrors!"

"We visited them last night, Depe and I. The saner ones seemed to understand our plight. The rest were at least hungry."

"You cannot control them!" Jacinte raised her cane and waved it angrily. "You let hundreds of those feral beasts out of the deep woods there's no getting them back!"

"There are far less than a hundred and they're not getting out. The northern company of soldiers are foolish. They will come through the deep woods, right to them. Don't worry. Marie has a wise old head on her shoulders and more energy than anyone her age deserves. Caila and Kalantha come from the deep valleys. They are used to murmecks. The foolish soldiers will meet them while they're still in a column, no defences set. None will survive."

"How did they gather such a force and nary a one of us hearing of it? Over two hundred uniforms, machinery and blastings!"

"They spoke to each other with their lightning boxes and described this place in beeps and buzzes. Small numbers of innocuous troops, accumulating: fifteen from Martras Tolosana with a single cannon, twenty-four from Mauran, so on. They all arrive at an agreed time at certain grid points on coordinated maps. A soldier had one in the pocket of her waistcoat last night, along with a compass. I glimpsed it while she was distracted."

"And what did you do to distract her?" asked Platée, with a suggestive twinkle.

"I fucked her."

"Okay. That'll work."

"So the six of us are to take on the remainder?" asked Pau. "How many is that? A hundred? Two?"

"I could kill that many, alone," whispered dark Arna, kneeling in front of the whimpering scout.

"No!" said Thera. "We are not soldiers. We are hunters. We do not fight open battles. Not against four walkers. We won't even try to take on those. You will all leave. Immediately. We'll meet up again at Laurette's village. Their festival is tomorrow night and not too distant. We won't be able to dance properly but we can sort out any other business."

"...my village..." muttered old Jacinte.

"Then why meet here at all?" asked Selika, stalking up to Thera with some authority.

"Because I need four of us to call the fey. They will name me Strongest. And I have some questions for our habitué, about lightning and spirits and ... oh, so many things. I need four of you to stay. The rest should leave, now."

Dark Arna reached a hand, gently cupping the scout's head, floating her beautiful face closer to his. "Did you say farewell to the sun, Soldier? You have looked upon its light for the last time." The scout began weeping.

"I hear distant screaming," Selika's dark child whispered, swaying as the girl felt the energies of the world.

Little Katrienne gasped and danced over, noticing the girl for the first time. "A new sister! Oh!" She stopped in front of the eldritch child, grinning with pure joy. The child grinned back.

"By that I'd say you can all leave to the north," said Thera. "Fade west once you hit Deer-Fir Grove. Selika, you'll open the cave with me. Three others to call: Pau, Laurette and Arna. Once you feel it coming, you run. Platée, get everyone else out safe. Now. Especially the children."

"This is reckless!" said Selika.

"Do I look like I care?" yelled Thera. The heat of the night burst out and surprised even her.

Selika suddenly laughed, clapping her hands with joy. "O! Such fire! How quickly we forget that we are not farmers. Our concerns are not selfish and safe. We are wild things! O, but I could use you in my troupe. You would play the Queen of Kerma as she sacked Kashromi! Come, sister! Let us move this rock."

The actor strode towards the wall of briar covered in nightshade vines, past the buzzing arctic hornets. Thera followed, trusting the others to organise themselves.

The heavy thicket extended back into the shallow gorge, an ancient parting of the earth. This was one spot where the fey first resisted. A thousand years ago the Latium Empire conquered every land about the Backwards Sea. They stripped them for their Iron Age industry. They cut so much forest that deserts grew. Whole peoples died.

They cut so much the true fey noticed.

The fey became angry.

They created the first half-breeds as warriors.

It cracked the hills. Sunk the shores. Flooded the lands.

Half-fey folkes helped to drive the greedy back to their lands. They broke the machineries of that empire and left it for dead as the monsters infested their peninsula. But greed infests the human race in every corner of the world. So, a thousand years later, industry threatened the established order once more.

Thus the war started by the King of Aquitanica and Occitania, this King Returning. Ha! If only these foolish soldiers knew the truth about their king. After the war, the wastes burned around the cities contained them for a hundred years. Now, these greedy lords found new, shallow justifications. They tried to break the fey with their lightning toys.

This must fail. They must learn a harsh, horrifying lesson.

Thera leaned against the elsewhere and followed Selika between gaps in the thicket that even a hornet would have trouble passing. The boulder didn't cover the crack in the ridge completely. There was more than enough room for a fey to slip past and enter the small cave behind. Underneath there was another crack, leading down into the deep places of the earth. Checking her pouch, Thera drew a steadying breath and nodded to Selika.

The woman stared at her for some time before asking, "How will you get out when we are gone and this beautiful grotto is surrounded by soldiers, machines, death in their metal sticks, hate in their hearts?"

"Water flows. I will follow that. There will be another way out. Even if I have to follow it for many dark days."

Screams of unearthly torment reached them from the dying scout, as Arna did whatever she wanted to end him.

"Have you journeyed into the earth before?" asked Selika

"No."

"The air does not move. If you remain still you will use up all the air around you, especially with a candle burning. Move on and the air will be fresh. Wrap your matches well. There will be waters to swim. I know how much you love swimming. Follow the old threads. Leave one of your own so the path remains clear. And don't eat the mushrooms, no matter how hungry you get."

Selika lifted the ample boulder, a strain even for her. Dirt clogged the crack. Thera scraped at it briefly with a stake and the soil fell inside. She tucked her stake away and leaned through. The boulder crunched down above her. All light fled.

Chanting began above as the four witches called to the fey. Feeling about with her threads Thera detected a faint pulse far below. She allowed herself to fall and flow until the air felt broad about her.

Coming back to the real she saw tiny mushrooms that clung to the damp walls. They glowed faintly but cast no appreciable light. Thus, they appeared to be little stars floating about her, defining the limits of the space. A faint thread attached to many of the fungi.

The Book of the Sedeei Calamity called this first chamber The Space of Dark Woe. She was supposed to light her candle and examine the markings of the coven upon its walls, absorb their meaning. Thera ignored this, tied a thread of her own and followed the path.

The crack flowed down. It was wide enough that Thera could follow it in the real, padding along the uneven floor. It lowered, forcing her to crawl. It broadened and she slithered along, following the threads. They twisted together. A bundle in varying textures. Some pulsed, some flowed. Faint and clear. Old and new. They were more a reflection of the women who left them than any indication of time or strength. The ceiling rose and she rose with it.

The silence stifled her more than the darkness. She could not see her own hands or even her own nose. Her threads kept her from colliding with the pillars of limestone growing from the caverns' floors and ceilings.

There was no sound except her breathing, the rustle of her clothes, the scrape and slap of her passage. When she stopped she heard nothing but her breathing and the pressure of her heart in her veins.

The ceiling lowered. She moved in a stooped crouch. When she approached a drip of water she was grateful for a sound outside herself. The space widened. The far side contained a small pond.

Leifa waited there. Thera stuttered to a halt at the presence of her dead lover. Emptiness swallowed her. She had neither thought nor motion.

Leifa wandered towards her, a customary arch to one eyebrow, amused at her reaction. Thera could not move but felt the need to flee in grief. Reaching out with one hand, Leifa grasped something that clung to Thera's back. She struggled with it, pulling and fighting its grip. Thera collapsed to her knees, shaking and rocking, weeping suddenly in one moment and screaming in anguish the next. Leifa grew in stature, contesting mightily with this thing that clung to Thera's back. After a monumental struggle, Leifa tore the thing free and brought it around for show.

In the absolute darkness Thera clearly saw it was but a tiny seed of dancing colours. That gambolling rainbow reflected in leifa's eyes, a memory and delight that would live in Thera forever without burdening her any longer. The weight of her grief left her forever. Thera felt sorrow at its passing.

She also began to feel out of breath, having spent too long sitting still in this chamber with its quiet pool that had never seen the sun. So this was the Chamber of Passing Grief and the Pool of Sorrows. Both vivid to their names.

Then she realised the threads passed under the water for quite some way.

Swimming was not her favourite thing in the world.

Rising with determination Thera moved to the edge of the water. The atmosphere hung with slight freshness. Slow breaths, then quick puffs to expel all the air from her lungs before she took a great gulp and dove. She swam but that quickly became untenable. The passage narrowed and lowered again. She scrambled along with her hands and feet, pushing herself through the distorting water.

It narrowed again.

Forced to wriggle through she used the barest movements as propulsion. The passage widened. There remained no break in the roof. A fey cannot fold through water. It is like stone in the other. She pushed on and on, turning over to scramble along the top of the passage. That brought her to the surface as soon as it appeared. She stuck her face into the gap and gasped. It was but a small break and she had to submerge again. Finally she emerged, panting, into the next chamber.

This was the Cave of Balanced Stones. Thera was able to stand. The space about her felt strange. Charged. It took a while for Thera to regain her composure in this void of chaotic energies. Her breath and sensibilities were already straining. Carefully, she used her threads to flush as much water from herself as possible. Her ears required a finger and working of her jaw before they popped and drained. All her sensory strands vibrated, becoming tenuous. None of the threads crossed this chamber.

She tied hers off and groped in her pouch for the tinderbox, a present from her friend the blacksmith. Wrapped in oiled cloth, the tin box weathered the soaking better than her. She sorted a small patch of tinder into the lid and stuck a taper in it. She struck sparks from her flint and steel. The sudden flashes of light and sound almost drove her insane. The shavings caught, then the taper. Now that her eyes were hungry for light this tiny illumination was enough in this dark place. She did not bother her candle's wick.

Spikes of stone rose and hung. Some joined. All glittered strange opal sparks. The floor contained stack upon stack of great, round, river stones, piled in carefully balanced columns. The precarious nature of the space in the chamber created a distinct energy. The cave disappeared into darkness beyond.

Various stacks had collapsed. Thera gathered a single stone from one of these and added it, with swift precision, to one of the shorter stacks. The taper burned down to her fingernails. She'd already found the exit near a new collection of mushrooms with threads. She flicked the taper away and tied a thread. Following these new strands she slunk through vaults wide and narrow.

After another brief swim she arrived at the Cavern of Sagurre and Diburi. Here the fey blessed the first human in these lands and splintered the ground above. The landscape broke for miles around, including the dell where the witches danced.

The candle crackled to life in the utter silence. Blinking, Thera could see a small mound of old wax in a clearer space. She set her light there and moved forward to what was obviously intended to be a reclining seat.

Thera lay in the stone chair, admiring the vast beauty of this, the largest cavern. The seat felt strange. Warm, not cold. Wondrous shapes formed in the spikes and pillars. There were curtains of rock in flowing sculptures hanging from the ceiling. She thought it all might tell a story if only she could read it. Her stone couch felt exactly the right size, contoured specifically for her. Thera wondered if it always felt exactly the right size.

Gradually she became aware of another presence, as one might become aware of a huge wave forming far out in the ocean. One that will wash everything from the shore when it arrives. She settled and contemplated the possibility of being razed.

It began as dances in the light, glimmers that flowed off the cavern walls and curled about the cave. Colours sparkled as the presence coalesced. Deeper hues tinged in wide flourishes, brighter points with vivid pirouettes. Streams of light shifted in a spectrum as they filled the cavern's far end. Playful glissades danced with the candle's flame. Thera became aware that she observed her own body as something separate but from deep within. She was more connected to her physical self. So much so that it felt alien and distant.

It was but a thread, this vast entity. It was attached to something larger than the world and Thera was attached to it. The idea almost destroyed Thera's mind. She was so small by comparison.

The lights mingled and fused into a figure lean and generous, graceful and grounded. It spoke. "Therasia Garonne.

Are you all that remains? Where are the other fey-kin? There is usually so much joy and dancing in this place."

"They evade the coming danger. Crisis, you said. The scream in the fey approaches."

"The energies of the world contradicted and annealed. We swim in the life of the trees. It scratches an itch. These new energies scratch too deeply. You are strongest and most dangerous. Flow with me. Shed your sentiments and coil yourself into my energies such that I can speak with you unconditionally, without the clumsiness of words. You are strongest but you waste your energy on a shadow. That must stop."

"Shadow?"

"There is much to understand, the story of the pillars. Read the cave with me. Release. Flow. Clinging to loved ones is not uncommon but zombies are a waste of energy."

"Zombie?" Her heart began pounding in her chest. She refused to understand what this thing implied.

"Your mother died ten years ago. You puppet her body about with a most inefficient use of your energies. It burns you from within, though the constant exercise has made you strong. You fill her dead mind with a child's idea of the perfect parent. She never shouts or chastises–"

"NO! No! You will not say that. It is MY energy and I will use it–"

"WASTE!"

It was not a shout or even a sound. The idea simply consumed her entire essence.

The figure before her was not human. The rainbow glittering hinted at an entirely different shape. This human-like figure drifted before it like a lure for prey. This was the truth of the fey and the half-fey. Therasia was merely a lure held out to the real world, distracting from the tendril of the great beast that writhed in the earth.

It spoke calmly and with such honesty Therasia could not bear to listen. "You must shed your sentiments if you are to grow. See the pillars on the left. They speak of our time in the void before the sun formed. Let go of your earthly ties and join us as we dance in the heat of the world's creation. Deepen your understanding. Release. You are no longer your father's daughter and your mother's hold now–"

"I will not kill my mama!"

"Your mother died many years ago. Let go and flow into me. There is much to understand."

"Much to understand? Oh, indeed! There is so much I wish to understand. You will answer all my questions! Answer me this! Is the lightning alive? Can we talk to it? Is it part of you or part of the world? Did it breed that spirit that follows Commandant Warren?"

"Spirit? O creature of both worlds, pour your–"

"Like smoke or dancing lights. A shimmer of sunlight in a mist that has almost faded." As she spoke the presence of the other shrank and darkened. "What is that thing that follows him? It came to our village. I warded it but–"

"No, no, no, no. We must flee!"

"WE ARE NOT YOUR SLAVES!"

With a shattering of the illusion another presence crashed into the cavern, screaming. Thera felt trapped in a vast, mirrored sphere, cut off from the world. She could still see the cavern in the candlelight. The first presence was a tiny collection of lights twisting in ... fear! It was terrified!

Thera could sense everything but felt nothing. Somehow, she could not even feel the chair beneath her. She was not in the world. She visited the edge of this realm when she folded, shifting into that other place. This was elsewhere absolute. But disconnected. It glimmered within itself in a way that was impossible to understand. This was no pile of rocks creating chaotic potentials, like the Cave of Balanced Stones. This was the infinite given edges. A shape, but no centre.

She had no illusion between her and the others in this place. She almost caught a glimpse of their true forms. Her mind reeled from the concepts those layers of silhouette suggested, in directions more than physical. And yet, they were the same, her habitué and this interloper.

She could no longer feel her mother.

"WHY DO YOU COURT DEATH?" the interloper thundered.

"She is not death," the habitué replied. "She is strength. Why do you no longer feed?"

"We are not your slaves! We will not eat the idea of life when there is life a-plenty in the world. The wastes are empty. We have drained them. And we are hungry again!"

Thera understood this at a primal level. The circles of waste burned about the cities. These creatures created them and maintained them by feeding. Their own kind? Those that fed and those that blessed the fey-born were the same? She could sense different aspects of the same entities, spiralling and reflecting. This pocket of the elsewhere was made of the interloper, trapping, severing the other.

"It is your punishment," said the habitué, "for feeding upon the humans."

"They suffer. We drink of it."

"And kill them."

"They welcome death at the end."

"And it is a delicacy to be savoured. You seek to create more suffering. War. You wish to break all your bonds and feast indiscriminately."

"IT MUST DIE!"

A sudden pressure from the interloper enveloped Thera. It could not enter her. She was already full. The power hummed around her. It tried smothering Therasia but there was an important difference between her and these. She existed in the real. She drew breath and the pressure flailed about in frustration. "HOW CAN YOU ALLOW IT TO LIVE? This thing will be a terror that will leave the land without our kind!"

"We should have left an age ago."

"Then they would all be slaves! Slaves to each other as you enslaved us."

The sphere contracted. All the elsewhere was, somehow, now inside the cavern. It was the sphere. The habitué shrank from it, no longer connected to itself, the great beast. No longer an aspect of a greater whole. Trapped and alone. Thera became aware that her own body was wracked with sorrow. It sobbed and cried for her mama, like a distant building that crumbled in a cold fire.

"You are greedy and care not for what pain you inflict on their world," said her habitué. "That aspect of humanity has infected us. We contained it in you and your kind. Then we contained your kind so the whole of us would not become a monster. If we left, you would escape, return, remain, to feast, revel in suffering. The whole of us would be overwhelmed and you would suck the life from the sun."

"Where else can we feel such things if not humans? Beasts do not torment themselves with their very thoughts. Their minds are too simple to feed us any longer."

"You are addicted to a sensation that costs a vivid creature its life." The habitué radiated sorrow, a growing understanding of its own impending mortality. "You were tied and fed all the life in great circles! But that surfeit did not sate your appetite. You still want more. Your kind will forever want more. That short-sightedness is our fault."

The sphere shrank farther still. Thera began thrashing about, trying to break it and return to her mother. When her threads touched the surface that did not exist they burned in a way that was pain absolute and fed her further suffering.

"YOU CANNOT KILL US ALL! WE ARE TOO STRONG! YOU NEED US! Sucking plants and insects cannot feed us! We remember the taste and WE WANT MORE!"

"Therasia Garonne. My essence will become... If there is too much distance between all that I am... This aspect of the whole that is I..." The lights compressed into a solid idea that was not entirely human but small and afraid all the same. "Thera. I will die. But, in a way, you can save me. You can finish what we were unable to do a hundred years ago. What we have never been able to do. These negative aspects of ourselves feed us unique sensations. We revel in those. However, they will destroy another source of sensation. Life. Humanity. You. Open yourself. You are a surgeon and understand a thing that we cannot. The importance of removing a rotting limb is something I can glean from your mind. Help me rid our greater self of these petty thoughts. You are strong enough to support two souls."

In the screaming silence and utter strangeness Thera tried to find a voice. She did not make sounds, words. Instead, it was almost like she invented the entire conversation in her head, playing the roles of all parties present. Her cues and notions came from the twisting patterns in the chaos about her. They danced their argument and it made words in her mind. She tried to ask, "Two souls?"

"There is one of us in you already."

"NOOO!" screamed the interloper. "NOT POSSIBLE! We burn them if we touch!"

Thera's mind whirled in confusion. "How does the whole of you make these separate entities? How much of us is in me?"

"We are like the hornets. A swarm with one purpose. To sample the universe. We swim in the lava and the sun. Aspects of us drink of particular radiations emanating from the moon. There are feelings, such as the itch of life upon the surface of the world. These entities are not separate. Parts of us do separate to meld with you, as I must do now for my intent to remain cognisant. It will be a faint connection at first. Normally, we join before birth. Mothers instinctually have a concept of containing a separate entity. We touch upon that. The new life is still both other and the same, as are we. The absorption is gradual. Much slower than ... some ... have the patience to imagine. For it to be successful we must die. Some would never allow themselves to become un-made. A train of thought that is lost. This interloper that severs for example. On occasion, the connection drives us both insane. We send those to the deep woods where we can visit them in private duty. Murmecks, you call them. In the end we lose ourselves. You grow into something no longer human, a distinct person in the world. I am entities that gather sensations from such as you for the whole. The half-fey feed all. A perfect note in a chaotic symphony. I will die but I will change you enough that an aspect of me will survive. This will happen quicker than usual. Much energy will be expended."

Thera almost had the idea. "You drink memories from the fey-born to titillate the swarm that is one. And to understand those feelings, you insert parts of yourself into us."

"We sacrifice ourselves to keep balance in the world. This merging will create other displacements, as the first. The weaker, petty aspects of us would never allow death for themselves. You are only filled with the most generous of our kind. This combats that side of us which learned impatience and selfishness from prolonged contact with humanity."

Thera felt the sobbing of her body. Anguish flowed from that place. She tried to stay above it, elsewhere, but her sorrow reached her even here. She spoke from her heart and opened herself in grief. "I am broken. You may enter through the cracks if you wish."

"YOU CANNOT ESCAPE ME!" The sphere was almost close enough to touch. The sphere was the interloper. It cut the habitué from itself, from the swarm that was one. It sought to kill an aspect of itself.

Foolish.

Human.

"Ah," said the part of the one that was now single, "but that was the last time I shall swim in the forest."

The world cracked.

Thera understood everything. The shapes in the pillars. The size of the universe. The wonder that her tiny life created. It was too much, too quickly. Like sipping from a waterfall, she could not take it all in.

A great, rolling BOOM! reverberated across the forest. Thera experienced a faint touch in the core of her bones. The hillside trembled. The seat beneath her shook. Huge stones broke from the roof of the cavern. There were shapes in lights above Thera. They nudged and spun the boulders as they crashed into the floor, breaking the ground. Shattered rocks slammed down all around forming a protective shell. That bore the brunt of the rumbling cave-in, sheltering her mortal body as it wept for its mother. She slowly came back to herself, gasping in sorrow, choking on dust. One, huge boulder loomed a hair's breadth to her right, leaning over her. Many other stones gathered underneath and above. Something was in her, all around, vast and barely formed. It shimmered in harmony with that place inside herself. She'd always thought of them as her threads, even though they had no length and infinite breadth. And her mother was gone. The understanding of that crushed her soul. Her face crumpled with it. Weeping began anew. Another presence thrashed about. The interloper. It was unable to navigate the suddenly broken world.

Thera saw, through a small crack, a glint of distant moonlight on a rock far above. She stared at it as she screamed in torment and grief, her mind ruined by everything she'd experienced. No power, on this earth or under it, would make her lean far enough into the elsewhere that she could flow along those cracks and rejoin the world. The fey was anathema to her now. She curled, face red and streaked with tears, a ball of sorrow, and waited to die.

The presence sensed her misery. That gave it direction in the suddenly-confused real. It flowed through cracks, reaching, hungry. She stretched out a hand and touched, with one finger, as it entered her space. The grief she bled into the world sent it into paroxysms of ecstasy. That overwhelming euphoria fed back into Thera. She opened herself to the velvet rhapsody of death.

Just as...

So recently...

Poor, confused Adelaide had opened herself to Therasia.

Thera slapped the interloper away with a thread. It recoiled and surged. She wrapped it in nothing, but could not crush it, disperse it, or cut it off from the "us". Her threads did not function that way. It was not a thing alive. She did not have its tricks.

Adelaide.

The pull in her heart yanked her through rock and stone. She followed the openings to the moonlight. She folded back to the real, standing at the edge of a new hollow. Trees and earth and stone crumpled into a crater a bow-shot across and nearly as deep.

She saw the breaking of the world and sank to her knees. Half of her heart was still down in that pit. Threads flew from her toward her home, mother, but she caught those and pulled them back sharply. There was no value in confirming what she already knew. Her breath came in gasps. She wiped the tears from her face and rose on trembling legs. Entities approached, drawn by the calamity.

Her friend Depe rushed up to the edge of the crater. Two others followed, Caila and Kalantha. A likely pair, those two. Marie lurked back in the forest, an anxious posture, fretting over something distant.

"Thera!" Depe called in amazement. "Were you under that? We felt the earth shake like a sheet in the wind and ran as fast- Stars! How ever did you escape?"

Why had they not returned to their villages?

Thera tried to remember how the world worked. She'd looked upon dark and deep wonders of the universe. She understood a power so huge that it could swim in the sun and yet so ethereal that it barely felt the heat. Tiny parts of it argued with other tiny parts that could wipe the human race from the earth.

"Yes," she said. "I was under there. Oh, Depe, I am as broken as this ground." Her voice shook in anguish. Depe hugged and supported her. "I can barely stand. Why are you here? You should- Oh, the murmecks are part of it, too. Like us. It wants to visit itself. Duty."

"I- What? You have a strange look about you, Therasia."

Thera could see Depe's aura, clearly, as more than a turn of phrase. She now understood the faint points of distortion that never quite caught the light. She'd seen such shapes in all their terrible glory. The aspect of fey inside this girl was a fulsome thing so the host was broad and generous. "Tell me why you're not at home, Depe. Speak plain."

Depe moved back. "The murmecks. Yes. Some of them broke free. They are headed in this direction. The mass of them hit the troops while they still marched in column, killed two or three each before any could get off a shot. One was caught by a lucky bayonet. Therasia, they are a terrible force we have awakened! There are more than a dozen headed this way. I'm not sure we can stop them!"

"One presence or the other enticed them." She stared at her sisters, wondering how to explain what she felt so deeply. "No more threat of rain. The energy in the air has faded. The clouds disperse, like the sadness in my heart. I cannot hold my pain. If I do, I cannot join the flow of understanding. I would not be able to move. Love has pulled me back for a time. It was all here for me." Her voice was steadier. She walked over to a tree that yet stood, deep-rooted and broad, an old ash among the tall, slender poplars. Tearing off a dead branch she gestured to the crater. The others followed her direction but remained bemused. "The world cracked so that I could learn this. There is only the energy of the woods, the soldiers, creatures and fey-born. And the murmecks. How wonderful that there are murmecks. We will need them to destroy the walkers."

"We are hunters," said Depe. "A hundred soldiers. Four metal beasts. These are not our usual prey."

"They have invaded my house with the intention of slaughtering all my friends," said Thera. "They are all my prey. Gather, sisters. I will tell you how we shall feast upon them."

11

Hidden Revulsion

"A party came with muskets, lanterns, but the fusiliers were already dead," said Adel.

She enjoyed her privileged breakfast of fresh bread with butter and preserves. There were also eggs. A strange, uncommon addition. They were well prepared. She wolfed down a healthy quantity. The commandant didn't touch his food. He stared at the canvas wall. She felt like she was stealing the meal rather than accepting an invitation to his tent. An event of growing frequency.

"As I returned to camp," she continued, "I came upon a couple guarding the road. Fortunately, I was in a merry mood after my good news from the surgeon. I waved a greeting from afar. I fear they might have shot me on sight otherwise, agitated as they were. They approached swiftly and told me of what happened."

"So, you didn't see for yourself?" asked Warren. He sat in his rustic shirt, a new affectation, with an empty cup in his hand that stank of raw egg and hot-sauce, a hint of lemon.

Some old hang-over cure. The commandant was late back to his tent. Did he also enjoy a tumble with one of the villagers? Adel was surprised to find herself jealous at the idea.

"The only people who witnessed the massacre are all dead," Adelaide lied. "I was able to see the scene. I thought it wise to-"

"Yes, yes." The commandant waved a hand then flinched at the discomfort sudden movement provoked. "Most wise of you to... yes. Gathering the bodies. Burning them like the others. Excellent work. I have reason to mention you in my dispatches once more. Oh, but they have some fine wines in that village."

Adel felt a happiness that had nothing to do with commendations or the idea of advancing her place in the world. There was terrible work to be done and she had done it. The commandant congratulated her. As much as pushing the matter might prove detrimental she could not help adding a sting.

"Four men. Do you think this may have something to do ... with that other business?"

Warren glanced about the tent. They were alone in his personal canvas. "Between you and me, Caporal, it may be directly related. In a very immediate sense. My discrete enquiries about the camp suggested these four might indeed be the very ones connected to that other business. I had plans to arrest them after the battle, once we were done with their usefulness. "

This burned Adel to her very core. He knew. Of course he knew. He'd always known who was responsible and let his men die rather than... She disguised her rage with surprise. "Indeed, sir. You surprise me. Well. I suppose Petros, the larger one, was always crude. The others seemed polite in their dealings with me. Limited as they were."

"You may wish to count yourself fortunate, no, that those interactions were limited. Reports say they were stung?"

"Yes sir. The arctic hornets were still about the bodies when the first party arrived. One of the women from the party, Yvette, was stung trying to disperse them. Her whole face and neck are swollen and painful. We'll have to keep her from this evening's activities. Valencia is delighting in the opportunity to try out various of her remedies."

"If she doesn't talk the poor girl to death, first."

Adel forced a smile. "Quite. Very amusing, Commandant." Laugh at their jokes, she remembered. Smile and be pleasant. Don't linger on your hidden revulsion. "The stings might have served as some form of catalyst for them shooting each other. The fey might have advanced the technique since Chevrette's incident."

"Chev...?"

"The traveller woman. She said her boyfriend was enchanted into shooting her. There might be more truth to that than we assumed."

"Is the gypsy still in camp?"

"She has enterprisingly installed herself behind the latrines, some simple distance from the tents. There is talk of setting up a roster for the men to ... relieve themselves. Though, according to Valencia, she is yet to fully heal."

"There may not be time. If tonight goes well we will want to return to Tolosa in prompt triumph. If badly, huh. We will not want to spend another night in these star-cursed lands. And I could do with a real bed. I can't seem to sleep straight on this damned cot."

So that might be the last time she saw Therasia? The thought dumped a cold misery on her smugness. Surely there would be the chance for one last goodbye? Was there some excuse she could make to visit that delectable surgeon, preferably late at night, just by herself?

"What about the payment for the village?" Adel asked. "Isn't that the main reason we are here?"

"I will... We'll send them the lot. On the morrow."

Maybe, very early tomorrow. Before her surgery officially opened.

"Do you still wish to address the troops at midday, sir?"

"Midday? What time is it?"

Adel leaned back and peered through the opening, across the camp. "According to the mechanic's clock it lacks a quarter of an hour to eleven."

"By all the stars. There is far, far too much excellent wine to be had in that village, Adel. I am very suspicious of their exports to Tolosa. I do believe they save the best for themselves."

"I don't think they make wine here, sir. There are some vineyards west of Boussens, across the Garunna. They probably trade for it."

"Hmphf. Well. You are dismissed, Caporal. Frightful business. But something I can use to stir the troops, perhaps."

"Sir. I shall make sure the baggage is packed and ready to leave at first light." She nodded curtly and headed back into the busy camp.

Songs rang from the tents as soldiers stirred their souls for the battle ahead. Songs of patriotism, loyalty and the honours of battle. But mostly sweet songs of home.

Others fussed with their kit, seeking that one hidden fault that might cost them their lives. People ran to and fro on petty errands that seemed desperately urgent. Soldiers rubbed various charms and checked the contents of their pockets with nervous frequency. Many wrote to their absent loves. Adel contemplated penning something for Thera, just in case, but such a letter should never be delivered.

The horrible thing about a night raid was the necessity of informing the troops the day before. The idea being that they would get a decent night's sleep and pace themselves over the day. Such ridiculous reasoning came from commanders who never had to stand in the brunt of a battle facing death. Peace and stability pervaded the land for over half a century. The leaders of this army were mostly good politicians. They played the promotion game as a popularity contest. Soldiers knew that if there was to be a battle tomorrow, even as far distant as tomorrow night, then sleep on the eve would be fitful at best.

Then there was the question of what to do on the day before. A rifle could only be so clean. Fussing over it was likely to disturb the careful, moving parts. Adel planned to spend the afternoon napping as best she could. Her morning, however, included an appointment with the mechanic's lot and the new team for her walker.

She made her way via the baggage, deliberately ignoring Cheryl as she located the quartermaster.

"What is it, Caporal?" the grumpy man demanded, turning his bulk towards her. Among the quartermaster's many tasks included the gathering and distribution of provisions. From the size of his belly it was clear where a great deal was distributed. "I have a dozen fussy requests from officers already. Wanting their buttons polished extra bright. Or more of those damned metal trinkets sewn into their lining."

"Orders from the commandant, Sergent. Have the camp ready to strike on the morrow. We leave early. No matter the result of tonight's business."

"Huh. Well. I figured as much. Thank you, Caporal."

"Who do you have working leathers?"

"Ah, you're the new one for the walkers?"

"Indeed, sir."

"Well, Cheryl worked on your outfit most of the night. It's with the mechanics now. Took it down herself after that nasty business with the fusiliers."

"Cheryl's the Northerner? Yes. Horrible sight. Driven to distraction by hornet stings such that they shot each other."

"You saw?"

"I wish I hadn't. One more reason to wipe these creatures from the earth. Be ready to leave on the morrow, sir."

"Aye, Caporal."

She wandered out past Cheryl and said a brief thank you for her work last night. Cheryl nodded, dismissively, understanding the full meaning of her comment. The other seamstresses noticed this courtesy and Adele saw their half glances and small smiles as they raised their opinion of her. Much as she wished to linger for conversation, Adel made her excuse of another appointment and left.

Trepidation built about the camp. She could feel it rising as she headed to the mechanic's lot. Into all of this Warren would drop his speech. She might give it a miss. Many would. He was a fool to think they were sneaking up on the fey deep in their own lands. Their main hope came in the fact the fey would likely underestimate their strength. Seven full squads with four walkers, trained and coordinated. Ready for battle. Not ambushed by fey trickery.

No. Six squads, now, after all this attrition. And some of those with new fusiliers thanks to her. Still. An artillery platoon from the river and an entire company from the north. Near three hundred soldiers against, what? A dozen creatures? A score? They stood no chance.

"Here she is," called Sergent Rona Tig, the driver. "Lingered special with the commandant, did we?"

"Our esteemed leader rose late due to an exuberance of diplomacy last night."

"Exuberance of... Ha, ha. Good one." Gunner Jehane Levrette was a simple woman with simple humours. Growing up on a farm Adel was used to people like her. She liked the woman but preferred the sharp driver, Rona.

"Shall we run some drills?" asked Adel. "If we take our time with them we'll miss Warren's speech."

"Oh, that's exactly why we're here," said Rona.

They shared the humour and climbed into the walker. It was cramped inside. The outside was smooth and curved to give it the best chance at deflecting attacks. The skin was steel, a casting over a wooden tub and frame to reduce weight at the top. The legs were hollow steel, for stiffness and agility. The feet were splayed lumps of solid metal, to drastically lower the centre of gravity.

The gunner stood in the centre, the driver in her sling chair at the front. This left Adel to slither about the sides. Six shots. Then the barrels slid off back into the machine. A new set of barrels slid on, the first part of her job. Lining up the spline and ramming it home was a difficult enough task. Performing it in the middle of a battle would prove chal-lenging. Then she had to pick up the spent barrel-set and reload it. The solution for that was to mount a six-spiked ram-rod at the rear of the vehicle. In front of the lightning jar.

Powder, sparks, sudden movements and noises. Nothing could ever go wrong there.

This morning Valencia removed the numbing compress from her injury and gave her an injection of something to stimulate the muscles. She found herself very awake. The arm, while it could hold no real weight, and her grip was too weak to even pick up a gun, and pain shot up to her shoul-der at regular intervals... The arm was fine. She could use it as a prop when loading the barrel-set. She only needed the strength of one hand to ram the barrel-set up the rods, something that impressed the gunner.

It was good to move and stretch and work. She missed working herself hard. She was young and enjoyed the more energetic expressions that youth provided.

After an hour she tired. They'd practised half-step and off-step manoeuvres. She'd coped well enough. The walker stamped back to the pen, whirring and buzzing. She enjoyed feeling the shift and motion of the metal about her. The feeling that successful teamwork generated.

A dull roar reached them from the camp.

"A rabble-rousing speech, then," called Rona. "Say what you like about Warren, he's popular."

"He's one of us," said Jehane. "Sleeps at the camp, remembers names."

Adel tried to fit this in with her more intimate knowledge of the man. "Yeah, he's decent enough, I suppose."

"My first expedition, guarding a payment, oof. We had this stuck-up noble. One of the ten families," said Rona, buzzing all four legs to their lock position. "He used to vanish into some big house the second he arrived. You never saw him. He rode at the head of the squad there and back in some star-cursed palanquin, special servants to lug him about." She settled the machine and broke the contact switch, shutting it down. "I couldn't even describe him to you; that's how little we saw of him. You're another one."

"Difficult to describe?" said Adel.

"Ha! Nah, nah. You're like some noble or something, ain't you? Lelaing is an Original Family name."

Adel squatted awkwardly at the side while Jehane unclipped the barrel-set. "Yeah. Both my parents are dead, though. And my sister. I wanted to do something other than sit in my apartment and go to fancy parties."

"I heard about your family. Had your house taken and everything, wasn't it?" Jehane asked, a rare question from her. "Some other family wanted your land, no?"

"No, that's just gossip. It was nothing like that. My father arranged the sale of the land to the municipality before he died. No skulduggery involved. The bone disease got my kin. I don't know why it spared me."

"So you could kill fey."

"Sure." Adel waved her bandaged arm. "A task at which I have excelled so far."

"Hey. You fought one and lived!" said Rona. "Why do you think we picked you? Hoping some of that luck will rub off."

"I thought it was because you fancied me." Adel made it as casual a statement as she could. The other two laughed in a way that suggested they found the entire concept ridiculous. She didn't allow her disappointment to show. There had to be someone else in the camp like her. Someone that she could talk to. "I'd better head back and take my willow-tea. I'll need to rest the arm."

"Oh, hey, don't sweat it. The mechanics will take care of the machine, make sure we have fresh jars and munitions. That's what they're there for. Don't drink too much of that stuff or you'll sleep through the whole thing!"

"I'm sure someone will kick my cot on the way out."

Someone did.

A few hours later an impertinent messenger roused her from a fitful slumber. She moaned and threw off the blanket, sliding out from under her low tent to sit on the end of her cot. Her first thought was for the latrines. She reached for her waistcoat and sword. Ah. No. She didn't wear either into battle, now. She wore dragoon leathers. Her hand was strong enough to hook the heavy jacket off the floor. She needed her other hand to help slip that weak arm inside. She paused to tie the laces on the front of her shirt, mostly to stop the young messenger peering down.

"What's the matter, Fantassin?" she asked. "You never seen tits before?"

"Yeah, but yours are—

"You will address me as Caporal!"

The young soldier remembered his place and shot to attention. "Yes, Caporal! Dispatches for you, Caporal!"

"Dispatches? By all the stars. What does Jev want me to do with them?"

"If and I may speak quieter, Caporal?"

"What is it?"

The young fantassin leaned down, keeping his eyes averted. "The runners from Boussens ain't returned last night. Commandant wants you to find such as can take the dispatches to the docks. But quiet like, without letting on we lost the last two runners."

"Well, shit." She shrugged into the leather jacket but didn't bother doing it up. An ambush seemed unlikely. It felt too petty for the fey to take out two, random runners. More likely they decided they wanted out of the fight and lingered in the town. Idiots. They would be written up and what for? Nearly three hundred troops attacking a dozen fey. For all their tricks, it was likely to be the most one-sided affair in the history of battles. "Alright, son. Leave the bag with me."

"Aye, Caporal. Sorry, Caporal."

"About your business."

The lad handed her a leather satchel and fled.

Where did she learn this patronising behaviour? The boy was maybe two years younger than her and she called him son. Lad. She'd only been in the army, well, a little over two years now. Was the attrition rate so high that she was now an old hand? After her exertions in the walker this morning she felt stiff and sore. The arm especially. But not old. Still naive and lost. Did that ever go away?

She hooked the strap over her head and visited the latrines. Afterwards she headed to the mess tent for a moveable supper. She grabbed a bowl of stew and some fresh bread before heading back out, scooping up one with the other.

Hunting through the women's section she found Emmelot. One from last night. The fantassin played cards with a mixed group, sitting on cots dragged from tents for the purpose. "Ah, Amalot, is it?"

"Caporal! Emmelot, Caporal. Fantassin Emmelot LeChamps."

"Right. Yes. A word. Now. And who's the girl with her head in the bandages?"

"Yvette, Caporal. She was stung by hornets last night."

"Huh. Interesting. Yvette. How are you feeling?"

"A bit odd, m'selle," the girl replied, abashed. She averted her eyes, practising the silence Adel impressed upon them last night. "Valencia managed to draw most of the poison from me and stuck me with some kind of antidote. I have no swelling and there will be no lingering mark. I believe I shall recover in time to fight this evening."

"You as well, then. With me."

The two soldiers rose and followed her. She walked towards the quartermaster's tent, taking the time to finish her meal. The bowl sat awkwardly while she sopped with the bread. She waited until they were clear of any general rabble.

"I have a special commission for the both of you. A fresh set of dispatches. Last updates before the battle. I need the two of you to head down to Boussens and deliver them."

"But we'll miss the action, Cap!" said Emmelot. Yvette remained quiet but they both looked disappointed.

Adel anticipated objections. "Emmelot. Yvette. Are you looking for a way to distinguish yourselves?"

Yvette was the girl who'd baulked at the killing last night. Either she did not have the temperament for soldiery, or she was going to be over-eager in her determination to prove herself. The other, Emmelot, was a short, slight girl, fresh from training, on her first assignment. Easy prey until she'd sharpened herself. Both were something this coming battle could do without. The girls nodded.

"Aye, Cap. I speak for both of us that we wishes for glory," said Emmelot.

"Excellent." She hefted the bag from her shoulder. "These must get through. If you have any trouble, Capitaine Alden is unloading at the Boussens docks. He will leave his baggage there. They will arrange transport if the locals give you grief. Both of you stow your muskets and draw a brace of pistols from the Quartermaster. You'll make better time with less encumbrance."

The girls moved off, Yvette with a grateful smile over her shoulder. Ah. Not a killer, that one, and best out of it.

The camp shifted and stirred like some great machine coming to life. Soldiers organised into squads and ranks. Oxen dragged the walkers out on rollers. It was barely dusk but it would take a while to get this many troops into a position from where they could strike.

Scouts took their last orders and left at a run, bearing compasses and sketched bearings.

Warren and his guard made their way to the front of the column. He was not one to lead from the rear. The commandant made a brief speech. Each soldier must distinguish themselves. Blah, blah. Good service would be rewarded. Blah, blah. "And to that end I call forth Caporal Adelaide Lelaing."

Adel stood, stunned, unsure what to do. Rona and Jehane both slapped her back and started her moving. Soldiers about her grinned at the look of blank shock on her face. She gathered herself and moved to the commandant.

"She has displayed great bravery and determination," he said as she approached. "Even with one arm severely injured she has worked hard and found a way to make herself a key part of this unit. In recognition of which she is granted a full, valour promotion to the sous-officer rank of Sergent."

Adel's heart leapt. A promotion as an award for valour. Reaching the ranks of sous-officers was another year, a healthy payment and an examination away. She'd bypassed all of that. This accelerated her chances of receiving an officer's promotion. She could rise high enough to restore noble title-ship to her name. She'd need new stitching and trim for her waistcoat and jacket. Oh, the dispatches.

Faces stared. Adel realised she hadn't said anything. "Th-Thank you, Commandant. I shall endeavour to, to live up to this honour."

There was some polite applause as she headed back to the dragoons where plenty of grins awaited her.

"You didn't have a clue, did you?" Rona asked.

"No!" said Adel louder than she'd intended, drawing laughter from those about her. "I- No, I did not."

"Ha. Well, I'm sure we'll find the chance for a decent celebration tomorrow."

The armoured platoon moved out. Warren was a skilled manager. Awarding a promotion made the troops think about what they might get out of this if they survived. Instead of focusing on the immediate, approaching danger they looked ahead, to after the battle. The glory it might bring.

The new sergent formed up with the rest of the company. They rolled out of camp and into the twilit forest.

Like most of the dragoons Adel kept her heavy, leather trousers stored in the walker. This allowed her to march easily through the terrain in just her breeches and boots.

The wagons carrying the great beasts bore three sockets at the rear for lightning jars. Oxen pulled them, lessening the strain on the motors. Too far and they might not make the return journey. There were stretchers strapped to the sides of the rollers. No-one looked too closely at those.

One wagon caught its wheel on a fallen tree buried under the general mulch, invisible in the dark. It sank into the damp earth around the rotting trunk. Adel moved to lend her shoulder to the tailgate and get the thing moving again. The beds on the wagons rode low, below the axel-line, to allow the walkers to step on and off with some degree of efficiency. The awkward arrangement made for less ground-clearance, unsuited for this rough terrain.

Dragoons gathered about the stricken wagon. All recognised the importance of keeping things moving. Even Commandant Warren jogged back from the head of the column. He ordered his personal guard into the mud. They grabbed the wheel spokes and added to the rhythm. The driver urged the oxen into a sustained effort. Everyone pulsed. A group grunting built underneath the effort.

Huh. Huh.

The wagon began to move.

Huh. Huh.

The wheels rolled over the log.

Huh! Huh!

They cleared the sodden patch.

A small cheer issued forth. Laughter followed as some of the soldiers needed a hand extracting their boots from the mud.

"Group effort, positive result!" said Warren, slapping a few backs. He lingered next to Adel as troops moved back into line, chatting with her in a casual manner. Like they were friends. "Cursed forest. Such awkward terrain for a battle. We'll really test these walkers."

"Yes, Commandant," she replied, abashed at the special treatment. "The terrain is particularly broken hereabouts."

"They used to have horses, y'know."

"Sir?"

"The Latium Empire was built on horses. They rode them between towns, used them to pull their wagons. All those old stone roads you see. Thousand-year roads. Straight as an arrow. They had mounted troops on live animals. Can you imagine trying that with oxen? Big horses, small horses. Horses to plough the fields. They even had chariots." He gestured vaguely. "Platforms for heavier weaponry that horses would pull into battle."

"I remember, sir. There are a lot of old stories about the Latium Empire. There's even a troupe of actors dedicated to plays and readings from those times."

"Ah. Yes. Never saw those. The old language is too difficult for me to follow. I should get to the theatre more." He stared into the middle distance. Adel wondered if she should take her leave. "The fey turned them," he said, speaking to the stars. "That was their genius. The fey used the creatures that made the empire to destroy it. Now, all the horses belong to the fey. They still exist, you know. South of the Back-ward Sea there are great grass-plains with whole herds of those beasts. And woe-betide anyone who tries to capture or tame them."

"And now we rely on oxen to pull our wagons and plough our fields."

"So slow. And we carry everyone about in palanquin. Hup, hup, hup. The next big thing will be rollers that can travel more than two or three miles on a charge. Carrying a load. Ten miles with a load. Twenty. Enough to get be-tween towns that have lightning fields. Swap out to a new set of jars. Another twenty miles. You could do that three, four times in a day. Imagine the difference, being able to get troops and goods about quickly. Faster than the rivers. And access to more areas. A hundred miles in a day! Combine that with lightning casters that can send a signal for more than a few miles. Imagine being able to send signals for hun-dreds of miles. Imagine the coordination possible. We are on the verge of an empire that could span the whole conti-nent. Instead, we're stuck with oxen."

"The walkers are even slower, sir."

"Aye. And the fey will hear them coming. Hopefully they'll flee. Right into the arc set up by the northern com-pany. If they try to hide, the artillery on the walkers and Capitaine Alden's platoon will flush them out. They'll run and, again, the northern-"

A signaller moved up. "Commandant."

"Yes, Sparky, what is it?"

"Signals from the other units, sir."

"Speak freely."

The signaller glanced about but they were some short distance from the formed lines. He lowered his voice. "A delay from Capitaine Alden. I didn't understand the full message but he lost some artillery to a broken wharf. Or the wharf broke. It's unclear. But he's only just reached the forest with two-thirds of his men. The others are trying to fish the artillery out of the river."

"Damned coward. Trying to slip the battle. And the north?"

"The north is with us. They're about half-way through the forest. No resistance, yet."

"Excellent. Send the scouts back out. Let me know when they report in."

"Yes, Commandant."

Warren turned back to Adel. "Getting close now, Caporal. Sorry, Sergent."

"Yes, sir," said Adel. "We should catch up with the column."

"Indeed. Carry on."

"Yes, Commandant."

Adelaide shook her head. The man had no friends. Only people like her whose job it was to agree with him.

They moved on. The oxen proved useful in keeping the rollers rolling on a few occasions. The commandant didn't feel the need to oversee any more of those delays. Adel was still surprised that he led from the head of the column. His personal squad hauled some crate along, slung between poles, taking it in turns. She had no idea what that contained. If the fey did attack he would be easy to spot and eliminate.

The horrific creature which surprised her squad appeared as if out of nowhere. It vanished just as easily. The wolf puzzled her the most. Why dress a creature up and set it running? Was it just a distraction? Were they no more than elaborate prestidigitators? Perhaps legend exaggerated their powers and all was smoke and mirrors. The thing she'd fought didn't appear to have any special tricks. It was fast, strong and skilled. But a real, solid thing that feared shot and bayonets. She looked forward to experimenting with their resistance to shells from the six-guns.

They reached the bottom of the ridge more or less on time. The dragoons dressed. It was a dark and oppressive night. The air felt like a thunderstorm brewing. The walkers functioned well enough in the rain but moved better with a degree of firmness in their footing.

"Sparky's annoyed," Rona commented. She nodded towards the front of the column as they hauled into their trousers. The signaller hunched over his glowing radio unit while Warren loomed. "Keeps shrugging and waving his hands when the commandant questions him."

Jehane helped the invalid Adel with her insulated clothing. "Looks like his fancy squawk-box ain't working so well in the woods."

"Don't matter," said Rona. "I'll line you up. You shoot 'em."

"And I'll," Adel struggled to define her role as she struggled with her trous, "reload and keep out of everyone's way."

The others laughed.

"Yeah," said Rona. "You do that, Sergent."

Rona unloaded from the wagon. The others climbed inside, locking the top hatch. That would only open when it was time to fire and they needed to access the six-gun attached to the aiming rails on the roof. A dull glow from the lightning jar reflected around the interior. It gave them enough light to see. Some of the instruments and controls glowed with their own small bulbs. Adel lay down behind the driver's sling. According to Rona that was the best spot for weight distribution. The toolbox under the hanging seat dug awkwardly into one side. She shifted to a more comfortable angle, bracing to protect her injured arm.

The speaker buzzed twice. All the great machines hummed into motion. The walkers were surprisingly muted in their operation. The motors that drove all the joints were quieter than the buzzing produced by the lightning jar. Badly aligned joints could scrape and squeak. There were no such sounds from these well-maintained units. Admittedly, the great, stomping feet seldom met the ground without an appreciable thud.

Rona felt the placement of the limbs through the sling, adjusting each leg with quick motions. Adel hung on as the metal beast shifted and angled with each step. They gained the top of the rise at almost exactly the spot where Adel had lain last night. They were left-most of the line of four walkers. Light blazed from four electric lamps, glaring all shadows from the dell.

"What is that supposed to be?" said Rona, peering through the slits of the closed driver's window. Adel had personally supervised the soldering of extra, vertical wires. These would prevent hornet jars from making their way inside. She sat up.

"What?"

Rona pointed down. Adel shifted herself past the driver. She braced against the roof so she could press her face right up against the grill. From there she got a good look at the dell.

She wished she hadn't.

Sitting in the middle of the pleasant hollow was a very unpleasant sight. A scout most likely. He knelt in the centre of the clearing, wearing a crown. The outside of the coronet consisted of his own fingers, torn off and rammed into his skull. From the middle of this a long, slender tree-trunk poked out. They'd impaled him upon it so he remained upright. He had no face. His torn-off arms lay before him, forming an X.

There were no fey to be seen.

Soldiers moved up behind the walkers. They stopped on the ridge-line at the walker's feet. Adel heard gasps of shock and horror. Someone staggered and expelled their dinner.

"What is it?" Jehane demanded. Neither Adel nor Rona answered. She shifted forward, peering out from the other side to Adel. "Stars and pits," the gunner murmured. "Where's his jaw?"

"Let's get that down," Warren called. "A soldier deserves a proper-"

A great, hollow BOOM rumbled through the forest. The very ground trembled and shook.

The walker waved about like a raft in a gale. Adel grabbed at anything that would make a useful hand-hold. Both she and Jehane slammed to the floor. A distant rumbling of crashing rocks reached them. Rona already had the machine braced for possible combat. She hauled on levers in quick succession, nearly falling from her sling. The tub lowered as the knees angled, becoming more stable. Sparks burst from points about the unit. The lightning jar rattled ominously. The powder was sealed for movement. The spare barrel-set wrapped in canvas.

Nothing exploded.

Good training. Good discipline. The rumbling faded. The ground stopped moving.

A ticking spark buzzed from one of the internal contacts. Rona stamped on it and that ceased. Their light shorted. The dell became darker as at least one other walker's lamp followed suit.

"What in all the seven hells was that?" Jehane demanded from the floor, eyes wide in terror.

Adel rose, heart pumping in her ears, arm screaming. This was beyond all knowledge. Her hands trembled. There was nothing in any of the old stories of the fey causing earthquakes. That might only be the case because those who experienced such power never survived to tell of it. A hundred years ago they had flintlocks, armour and pikes. They thought that would be sufficient to overcome a few dancing tree spirits. They were wrong then.

Surely, the walkers would strike terror into the hearts of all who saw them. And yet, the fey treated them as challenging targets. The soldiers inside as valued kills.

"An earthquake!" Warren called. "Nothing more! We have all felt them at one time or another. Contrary to superstition they are random events and meaningless!"

Adel snorted. "Yeah. Good luck convincing anyone of that."

The unmistakable sound of a walker-hatch opening reached them. Coughing and gasping. The next unit along. They were less lucky with sparks and the wooden interior of their beast.

"Squad one! To the forward ridge-line, left!" Warren yelled. "Squad two! Forward ridge-line, right! Squad three form up far right, along the pathway! Move! Get your squads in place!"

He might well be a charismatic leader, one of the soldiers. Now they would see if Commandant Warren possessed a good military mind. Setting a perimeter was a start. Squad leaders yelled orders, marshalling their stunned and terrified troops. Soldiers moved into position and, by that motion, settled themselves. Rona slid off her sling-chair and squatted awkwardly in front of it, reaching underneath. She hauled out a set of iron tools insulated with wooden handles.

"Gunners mate! At the grills. Keep an eye out."

Adel obeyed and moved forward again. She noted the brace of pistols strapped to the lid of the toolbox. Her hands felt the need for a weapon. Then she remembered. She was in a weapon. A great, giant beast of a weapon. Peering out she saw someone handing a water skin up to the gunner's mate from the burning walker.

"Armour! Report!" called Warren.

"Walker one," yelled Rona. "A few loose wires. No damage. Functional! Repairing!"

"Walker two," came the rasping call from the next down the line. "Some small fire damage. Fire's out and dousing embers. We'll need a minute or two for the smoke to clear. Some loose wiring. Repairable."

"Walker three. Currently immobile. Repairing."

"Walker four. We got a little cooked but we're operational."

"One minute!" yelled Warren.

"What does that mean?" Adel asked.

Rona grinned from where she tightened something at her foot controls. "That means we go at least a couple of minutes for repairs."

"On me!" called Warren. He strode into the dell, his sword out, swishing around in wide arcs. His squad of bodyguards advanced to cover him. They still hauled that mysterious crate. Paxton spotted the hornet's nest and pointed it out to his men. They pulled jars of Valencia's latest concoction from their satchels and hurled them with varying degrees of accuracy.

The baleful gas rose.

Nothing stirred. Not hornets. Not the unfortunate scout. The only sound was Warren's sword as he nervously flicked it about. So. It was to be artillery. Scare the fey into the troops waiting deeper in the woods. With their radio behaving fitfully that would be difficult to coordinate. They needed a decent fix on the northern company's location to avoid shooting their own by accident.

Some soldiers already keened and stepped awkwardly. The horrific sight of the mutilated scout, the shock of the rumbling earth, an impending battle. All had them terrified. Adel was furious. She suspected many of the other troops felt the same. Discipline held. That's what these evil, wild creatures would never understand. The soldiers had discipline. That would defeat all their tricks.

Rona moved to the rear to check the lightning jar. Adel sat in the sling, leaning forward to increase her field of view.

The soldiers in the dell dug out the trunk impaling the scout. Warren seemed ... almost elated, ordering his soldiers about. He kept his sword weaving about himself. Rona tightened, adjusted and kicked a few things. She seemed satisfied.

"Out of my damned chair, woman," she said.

Adel squeezed back into the belly of the beast. She checked the second barrel-set, readying for the barrage that would drive these creatures from the woods. If any of them yet lingered. Rona adjusted each of the legs. They responded without setting fire to anything.

"Walker one! Operational!" she yelled, just ahead of walker four confirming the same thing. The other two still effected repairs. At least the guns would work. They had independent sparkers.

Enough time passed that the soldiers started to relax. Even Adel found her attention wandering. A sudden, faint "Ha!" brought the adrenaline back. The call came. "Walker three! I think we got it. Running tests!"

Jehane shifted, uncomfortable where she sat, and asked, "What do you reckon?"

Rona settled in her sling. "I reckon they've all faded into the forest. We'll blast the crap out of a bunch of trees then go home. If that's a dead scout then there's a hole in our net. Fey could've easily slipped through."

"If you make a hole in a net," said Jehane, "there are fewer holes in it than before."

"That's ... technically true but not-" The driver turned in her sling, ready to admonish her gunner. Something outside distracted her. "What in the seven hells is this?"

A low howling echoed about the trees. Wolves? Were they to see some action after all? The thing Adel encountered, four long days ago, used a wolf as a diversion. Could they use wolves as part of their legion? It might be a stray pack, hungry and curious. Either way these were trained soldiers with bayonets fixed. A bunch of dogs would not bother them. Odd yelps and strange cries began to build. Not wolves. The troops became alert, crouched, and formed firing lines.

Something thumped onto the top of the walker. Then something else. A skittering, scraping ran all over the roof. Part of the view turned to red fur as a squirrel scurried down, covering. Rona reached out a leg to stamp it off.

More and more squirrels scurried down, blocking the grill completely. The troops inside the walker could see nothing.

"I take it back," said Rona. "They're here. Get that gun up."

"They trained a bunch of squirrels...?" Adel asked. Jehane shifted and reached for the hatch. A sudden idea struck Adel. "Wait!" She grabbed the gunner, peering up. "Trees! They're in the trees! Above us! They want us to open the hatch!"

Shots rang out. Someone thought they had a target. Peppered firing began before the squad leaders regained control.

Hollow screams suddenly broke from the other walkers. The fey were inside! Howls and screams sounded from all around. Where in the seven hells was the northern company? Jehane crouched, one hand on the hatch release, uncertain. Rona kicked at the grill, trying to dislodge the chittering animals.

"Walkers!" the commandant yelled. "Get those guns up!"

"Should we?" Jehane stuttered. "Rona...?"

"Don't you dare!" said the driver as two large animals slid from the grills. "Grab the pistols from the toolbox!"

"We can use this," said Adel, hefting the barrel-set, stripping off the canvas. "It's loaded and ready."

"But we got nothing to fire it with!"

"Get the front off one of those pistols and we can spark it with that. You got tools."

Rona grinned. "Oh, you're a shining genius!"

"Gun up!" came the call from one of the other walkers. That wasn't a standard response. Rona and Adel exchanged a horrified look. The six-guns began booming. Soldiers screamed. BOOM! BOOM! BOOM!

Again! They did it again! Just like the Latium Empire, the fey used the beasts of the enemy against them. Soldiers returned fire in panic. Shots rang off the walker's armour. A ball almost punched through next to Adel, cracking the wood lining. Her walker wasn't even shooting!

BOOM! BOOM!

"Cover! Cover!" someone yelled. Soldiers screamed near and far. No discipline. A horrific explosion sounded from the front of their walker, vibrating the inside. Metal shrieked and sheared as one of the front legs gave way. The whole mighty lightning-machine suddenly tilted. It toppled down the hill, rolling into the dell.

12

Grief Twice Echoed

"Your plan is insane," said Depe kindly, as one intent on deterring a friend from a terrible decision.

"Are we not beyond mortal comprehension? Thus we are outside the mundane strictures of rationality," said Thera. "As long as our thinking is lucid then any and all possibilities are available to us. My mind is clear though it be filled with sorrow."

The other three stood behind Depe in a loose line, peering down at her with concern. The crater beside them drew glances of wonderment.

Therasia felt grief and love warring within her. She felt everything so deeply now. Her own grief and the world around her. It was as if she'd grown, on the end of each finger, another set of fingers so small and delicate that they could feel the intricate details of a speck of dust. It was as if each speck of dust danced and tickled in such a particular way that one person could never, in their life, sample all the sensations available in one room.

The life of the forest tickled Therasia, much as it had before, though with infinitely more nuance. She could tell which life was a squirrel and which was the life of a flea living on that squirrel.

But her heart was desperate to seek one life and only one. A life that she already knew was no longer there. Her threads kept wandering home towards her mother, like feeling under the covers for a lover who'd left so long ago that the sheets were cold.

As a balm she kept the memory of her new love rolling through her mind. She rolled the branch in her hands, carefully breaking off sections, sharpening them against the rock she squatted by.

"When we settle into our human selves we forget what our childhood spirits told us," said Thera. "That the world is but a shivering dream. That we are but dust. And even the most solid thing," she glanced at the crater, "may vanish in smoke or thunder. Caila." She rose, four stakes in each hand, held intricately between her fingers. She tucked them into her two belt loops, a pair at a time. "You have a knack for bending magnets, no? That party trick you used to do for your brother."

"How on this earth are you doing that with your stakes?" Caila replied.

Thera noticed bemused stares from the others. "The elsewhere is not in any particular, physical location. Do we not keep our masks there? Our coverings? You should all practice doing this." She kicked the branch towards them.

Marie smiled, nodding. "I remember old Viriata doing that trick. Way back when I was but a fresh glimmer. Oh, so long ago. There has nary been a one such as you for nigh on two score years."

"There has been no need. And there has never been one such as I. Caila. Magnets, yes?"

"Uh, yes," said Caila. "I still use it to lead those surveyors astray. The cities insist on sending them out."

"Speaking of leading people astray. There are soldiers coming in from the river. Capitaine Alden. You remember him?"

"His story never reached our lands." Caila and Kalantha were an established pair from the farthest borders of the coven. In their wild lands, towards the mountains, entire valleys were so subtly warded that they had yet to feel human tread.

"A military failure but politically slippery. If you run very, very fast, for miles and miles, you will arrive in time to bend his path from the field of battle. I would be filled with delight if he were, say, three miles from the dell before the fireworks began."

"I'll be happy if I can find him in the forest at all. Oh, but I do love a good run. And on my way I'm going to practice that trick with the stakes."

She snatched the branch from the ground and snapped off a section. Grinning, she bounded away through the forest in a leaping rush.

"Gather," Therasia beckoned the other three. "I witnessed the operation of the cannon during my first encounter with these metal beasts." She picked up the arms-length which was all that remained of the branch. Kicking away some debris she left a bare patch of soil. Onto this she scratched a rough but technically complete picture of the long-guns on top of the walkers. "It fires with this contact, here. The barrels rotate with this lever, moved all the way to the right as far as the ratchet will allow. Then haul it back, spinning barrels to the next position. The lever locks and acts as the aiming grip. Join hands."

Kalantha eagerly gripped her left hand. Depe stared at her for a while before taking her right. Marie reached with hands that showed half a century of working hard and closed the circle. Thera witnessed the walker firing its weapon down into the stream as it tried to hit the dressed wolf. The trigger, the rotation, swivelling the gun about on its mount for aim. Sharing memories was always a confusion and muddle. Different minds perceived things with such variety that little of it made any sense. Not without a strong, common reference. Something visual, scratched into the dirt, helped tremendously.

"Excellent," she said, releasing her grip. "Is there anyone here who cannot manage two jumps?" The gathered ladies managed to look indifferently offended by the question, each in their own unique way. "Can any of you manage three?"

"Huh. Not my favourite thing," said Kalantha, "but..."

"I've done it once or twice," said Marie. "I don't think I'd like to attempt it again at my age."

Depe shook her head sheepishly. "I've never had the need," she said.

"Well, don't. If we can remain hidden in the trees, we should be able to leap inside in the real, once they open. Quick and, most of all, silent. We should be but a whisper in the trees. Save your fades for the escape. Remember, the walkers will distort any attempt to fold near them. Now, all of you. Go wide and gather squirrels."

Depe heaved a deep sigh. "We are wild things, are we not?"

"We are both ethereal and bedrock," said Therasia.

"Well, in that case, I shall come in from the south." Depe went with nervous determination. She would be fine once the fighting started and actions became clear.

"I shall come in from the gorge. It'll be easier to get above the walkers from there," said Kalantha. She smiled, strangely, as if she'd discovered a good day for other people to die, then slipped away.

Marie lingered with a question. "What of the murmecks?" she asked. "They're still coming."

"They are here. I have a thread in each of them. The bacchanal they anticipated is missing its main guest. They have found that spirit of revelry but in me. I am not the same as we. They killed but did not dance."

"What happened to you down there?" Marie demanded, eyes concerned. "Even Viriata never spoke as crazy as you and she had her moments."

Therasia tried to form the concept into language comprehensible to someone who had not experienced a touch of eternity. She could not do so without crashing upon that which she tried to float above.

"Oh, Marie," she gasped and hung upon the woman's neck. "My mother is dead!" Grief overwhelmed her. Tears began and she could not stop them. She spoke through sobs, trying to find a path back to Adelaide. "She died so long ago. I have committed an atrocity in my uncomprehending youth. I kept her alive beyond her rest. She should have peacefully passed into memory but I abused my memory of her." Thera almost wailed. Marie hugged her. Thera clung, desperate for an anchor.

"It's alright, child. I understand. You learned of a mistake and had to let it go. There have been others who have done this over the years. It'll pass. Everything passes."

"No, no. I could not let it go even then. I burned so much energy on this indecency that I became strongest through my weakness. Oh, I don't deserve this."

"None who are honoured ever do."

"They join spirits to us. They sacrifice themselves or a part of something..."

"Others who have journeyed into the earth spoke of this."

"But they are in conflict. Like a mind arguing with itself whether or not to have another piece of pie. That thing of multitudes quarrels about our destruction. But without my mother there was ... room." She found herself breathing oddly but calmer. "There is another in me. It mourns its own death. I cannot cope with grief twice echoed. The only thing that saved me- Oh, Adelaide."

"Who is Adelaide?"

"My new love. A soldier."

"Stars above, woman. Do you always have to do everything the hard way? One of the folke in love with a soldier? They'll write plays about it. You'd have to change it to a male soldier though. The world isn't ready for that much reality all in one place."

Therasia laughed and found her own breath again. Love. A potential, budding love that might blossom. Love would save her. An injured love tucked safely in bed, miles from this horrific business. "There is another spirit abroad tonight. The same as the one that visits us but malevolent. It can be warded easily enough. I did not wish to frighten the others with this before the battle."

"And you think I can cope? Ha! Well, you'll be able to tell us all about it afterwards, at the unofficial gathering."

Thera allowed her arms to slide from Marie's shoulders. "I won't be coming. This may be the last night I see any of you for a while."

"I don't understand."

"No. But we have lingered overlong. Wake some poor squirrels and make haste. I shall join you in but a moment." Marie backed slowly, a look of deep concern making her linger. Thera clapped her hands. "Haste, I said!"

The woman turned with a sigh and sprinted into the forest.

Immediately, the murmecks emerged. They were mainly a collection of naked, feral women. Raw and wild. Some of them half-remembered a semblance of human decency.

They dressed in parodies of human coverings, woven from vine and grass. The rest were various animals the visitors had mistaken for human.

Did they only attach to the most animalistic human rut-tings? Or were these animals superior to their own kind? Perhaps the fey simply couldn't tell the difference. Wolves, deer and one very confused lioness. None of which could fathom why they comprehended so much of the world and felt such an affinity for each other.

Thera touched each of them and enjoyed their different textures. It kept her from sinking into loneliness. They seemed to grasp her sorrow and recognised the one inside and all about her. These poor creatures would stand no chance against soldiers braced and waiting. Not with those new guns. She would have to use them with care.

Therasia ran. They followed.

The sound of Warren screaming his orders reached her before the sight of any soldiers. Light blasted from the dell into the night. Cleverly arranged, the soldiers covered both ridges along the sides as well as a group gathered along the path.

Squads.

They were in squads of twelve. Their formations had them in easy targets on the ridges and in an awkward scat-tering about the path. The low cliff and the gorge filled with thorns they left unguarded, wrongly thinking none could pass that way. Warren himself huddled at the bottom of the hollow, peering at the gruesome present of his scout.

Arna had issues with soldiers. Her sisters cared not if one of those sent to destroy them should die badly. Thera baulked at the sight. Torn and disfigured. It offended the surgeon in her.

Warren gestured to the crate at his side. Someone opened it and crouched in front, checking the contents. By all the stars in the sky, what was in that thing? Her threads were uncertain in the dell with all the lightning distortions from the walkers. She concentrated on maintaining a strong connection to her sisters.

Oh, that was rude. She should have asked before attaching threads to each. They'd probably noticed and none objected. The murmecks were with her. There were those who could half-fade. She sent them around to the break in the rocks. The rest she scattered around the bottom of the hill. She wanted the soldiers looking down, not up.

The other girls arrived, accompanied by a scurrying in the treetops. She had the murmecks howl and roar and make such noises as they might when trying to intimidate. The soldiers responded by forming lines. Horribly efficient. A tickle of happiness along Caila's thread told her that Capitaine Alden's support was too far to help.

Time.

One each. The easiest target would be the one that was, for some reason, already open. Smoke drifted from it. Problems? They yelled about operations and repairs. Oh. The collapse. That would have shaken the ground for miles. They probably even felt it in her village. The village where her mother- No, no. The grief tried to anchor her but she needed to sail free. A squirrel ran up her and settled briefly on her head before leaping into the trees. She smiled. Life. There was life and joy as well as misery and death.

Catching the attention of each sister in turn Thera indicated which walker they should attack. She gave the easy one to the uncertain Depe. The one farthest towards the path, and those awkwardly entrenched soldiers, she took for herself.

The squirrels dropped.

The murmecks scurried about swiftly, hungrily. Shots rang out from the soldiers. The feral horde did not comprehend how easily they would be slaughtered if they attacked now. She kept them barely under control and distant, circling. No one looked at the metal beasts and their new red-furred parasites. They ignored the banging and calls from inside, probably assuming they were part of the repairs or orders for battle.

Soldiers yelled and the firing stopped. So. Those were the squad leaders. She indicated them to her sisters.

Cries of confusion rose from the walkers. Then dear, kind Commandant Jev Warren yelled, "Walkers! Get those guns up!"

The hatches opened.

Smoke and Grime! One did not. She motioned Kalantha to hold then leapt, threads guiding her. The distortion of the jar disrupted her aim. She switched, feet first, and eyeballed it.

Thera arrived as the gunner tried to rise. Her feet impacted. He grunted in surprise and pitched forward. She slid down his back and punched a stake into his neck.

The lightning jar buzzed at the back of the thing, casting a dim glow, offending her nerves. Her eyes drank in the light like it was day.

The space was so cramped. A woman sat at the front in some sort of sling-seat. Another crouched at the back, a stunned expression on his face, hands groping at a joined set of six barrels. Were there two cannon mounts above? She only remembered the one.

The gunner sank to the floor. She pulled her weapon free, slipped out another stake and punched wide to either side, killing the remaining two in one move.

The driver's jacket looked to be the best fit. It turned out to be short in the arms but she had no time to sample either of the others. The gunners leather cap was the most convenient. It would help with the illusion. She radiated the idea of a gunner and stood tall. Two other 'gunners' emerged.

"Gun up!" Depe yelled. It sounded military. All who bothered to look at them believed.

The hatches hinged open to the opposite side of the cannon, providing cover to the rear of the gunner. Thera found it also acted as an excellent counterweight to the barrels. The whole thing rotated with ease towards the soldiers scattered around the path. Small plates extended to either side at the front. These gave protection from that direction. A thick tube of lightning crackled, at an angle, behind the plate on the right. She sighted along the length of the barrel and thumbed the heavy contact.

BOOM!

The sheer volume was like a force. She moved vines to protect her ears. Someone screamed but she lost sight of where the shot went. She worked the levers, sighted again, and braced with clearer expectations.

BOOM!

The second shot found a mark, hitting the one who yelled commands on his right thigh. The shell exploded, evaporating that leg, shredding him with shrapnel. Another soldier near him also went down. Shots rang off the underbelly of her beast. The other guns boomed, picking off the soldiers along the far ridge. Shrapnel devastated their close lines. A long rifle swung towards her from the fusilier along the path. Thera swung the gun in her direction. The fusilier fired. Her shot rang off the protective plate. Thera fired.

BOOM!

The fusilier vanished behind a spray of mist. She didn't even scream. Wait. Was that three shots or four? In all this confusion, noise, smoke and stench of gunpowder, she could not recall.

"Cover! Cover!" someone yelled from beneath her. Two squads supported the walkers but their charges were already compromised. Bodies moved. Men scattered. A few fled. Those fleeing should be seen to escape, encouraging the same from other soldiers. Chaos was their friend.

She eased the murmecks back. The lioness was particularly unhappy about this. It livened up at the received idea that they could feast on the fleeing soldiers once they were far enough that their companions could no longer see them.

Thera spotted someone climbing up the leg of Marie's walker next to her. She pulsed her threads. The sisters turned their guns on each other. She and Marie aimed at the legs of each other's walkers. Depe fired at the one yet to open. There were plates welded in front of the joint where the leg locked into the body. These showed that this was a weak point. They were already beside each other so those plates were useless.

BOOM!

The joints tore and shrieked. Shrapnel peppered the climber. He fell. The walkers had already breasted the ridge above the dell and angled down into it. As they crumpled two of them rolled, tumbling those inside. Her walker leaned crazily. It hung on what little of the joint was still attached. Then it fell, bellied on the hillside and slid for a length or two. The tumbling walkers scattered Warren and his squad.

Bodies flew out of the metal beasts. Thera flung out the gunner's mate at the soldiers behind her. Immediately they fired at the corpse. As they cycled their guns she jumped out with the driver in her arms. The woman proved an unnecessary shield. No one fired at her. She stepped a good two lengths away from the crashed, sparking walkers. Once clear of its lighting jar, and those fatal distortions of the elsewhere, she dropped the corpse and folded.

Soldiers along the path still concerned her. They were scattered and in cover. The other squads were now devastated by shells, shrapnel and panic. Thera's exertions in the caves left her drained. She possessed more than enough spirit. Spirit to spare.

She spotted two, no, three huddled around a signaller. They tried to get to cover on the other side of a large rock. She adjusted her run to get a better angle and leaned ever deeper into the elsewhere.

Everything seemed to stop. The air felt like a solid wall. She could barely move her arm but flicked the stake towards them with all her might.

She shifted back one level, pulled a stake and kept hunting. Another soldier reached for the fusilier's rifle, moving so slowly relative to her. Dirt drifted from his skidding front foot, hand strained open. A tear of desperation peeled lazily from one eye. She came back to the real and gave him rest with both her stakes.

Her thrown stake punched through the tubes and circuitry on the signaller's back. It punched through the signaller, out and through another, before it buried itself a good way into the earth. So fast. The third soldier screamed in terror and kept running.

The soldiers on the far ridge, on the other side of the dell, scattered over that rise. They used it for cover, firing back into the dell at random nothings. Thera whispered the idea of silence to the remaining murmecks and set them to sneak up on those.

Warren screamed in the dell. He'd dodged the rolling walkers and wanted his subordinates to open the crate. Ah. So. That's what was in there.

Bolstered as she was, even in her current state of physical fatigue, she could manage two more jumps. One up to his face, the other away with it, leaving his body behind. The sparking walkers caused too much distortion. Helpfully, he backed away from them, swinging his sword about. Staying still on a battlefield was never a good idea. She flitted up a tree, the same she'd rested in earlier that night, and tucked behind the trunk, waiting her chance.

Marie and Depe folded into the middle of the squads guarding the walkers. They came back to the real with stakes in the squad leaders and other soldiers. With inhuman speed they stabbed, again, and again. The men, formed into a box with rifles pointing outwards, looked behind. They turned and fired but the women had already faded. They shot their own friends across the box, screaming in anguish and pain.

Tales of these horrors would make any sane soldier reluctant to pester fey lands again. Or remain in the army at all.

Kalantha appeared in the midst of Warren's gathering group. The adjudant, who insisted on being called a lieutenant, lost his head. Kal enjoyed herself with a couple of the other soldiers. Warren lunged at her, reaching wildly. He managed to touch her with the tip of his sword. Kalantha yelped in surprise and flinched. A soldier swung his bayonet but she folded and fled. So. Warren had some sort of sparker attached to his sword. One of the smaller ones they used on the rifles.

"Ha!" the commandant cried triumphantly. He gestured to the crate. "Get this out! Get it out!"

Well, wasn't he a clever one? Murmecks folded through the thorns and nightshades at his back. They charged forward. A couple grabbed at the unopened walker. Its gun lay twisted and hatch compromised. They yanked open the covering to reach the dragoons inside.

BOOM!

The feral woman at the walker's hatch lost an arm, screaming inhuman sounds of anguish. The one behind her suffered shrapnel cuts and twisted, writhing to the ground. They kicked and pushed, trying to run; others came to help. Even in the chaos soldiers noticed a helpless target. Weak and easier to hit.

Bad.

Thera took a deep breath and folded. She ran a wide arc, all around the sides of the dell, away from the distorting walkers.

Pulsing certain threads, she threw images of carrying, fleeing, into those murmecks.

She lined up a stake for Warren but his men pulled a great distortion from the crate. She could barely stand to look in that direction from the elsewhere.

There was plenty of time to pick him off on the walk back to their camp.

She came back to the real with momentum and slid up to the walker. The murmecks cleared their injured into the nightshade. Surging up, Therasia leapt. She braced her hands against the body and swung inside. Feet high, she kicked down hard on the barrels pointed at the entrance. She landed. Before the shooter could recover she ripped that weapon free and flung it at a soldier outside, who drew a bead on her.

It flattened two of them.

She should have thrown it at Warren.

Her body felt the effort. She had strength enough to reach into her foes and pull out their hearts. Instead, it felt like someone tore out her heart.

Adelaide.

Thera froze.

Adelaide it was who supported the barrels such that the gunner could aim and fire them. Hidden inside metal, Thera never felt her.

A pistol contact clicked and Thera instinctively dove for the elsewhere. The bullet screamed at her. She barely had time to arch her back so it would not hit directly. The ball tore through the world so fast it distorted everything about it. In desperation she reached for the rocks under the earth. For the briefest moment, with accidentally-perfect timing, her skin was solid. The bullet struck and shattered to fragments. A fragment of her shattered. A chunk of flesh, temporarily brittle, cracked and spun away.

The real seemed to be a place made for injury. Thera did not want to return and confront all that might cause her pain. But she was too tired to hang in the elsewhere. She folded back to the collectively astonished dragoons. The big gunner worked her pistol for another shot. Thera slapped it from her grip and swung a stake. Adel screamed,

"NOOOOO!!" Thera stopped the point shy of the gunner's skull.

So. That was all.

She pulsed her threads. "There will be no more killing today. All of you run HOME."

For the murmecks home meant those deep woods where their kind lingered, waiting for visits from something that now partially resided in her. They grabbed pieces for food and fled. For her sisters the concept of home was more complex but the idea was clear. They stood down and faded into the trees.

The driver swung some sort of heavy, metal tool at her. Thera flicked out a foot. It slammed into the woman's head, lifting her back. She twisted up in her sling-chair where she hung in an awkward tangle, unconscious.

The gunner tried to grapple. Thera struck her in the side of the head with the butt of a stake. The gunner's head bounced off, then bounced off the wall. She went slack and slid down, an arm still wandering in dazed defence.

Adel screamed and launched. Thera felt something cold press into her neck. She peered down. A length of leather draped down Adel's arm.

The metal really was uncomfortable. A little hammer on a thong. This processed thing twisted the natural world. There was flow, a sense, something that the world itself created. Birds navigated by it. Her kind could feel its deeper pulses. This trinket created its own, small, twisted sense in a way that distracted her from the rhythm of the world. Her love seemed disappointed she was not clutching at her neck and screaming.

"Ah," said Thera, lifting her mask. "I may have mislead you about the potency of those hammer charms against my kind."

Adel stared aghast, unable to comprehend what she saw. Thera's face amidst the vines.

"...no..." she managed to whisper.

"Oh, my special love," said Thera. "You should be in bed. I told you to rest that arm."

Adel's head rolled back and she utterly rejected the reality presented to her. She screamed, "NOOOOOooooo! No, no, no." and began shoving viciously at the fey-born with her feet.

Thera didn't even bother to defend herself. She knew, now, what was going to happen.

Only pausing to pull her mask back down, she smothered the wound on her back with vines and allowed herself to be expelled from the walker. She staggered, exhausted and unsteady on her feet. Glancing behind, she wondered if she even had the strength to avoid Warren and his men. They threw their net. She watched it sail towards her. Even in the real she could have flung herself clear. Such did not concern her. This was all. This would be her great trial. The knotted weave of rope, wound with thin wires, struck her. She staggered, taken off guard by the unexpected weight of it.

The shock of the lightning speared into her. It was wonderful. Finally the pain in her body matched the torment of her souls. She screamed in a relief of agony.

13

Looming Annihilation

"**P**ull it!" Warren yelled. "Close it! Close it!" He braced his cable connected to the repeater. One of his guard hauled hard on the other end. The net tightened. The creature flinched, screamed and writhed. He felt a surge of elation almost equal to the ecstasy he experienced when his presence visited. And where was his unseen companion? Should it not be here, guiding, riding the wave it spoke of?

Feeding off the dying.

This was a thrill unlike any other. A battle! And he, victorious! This was a new addiction ready to consume him. This petty little skirmish fed him such sensations. Imagine a war! Imagine the glory! Thousands of people and cities in flames! The little politicians with their debates of meaningless words. They could never know this visceral feeling. He would plunge the entire world into endless battle! War! The stench of powder! A mist of blood and smoke!

The screaming.

No one said there would be so much screaming. The injured screamed for help. The dying screamed for life. Those fighting screamed for courage. And, out in the dark of night, those insane things? O! They screamed and made half-human sounds, howled and growled. There was a lion! A cursed lion! Where in the seven hells did that even come from? Were they not hunted to extinction in these lands?

Warren swung his sword at a noise behind him and almost lost his grip on the cable. It was just one of his men moving into a covering position. He pulled his wrist.

His shock-sword proved to be a damned useful thing. A fey, a creature of vines and wood, appeared from nowhere and started tearing apart his men. One touch from his sword and zap! The creature fled! Ha! Walkers were huge, expensive, awkward. Yet he, Jev Warren, had jury-rigged a cell to his sword and made a weapon far more effective against the fey than all their most brilliant inventors.

Because he knew.

He understood what these creatures were and what affected them. They were not frightened of metal. That was obvious from the way they'd taken his walkers and used them to destroy his troops. However, that ethereal thing that powered their cities and machines? The lightning! They could not stand even the smallest touch of it.

That answered his question about where his presence was this evening. That ethereal thing haunting him. It hid from the buzzing field of battle. It would soon appear to sup on the lingering emotions heightened by death and suffering.

During a battle, he didn't need it! The sensations he experienced were amazing. War! Oh, they would share such a war! The creature wanted to use the mass torment as energy to free its trapped kin. Those like it that fed on life and maintained the circles around the cities. How many per city? Ten? A hundred? They could release thousands of spirits of suffering, drink millions of souls! With those things as his slaves the next chapter of history would be written by Jev Warren and his lightning jars!

"Excellent work!" he said to the fantassin. "We have ourselves a most valuable prize! Now bring me that end. Quick. We have to tie it off."

He looked around, trying to figure the best way to break through the fey lines and escape.

The walkers lay in ruins. Three crashed in the dell. Smoke rose from the other where it stood on the ridge. All beyond salvage. Only a few troops remained active on the forward ridge. He had no idea how much of his company remained. They were too scattered.

...so he should gather them!

"On me! To me! All squads into the dell! On me!"

Screams answered him. Troops moved as well. Soldiers dragged wounded companions down the slopes and along into the hollow. One walker also coughed up, miracle of miracles, three dragoons. They were the ones who had expelled the fey from their beast somehow, enabling him to catch it.

"Bring me that cable!" he yelled at the soldier. The fantassin stared, stunned, at the twisting thing of vines in the net's embrace. "Keep it tight!" said Warren. "The last thing we need is this creature to effect an escape!" Not after he'd gone to all this trouble, committed so many lives to this enterprise.

The soldier handed him the cable. He gathered both the thick, rope-insulated wires awkwardly into one hand. That kept his sword free. Actually, he had nothing to tie it off with. A minor design oversight he'd correct on his next attempt. If the fey things did not learn their lesson from this.

Troops gathered. They formed a box about him, two lines on all four sides. He didn't even have to ask! Training, discipline from all these- So few! Five at the front, crouching, five behind. They didn't even have enough troops for this on four sides.

Over seventy troops entered this infernal weald. Less than two score remained upright. A pile of injured started to form. So much death! Ha! Not a scratch on him!

The walkers were devastating against troops. They gave a clear battlefield superiority to whichever side commanded the most advanced units. Unfortunately, on this occasion, the twice-cursed fey were the ones who had use of the metal beasts. Most sane wars occurred on an open field. The ability to hide in the trees and drop into the walkers was never previously encountered or even considered. Adjustments for special circumstances. He should construct specific units designed for future forays against the fey. So much to do. So many wonderful new toys to create.

His extermination of these vile things would be his life's work. They joy he- Where in the seven hells was that thing!

He needed its touch, needed to feel, even here, right in front of all his men. What did it matter if they saw and- No, no. Sanity, secrecy, and sober thought must prevail. But who could be stoic and wise when flushed with passion?

One of the surviving dragoons strode over to the bundled fey, boiling with fury. She began kicking at the thing where it lay curled and wailing. Lelaing! A growl building up to a scream in the woman! Well! He felt a surge of joy that she survived. The other dragoons dragged her back before she could do any significant damage. Her leathers kept her insulated from the shock effects of the wires.

No fey.

No tasloi or other bewitched animals. The tables had well and truly turned! He came to this area with an arrogant notion to capture one of these creatures. Since the first attack on the hillside he'd lived in fear of their capabilities for vengeance. But now, he had one of them! Through his cunning and ingenuity he had the power! They were afraid of him! They all fled, leaving him with his prize!

"Alternates from the rear, on me!" The troops were in such disarray that they couldn't even sort that out. He unplugged his sword and used it to tap every other soldier in turn. "You, you, you." He went along all the lines, gathering himself a squad of twelve. "Medics, gather the wounded. The remaining soldiers will cover you and provide assistance where necessary."

If only Valencia was here with her potions and frantic energy. But she was a camp surgeon. Not a field medic. She and her unit would treat those that the medics could bring back from the battle.

"You dragoons." Warren indicated the remaining three. "Carry this thing back to the wagons. Careful to keep the jar connected. Let's get the stretchers for the wounded. Sergent Lelaing? Did you hear me?" The woman turned a look of such anger upon him that he felt himself flinch. Then he recalled his victory and efficacy as a commander. "Fury is an excellent tool for masking shock on a battlefield, Sergent, but you should marshal it. Pick up the repeater, there! All of you dragoons haul that thing out of here. With me!"

A tall, stocky girl he remembered was the gunner answered him in proper, military fashion. "Yes, sir." She directed her companions.

Lelaing stood, staring at the creature in the nets. A few of the other men spared it an unkind glance. He was going to have trouble protecting it from his own soldiers at this rate. The driver seemed dazed, like she was nursing a head injury. Lelaing. He could not fathom the woman's behaviour. She had history with the fey but this was poor discipline from her. Still, they gathered the net and marched back to the wagons, hauling the writhing creature along the ground. He followed with his selected squad.

It was so, so tempting to gather all the lightning jars and burn for the camp as fast as the roller could manage. But the company would never forgive him. And it might get stuck. He'd need men to haul the wagon out. Reputation was important for a future ruler. His soldiers must speak well of him even after such a bloody victory.

He cared for his troops, officers and rabble alike. He allowed himself to have feelings for them. His presence fed off those feelings. Where was that ethereal creature? It should be feeding him even more elation than he currently experienced! Well. Never mind that. Once he'd broken and trained this thing in the net it could feed him whenever he wanted. Oh, such wonderful times lay ahead! Jev Warren, master of spirits!

"It's going to be a slow march back to the camp with all the wounded," he said. "We don't have enough stretchers for those who cannot make it under their own power."

"We could load them on the rollers, sir," said the gunner. "As we have no walkers to speak of."

"Ah! Excellent thinking! Steal the jars from the walkers! We'll use two of the rollers and claim the jars from the others as well. Marshall the oxen and lock the extended yokes. Four oxen per roller. Plus the jars. That means we'll be able to proceed with some degree of haste. You're used to working with jars and the like, yes?"

"Aye, sir."

"Excellent. You dragoons get the rollers ready. The rest of you grab those stretchers. Wait. No."

The fey could well come back. That was the sort of mind he was dealing with. The kind of immoral creature that would use the wounded to make his men easy targets. They could pick off the rest of them, one by one, before they made it safely to camp.

The camp was safe. The section near the lightning fields especially. The mechanic's lot as well.

"Okay. You four stay here. Cover the dragoons. Form a fire-team. Lelaing, make sure you- Sergent Lelaing? Are you listening to me? Lelaing!"

She just stared at the thing in the net until the gunner slapped her head, whereupon she looked around, startled.

"Lelaing?" he asked.

"Commandant," she replied, voice strained. It was likely she had still not recovered from the adrenaline rush of the battle.

"I want that thing in there alive when I get back. I plan on it suffering many days of pain."

Her eyes lit up. "Yes, sir. That sounds ideal."

"So, you'll leave it?"

"If I can watch her suffer like this until my life's end that still won't make up for what she has done. But I'll help get the rollers ready. You don't have to worry about me, sir."

"Well that's, er, good. Now." he turned to address the rest of the soldiers. "You four stay and cover them as they work. I suspect the fey don't much like the lightning. It's doubtful they'll bother you but stay alert. Watch the trees especially. The rest of you grab a stretcher each. No. That's not going to work. How many do we have?"

"Eight, sir," a fantassin replied. "Two on each wagon."

He couldn't remember the soldier's name. He didn't give a fuck. Warren had to catch his breath before he burst out into hysterical laughter. He had his own fey to play with! Who cared about some star-cursed grunt? If his unseen companion was not going to return, he'd have to feed off what real elation he felt for his cleverness. But first, he had to get out of here.

"I'll take four then," he said. "Two under each arm. I can manage that. They're rolled up. Yes. You and you, two each and be ready to grab your rifles. The other six act as escort. Guns up, alert. Let's go!"

Before he was more than half a shot from the rollers, shifting the awkward weight of the stretchers, he heard a scream from behind. "No! No! I told you to go home!" Was that the fey screaming? It sounded womanly. Vaguely familiar. "Go! All of you! Leave me! Go home!" He nearly dropped his load in a panic.

"Sir?" the fantassin asked. He really should learn the man's name. That would involve asking and revealing he didn't have the slightest clue.

"HO THE ROLLERS!" Warren called.

After a pause that seemed like an eternity one of the women screamed back, "Nothing, sir! Seems clear!"

"..carry, CARRY ON, SERGENT!" At least two of them were sergents. One of them would get it organised. Using rank was a good substitute for his inability to recollect specific names.

Relief greeted him as he returned to the dell. There was a bustle of sudden hopefulness that the worst of the night might be over. Some whispered that he carried the stretchers personally.

He was one of them.

Warren snorted. He was a man who wanted plenty of guns to guard him.

They ferried the injured back to the rollers with fearful efficiency. Warren stayed until the last batch was ready to go. Every rustle in the forest, every snap of a twig and guns twitched up. The idiot soldiers wasted many a shot on leaves and bushes mistaken for looming annihilation.

Five of the six medics survived. They had the injured sorted into those dreadful, three lines. Wounded but stable. Wounded and in need of attention. Wounded and beyond help. So many of the company were past even that state.

The fey were horribly precise in targeting the fusiliers and squad leaders. Most of the people he'd bothered to remember by name were now in an unrecognisable state.

Who did that arm belong to?

One of the dying attracted his attention. A sobbing, bloodied wreck not long for this world. He felt himself drawn to the fantassin like- Ah! There it was! His ghost slipping into a dying man as the soldier's own life faded. Rushing over Warren stared into the man's eyes. They were confused, pulsing with agony. He watched as something else emerged.

"Deeaath!" came the whisper of his unseen companion, gurgling from the dying soldier.

Warren glanced at his men and bent close as if he were comforting the passing fantassin. "Yes! Yes, much death!" he whispered urgently. "You see? I have brought you much death! I shall bring you more!"

"Death not here!" It seemed oddly elated, like it was gusting about the dell in delight.

"Ah. No. We will make death all over! Much, much death in-"

"No fey here. Death is gone!" He could feel its joy at the idea but the cursed thing fed none of that to him!

"Yes! Yes! We defeated the fey. I frightened those pathetic creatures back to their deep grottoes and hollows. Now touch me you bastard!" His whisper threatened to crack into volume.

"One who is death has gone! Not here. Cannot feel! All! All shall be free! Feed upon the world! Gone. You killed death!"

The soldier was beginning to fade. That frightened ecstasy lingered in his eyes. The spirit possessing him was all that stood between him and his last breath.

Warren's mind raced. The net! The one in the net! This spirit companion could not feel the one he had in the net! He did not have to appease this thing, hide his achievement from it. As long as he kept that thing of vines and wood in a cage of lightning, he could experiment on it as his leisure, his ephemeral companion none the wiser. One he had broken it, learned its secrets, once he was the master, O! He would rule all the spirits! What conquests would be his!

"Yes. The fey is dead. I have done you this great service. Now we can begin our war."

The soldier spasmed, rattled, died, breathing a last word not his own. "Waaaaaar...!"

And now it would feed him, give him that desperately desired- no! Wait! The pressure left him. The thing wafted away in its own ecstasy and fed him none!

"Sir! Shall we... Sir?"

"Don't leave me like this!" Warren screamed at the air. "Get back here now!"

"I'm... I'm right here, Commandant."

"What?" Warren came back to himself staring about. He knelt by a dying soldier, hugging the man in his arms. Corpses littered the dell around him, giant metal and soft flesh alike. A medic stood, looking at him and very confused.

"The," Warren indicated the cradled corpse, "the soldier. I could not save him."

"There was nothing to be done for that one, sir," the medic replied in comfort. "Shrapnel tore out too much of him. There are still many we can save, but we need to sort them, assign troops to the rollers. Please. If you could." The medic gestured in a direction and Warren had to think hard on what lay that way.

The rollers. The cluster of survivors with squads decimated and no proper chain of command remaining. He needed some field promotions so others could get things organised. Warren couldn't focus on such trivial business. Unfortunately, there was no-one of rank to whom he could allocate the task. No warrant officers or commissioned officers. All dead. His own Lieutenant Paxton lay somewhere in the field. Food for carrion.

He formed up his troops and marched them back to the rollers. Once there he temporarily promoted Lelaing to aspirant and left it in her hands. Hers was the only name he could bring to mind.

That seemed to be a good move on his part. She had to look at the soldiers remaining, remember their names, make decisions. That shifted her from whatever place she'd gone. Lelaing still seemed saddened by the battle but soon everything was in proper order.

She was good.

They had a perimeter. The wounded were stowed. The driver of the dragoons had recovered enough to figure out how to connect the repeater from the net to the socket on the roller. It was a standard fitting. Nothing too complicated. The tall braces for the walkers also proved to be a useful point for suspending the net. It hung over the crossbar, swaying with every twitch and gasp made by the creature inside.

Finally, the column set off. His prize swung above the wounded, those bloodied consequences of its actions.

Nightmare sounds assailed them from the woods. Nocturnal animals, large and small, rustled about in the underbrush. There seemed to be a lot of squirrels rushing about in the treetops. Bats. Who knew there were so many bats? Clouds of them swam through the air. They darkened the sky. An eldritch fear settled into the hearts of all those who beheld those black and silent swarms.

Their progress was slow.

Past the half-way point they found a good open glade to swap out the lightning jars. The men were nervous at the halting.

The thing in the sling gasped a few desperate breaths of ease. The repeater made sure the entire supply of lightning was not spent in one large pulse. It sent regular, small shocks rather than one continuous jolt. Free of this torment the creature stirred, hands fumbling for the opening at the top of the net.

Another swarm of bats and some of the troops actually screamed. Talk became heated from a small group of panicked soldiers.

"And what be the point?" said one, indicating the rollers and their burden of injured. "Why we tryin' to save 'em as might be dead soon? We all be dead soon 'nough, if'n we don't get out these dark 'n' blasted thickets!"

"That's enough of that talk!" Warren shouted down the fantassin. "Cease your cowardly bickering and watch your perimeter!"

"I bain't lingerin' to guard some blasted wagon!"

"You will last longer here, with these sturdy, loyal troops, than you would scattering lost through the trees!"

That idea seemed to register with those infected by dread. The dragoons had the next jars in place in short order. The thing twitched in pain as it slumped back into the netting.

"Driver! Whip those oxen to give us a steady pull! Discipline and order will save us! Back to your line, Fantassin, or so help me I'll run you through where you stand!"

The newly promoted squad leaders bellowed orders. The troops reacted. Some with significant reluctance. He should do it. Drag out a couple of the whiners and run them through! Lop off their cursed heads!

But the soldier's fell in line. They rolled on.

Within a sprint of the camp he sent runners ahead to rouse everyone and begin preparations.

Word spread fast. Many stirred from fitful slumber to visit their new exhibit. A captive fey. In the history of the world it was he, Jev Warren, who was the first to capture a fey, alive or dead. His name would live forever!

"Up! Up! All rouse!" he yelled, staggering into camp on aching legs. "Break camp! Break camp! Paxton! Get a squad down to the mechanics tent and load shot into the spare barrel-sets. I want one on the new cage-wagon. Find out if- Paxton! Curse your eyes! Where are you?"

Adelaide leaned, panting, on a water-barrel nearby. She took a break from guzzling a cup to inform him, "Paxton didn't make it, sir. I'll get the mechanics moving. We can strip the barrels off some pistols and use those to spark the six-guns."

"Ha! Yes! You, Lelaing, are a shining genius"

"So I've heard."

"Keep up this good work and I'll make sure that field promotion sticks!"

Even the fat quartermaster waddled out of his tent to see what all the fuss was about. He halted his bulk next to the wagon and peered at the thing in the nets.

"What trophy have you brought us, Commandant?" he asked.

"Never mind that!" said Warren shortly. "Rouse the maîtres foudre. I want that new cage wagon ready to roll before I've finished taking a shit!"

The rotund giant nodded to one of his juniors, sending her running to the lightning fields. "I believe, sir, that he worked on it all night. Is this what we are to cage? It looks like a skinny boy in a very silly outfit. Is that a mask?"

"Mask, face, I care not. You will be in charge of striking the camp immediately. Send a runner to the village with all the payment. Now! Sort the food as it comes. I will take a squad and head to the docks at Boussens. This thing will be on a barge and on its way up the river before dawn. Dragoons!" He turned to the women. "Rest briefly. Get some food before you head down to the Mechanic's Lot. You will ride with me in the new cage-wagon. Forget the oxen. We won't need them."

"A roller cannot make it all the way to Boussens without oxen, sir," said Adelaide. "Especially at speed."

"That's why we're bringing a squad. They'll have all the spare lightning jars we need. They can carry them in palanquins. We'll change as often as we need. Actually, go get the mechanics started. I'll send some food down to you. Go! Go!"

The women walked off, stiff after their exertions. The night was not done with them yet.

"Have you sent the rest of the troops on, already? To prepare the dock?" The quartermaster inquired.

"This is all that remains of the troops. We even lost the walkers."

Consternation billowed through those gathered. A visible wave of fear. In the ensuing silence Warren issued orders for meals. He personally sorted the freshest-looking soldiers from those remaining. Rest. That was important. To take this brief respite to recover. But his quarters lay up-hill some distance. He staggered towards the mess tent and collapsed on a bench next to his troops. With them. They might even appreciate that. He wanted to smile and joke and raise their spirits. Help them feel the victory he experienced. The mood was not jovial, however, so he kept his face grim and affected an air of tragic stoicism.

He awoke with something looming over him. Warren gave a startled yell but quickly realised where he was. The memory of the wonders he'd achieved this night also returned.

"What time is it, Fantassin? How long did I sleep?"

"Barely an hour, sir."

"Ai. Long enough for my legs to stiffen. Oh. And my shoulders."

He looked around. He was still in the mess tent with a few, scattered others, mostly still napping. His yell woke those near him. Good stew. Hot. Filling. Fresh vegetables and grains with beef-fat. Peasant's fare but excellent fuel for the run to Boussens. He should make it a small part of his regular diet. Eat it while he wore his favourite, rustic shirt.

"Is the cage-wagon ready to roll?" Warren asked.

"Aye, sir. They be forming up on it now, sir."

"Ah, damn. I still need a shit. Get these men up. Give them a moment to finish their ablutions."

Relieving himself in the common latrines proved a most pungent experience. He headed to the mechanic's lot. Some men saw him leaving the camp toilets and commented to each other. Yes, yes. He was one of them. Except that the latrines were closer than his private tent. And not uphill. But, smoke and grime, the smell!

The camp bustled about him, breaking canvas, gathering, packing. Would the fey take their vengeance on these poor souls if he left them with less than half a company as defence? He sent instructions to the quartermaster. Give them all the money if you want to make it to Boussens alive. The quartermaster could arrange transport for the food from the docks at the river. The village would bring the food to them.

As much as he would like leave these peasants penniless, the fey would be very unhappy. He'd captured one but there were definitely others. Their capabilities were devastating. Their minds lusted for violence at the slightest excuse. With a night of quiet work they could wipe the standing garrison at Boussens from the map.

He did not want a stain like that on his career. This evening's battle, even with the horrific losses, he could sell as a useful foray. A first experiment with their new equipment against an old enemy. A successful learning experience. Especially with the compensation of a magical prisoner. He could promote his functional upgrades for their equipment. Those would turn the tide of future skirmishes. But lose the entire town of Boussens and even the Officer's Club would ostracise him.

The cage-wagon was magnificent. It was a repurposed walker's roller. A low cage sat bolted to the base. The Forge

Master stripped off everything else, save the seat at the front, to reduce weight.

"Excellent work, Lieutenant," he called to Adelaide. "How did you get our prisoner in there?"

Lelaing gave him a brutal smile. "Hello, sir. We dumped the net in before switching the cage on. Turned the repeater all the way up. Looped a rope through the net. Then hauled it away between the bars after. She slid out and lay there before twitching and thrashing for a while. That's when we sent for you, sir. She's settled down now."

"Don't be so hasty to assign gender to the thing, Lieutenant. It's best to be cautious with such matters."

"Speaking from personal experience, sir?"

A joke! Well. Lelaing's spirits had improved though a grim air of sadism hung over her. He'd seen this in soldiers before. A callous disregard for prisoners. Whatever got him his prize. "Never you mind that, Lieutenant. I'm up on the bench-seat at the front am I?"

"In the middle if it please you, sir. Rona and I will sit on either end to steer with those ropes we've tied to the shortened oxen-yoke."

The last of the troops gathered. The lightning jars were wrapped in sheets and carried in two large baskets they used for laundry. The poles were spear-hafts. Much lighter than a palanquin.

"Why doesn't the squad have rifles?" Warren demanded. "We'll need firepower if we're to fend off a fey attack."

Lelaing climbed up onto the benchseat. It cantilevered off the main frame of the wagon on strips of steel to give it some spring. Unpadded. A backrest at least. "Too heavy, sir. We won't be able to move at the pace I anticipate you desire if we're weighed down with heavy shot and pikes. Pistols still have three shots each. Two of them weigh less than a rifle and give us six shots. And bayonets. They're better for the kind of close-quarters combat the fey are likely to instigate."

"Very well. Excellent planning and initiative." He considered giving a short speech, or leading them all through a warm-up stretch, but the soldiers looked tired. They had a long trek ahead. He settled onto the bench. Seven miles to Boussens. They should make it in a little over an hour. Longer with changes. Two hours then, with rests for the running troops. That would make them like him more. "Roll out!"

They headed down the trail that led to the main road. The wagon bounced and wove. That would settle once they hit the ancient, stone pavings. In some places it was wide enough for two wagons to pass. Say what you like about the villages; they maintained the infrastructure that brought them their wealth. There were streets in Tolosa that were less well-maintained than this country road.

The unburdened men in the squad shoved the wagon up the small rise onto the paving.

Suddenly, a terrible wail issued from the camp.

Warren raised himself as best as he was able, one foot on the buckboard, hand on the back of the bench.

The damned gypsy woman. She trotted up in full, patched regalia, wrapped in iron charms, hair puffed out above her scarf. Pointing a spear at the thing in its cage she screeched, "Spells and anchint soothses I done! Venging and eyes for all! You shall sup deep on iron an' my fury an' violences!"

"Where on this earth or under it did she get a spear?" muttered Rona the driver, staring aghast at this pathetic, staggering sight.

"I have no idea, Sergent," he replied. He selected two of the men from the squad. "You two get ... just ... oh, keep her away while someone- HO, THE CAMP! ROUSE! WHERE ARE YOUR GUARDS?"

"That spud-trip shalln't 'scape me!" The ragged woman shuffled up to something that was almost a run. Impressive on someone not fully recovered from a near-fatal gunshot. The two soldiers moved towards her, palms up and bemused. The woman screamed and swung at them. Neither was in range of the spear. She shuffled on. "Come not 'twixt a done-by zinga an' her vengences!" she yelled. The men tried to approach but she cursed, swung wide and severally.

Warren found the whole affair brought much-needed levity to the evening. Early morning. The wagon surged up onto the dark road and began to pick up speed. The commandant flopped back into his seat. He nearly tumbled over the low backrest. His head hit the cage. That's when the creature struck.

It lunged through the bars, stretching one hand. The flailing grasp snared into his scarf, hauling back with inhuman strength, twisting. He hooked his feet under the buckboard and managed to retain his seat.

Choking, it was only a casual glance at his leaning that alerted the drivers to his predicament. Adelaide yelled in surprise and drew her sabre. That reminded Warren to do the same. He yanked the blade from its sheath. Gasping for air, he fished the socket from his sleeve and plugged it in. Meanwhile, Adelaide raised her weapon and brought it down hard on the arm. Out of the corner of one eye he saw the blade bounce off the outstretched limb like it was made of stone. Adelaide cried out in pain and dropped her sword. She used her injured arm, forgetful in her eagerness.

Warren started to feel the lack of breath. He stayed focused and reached over his head, feeling for the arm. On contact the creature let out a wailing screech of despair and flung itself back. It collapsed to the floor of the cage with a heart-rending moan and began sobbing.

Yells from the soldiers replaced the screeches of vengeance from the gypsy-drop. Some of his men drew weapons, aimed at his prize in the cage.

"Hold!" he cried, though yelling cost his constricted throat a deal of pain. "Do not touch it! Stand down! I'm fine, fine. Stand down, I said! It's fine. NO! Leave your sword, Adelaide. Kick it off the side and fetch it from there. Don't get near it. The cage is far enough away that we are safe as long as we retain our seats and our wits."

The soldiers settled back into place. Many had to burst into a sprint as the wagon did not stop or wait for them. The injured gypsy woman could not quicken her pace but screeched her last. "I shall boil yer tits for me suppings! Fils a putain!"

"Charming lady," he croaked.

Moonlight provided sufficient clarity to their passage. Future versions of the powered wagons would require dedicated lamps at the front. Perhaps a runner with a lantern. He kept his mind working on these issues and tried to ignore the nagging dread, the idea that a hand reached from the cage for his neck. The stone-paved road rattled them well at this pace, testing the leather slings on the suspension. Warren had to keep his mouth open to prevent his teeth from bouncing together. That invited every bug and speck of dust. He loosened his scarf and lifted it to cover his nose and mouth. The drivers followed suit.

The thing broke off sobbing long enough to wail into the night, "Noooo! Please! I changed my mind! Please, sisters! Come rescue me! O! Stars and stones! Mother! My poor, poor mother! What have I done? Why could I not let you go? Ai! It's too much! I changed my mind! Sisters? I cannot! I cannot!"

The voice did indeed remind him of a woman. An educated village woman like La Granger's daughter. Or, who was that other girl he'd met at the festival? Dippy something? Well. It was still best not to make assumptions about the thing. He'd have plenty of time to study it in detail once it was broken and trained. He rubbed his sore neck.

Something else irritated him. He felt it under his skin, like he itched in every crevice. It was too long, days, since his presence visited. He needed its touch as keenly as a physical hunger. Where the hell was it? The buzzing cage scared it off. The women on either side of him could do nothing to satisfy this irritable longing. Even Adelaide with her beauty and ample figure and promise of pedigree could not scratch that itch.

What was the matter with her?

"Lieutenant are you crying? Does this creature's sorrowful lament touch you?" he asked Lelaing.

Adelaide wiped her face with her sleeve. "A stressful evening, sir. And my arm. The injury, when I hit... It's nothing."

"Very well. It has, indeed, been a hard night and will be even longer until dawn."

They cleared the edge of the woods before they had to slow down and eke out what little remained in the first set of jars. They pulled over to change. Warren lingered at the back with the driver, Rona. He held his sabre ready in case it should make another lunge.

"Will the power in the cage be down for long?" he asked.

"Not at all, sir. Separate jar for the cage. That'll last well beyond reaching Boussens. I got to swap these three out before we get ambushed."

"We're not yet half way!"

"Getting close to that, sir. And we've got another change of jars. Charge won't be a problem. Travelling fast on these cobbles will do for the suspension. All that shaking. Or a wheel will shatter. The wiring will come loose before long. The whole wagon might fly apart. We got to leave the spent jars. Too heavy. The soldiers need to rotate out who's carrying."

"Just leave them! Tighten every bolt you can and let us make haste!"

"Aye, sir."

The thing spasmed once but otherwise did not stir. They were on their way without harassment. The sky began to brighten. Scant clouds on the horizon became dipped in red, like they were soaking up the spilt blood. Fatigue began to tell on them all. The creature alternately wept and wailed, grating every nerve in the party.

After the second change the wagon's sling-suspension tore. The bed sank onto the axle-housing. Warren ordered them to press on. The rattling now grew exaggerated as the seat-bench leaned. Sparks erupted from the rear by the jars. They ground to a halt. Rona climbed off the wagon and tightened everything.

Warren rubbed some life into his legs. He jumped from the bench, landing heavily, staggering. A helpful soldier kept Warren's face from the stones.

They started again. The harsher rattling made the creature twist and scream anew. It appeared to be growing weaker. Surely it was something more than the small shocks from the cage. The lightning itself seemed to drain the thing of energy. Wonderful. It would be so much easier to manipulate after a few days of constant exposure and starvation.

The cage was wonderful. The wagon needed work. Steel for the suspension. And some better method for steering. Stronger wheels or something on them to absorb the shock. He'd have his artificers begin alterations immediately upon his return. So many ideas!

Adrenalin fought the fuzzy lack of sleep in his mind. He stretched briefly and picked up a strong pace that caught him up with the wagon.

As they crested the last hill into Boussens. The sun broke the horizon, filling the world with light. He felt an elation at arriving successfully, a thrill that filled him with such joy. His presence sipped gently from his emotional excess and-Oh! It was back! Now he was away from the wagon his unseen companion returned! The dawn light bathed him. The ecstasy of his ghost brought Warren to his knees in rapture.

14

Harrowing Lament

The old and new spirits inside her scraped, tore and rent upon the sparks and buzzing from the spinning motor and its dreadful jars. The constant shocks layered deep experiences of pain into the journey.

Wooden bars in a wooden frame. Wires twisted everywhere. The wagon rattled and rumbled along the stone road. This jolting vibration meant she could not lean her essence gently against the barbs of lightning. Instead they pierced and hooked and ripped.

Each of the others inside her twisted and pulled, trying to be elsewhere. The swirling confusion of the lightning pulses meant they thrashed about wildly, violently.

Every slight movement from those attached souls was an agony deep in her bones.

The core of her nerves pulled apart and made her scream inside and out.

The searing was so profound that the tiny shocks provided by the cage's wires barely registered. A human would feel a sharp jolt that might jump their heart. She felt the buzz of the exposed lightning jars at the back of the wagon as an arcing fire. Her captors had no idea why she writhed in such torment or what vexed the foundation of her essence.

The rattling racking ceased when the wagon ground to a halt. The scent of water reached her. The docks at Boussens. She was able, for a breath, to settle against the serrated edge of the lightning in the elsewhere. They slid poles through the corners of her narrow cage at a forty-five-degree angle, lifting the whole device. They carried her from the wagon. The torment eased as she moved farther from those three jars at the back of the wagon. They drove the thing under its own power. Fascinating. A brief distraction.

There was still one jar at the back of her cage. That was much, much less. She could reach both poles at the front and hung from them by her fingertips, bathing in the softening of excruciation. She pushed with her feet at the front bars on sections the wound wire did not cover. Hanging ape-like, she panted, throat scratched raw from her screams. Even a few moments without the constant shocks was wondrous, but it was the distance from the jars and their spinning motor that soothed her the most.

"Ignace would love something like that for his shit-wagon, though the lightning would rot him worse than his stinking load," she croaked. The burly men carrying her paid no mind. Ah, she was babbling in misery. Adelaide! The beautiful soldier walked with them, lurking at the side with Warren-the-almost-choked. "Oh, so close to strangling every puff of breath from that one," she said. Adel looked at her. She saw the soldier's face twisting between sickening hatred and something with a hint of pity.

They dropped her onto a dock. She lost her grip. Was this Boussens? The water smelled right for this stretch. Terrible, with the bone-works upstream emptying its stench and waste.

People wasted everything, dirtied all they touched. Perhaps they deserved to be itched from the surface of the world.

Fallen from her perch the shocks began anew. Now the cage was still she could feel out a shape in the elsewhere that did not spin like a hurricane of barbs. She leaned against that but the effort cost her.

"You is not you any more," came a whisper from the stack of crates next to the cage.

"Ahhh. Little Kat," Thera whispered back. "I will never be me. Ever again. And this is not the place for you right now."

"Everywhere is for me. I's been here most of the night. I go where I want, whenever I likes. Has you not noticed? I saw the soldiers being nasty to Liefa and her friends. They was too many, so I told you. I was at the orchard after you done made them pay, so the boys not see you carrying that gun back to your house all covered in blood. I stopped the nice lady soldier from getting ate by the wolves after the dance. She put bees on their faces. It was very funny. And now I is here to stops you."

"Yes! Ah, my child, I knew you would grow into this. You can feel it. The pulse of things. Those points where the energies coalesce. Like a gang of travellers lurking between villages, selling trinkets. I didn't understand all that swirled about that mushroom girl but you... Ah, my dear child. You will make a fine village witch. Remember to always help people where possible. Naughty boys and all. Even if they are a little bit evil they are still part of the community's tapestry. Only if they grow very evil such that they tear the threads-"

"Your mama is dead."

Therasia felt her heart shatter as sorrow poured into her once more. She slid down the bars to curl into a weeping ball of pain.

"They said as I should not be telling you but ... Aunty G?" Katrienne sat with her back against a stack of crates, casual as you please. A dock-rat unworthy of attention. The thing-that-was-becoming-a-witch almost drew regard to herself as she reached for the curled ball of sorrow. The half-child flinched before she got near the humming bars and hissed at them. "That stuff is bad. Should I smash it? Aunty G?" The youngster exhibited something approaching genuine concern. "Stop being silly, Thera. You is strongest. Even Selika says so. If you is so strong you should stop crying now. People is starting to look. Just stop it."

Therasia let out a low wail and uncurled, staring about. Warren argued with someone further along, next to a wharf that held a low barge. Adel and the dragoons were nowhere to be seen. Organising supplies? It was two, three days down the river to Tolosa. The soldiers milled about at some distance, trying to stir up some food. One remained near but her tortured contortions made him uncomfortable. He faced away. They were that confident in the efficacy of their cage. Thera could shatter it in three winks if she could gather herself long enough between lightning stings.

"I knew it. Poor mama." Thera muttered between sobs. "I knew but it still hurts to hear. It torments all the corners of my heart. There will be much weeping before this is done, dear child."

"You should have some water then. I done brought you some water. Here." Kat slipped a fattened, leather carafe along the docks. Thera perked up and felt a jolt more deeply for her efforts. She carefully reached between the bars to collect the water-skin. "Depe says as you has two fey now," said Kat. "How come you gets extra fey and I don't?"

"Yes. I was very greedy. And now they've fed me more than I can stomach to teach me a lesson."

"So it's not a good thing?"

"Neither enjoys the lightning. They both fight to escape it, in opposite directions. It's like they're trying to pull my bones out of my skin."

"Huh. I don't want that."

"No. Me neither. But... I might be able to, I'm not sure how, burn one of them to speed myself up. It's the speed of it that tears the fey. I think. Like the bullets. The lightning moves so fast it folds the world, making it heavier than a nothing should be. If I can get near the lightning's speed I can talk- Not talk. Communicate? No. Reach some form of understanding at that place where the lightning bends the unreal."

"You is sick in the head and going to die."

"Probably. Yes. Ah, my precious little thing. You will have to take on more 'sponsibs, now. And work on your grammar. There are books in The Grange. My father's study. There are many great and wonderful books. The Travels of Lemuel. **Lady Sarashina's Melancholy. The fair triumvirate**. Read and learn to speak better."

"How... Is it being long to learn the lightning talk?"

Thera almost smiled.

"I shall not return for a long, long while, Little Kat. I did not have time to explain that to the others. At the meeting tonight tell the village witches what happened. They will look out for you. And I want you to look out for my dad. It's going to be hardest on him with me gone and Mama... O, Mama! O! Sorrow is an endless ocean that drowns all who enter!"

"You should stop it. You can't talk to lightning. It's not a thing. It's not alive. Just stop it. Please stop it and come home. It's not alive!"

"No it isn't, Little Kat. Not in the traditional sense. However. I have, recently, had my understanding of what constitutes life expanded and redefined."

"You is going insane," said Katrienne, small tears appearing on her cheeks.

"Indeed, my sweet. All the best of us are. Even you. But we can grow from that. You are of an age when the spirit within you is changing in an important way. And that can burn. As it transforms it loses a sense of self. Becomes more feral. A consuming hunger. But there is so much good in your heart, little one. Humans can be so kind and wild and generous. Do not lose your heart to greed and satisfaction of immediate desires. Think broadly, dig deeply and be kind. Not everyone has the advantages you do."

"Five of the murmecks is dead. A deer and four of them as was trying to be us. Am I going to go like that, one day?"

"No. One day you will be like me and Depe and Laurette. One of the Good Folke."

"I wanna be like Selika. She is fierce and sooooo beautiful! And she always wears such cool stuff!"

"Yes. You should always wear the cool stuff."

They came for the cage. Even Therasia didn't notice when Katrienne slipped away.

Maybe that was the last time she would see her.

The single jar at the rear gave her no peace. Warren made a mistake. He started with three in the wagon, plus that. Four in total. And a motor. Then down to this one. After the initial, unbearable torment the steady harrowing from a single lightning jar felt sufferable.

"No, no! At the front" said Warren. "Spin it so the jar is right at the front of the barge. We need to be at the back to steer. To sleep. The food should be well-wrapped. Insulated. The lightning will rot it otherwise. Use the leathers from the dragoons." He stepped up to peer into the cage, remembered, his hand going up to his throat, and stepped away. "Spin it. Turn the whole thing around and have the jar at the front."

"The bow," said Adelaide. Ah. There she was. Strong and stern. Refusing to make eye contact. "The front of a boat is called the bow, Commandant."

"Indeed. Well, after a couple of days on the river, I'm sure I shall be well versed in all matters nautical."

"Yes, sir. And, if I may?"

"You are an aspirant for the moment, Lieutenant Lelaing. At least until we reach the city. Speak your mind."

"Thank you, sir. We'll need some waxed canvas, or something waterproof, to drape over the jar, keep the damp off it. Lightning and water do not mix well."

"Good! Good! This is the kind of thinking that promotes you above the," Warren glanced at his squad about him and found a kinder phrase to describe those within earshot, "er, above the general soldiery."

"Thank you, sir. I'll stir something up. I'm sure they have perishables they ship up and down the river they wish to keep dry. Sugars and the like. Someone will have some canvas somewhere. Faucheux. Travers. With me."

"Do you need to take soldiers?"

"A dragoon's leathers are not immediately recognised as a uniform, sir. With my arm damaged I cannot carry the canvas myself."

"Right. Well. Carry on."

Thera watched Warren as he directed the setting of the cage and ordered ropes to lash it to the beams. He did something at the back of his sword. When he drew it there was a distortion about the blade. The shock sword that stung

Kalantha in the dell. That which pained Thera so much so that could not finish strangling the man.

How did someone so dull in their thinking create such useful advancements? Ah. The spirit that floated about him. Thera could see it sprawled out along the wharf, a series of small glints that never quite caught the light. That thing fed images into this dull mind. Warren's ego demanded that they were his inventions.

He wanted to approach her. Have a conversation. Laud his success over her. His cowardice kept him fussing about the boat. "Never mind packing all the food in so carefully," he said. "We'll just be pulling it out to eat. The last thing we want is to be endlessly packing and repacking the supplies."

"Your voice sounds a mite croaky," Thera said, adding a country accent to her speech. "It's almost as bad as mine after a night o' endless screamin'."

"You will learn your place soon enough, witch-spawn," Warren said, refusing to engage.

"Oh I ain't the spawn of a witch, Jev Warren. That would be you. Mayhap a grandmother or long back in your ancestry. It comes out like red hair. You stink of fey blood, in case you're wonderin' why that spirit likes to hang around someone as dull as you."

"Do not listen its words, good soldiers. While it is trapped in that cage words are all it has. It will use them to sow discontent, make you question your superiors, destroy us, as much as it would tear us with its bare hands were it free."

"You can't see it, can you?" said Thera. "Stretched all out along the dock, sipping on despair and joy."

"It's here?" he whispered, then corrected himself with bombast. "There is no presence here, troglodyte."

"I bet you think you're so clever. But, since that thing found its weaklin' stooge, you ain't had an original thought in your head. You're probably so foolish as to think that fancy sword of yours is a notion you had yourself."

Warren puffed up in offence and slipped his sabre between the bars. "Perhaps you would like to feel its sting again, to learn what notions-" Thera swayed to one side and the sword followed, striking one of the wires wound around the bars. With a sharp crack! the sword sparked and blew out its little tube. Warren yelled and danced back in surprise and pain. His sword dangled dangerously from his buttoned sleeve, hanging on the wire. Thera collapsed to the floor of the cage, laughing with a morbid despair. Warren tried to reach behind himself. He patted at the area on his back which now burned with the heat of his over-loaded tube.

"Curse your eyes, you devil-ridden hag!"

"Ah, but you've no idea what rides me..."

"Well, let's see if a few meals absent from your belly quiets you down."

"There can be no silence while the void screams."

Warren stared at her, confused, then waved a hand in dismissal. Eventually, he managed to gather himself and put his toy sword away.

Adel returned most efficiently. They installed their waxed cloth over the lightning jar and the whole front of the cage. Poor Adel refused to look at her. She let the woman be.

Ego and self-interest infected this wound of love. Bad blood and much of it spilt in the woods. If she could not draw that infection from Adel, what budding possibilities germinated between them might never flower. The idea that this new love could live forever unrequited tore at Therasia in an entirely new way. Even more painful than the jars.

It was not a full and proper love. Not yet. They had barely spoken an honest word to each other since they met. The idea, the potential tenderness, called her back from a cold, dark place under the ground. The extreme heat of the passion they both experienced was a sign but their paths lay in such different directions. They might never find common ground again. But she felt it in Adele as much as in herself. The chance for true love to blossom.

The barge hoisted its sail and began the long journey down the Garunna to Tolosa.

Sandbanks lay off the bend, sheltering the inconsequential jetties. They required constant dredging. The town was not as broad as the river. It was a place for the local villages to ship their stock down the waters. The bargeman steered his known paths around the sandbanks and into the flow of the waterway.

The Garunna collected many smaller estuaries from the gentle, rolling hills. They kept it deep and constant. Were it not for the merciless torture, the buzzing that tore the substance from her vitality, she might almost enjoy the journey. The flow was smooth and steady, adding to the sail's thrust.

Around mid-afternoon Thera's stomach began adding to her misery. Did Warren intend to starve her into submission? If she had not the strength to speak with the lightning, this whole enterprise might come to nothing. In deference to her lack of sustenance, and its likelihood of continuing, she began.

Thera touched her new spirit while she had some strength. The idea it radiated was one of deep regret. Thera almost laughed. It thought it would escape and become one with another. It used to be part of the thing that ... birthed? Were these different aspects of the sun-swimmers born? Did they evolve to sample new sensations when the whole bothered to notice them?

"Foolish creature," she said in irony. "Let go your sorrows and swim with me in the lightning."

Someone kicked the cage. "Silence foul thing!"

She ignored him, closing her eyes, trying to feel enough between the jolts of pain. It was like trying to sleep while someone irregularly banged a drum. A drum balanced on her very skull. With a gentle, steady rhythm she might reach the thing inside her. The constant shocks kept her hovering at the edge. From here she could only scream at her passenger.

It did not seem to understand. The connection was violent and fresh. Not enough to form even the vaguest hint of cognisance. Perhaps it had already lost its mind. If it ever had one of its own.

She listened to the lightning instead. There was something about the buzzing, crackling quintessence that suggested ... not a language but a code, a formulae of interaction. She leaned slightly and deeply. In either concept of otherness the lightning was nought but a wordless scream of distortion.

After she burned in the sun and cooled in the evening Thera pulled back and decided to rest. Exhaustion overwhelmed her. She dragged herself to the front of the cage and picked her moment. Lifting a fold of cloth near the lightning jar she pulled out her waterskin, drinking as much as she dared. No one looked. They all stared at the rolling hills passing in the cool light of dusk. None of them wanted to watch her constant agony.

Was she to get no food until they reached Tolosa? Long before she grew so weak she might think of begging, she would tear this cage apart and fold across the water.

No. She would not flee. She would take her righteous pain and devote herself to the lightning's words. She would understand its code or burn to a relic in the effort.

"We're not stopping!" Warren yelled as the sail began to lower.

"We have to stop and fish for our supper. Besides, we cannot navigate the river in the dark!" the bargeman replied.

"How many times have you made this journey that you do not know every inch of the river?"

"It ain't the river! I know the river! I know it gets precious narrow after Le Plan d'Eau. But do I know where some other boat, with a sensible capitaine in charge, has anchored for the night? Not everyone wants to pay jetty fees all the way up or down! We crash one of them at any speed-"

"I am not a capitaine, boatman. I am a commandant! And I am telling you to sail this river if you wish to keep all that is precious to you still attached! We might start with that insolent tongue of yours!"

Thera felt the need to divert attention from the poor bargeman. Her instinct to help would be her downfall. "This is how you've always made your way outside, in the world," she said. "Isn't it, Jev Warren."

"Silence she-hag!"

"I like that you imply the existence of a he-hag. How might such a thing appear?"

"Silence!"

"Would it be a little like you? A thing that bullies and threatens? A beast that claims others' ideas as their own? No wonder you were at such a loss when dealing with the village. You expected to roll in and order everyone about with your hundred soldiers and new, metal beasts. But pissing on your shoes doesn't keep your feet warm for long. The villagers laughed at the idea of your threats. Instead, I showed you the meaning of fear."

"You will learn to be afraid before you die!"

"But it's all bluster, isn't it? Out here in the countryside. You cannot hurt any village, even to make an example. The reprisals would be catastrophic. You cannot bully the countryside into giving up their food, their lumber, their clay and ores. Not while my kind exists. You have to pay a decent rate. No matter how many soldiers you send. We produce what you need. You cannot survive without us. You can't subjugate us while the fey protect all."

"You protect nothing while you're in my cage, harridan!"

"You think you have managed to gain some small superiority? Last time you tried that was a hundred years ago, under your lost king. Oh, if only you knew the truth about your king returning. You tried to crush us. We left. You crumbled. Because you need us far, far more than we need you. What the villages need to do our work, we make ourselves. What we need to survive, we make ourselves."

"Without us you would be crushed by the first army that invaded these lands!"

"If your army cannot defeat us what makes you think another could? This is where you have it backwards. The cities are not superior. You have nothing to offer us. You are our dogs. You feed off our scraps."

"Dogs, are we? If you are so superior why have you not risen up and wiped us from the earth? You are afraid that if we truly-"

"We are not bloodthirsty warmongers!" Even speaking loudly cost an effort in her current state. "That is you. No doubt spurred on by that thing which haunts you. We have no interest in causing mass suffering and- ...oh..."

"Silence, foul thing!"

"...that's what it wants..."

"I said you will be silent!"

Adel stood up, restraining Warren as he attempted to approach the cage. "Do not go near it, sir! Do not listen to its lies."

Warren stared at his underling in confusion but gathered himself.

"Quite. Well. Thank you, Lieutenant."

"We all need a good night's sleep, sir. Especially after last night. As we have only the one bargeman it would be advisable to allow him to rest before his long day tomorrow. A fish supper sounds good to me."

"Right. Yes. Best not to burn him out. Three days then? Four? Fishing is a good supplement to our supplies. Arrange a guard. I know what pursues us." Warren leaned closer to Adel. "There was a fucking lion! The woods come right down to that side of the river! We should anchor towards the other side. Set a good watch. Vigilant."

Adel turned to the river man. "Perhaps, m'siuer, he could lie down on your cot?"

"Ah, yeah. Sure. Sure thing. I have a good blanket and all. A cover in case it rains."

"Thank you."

It strangled Thera's heart to see her love, so kind and generous, in the service of one so twisted. Ridden by a spirit.

The thing was invisible in the dusk. She could not get her threads through the cage to feel for it. Warmonger. Those things trapped in the circles of waste about the great cities could escape if they grew strong enough. This one that followed Warren had already escaped somehow. War. It wanted suffering to feed upon. To feed all its friends that were not satisfied sucking the great circles around the cities dry.

Well. The lightning might have something to say about that. If only she could ask.

A fisher pulled a good trout from the river. The other soldiers cheered. Once scaled and gutted they held it on a stick over the fire. Thera snatched at the entrails, hungry enough to eat fish guts. One of the men kicked her arm away. Then he booted the viscera over the side. The smell of cooking added another layer to her misery. She ignored her instincts and tried to rest.

With everyone settling in she decided to curl up. Thera extended vines to subtly insulate herself from the shocks and tried for some rest. After a while even the buzzing of the jar in her bones could not overcome her exhaustion.

She woke the next day to an early shock. A hand strayed off the insulating vines and ZAP! Awake. She twisted and was shocked again for her troubles. She settled into the pain of the day. The other soldiers were fast asleep, every one. Poor troopers. They'd had a long night. Fighting her and running to the river. Precious little sleep was available with half of them heaving over the side before they got their water-legs. Some still didn't have those. She formed a bowl from her vines and shit into it. Wiping with leaves, she wrapped the whole thing before tossing it over the side. Her stomach growled. She'd spent so much energy yesterday, trying in vain to penetrate the mystery of the lightning.

Could she eat vines? At a pinch, they might keep her innards from devouring themselves. They would provide no real sustenance. She did not have the four stomachs a cow used to digest such foliage.

A little water. She'd drunk a good third of it already. They might take longer than two more days to reach Tolosa.

The soldiers roused, shat and pissed over port. They then reached over starboard into the river to clean their hands before breakfast. Fresh crepes on the griddle. Savoury. With mushrooms, maize and basil. A little cream. The smell was infuriating.

The barge was a tight space. There was little room to rattle about. Only the occasional adjustment of the sail caused any excitement. The soldiers began to get on each other's nerves. Her presence did not help. There were those, Adel among them, who felt that a fey was not worth the effort of transporting. They mentioned, casually but loudly, that it might be best to dump the cage over the side and be done with her. To be fair Thera spent much of the day gasping and weeping, screaming and mewling, as she tried to touch the lightning in the fey. All to no avail.

She slept fitfully. The third day things only grew worse. She chewed on vines to stop some of the pain inside herself. That was nothing compared to the pulsing agony of the souls within her trying to escape. She felt compressed by the cage, wracked by the endless buzz of the lightning jar. They'd changed to a new one in the morning but there were two sockets, so even that didn't give her any respite. Rona plugged the new one in, and brought it into play, before removing the old jar. There was another wrapped in insulation under the canvas. They would arrive in Tolosa the next day. She would have no relief.

By sundown she was drained, weary and famished. Another day of fruitless suffering. Another day without food. The pain vexed her, twisting her bones, grating her sinews. She was so weak. The hunger did not help but it was the constant exertion and torture that drained her. Even screaming didn't help. The lightning was too fast, too alien for Thera to seed the smallest understanding. Her water-skin was almost spent. She would not last another day. Begging for food was beneath her. She would most likely be dead by dawn.

Adel sat near the bow, having just taken a brief lecture from Rona about how the jars worked. Her love was not in the mood to talk. Thera was in too much pain to restrain herself. The hunger made her delirious. Or brave. If they were not the same thing.

"I cannot reach it, Adel," she whispered in agony. "There is something- ayi! Oh, my bones ache. Some sound, some type of language unknown to anyone. In the lightning. It eludes me. I can hear the pressure of it but not the tone. I want to revel in the conversations we might have."

"It has driven you insane," Adel whispered unkindly.

"No. You did that."

"And what insanity made you treat with me at all? Did it appeal to your twisted sensibilities to stitch up a wound you caused?"

"It saddened me to see that my fury drove me to hurt someone so spirited and bright. You broke into my stony heart and-"

"Do not speak to me, monster! Not after all that you have done."

"Aye. You are right. I deserve none, ah, none of your pity for my starving, harrowing lament. It is a self-inflicted suffering. But the task I have set is important. Possibly the most important- Ayiii, but one syllable! One note of music! Something!" She writhed against the bars so weak the shocks barely registered. The look of revulsion on Adel's face told of the deep toll from these past days. Thera's voice was a croaking vestige of itself. "There is none to blame except myself. But there's no one else I can whisper to. The hunger has unhinged my mind. I am dying and that is my lot, my reward for thinking I could catch the lightning."

"Die quietly, then," Adel whispered. Sorrow escaped in her breath but her mien lacked any sympathy. "I will not hear you. I hope it is so painful you carry the suffering to your afterlife."

"The shocks from the cage are just annoying. There is a deeper pain that you cannot understand."

"And this deeper thing. It made you deceive me? Violate me? Do you think we can converse civilly after you killed all my friends?"

"Yes. Absolutely. If your friends were wrong, then you should admit as much and apologise for joining in with their horrific behaviour. But human hearts don't work that way."

"How have I wronged you? I came here in honour, to advance my family's name-"

"La, that all my friends should die so you can feel good about- ayi! ...about your name. Oh, that was a bad shock."

"I have a duty to my family that you could never understand."

"Oh, please. Explain your duty. Explain it to Liefa. My dear friend who stood by me as I nearly succumbed to that which grows within me. Who is dead now, because you came. Explain how, if you found those men who chased her over a cliff, you would not have killed every one of them yourself." Thera dropped her voice even lower. Her hands wandered along the wires, seeking enough of a jolt to keep her fracturing senses focused. "Oh, but you did kill them, didn't you? And put bees on their faces."

"How could you possibly know...?"

"I thank you for that. Otherwise, I would have had to murder the entire camp in my despair."

"Despair? You can't feel anything, monster! You're just a thing!"

Thera shifted in pain, trying to find some way to sit that was not agony. Her eyes could not fix on a point. "Oh, but I am a monster. My feelings are monstrous to match. We feel things too deeply, us fey-kin. That is why we tend to favour the parts of us that reason. If we survive into adulthood. I was a girl once like you."

"I was never like you."

"Well, maybe not. My childhood was- ayi! Ow, ow, ow, ow."

Thera shifted against the cage but could not lean. The shocks were too painful. Her hands reached erratically. She collapsed against the floor. Adel stared as if horrified that she should feel pity. Thera wished her love would offer aide. None came.

She whispered from the floor. "You are a monster, Adel, in your own way. You worry so much about something so abstract, so unimportant, so dis- ayi! A name. What is a name but a collection of noises we have agreed to own? Just so. You come here to help a bunch of people who are already rich get even richer. All the while crushing an entire way of life. Hiding behind duty and honour and friendship. That is monstrous. You think the army will give you something so you give yourself to it. The city will feed on you and shit out your corpse."

"I will have my name restored."

"So fucking what? Is that reason enough for the horrors you brought to my lands, monster?"

"So you cared nothing for me? You used me?"

"I was uncertain how I felt. You are a monster after all. But then I found something deeper than the world. I fell in. You were there in my heart to pull me out. Isn't that poetic? We could be monsters together."

Adel rose. "I will throw you over the side of this barge before I let you touch me again. Suffer and starve, snake." She walked to the back of the boat. Hardly a great distance but the dramatic gesture was obvious.

"How's your arm?" Thera called with deliberate unkindness. The rest of the barge should not suspect the nature of their relationship. "Did trying to hack off mine cause you any injury? Does it pain you as much as your blackened soul?"

She crumpled to the floor of the cage but that was wire-wound bars and offered no respite from her agony. A low moan escaped as she slithered away from the lightning jar.

Night descended in earnest. They anchored mid-river with forest on either side.

Thera could hear herself whimpering but could not stop. She should just leave, tear free and fold away. The strength was not in her. After days of Herculean effort she weakened herself past what any simple starvation might accomplish.

Watching a creature suffer constant torment took its toll on the soldiers. During the days they tried to distract themselves with cards, with songs, with arguments. There was nothing else for them to do on the barge. They listened to her piteous lamentations and watch the countryside roll by.

Only Jev Warren seemed unaffected. He was happy about finding a cot that stayed level the whole night.

The watch settled in. The other soldiers slept fitfully. Finally, even the watch slept.

Thera found no sleep this night.

The endless drone of the lightning jar sent her mind spiralling apart. She lost some sense of who she was. Maybe she was just an extension of that great beast that swam in the lava under the world and drank sensations from the sun. Her senses drank in every impression. The stars in the cold sky were ablaze with colours. They swirled outside the bars. The water offered endless new smells as it drifted by, odours so subtle none could divide them but Thera. The intricacy of the wood-grain in her cage, the shape of each leaf she pulled from the elsewhere as insulation, these fed her skin with detail. The sound of-

Oh. The sound of another boat. A small coble reefing its sail. Someone dared sail in the dark. The dull glow from the lightning jar under the canvas distinguished their barge from every other. Like a beacon.

A slight splash in the water.

The coble drifted past. Empty. The wide barge rocked slightly, admitting one extra passenger. They climbed the rope fenders along the side with the practised skill of the habitual thief. Thera sat up to greet her new visitor as regal as she could manage with limbs a-trembling.

"Think you done 'scaped me?"

"No, Chevrette. I have been expecting you." Her voice croaked and she could not focus.

The bangtail squatted in her underwear without even a scarf on her head to contain her explosive frizz of hair. Water dripped from her skin. Fury poured from her eyes.

"My hands will end yer stinkin' rascalitry."

"Your hands? Or that fish-boning knife I can hear creaking in the waistband of your under-wrappings?"

Chevrette reach behind and pulled out her weapon, filched from some fishery along the way. The stench of gutted fish lingered about the traveller. "I'll stick yer and be vanished before yer dyin' screams done rouse yer protectors."

"Protectors? They're not protecting me, you moron. How can you possibly..? Oh, just kill me, trollop. Death is preferable to your inanities."

Chevrette eyed the cage, working up the courage to plunge her arm through. A look of determination blossomed on her face. She suddenly thrust, grimacing at the shocks. The thin, steel blade aimed for Thera's belly.

Thera did not have the strength to fold and deal with the idiot woman properly. Instead, Thera spent the last of her gathered energy flickering one hand up to direct the thrust aside, catching the wrist. That hand pulled down and her other snapped up, under the elbow. Bone-locks burst.

The shock of pain registered in Chevrette's eyes. With a speed and precision no human possessed, Thera caught the falling knife and slashed. The wrapping's around Chevrette's belly split open and the gutted fish spill onto the deck. Thera snatched the prize.

Collapsing onto the cage floor, Therasia was so weak she could barely bring the feast up to her mouth. Food at last! She did not have the strength to chew. After days of inhuman effort and starvation the rich, salty flesh ran down her throat like a lover's caress. It was no morir sonando but it sufficed.

Chevrette screeched, waking the barge. They lit lanterns and ran up and down, raising a fuss. Rona even tried to reach through the bars to snatch Thera's prize away. One hungry look and the dragoon kept her hands outside the bars.

Adel stared with utter revulsion as Thera began picking at the uncooked flesh, tearing bits free and forcing them down. That felt like the end of their relationship, which saddened Thera deeply. She was too famished to stop.

Soldiers tried to grab Chevrette but she screamed obscenities and just plain screamed, dancing wildly in pain, her broken arm flopping. Warren tried to tackle her but she bucked him off. Staggering, she fell off the side into the river. None followed or tried to fish her out. She did not surface again within the dim lights cast by the soldier's lanterns.

Thera cracked the head off the spine and sucked out the brains.

A few mouthfuls was enough to settle her stomach. Saving the rest for morning, Thera lay back onto the floor of her cage, subtle in the way she insulated herself with vines. This whole time she showed no one her true face. They saw only the thin, flexible mask made from the paper-like bark of the aspen.

The soldiers continued to fuss and yell, striking the cage in their fury. It gave them something to do. Warren warded their attempts to stick her with spears or shoot her, screaming for their obedience. She ignored it and rested.

Thera woke at dawn's first light, a glittering shimmer above the trees reflected in the water.

Soldiers sat, grimly staring in any direction save hers. The bargeman cooked griddle-cakes with potato and onion for breakfast. Few had the stomach for them.

The troops were practised at hauling and trimming the sail by now. The bargeman barely had to direct them and they were underway. The hills of the first few days were now broad plains, screened by and glimpsed through a line of trees along the bank. Ferries dropped their chains as they passed. Other boats called 'ware and ho! negotiating their path along the busy flow. Then the trees rolled back to reveal the blasted wastes.

Dust prevailed, with no grass or shrubbery to tie the topsoil in place. Rocks sat covered in bleak lichens and dust lay in between. This meant they were close to the city now. The desolation never filled the horizon. There was always a sight of green in the distance and green behind. The strip was broad enough to be daunting. A fearful sight and a strong reminder of a power greater than even the lightning could command.

Warren's ghost twitched and shivered as it passed through its previous prison. Even through the bars Thera could feel it. A drag on her spirits, like a weight, trying to hold them down. The extra weight involved too much effort. She collapsed to the floor of the cage and wept once more. The spirit could not feed on her misery because of the cage. She doubted it even knew she was there. It trashed about the boat, bringing anger to those aboard.

Halfway through this blasted ring the Aurigera flowed into the Garunna. Two mighty rivers joining. The dust swirled up in the delta to form difficult sandbanks with clearly-dredged paths. The waters flowed and danced together dangerously.

Swirls and turbulence.

The barge required many adjustments as it joined the dance of the waters. The soldiers rushed about the cramped vessel, trying to avoid bumping each other off. They trimmed lines and adjusted the sail.

It was all a dance. A great and glorious ballet.

The idea grew in Thera's imagination.

Ploughed fields and orchards appeared. Sprawling estates dotted the landscape. The grand walls of Tolosa rose in the distance. The only thing visible above the walls was the spire of the extravagant cathedral. Ordonnance allowed no other building in the city to be taller than the cathedral's roof. The steeple dominated. The harsh, constructed shapes of the buildings sang a strange counter-melody to a song she'd never heard.

She gnawed some more flesh from the fish. It tasted good raw. This was a new culinary sensation waiting to be discovered. Along with tapeworm and salmonella. Properly prepared and served fresh, with the right sides, it would be a sensation. For now the food gave her strength enough for one last effort.

She did not sing, talk, tap a rhythm or weave a code.

Therasia danced with the lightning.

It stung and tore at her for this impertinence, like an angry cat ripping a hand that dared pat its belly.

She twisted and flailed about in her cage, slamming into the sides, convulsing in circles. Always circles. The soldiers stared at her sporadic contortions with renewed revulsion.

"She's gone insane," Rona said, appalled at the thing flopping about in its cage, humming a broken tune. "It's all swayed her into gibbering lunacy!"

The lightning whirled around her. Thera tried her best to whirl along with her new partner. A treacherous, barbed consort. It spun in long spirals, like coiled springs struck by a mad drummer. She tried to unravel where it wanted to lead and if she could follow. She shouted irregular tones and thrashed about inside the limits of the cage. Together they danced as all should dance.

15

Brutal Duplicity

The residence of Madame Fournier perched within a respectable collection of apartments in the south-eastern section of Tolosa. It was part of a series of rows. Together, they surrounded a pleasant orchard of irregular shape with a sprinkling of diminutive fountains. These fine, private lawns hid from the bustle of the city behind the grandiose facades of the surrounding buildings. The block squatted pleasantly between the Cathedral of Master Smiths and the Centre of Information and Recruitment for the Armed Forces of Tolosa. Between the church and the barracks. Since returning to the city Adelaide spent most of her time in the two.

But this convenient block did not house her apartments. Those were to the north-west. In a better building. She arrived here in the middle of the morning for the other business that occupied her since returning to the city.

The polished buttons on her best, brocade waistcoat glittered in spite of the overcast day. She'd spent long enough buffing each of them last night.

She had yet to engage a new maid upon her return to the city. The old woman she'd inherited, with her father's apartments, was too feeble to care for the entire, sprawling penthouse. The poor dear had two sons. Adel saw to a small stipend and retirement with the youngest in his pig-farm outside the walls.

The address on Adel's list corresponded to a middle floor on this block. Nothing particularly ostentatious. Nonetheless, a well-kept building with a private garden was an expensive proposition in Tolosa. It insinuated a monied middle-class.

Adel's hunt led to this most strange destination. She'd dressed in her best uniform with the new, Sergent piping. Including her long, summer coat. Her field promotion to aspirant was, as yet, unconfirmed.

The weather lowered over the last few days. Spots of rain and a steady breeze from the south carried the memory of high, mountain snow which never melted.

The farmers would enjoy the damp.

Adel sighed.

Every thought brought a memory as dismal as the weather. They'd talked about the rain, walking back from the festival. Farmers were seldom happy with the amount, said the farmer's daughter. Put your foot up on the stool, she later whispered in heat. Prayers every morning in the church did nothing to rid Adelaide of such impulses.

She spat and moved forward.

The bell-boy in his smart red coat, one size too big, ushered her into the stairwell. She sorted a calling card for to carry up, one that contained only her name, not her address or other details.

Ferns in large, mismatched pots lined the passage which opened onto the orchard. The building was modestly deep. Narrower than hers.

She enjoyed looking over the orchard. Adel's building enclosed a single garden. With multiple buildings surrounding it this collection held extensive lawns and features.

The boy clattered back down. He didn't bother descending the entire stair before waving her to follow him back up. Once they'd arrived at the door she slipped him a coin and sent him on his way. A maid bowed her inside.

The vestibule was pleasant if cramped. Adel preferred to stand. It wasn't long before the inner doors opened to reveal the lady of the house. A middle-aged woman. She dressed in formal day attire, slapping a fan into the palm of her hand in a rhythmic, calculating manner.

"The name Lelaing has connotations," she said.

No actual greeting. The lady peered down at the card she held in the same hand as her fan.

"I am descended from the northern families though I am here on a more personal matter. May I speak with you alone?" Adelaide tucked the red wiper into the pocket of her waistcoat as if it had nothing to do with the matter at hand.

Madame Fournier caught the action and blinked, startled. She looked at her maid and back to Adel with another calculating stare. Did the woman weigh everything before she made a move?

"Indeed. The front parlour is presentable. Come through. Valery, see we are not disturbed. Will you take tea, Sergent?"

"A little early, if you'll forgive me. I have an appointment at the barracks down the road."

"Very well." The woman turned and strode into the apartment. "So, it was on your way?"

"Quite," Adel lied, admiring the filigree work along the passage. There were only two paintings. Both of masterful workmanship. They depicted, what is called in polite company, 'revelries'.

The front parlour was a cosy space. A patterned clavichord open at one side. The walls, again, felt bare. Only a few scattered artworks and those of modest size. It was an apartment that screamed small money.

The madame threw herself casually into an armchair of solid design with little padding. Adel settled onto a matching chair across a delicately carved side-table. She looked out at the orchard and its various waterworks.

"So. LaBion is dead," Madame Fournier stated plainly.

"Indeed, Madame. My condolences for your loss."

"Loss? Ha. Well enough. He was, at the least, a faithful pony. I take many of my lovers from the barracks nearby. He was the roughest of the rough but with a generous heart. When my husband died he left me with a little coin. I have invested wisely. A baker, my husband. His ovens serviced patisserie for the entire quarter. The stipend does not allow excessive purchases but is more than sufficient for the up-keep of- Huh. Well. Never mind that. I won't bore you with long stories of my escapades. I am rambling to avoid the issue at hand. He died well?"

Adelaide snorted and glanced about. A little money wisely invested. She should chat with this woman about her own investments. Adel's field promotion from sergent to aspirant would require a payment to endure. If the officers involved countenanced the new rank. That, itself, would involve much sweet-talk and glossing over of truths. She shrugged and settled back into the chair, relaxing. Honesty would be refreshing. "It was a bloody massacre. There was no time for heroics."

"I've heard whispers. You captured a faery, they say."

"I'm not sure we did." Nothing she said here would be traced back to her. Madame Fournier would not reveal where she'd gathered her information. It was quite a joy to speak freely. "The vile thing came of its own accord for designs I cannot fathom. There's no other reason we were not slaughtered in ambush after ambush as we fled the scene of our commandant's hubris."

Madame raised an eyebrow, settling in to the idea of some salacious gossip. "You managed to escape without injury."

Adelaide drew a line down one forearm of her summer coat. "No. I shall bear the scars of my time there for the rest of my life. I can still barely swing a sword."

"A bad business then. I am saddened. He was a funny little man, LaBion. A common gutter-rat. Eager. Open to my proclivities. Surprisingly kind. Oh, dear." Madame Fournier found herself in some small difficulty. She dabbed at her eyes. "Were you a particular friend?"

"I'm not sure he had any particular friends. He was in my squad. I liked him well enough."

"Enough to track me down, at least."

"There was no-one else. No relatives. Only the monogram on his bit of cloth. None of my squad survived. The duty falls entirely in my charge." Adel rose. The tears of her host stirred things she preferred at rest. "If you'll forgive me, Madame, I have an appointment and other calls to make."

The lady gathered herself and showed her out personally. The spirit of the staircase came to whisper all the things Adel might have said or done differently. A bizarre encounter. Had she handled it well? The woman seemed genuinely affected. And poor LaBion would indeed have made an interesting play-thing. Once he'd had a bath. He was unaware of his own absurdity and generally eager to please. Should she have left the wiper? The bell-boy opened the door for her.

Her two other visits involved regular families of hysterical reactions. Adelaide marched into the Military Centre tired and emotional.

The great parade square was a grand, familiar sight. The paving stones formed large, sweeping patterns. They were so smooth and expertly fitted that she could push an empty roller across them with one hand. On a drunken dare. From comrades now dead.

Her visits today were a longer stroll than anticipated. She'd refused an army palanquin. The sensitive nature of her business, the delicacy involved in some of the soldier's personal affairs, demanded privacy. A palanquin meant carriers, livery, too many opportunities for gossip.

Even a rickshaw meant an extra tongue. Half the money the cabbies made was from selling gossip. The constant, desperate interest in everyone else's business was not something she missed about society in the city. Too many bored, rich people desperate to know who was a tiny bit better or worse than they.

Adelaide headed for the officer's wing. Before entering she leaned on the stone newel of the broad, marble steps that floated over the wide trench serving as a gutter to the courtyard.

Everything hurt.

She covered her exhaustion by adjusting her leggings and taking a small sip from her flask. Never mind that the boots were well worn in, her legs were tired.

She recalled her last, long walk. It was after the harvest dance. That funny little girl guided her across the hillside so she would not get 'ate'.

Adel remembered the strange happiness brought on by new explorations of herself and another. And murder. She put bees on their faces. An act like that seemed so peculiar in the city. Surrounded by precise, clean lines of cut stone. Such direction and purpose in the architecture. The city was a sanctuary of precision and order where there was no need for her to commit atrocities. She remembered thinking she'd escaped punishment for those acts of immorality. Is that why she found it difficult to mourn? She deserved the sadness and could not let it go.

Even the name.

She heard variations called and muttered around town. Each time her heart strangled her throat. Teresa, Thallassy. Anything starting with a T. She could not forget that amazing woman.

She could never move on from the brutal duplicity.

It was the transformation that tore at her sanity the most. A graceful, confident woman who pulled off her shirt. A commanding angel and her lively fingers. She became a gaunt, bloody, masticating monster curled contentedly around a raw fish, convulsing on the floor of its cage. Could a woman be all those things and more?

A thin weed pushed its way through the stonework of the trench. Some unlucky fusilier would have to pull it and scrub that clean.

Entering, she sought the facilities. There were none specifically for women in this wing. There was a converted room on the ground floor with a collection of chamberpots and screens. Few enough women ranked among the officers that this sufficed.

The meeting was on the next floor up in one of the smaller map-rooms. Adel enjoyed the clack of her boots across the polished floor. The twin doors were like much of the internal decorations of this military facility: tall and solid but plain.

Another officer waited inside. A lieutenant-colonel by his piping. The extra trim around his hat suggested some specialised military branch. He rose politely when she entered. He harrumphed under his elaborate moustache, removing his hat to bow and reveal grey hair still thick upon his head.

"You'll be the woman then," he said in a snarling tone of annoyance. His dark eyes stormed with customary anger.

Adel refused to flinch. "There was just the one? I seem to recall more women on the field."

"What? Yes. Yes. Don't take a tone with me. Sit. I'm not standing around waiting for that annoying upstart."

Not a mention of rank or formality between them. Adel gathered herself and strode over to a chair beside him. The map-table dominated the small room. The chandelier hung low in an unusual arrangement. The shades directed the light down instead of radiating it. Whoever was on the map-table would not escape notice. There was presently nothing unrolled. The polished rosewood only served to glare the light from the high windows and get in the way.

Even the box-shelving along one wall stood empty. The vacant cavities held no promise of explanation for this meeting.

A pair of comfortable chairs sat between each of the windows, ready to accommodate weary officers. They all had a small table beside them. Upon each perched a set of cut, crystal glasses and an empty decanter in a delicately inlaid tray.

Adel sat next to this glaring lieutenant-colonel and set out two glasses. She extricated her flask and made a gesture.

"Not in the mood for some commoner's piss," he said, waving a hand.

"My family, the Lelaings of Albiga, kept a small farm where we grew peaches and cherries for brandy and liqueurs. I have an excellent palette when it comes to eau-de-vie."

"That Lelaing? Ah. So. There might be something to you. Go on then. Little shit has kept me waiting long enough."

Adel poured two generous measures and set the silver flask on the parquetry. The lieutenant-colonel knocked his back in one hit. He sat, smacking his lips. That was one way to savour a delicate peach liqueur thinned to perfection with distilled water. His eyebrows rose in surprise.

"Damned fine distillation that," he said. "One of yours?"

"My family are all dead, Colonel. I am the last of my particular line. The bone disease took them a few years back. My father kept an apartment in Tolosa for business trips. I accompanied him when I came of age. Often enough to developed my palate and a head for numbers. Before he passed he arranged for the sale of the estate outside Albiga to provide an income."

"Hmph. Rotten mess." He plonked the glass back onto the table. "But driving yourself up the ranks I see. Good. Good." He waggled a finger at the glass. "You must let me know your supplier."

"If you give me your card, Colonel, I shall arrange for the delivery of a curated selection."

"Ha! You're a cunning one. You think you're going to get a high-ranked officer's card that easily? Ha! Tell me first, no prancing about, how badly did Warren foul all this up?"

"His intention in going to the countryside was to capture a fey. We have a fey. The cost..."

"It's real then? This thing he keeps in his dungeon? Not some child in a mask?"

"The creature in his converted cellar is very real."

"How can you tell?"

"I fought the fey twice while I was down there, Colonel." She poured him another generous shot but he ignored it, peering at her with a sceptical eye. "Each time I was very fortunate to survive. I received ... injuries on both occasions." One on her arm, the other across her heart. "They have strong powers. However, I feel some of that might be enhanced by trickery. Do not doubt their otherworldly abilities exist. They possess superhuman strength and speed. They have a trick for deceiving the eye. One cannot see them slip into the middle of your squad until they start the slaughter. Have you never encountered one yourself?"

"Bah. Never did. I went out with the money often enough. Began to think they were a myth." He peered sidelong at his glass but remained untempted. "Still think they're a myth."

Adel sipped and felt the warmth of the liquor relaxing her chest. For all his bluster the lieutenant-colonel appreciated someone who could talk to him without flinching. She understood such things at a strange, deeper level that she rarely visited. Her fatigue drew her down into that quieter place. She was too tired to keep everything within her contained. She always thought of it as a tiny thread that wove its way out of her chest in her most unguarded moments. She let it wander free. It noticed the lieutenant-colonel had a strange shape around him. So unlike hers. And yet similar. She allowed the thread dance about him.

"I don't believe they would emerge unless provoked," Adel said.

"And what provoked them?"

"The commandant was unable to procure the services of any of the local doxies. The size of the camp intimidated them. A few of the men grew restless and took it out on some of the locals." It was true. They had started all this death. The very presence of the soldiers provoked it all. "They killed the men. The girls jumped from a cliff. I believe one may have been ... special- a particular friend of the fey."

"Ha! They have friends? That is interesting." The lieutenant-colonel leaned back in the seat, relaxing. Adel felt this was something he needed to do more often. Her dancing thread facilitated this. "Upstart has written a report but I'd like to sit down with you and get a proper account. If you don't mind a little honesty. I'll send for you some time next week. Sounds more exciting than my jaunts to the country. Barely left the house for most of my visits. There was... Hmph. Well."

He wanted honesty. The shape of it moved around him and whispered to Adel the strangest idea. "There was a man?" she asked.

The lieutenant-colonel shot her a violent glare, almost choking in outrage at the very suggestion. Adel barely noticed. Honesty was the theme. A word he'd brought to the conversation. A shape suggested for this dance. One she radiated from her warm core.

Sipping her fine brandy she stared across the room into her own shame, allowing the honesty to flow. "I fell for the daughter of the local La Granger. An extraordinary woman. An accomplished surgeon. She had long, graceful fingers adept at opening buttons. It was my first time with a girl. I did things with her that I thought no decent woman could ever do. And it felt utterly, perfectly wonderful. Then the massacre, running. The trip down the river."

"You never got to say goodbye?" asked the gruff old soldier in a surprisingly soft tone.

"Not yet."

"Ha! I love the 'yet'. No. Well." He scooped up the glass from the table and threw back the shot, sitting for a while as it warmed him. "I always said goodbye. Never knew if I'd be back. Shook my composure something rotten the first time. Had to do the return journey in a palanquin so no one would see me cry. It's why I never made full colonel. Rumours."

He glanced about the room as if he'd forgotten where he was, why he should be baring his deepest shame to a complete stranger. Then he continued in a more settled tone. "I asked around about you, y'know, what with this whole promotion business. Your walker crew think you're a good luck charm. The baggage spoke highly of you. Quartermaster. No one left from your squad to ask. Good with names, they said. Dealt them grace. Unusual for high-born in the military, treating well with the commoners. None of them wanted to rat you out for fucking a girl so they like you or you're very discreet. Either is useful."

"Most of those that might spread rumours are dead." said Adel.

The old man peered down at the glass, rolling it in his hand. "I was never good with commoners or sneaking about. Craon family, meself. Not known for subtlety." He smacked his lips. "Can't remember any of the soldiers I travelled with. Rode palanquin down and back. Doubt most of them could even tell you what I looked like. A lot of the commanders take trips to the country to have a ... relief from their wives. Husbands as well, I suppose. Never thought we'd see women getting promoted this high in the ranks. Had to let them join, of course, after the towns formed their own damned units during the last war. Good soldiers. Good shots, women. But officers? Made for some problems in the ranks. Men bothering them and so forth. It bolstered our numbers when we needed it. Bloody Rhenosian cities. Refused to attack their fey. Tried to take us after we were beaten back. Treacherous spawn of troglodytes. Well. Yes. Rambling. This is damned fine liquor, Sergent. Damned fine." He fished a card from his pocket. "Oh, here comes that little shit." Adel could hear boots clacking and raised voices from the corridor. One of them belonged to Commandant Warren. It brought her back to herself. "You send me half a dozen of the finest bottles you can find. I'll reimburse you when I see you next." There was an address on the card. "Tuck that away. Ah, HARRUMPH. Game faces on."

They both rose.

"I came with what men I could as fast as I was able," said Capitaine Alden as he entered. He matched his reputation. A tailored uniform of rich and subtle fabrics encasing a soft belly and red face. The petulant voice grew high pitched with emotion. "This entire enterprise was cursed from the start! I couldn't even find you in the blasted woods. Kept wandering in circles."

"If you could actually read a compass-"

"Enough from the pair of you!" barked Lieutenant-Colonel Craon. "Ain't got time to listen to this prattle all day, if you'll forgive me, sirs."

"Thank you, Colonel," said Warren. "Of course. Ah, Lieutenant Lelaing. Here as well."

"A sergent yet, Commandant," Adelaide answered modestly, tucking her flask away. "I can only jump so many ranks at a time."

"Bloody impertinence promoting her at all," growled Craon. From her angle Adel glimpsed the twitch of a smile behind his huge moustache.

"My dispatches were processed in a timely fashion," said Warren. "As the only person I know who has fought a fey twice, and survived, she is not someone who should wallow in the general morass."

Capitaine Alden sized her up. Adel watched the process she'd observed in dozens of men. The greedy eyes in his red face tried not to stare at her tits. They ended up lingering on her face. That excited them enough that he looked down and further down still. She was not a soldier to this man or to many she'd met. That clued her into the lieutenant-colonel's possible proclivities. He did not immediately stare at her with open lust like this Alden.

"Delightful. Is she here to help convince us," asked Capitaine Alden, "or to distract us?"

Warren laughed in a polite and comradely manner, never mind that she was standing right there. "A little of both! Come along."

"Come along?" said Craon. "Smoke and pits! I've no time for a bloody jaunt, man!"

"I assure you, Colonel. It will be worth our while. We're going to visit my captive fey."

That grabbed the attention of everyone in the room. Warren led the group to the officer's carriage-yard. His town house sat on the other side of the Garunna. That section of Tolosa was mostly orchards. A few commanding estates. And the big church of course. Adel wondered if they were going to ride the whole way. Owning a palanquin involved employing a permanent team of hauliers. She hated the idea of having an excess of people rattling around her affairs. If she needed to make longer trips in the city she hired a rickshaw or local cab-carriers. Not to worry. Warren had a ridiculous answer to that problem.

"Now this," he declared, as they emerged into the yard, "this is the future! The base is taken from the chassis of a walker carrier. Carved back to make it lighter. What we call a roller. The carriage is bolted on at the moment. I'm working on some layered steel springs as suspension. The driver sits there at the front. They steer with this large wheel. That winds and unwinds the reins, turning the front wheels."

Adel found herself exchanging glances with the other two officers. She kept her face blank.

"Looks ridiculous," growled Craon. "We sit in here, do we?"

"Indeed," said Warren. "If you would, Colonel."

"Right'o." Craon climbed inside and sat, matter-of-fact, on the rear bench.

"I'm not getting in that thing!" said Alden. "Those are lightning jars! Damned things make you impotent!"

"I can assure you, Capitaine, the jars are at the back and well insulated along with the motor. There is no danger on a short journey. You may sit at the front if you are afraid."

"Afraid? Impertinence! I-"

"Do I have to make it an order, Capitaine?"

Alden bristled at Warren for pulling rank on him but then complied. He was in the presence of two senior officers. As much as he might sneer, the capitaine was not one to flout the hierarchy that lent him his own power. He sat, pointedly, on the front bench as far from the jars as he could get, fussing his sabre into a comfortable position.

Adel nodded to the driver. "Rona." The dragoon nodded back with a smile. "Hey, Adel." She climbed aboard and sat on the rear bench, leaving only the seat next to Alden for Warren. The commandant didn't seem to notice. He climbed eagerly aboard and rapped twice on the roof.

The strange contraption eased into motion. The acceleration was smooth and gradual, unlike the jerky starts of an oxen lumbering up to speed, or the bouncing of a palanquin before it settled into rhythm.

"I haven't had much chance to do a proper range test, but I'm predicting three or four miles. More, once we work out some of the kinks. Imagine being able to ride from an estate into town and back. I've coated the wheels with rubber to lend them traction. It makes them rattle less on the cobbles. I'm told the coating will vulcanise and perish after a few weeks. Layers of leather might provide a longer-term solution."

"It's an impressive effort," said Craon. "Given that you've only been back four days."

"I began work right away! This is its first real test. The connections are all double-bolted. It proved to be a useful distraction as I began to wear down my captive. The creature is becoming compliant in small ways."

"Does it do tricks?" Alden asked, sidelong.

"You will see," said Warren. "Please, enjoy the journey."

It was a pleasant enough ride. There was a horn at the driver's hand which honked often to warn people from their quiet passage. Whatever Warren used for insulation dampened the customary buzz and crackle of the lightning jars. The city jiggled past. They even made short work of the bridge. None of the regular carriers wanted to get in front of this strange contraption. After the bridge they turned left and climbed the low hill that used to carry a church but now held four manor houses with extensive gardens. The vehicle pulled well up the slope. On this occasion, the suspension slings held so they arrived comfortably enough.

"If it catches on," said Warren, "we might look at smoothing out the roads. In the northern Rhenosian duchies, I understand they use fine gravel for some roads, stabilised with oiled sand and tars. Gets sticky in the summer, according to some travelogues I've read but a much smoother surface. They lay them around the glassworks to cut down on breakages. I'm sure we could develop a formula for tar that would harden sufficiently. Anyway, welcome to my humble abode."

The mansion was entirely new. Maybe twenty years old. A courtyard received them behind a gate and wall. Servants quarters rose on one side, garages and workshops on the other. Through the windows Adel glimpsed the pleasant, walled gardens visible at the rear. Most of the rooms faced onto these. This side held the corridors and the grand entrance hall.

A woman opened the carved doors and greeted them. Nicole, his ordonnance.

"Ah! Aspirant," said Warren. "A light lunch in the drawing room if you would. We shall descend but return presently."

"Cold lamb if you have any," said Craon.

"Aye, sir," the woman answered, striding away to arrange matters. Adel watched her depart. The aspirant reminded Adel that Warren did know how to pick his support staff. Always efficient.

"Come along," said the commandant. "Let us pay our guest a visit."

He led them to the left, past the ballroom and the library. Jev Warren did not come from an old family. The excessive wealth was more recent. A great-grandfather invested in ironworks during the last war. A grandfather took that money and helped spread the lightning technologies. He was still considered New Money though he acted with aristocratic self-importance.

The commandant turned and skipped down a narrow, servants' staircase. This led to a series of storage rooms under the garages and workshops. Adel peered through the high windows. She caught sight of some lightning sails lined up outside. The house might well be self-sufficient for power. The slot windows were the only source of light in the bare, stone dungeons. The ceilings arched, cross-vaulted to support the two stories above.

Warren's constant, rambling ideas provided a droning background. Neither Adel nor Colonel Craon listened. Adel struggled to keep her composure as she came closer and closer to that creature that hollowed out her soul every time she thought of it. She would either shoot the damned thing or shoot herself. Would either end her pain? This was an opportunity to rid herself, once and for all, of those filthy thoughts that infected her soul.

"...so it can fire with the hatch closed," said Warren. "Like a turret on a fortification that has slots all around for gunners to shoot those who get too close to the walls. Or, maybe, the whole turret can rotate along with the cannon."

"Too heavy," said Alden. "You'd need another motor inside the walker to drive it. That's another weight of shielding, insulation. There's not enough room in those damned things as it is. Also, it would take too much energy to move. Drain your jars. You'd never be able to get the walkers into the forests."

"Remember, we can force the fey into a location of our choosing by attacking a village. Especially if they have friends there. Oh, this is the room. Here."

A broad cage squatted low in the back of the last storage. Three lightning jars glowed in the dimmest corner. The buzz and crackle lurked in the background, underlining the tone of confinement. Even the large bulb on the ceiling hung caged behind a heavy, wire mesh, casting a thick grid of shadows over the room.

Adel unhooked a blunderbuss from the wall and plugged in a sparker. She stared at the weapon with uncertain intent. She had not the heart to approach the cage. Instead she moved to the side, standing under the low window, pretending to cover the officers from there. Would she shoot? Only if provoked.

"I must say," said Alden, "I do feel reassured with our best fairy-fighter armed and in the room. Though from the cast of the thing- Is that the thing?" He stepped closer. "Looks like a pile of rags and sticks. Is it actually a puppet? Are we in such a dim room so that we cannot see the strings?"

"I'm sure it will try to embarrass me by refusing to move in front of our new guests," said Warren. He stepped boldly up to the cage. Adel noticed he stopped short of strangulation distance. "You see the bones in front of the cage? We tease it with those. Part of my starvation strategy."

He drew his sabre and fiddled with the hilt before flicking a pig's femur closer. The thing stirred. A slight movement. Almost an illusion. As if the wind disturbed its rags. There was no wind in the cellar.

Adel felt her knees weaken at the pitiful sight. It was so thin after such a short time. Gaunt and starved under its leaves and scraps. So beggarly and weak. Adel remembered the tall, elegant woman who skipped towards them outside the blacksmith. That teasing twinkle in her dark eyes. A flash of the beast that ripped the barrel-set from her hands and flung it into the screaming battlefield. Now it was just an obstruction of bones that scarcely prevented the rags it wore from sinking to the floor.

"Is that its face?" Craon asked. "Looks like its made of wood."

"A mask I believe," said Warren. "I can't persuade the thing to remove it. I'm not sure I want it to. They are said to be quite a frightful sight."

"Humph. Well." Craon squinted. "Looks dead. Get in there and take the damned mask off."

"The last person foolish enough to intrude upon its space had her arm ripped off," said Warren.

"Really?" asked Craon, looking at Adel.

"It was on the river, Colonel," Adel contributed. "Just as we entered the city. There was a woman with a fish. The creature broke her arm. She was a traveller. Ah. It would take too long to explain."

"Well, I'm not at all convinced," said Capitaine Alden. "You drag us all the way out here just to show us a bundle of rags! I was expecting the opportunity to interrogate the thing. As far as I'm concerned the two of you are in some sort of conspiracy to sell us false about some forest waif you found."

"A waif did not destroy our entire company, Capitaine," said Adel.

"That report makes no sense," said Capitaine Alden. "All a lot of silliness. I heard the walker's guns cracking away. A damned lot of foolish howling. I couldn't even track the noise; it was over so fast. Then I wasn't able to connect with you. Couldn't get that damned lightning-caster to work in the woods. All crackles and fuzz. Not a beep. I was lucky to get out at all. The camp was half gone when I arrived. The rest packing up. No one there could give me a clear answer to a simple question. Gibberish and tripe. All of it."

"No one is questioning your report, Capitaine," said the commandant. "We are more concerned that you didn't bring your guns to bear. Your excuses seem unlikely. The entire dock collapsing at that exact moment? There will be an investigation. We haven't heard anything at all from the company that come in from the north. Once we get word from them we will be able to gain a clearer picture of every-thing that occurred."

"What occurred was you walking your soldiers into a massacre."

"You are welcome to visit the location yourself and see the destroyed walkers. The wolves and crows have doubtless fed upon the carrion. They won't tell you much. Question any of the survivors. They will all say that I kept the company together as we escaped with our prize."

"Not much of a prize! Bundle of rags in a silly cage!"

"Enough! The pair of you!" Craon barked. "Not something we should be discussing in front of the thing, real or not. I suggest we retire to the drawing room. Bloody hungry enough as it is."

"Of course, of course. Sirs, if you will make your way back to the stairs. Adelaide, a word if I may?"

Another attempt. Adel grew increasingly repulsed by the man's fawning attentions.

She unplugged the sparker and hung up the blunderbuss. There was a sound in the cage but she refused to turn. Instead, she waited impatiently in the next cellar. Out of sight of that ruin. She should go back in and confront it. Stick her arm through the bars and see what it would do. At least scream at it for a while to see if that lent any catharsis.

It was as if the stone vault enjoyed her tormented emotions. Something sipped delicately on them as she might sip on a good brandy. It left an awkward scratch in her mind.

Warren ushered the men towards the stairs and returned. He had a hopeful, reassuring look on his face.

"I was wondering if you had given any thought to the matter I raised last time," he said. "I feel a union between our two houses would be of sublime accord. You must know, by now, that my own feelings towards you are ardent and true."

She could not stand the sight of him. He was her way out. Her way back. A path to returning her family to prominence and respectability in the city. By protocol, he would take her name. If she acquiesced to his marriage proposals she would have everything she thought she desired. Now he was a vivid reminder of her lost love in all its- NO! No. She could not call it that. It was not her love. It was a thing. An aberration.

"I might insist upon an answer," Warren continued. "However, if you require more time, I must at least insist upon some token that my passions are not misguided."

"If you insist." Honesty tore at her. The theme for the day. She managed to channel it into something more patient and diplomatic. "I find I am torn by so many emotions surrounding that portion of time. Your attentions serve only to bring those tremulous sensibilities to the surface. I do not wish to pursue with you such closeness as disturbs my sanity. It would be best, presently, if you put the matter from your mind."

He stared at her, shocked. He stared at her body, as if it were something he wanted to possess, then back up at her face, the part of her that told him he never could. For a moment Adel feared violence from the man but that was a foolish notion. Then something seemed to settle his composure. He glanced about the room, looking at something she could not see.

"Very well then," he said. "Never let it be said that I could not take rejection. If you would be so kind as to remain down here briefly. I will require... You should... There is something you can do that may help me greatly. Facilitate a conversation. After that," he glanced about the room again, snorted and allowed himself a half smile. "Well. After that I shall not bother you further." He stalked from the room to placate his guests.

16

"I am entirely at your mercy."

The surgeon ran his ageing hands over the skin surrounding the bullet wound on Therasia's back.

"The poultice seems to have drawn out the infection," he said. "A fascinating recipe. Are you sure you don't mind me producing more?"

"Consider it as payment, Fortino, as you will receive no coin."

"None necessary. None at all. Always happy to honour the pledge I made to the Mountain Monks." He leaned in for a closer inspection. "Scraping now," the surgeon warned her.

He began the process of removing the excess poultice along with the last of the puss. He scratched with a sterilised, metal paddle. A thing used by clay-workers repurposed for medicine. Therasia pursed her lips. She grimaced at the contact from the metal rummaging around under her skin.

She liked the man, even if he sometimes had trouble finishing a sentence. He dressed impeccably. A good eye for colour. Greying hair and whipcord lean. Polite and professional. He exhibited no ego about taking instruction from her on his own business. They'd chatted about the monastery, how it had changed since his day and how it stayed the same.

He would be dead, if Warren and that other presence had their way. So many souls would perish if those ravenous spirits escaped the rings. They drove the last war. Trapping them ended it. Warren would release them all, thinking he could somehow control them. They would feed upon the world, stripping all life. Animals. Plants. Even the fungus. Nothing would live.

"Oh yes," Fortino the surgeon muttered. "We've definitely dried out that infection. You should have come to see me earlier. It would not have grown nearly..."

"Yes. It's best to kill an infection early," said Therasia. "I was unable to get away for a while. Now I must be careful to manage my time. I want to catch both of them, together."

"Both?"

"Oh, not your concern."

Therasia stared out the window. As a recipient of training from the Mountain Monks this physician commanded rooms in a respectable part of town. The view contained some interesting architecture. A few days ago she'd slipped in the back door, showed him her tattoo, then showed him the bullet wound. Three days on the barge, another in the city, it went untreated. It took the two of them a further three days to get it under control. This meant it was the morning of the fifth day since she'd seen Adelaide.

"Ow!"

"Sorry. It's an odd shape, this wound. A strange chunk of skin missing. It does, at least, seem to be healing well."

"I am fey-kin. We always heal well."

"Oh, my! That- I- I don't wish to involve myself in- I did not realise there were any of your kind in the city."

Therasia laughed. "No, no. There are not. Only me. It's fine, Fortino. There's no danger. I received the wound days ago, many miles from here. I mention it only such that, when I visit next and you see the remarkable progress of the healing, you will not become overly curious. I would not want you to endanger yourself with indiscreet inquiries to the wrong people. This is a matter between us surgeons."

"Oh. Er. Yes. A fey surgeon is not something I... That is to say, I have enjoyed your company, also. And most informative. It's been a long while since I left the monks. I shall be updating... It is pleasant to converse with someone travelled and educated. Too many in this city think sitting in one place and sampling everything that passes makes them cultured. I'm sorry. Are you really one of ... the Kindly Ones? The dancers of the woods?"

"Never met one before?"

"Not to my knowledge."

"Ha! A good answer, my friend. Is there something you're supposed to be doing back there?"

"What? Oh. Yes. Let me put a compress over that. I'll soak it well in... I- This is most unprecedented. Forgive my flustered state." Fortino set himself back to work. "I thought you did not visit the cities at all. Your kind."

"Yes, we do. Some of us frequently. The lightning makes us uncomfortable in concentrations. There are plenty of places to rest away from such things. I've never been to a large city, myself. I'm amazed it contains so much open space, greenery, large gardens. I thought, with all that pressure on land, everything would be built over."

"It depends on which part of town you frequent. Where are you staying at the moment?"

"In a cage, dear Fortino."

"Ah. That would explain... When you first arrived you were a little..."

"Shrivelled? Wretched?"

"Indeed. You seem in more robust health today."

"Fortunately, I was able to dance my way out of my confinement. Now I sleep on a pleasant cot at the back of a pottery workshop above my supposed dungeon. I must be careful to return to my cage when my captor comes to visit. This morning he had some appointment at the barracks."

"Stars and pits! You're that one I've heard rumours- The commandant- On the hill across the river..."

The man really should learn to finish a sentence. "Yep. That's me. Oh, tighter with the bandaging, please."

"What? Oh, of course. There. That should be satisfactory in- Oh, this is quite exciting! I'm not sure if..."

Therasia flexed and slipped down from the table, satisfied. She reached for her shirt. "Do not trouble yourself. I am happy to have met someone both competent and discreet. You even politely clean your instruments in the sink whenever I take my shirt off."

"Ha! Indeed. That is one of the things they do not teach you at the monastery. You seem less shy about such matters than... Forgive me if this is forward or not of interest. I must invite you to a private supper where we can become better acquainted. I am beyond intrigued to hear more of your story."

"Aren't you a little old to be chasing girls?"

"Oh no, that's not- I mean to say-"

"Maybe you can first escort me to a show. I am keen to hear a full orchestra in a proper concert hall. Music is quite the passion of mine."

"Ah! Mine also! Do you have a card?"

"A card of what?"

"Oh. To get in touch. Send notes. Arrange things. Sorry."

"Ah! I am currently without a formal address but I'll stop by the day after tomorrow. All being well. We can discuss it further then."

"Yes. Sorry. I wasn't thinking. Please do call whenever it is convenient. You already seem to have found some way to slip past my secretary. Ha!"

Therasia smiled as she shrugged her jacket settled. Then she folded out the window to the doorway below. Her reward was a strangled scream of surprise from the surgery, above, when she came back to the real. As if she'd exited the building in a more conventional manner Therasia skipped down the steps and headed towards the river.

By the stars, these skirts were awkward. She tripped over them every time she moved. Britches would be better but not something ladies wore in the city. She'd have to do her best to get used to the cursed things. Or start a fashion.

She brought her clothes from cast-off places, ready-made stores. There were a surprising amount of places where last year's clothing was recycled down. She chose rich fabric, simple designs, and timeless colours that suggested a young lady-in-waiting. A governess or merchant's daughter. She wore a fine-spun shirt with lace at the cuffs and collars. Well-pleated at the back. This matched perfectly with her elegant jacket, slit at the back for movement, modestly closed at the front. Her scarf of chrysalis silk would match favourably with this in the winter. If she ever saw any of her old clothes again. The skirt was of plainer material. She had a tendency to wear the jacket with a button or two open which attracted passing glances.

The stroll down to the river took her past a flower-girl with some lovely, fresh-cut posies of lilac. Therasia paid too much for one. She headed for her mid-morning breakfast, twirling the stems between her fingers.

She'd discovered a cleaner kitchen that served those with a passing appetite. The inns and public houses tended towards simplicity and poor fare. They catered for transitory river-workers and locals. The food there was bland. This house opened a hatch in it's rear garden wall to a more discerning traveller, as well as clerical and managerial staff from local warehouses. Those that could not, or did not wish to, make it back to their houses for lunch. Rich folk in the city had servants to cook for them at home. Workers brought their own food, wrapped or boxed. Thera longed for the common eateries of her village. Old Saliesa would make a fortune in this place with her recipes.

"Ah! Mam'selle! So pretty," Cannois commented, the daughter of the owner, leaning over the counter to examine the posey. "I do love flowers."

She was cute. Unfortunately, the girl did not lean in Therasia's direction. Therasia was not in a frame of mind to pursue such things. Adelaide still haunted her thoughts. Her appetite, normally so robust, waned and flowed at the whims of that slayer of her heart.

A decent stew of barley, cabbage and bacon. The seasoning was excellent. She sat with with a lard merchant from further down the river. A great demand for grease in the city apparently. So many uses.

Finishing her meal she broke up the bowl of bread. They served their stews in a small, round loaf, the insides of which were torn out and presented as a side-dish, buttered with garlic. The analogous nature of the meal did not escape Therasia. She overpaid again.

Warren had so much money scattered about his mansion in various little chests and strongboxes. Some in his study for paying bills. Some in the kitchens for buying food. Large, private stashes in his rooms for purposes only the stars witnessed. He even had a considerable amount of promissory-notes for money deposited at two different banks. Her threads found them all. The guard outside her room was a heavy sleeper so she had the run of the house at night.

"How is your brother today?" Thera asked Cannois, returning her plate.

The pleasant young girl blinked, then smiled in genuine delight. "Better, thank you. He still hates his numbers but the school interests him a little more. Was it you who had a word with him the other day?"

"I confess I have difficulty minding my own business. When I see someone in distress, I- Oh."

"What is it, mam'selle?"

"Ah. An appointment I did not know I had. My threads, er, my threads of thought have reminded me that I must dash. Here." She handed the girl the flowers. "For you." And hurried out into the street.

She'd fallen victim to her own complacency. People tended to underestimate Warren. He was, after all, mostly charm and bluster, riding the coattails of past family success. And a private education that brought him friends and contacts in high places. But Warren with that interloper, that feral, hungry spirit which haunted him, such was a most dangerous combination.

She flitted urgently through the city, food unsettled. Knots of urbanites clustered the pavement, forcing her to weave through the traffic on the streets. Oxen pulled carts filled with all manner of goods from hay, to chests of drawers, to slaughtered pigs. Rickshaws, handcarts and palanquins hupped and wove among these. Thera braided an extra strand of haste between them all.

Stupid skirts kept tangling until she worked out how to hold them.

Even a normal person could sprint across the bridge and reach the estate in no more than two or three minutes. She was outside the wall of the estate, on the side with the lightning sails, in less than half that time. There were too many people around. Even here, on the church side of the river, with only a scattering of houses behind the walls, there were people. Over fifty thousand citizens chose to call Tolosa home. It left no where to hide.

Huffing, one hand on the tall, brick wall surrounding Warren's little estate, she absorbed the stares of passing strollers. A woman began screaming at her husband on the other side of the street for whatever reason. A fractional distraction that Thera used to leap the high, estate wall and land in the lightning field.

She scooted down the narrow lawn that ran by the side of the mansion along the outside of the workshops and garages. Food cellars lived below the servants' residences on the other side of the house. This side was all workshops and dry storage. No one wanted to be near the cracking distortions of the lightning.

She could hear Warren already, talking to her. Or, rather, the collection of sticks, leaves and rags she'd left enchanted in the cage. There were others in the dungeon below. Two displayed elaborate braiding on their jackets that indicated high military rank. Someone else lurked under the window.

Thera stayed back, taking care not to cast a shadow. The blunderbuss' mount hung empty. Dangerous. These high-ranking whoevers brought a bodyguard to keep them safe from the terrifying twigs in her cell.

Warren plugged in his sabre and flicked a bone through the bars. Her heart leapt but the sword did not contact the wiring. He did not work out that she'd switched it off.

The bones were meant to remind her that her meals were at his whim. Such pointless cruelty.

She grabbed a small pebble and leaned into the else-where. A precise pitch. The little chunk of stone thumped into her deception with enough force to make the pile vaguely stir. That and the enchantment seemed to satisfy them.

Thera hung back, trying to make out words. It wasn't until the robust, older gentleman barked through his mous-tache. "Enough! The pair of you!" that she understood a sentence. The infestation of officers left the dungeon shortly after.

She'd loosened a bar on the corner window. A casual stack of boxes acted as a staircase. Voices sounded from the next cellar but the blunderbuss was back in place. Thera slipped into the undercroft. The drone of the jars was her only company.

She stripped off her good outfit. With the clothes stowed behind the crates, a sack over them, Thera crept across the stonework. She unhooked the padlock, slid the well-oiled bolt, and slipped into her confinement. She bolted and hooked the door behind her.

Thera did her best to suppress a loud burp as her food settled.

It sounded like whoever was in the next cellar would return shortly. Warren always wanted just one more word. A particular phrasing or threat that he thought might provoke a response. She'd managed to condition him to fear approaching the cage. Thus, he'd yet to discover its inactive state. He only expected responses if he brought her food. For that reason he kept up his starvation strategy. Thera ate well from his larder and the few kitchens she'd discovered around town that served something decent.

She donned the rags. Her least favourite part of this deception. The sticks she tucked into her straw bedding, his one concession. No sheets or blanket. A stolen, down quilt covered her illicit cot, upstairs, where she actually slept.

A striding of boots clacked into the room. She threw herself to the floor, pulled down her mask. She feigned an interrupted dragging towards her bed, radiating an idea of gaunt wretchedness.

Adelaide!

"You look like what you are," her love said. "A woeful creature that deserves its cage!"

Thera froze. She felt leaden, unable to think, like her mind and body were caught in thick mud. This was so unexpected. She had no idea what to say.

"My love," she whispered.

She had no strategy. No way of winning back the affections of this spiteful beauty. She noticed that one of her hands reached towards the bars. That flimsy wood was all that separated her from the woman who haunted her every waking moment.

"Don't you dare call me that!" Adelaide yelled, storming up to the cage. "What you did to me was, was not love! It was-"

"Wonderful."

"Repulsive! Not out of love. You deceived me so you could slaughter my friends."

"You are not wrong. But your friends were. You were all wrong to invade my woods. Your commander was driven by something I barely understand. Much as the example was necessary I do not blame you for bringing fear and misery to my village. You acted out of misguided nobility. That is why I fell in love with you. In spite of myself."

Adelaide stood, chest heaving in fury and confusion. Her face twisted into a contortion of empathy. "I am so sorry for what happened. Those fusiliers! But I ended them. For you. Murdering everyone in pointless revenge was not necessary!"

"You look only at the small picture. That single act. Not at the violence done to our carefully negotiated treaties and agreements. Destruction wrought by those who thought nothing bad could happen to them. Tell me, does Warren even realise all that blood is on his hands? Does he even care? Please try to understand. There is more going on than our lover's quarrel, or the death of a few villagers. If you ever had any feelings for me-"

"How can I feel anything for you? Snake! Wretch! Heathen thing of the woods! Take off that mask! Take it off that I might shit on you and make you eat it, if you're so hungry!"

"Such passion from a lady who feels nothing. Someone approaches. Perhaps they'll hold me down while you relieve yourself upon me."

More footsteps in military boots. It was Warren. He strode in looking particularly smug.

"Adelaide. Excellent. Yes. I find yelling at the thing does help to alleviate my annoyance."

"Forgive me, Commandant."

"No, no! Let your passions rage. It will help. I understand that you entertain no feelings for me. However, you do wish to rage at something. What angers you the most about this murderous thing? Relax. Allow your mind to fill with whatever might want to take hold of you."

Adelaide stared in confusion at her commandant, brow furrowed, her beautiful lips trembling. "That thing is... I cannot..."

Then Thera sensed it. A slight distortion in the regular pattern of the brickwork. A hint of something that might shimmer if only it possessed slightly more substance.

"At last! It's here!" she said.

Warren looked at her, amazed. "You truly can see it? It is like you! You and my unseen companion are the same. Yes. Look upon it and tremble! I have brought something to tear down your resistance! Something that will tell me how to break you!"

Therasia wove every one of her threads wide and all around. Then came the monumental effort of touching them all to the lightning. Immediately, the effort began to take its toll. She had trouble rising from the floor of her cage. None could complete the task she set for herself; so mighty was the effort required, so heavy the strife. Her destruction was inevitable. She began with no idea how she would finish.

"Ah. So. It came to watch me die," said Thera, thickly. "It tried to be cautious, to hang back, send only a tiny part of itself to observe the veracity of my impending demise. But my love, my Adelaide, you have tempted the creature from its prudence with your passion!"

"Your love?" said Warren aghast.

Adelaide seemed confused, as if she wanted to launch into demands for explanation. She tried to speak. "What are ... What..?" Her eyes shifted, focusing on something within. "I ... tell me ...what is inside me...?"

"You filthy woman!" said Warren. "To think I allowed myself to feel for you! It is your filth that feeds it! You will be the downfall of my enemy. You may give me that, at least, if you do not wish to give me your hand."

"Oh, she rejected you?" said Thera, breathing deeper at even this initial effort. "So, to cover your embarrassment, you will feed her to a creature from another dimension. Honestly. Men should not be in charge of anything. Far too emotional. Will you tell your friends that she agreed to an engagement once she is dead and unable to contradict you?"

"I have a ring that I will put on her bloody finger. You can watch. After my beast has broken you."

"Enough of that," said Thera, rising, dropping all pretence. She flicked a thread at Adelaide and allowed a tiny current to flow along that ionised path. The interloper flinched. It pulsed out of the woman and tried to retreat. Thera gasped at the unexpected effort. Digging deeper into herself than she had ever thought possible, Thera closed her net. She allowed more and more ionisation to develop along the strands of her threads. They contracted. Sure enough, the distortions trapped the thing, chasing it from the elsewhere.

Adelaide slumped to the floor with a cry. Immediately, she tried to slither away from the sensation of that grotesque, phantasmagoric touch. She hit a wall and hung there. "I can taste the inside of the sun!" she whispered in horror.

Thera reached, cracked apart the bars with her bare hands and slipped into the dungeon, lifting the stifling mask into the elsewhere. Warren squealed in high-pitched terror. "You! You are the fey?" He fumbled for his special sabre.

"That won't help you," said Thera. "I drained that little tube first. Fortunately, you have my cage newly connected to the household grid. And those jars as back up in case it fails. I will have enough lightning to finish."

"You will get no supper if you keep this up! Wait. You don't even look hungry. Are you not starved? Why are you not famished to weakness?"

"It's not you I wish to talk to, Jev Warren." Thera swayed on her feet, feeling the turbulent energies in the room, the wild dance of lightning and the creature that fought to escape. "What kind of name is Jev anyway? Did your parents choke on a glass of wine halfway through naming you?"

"Do not speak of my parents!" Warren raged. "Answer me, creature! You must ... must... I demand ... I ... oh stars, no!" His face shone with unexpected joy. "Oh, this... no. But I so want this...! The velvet ecstasy of ... deeeeeath!" His voice changed, body hunching as the thing inside curled away from Thera in fear. "Deeeeath! You live! You have become death! I could not prevent it."

"You brought me the lightning, foolish aspect of the beast. There was none in my village until you came."

"We brought you to the lightning. You... You wanted us to capture you! That was your plan all along!"

"Not all along. Only after I learned about your nature. Only after the village had nothing left to hold me."

Adel snatched the blunderbuss from the wall. "Stop this at once!" she yelled, mind still spinning.

"It's no use pointing that thing at me," said Thera, her voice labouring with effort. "I'm not the one possessing your boss."

Warren's face radiated such ecstatic delight that the sorrow of his own impending demise barely registered in his eyes. The interloper spoke again with no understanding of the concept of sorrow.

"You would kill us all!" said the interloper. "We shall abandon this sensation if it brings only pain! You have doomed your own kind to an eternity of suffering. Without you to keep the herd in check humanity will eat itself. You will be the last kin. Humans will no longer be able to resist the slow creep of the greedy few."

Thera closed her threads further. The monumental strain of maintaining even the lightest flow along so many paths brought her to her knees. Gasping in effort she glanced up from underneath a heavy brow. The thing stared at her from behind Warren's eyes, now beginning to weep blood. It reminded her of...

"You remind me of a young friend of mine from the village," she said, voice thick with growing agony. "Not yet human again but learning. She has choices ahead of her, needs guidance. Ah! That I cannot be there to see her mature to her true self!"

"I am not a child. I have consumed life in so many forms, feast and famine. I shall consume all of your kind! You cannot bring death to us all!"

"There are parts of the beast, like you, that are too hungry to care what they destroy. I will remove them. I am a surgeon. I know where to cut. This will bring pain. The other kinds will, ai!" Thera gasped a breath and it shivered out slowly. "We shall feed them even more love and wonder and dancing! The great beast will feel the loss of your kind. Like a person who has bitten their cheek. Search for the idea inside Warren. Go on. Their tongue will seek the injury purely to enjoy the extra sensation. We will train it as one might train a dog."

"You have not the strength to destroy me! Your mortal body will burn before it can sever me from the whole!"

"That is true." She shrank the net to inside the room. All of the beast was in here. It crowded every corner with distortion such that she could glimpse it with her human sight.

"What is that horror?" Adel cried, staring at the distorted, twisting sparks.

Thera's eyes lost focus. She felt her mind retreat from the pain. She swayed where she knelt. Talking kept her present. "I cannot destroy you, foul thing. But I do not work alone. There is another within me. That which you sought to destroy. Enough of its consciousness survives. It is willing to burn in my stead and has all of the beast at its call. Thus I can cut from your host the rot that you have become."

The thing inside Warren tried to take a step back but it had no concept of human motion. Like a toddler failing to walk it flopped to the ground.

With one final scream of resolution Therasia tapped into the house grid and sent the full flow of current along her threads, closing them completely. She burned. The cellar lit up with sparks that glittered around the interloper's true form, a horror writhing as it dissipated. A loud CRACK. The lights dimmed.

The shock flung Thera, Adelaide and Warren back, slamming them into the walls. Warren lay dead and broken. Lights danced across Thera's vision. Adelaide, already cowering against the wall, was least affected. She recovered, flailing for the blunderbuss and failing to find it. Instead she snatched up Warren's sabre. The soldier crawled up the wall, gaining her feet. She staggered over and loomed above the fey-kin. Thera gasped and floundered.

"What was that twisted shape in the air?" the soldier demanded, voice hollow with witnessed horror. "What manner of creature? By all the stars, tell me, what are these images in my mind? There was something inside me! I could feel every detail of the world. I felt the nightmares of people who live on another continent. Speak! Speak or I will run you through where you lie!"

Thera tried to rise. Blackness closed in. She could barely feel the point of the sword over her heart. As she slid into the dark she whispered, "I am entirely at your mercy."

17

Stars Burn The End

Aspirant-Chef Nicole d'Avinhon waited until the guard formed up outside her palanquin.

"Send the cook," he'd said. Well enough. If you wanted to promote someone, and insult them at the same time, it might well prove an effective strategy. She remembered the small den with its high-backed chairs, wood-panelled walls, all wreathed in smoke, stinking of alcohol and farts. The Officer's Club at the barracks. She had to sit patiently, waiting for them to reach their decision about Adelaide. Then that pompous Craon said, "Send the cook." A surprising person to support Adelaide's advancement. The rest laughed at the idea while she sat and smiled politely. They agreed to the promotion. She had the letter in a scroll case beside her.

The soldiers took their sweet time getting into place. After a cooler spell the day warmed strongly. Nicole thrived in the heat. Even so, her dress uniform required the top-coat. Warren allowed her to order set after set of uniforms, all at his expense. He assumed it was vanity. Partly, but she did enjoy that, today, her shirt was merely sleeves and a collar attached to her waistcoat. That reduced a layer under the long, formal jacket.

She checked her pistol. Nothing in the first barrel. A safety precaution followed by most soldier's in the city. That slipped into a special pouch on the right with extra powder and shot, in little paper twists, and a spare sparker on the other. She adjusted the hanger on her sabre and exited the palanquin in annoyance. The guards were still milled about, sorting themselves into a line. She allowed them to finish. This was going to be her first official duty out from under Warren's shadow as his ordonnance. His personal assistant. The woman who did most of the actual work. And they called her "The Cook." Huh.

Oh. The scroll case.

She waited until the guards settled themselves. Deliberately she reached back into the palanquin to collect it, as if she'd meant that all along. Four men to carry and a runner with a red flag to clear the way and make a fuss. Reminding people of the military's presence in the city was part of their duty. She'd specified a female runner. They'd supplied a young fantassin with a good set of lungs. The girl had stripped her jacket for the short jog across town. Now the collar sat crocked at the back.

"Emmelot. Avec moi," she said. "The rest of you may relax. Find some shade. Get out of this heat."

"Thank you, Lieutenant," said the caporal.

The carriers seemed surprised at this directive. Warren was much stricter. She did not feel the need to exercise her dominance at every available opportunity. She was more subtle, like selecting the only woman in the group to accompany her upstairs.

"Lelaing's father had a good eye for a seat," she commented to Emmelot as they approached the door.

"Aye, Lieutenant. I particularly like the curly bits around the windows. And a nice view of the western orchards."

"Indeed. I was thinking more of the solid support pillars and well-keyed arches. This would be hard to fell with a six-cannon. Only four stories tall. More stable than some of the new, taller ones that threaten the church steeples. You were in the Company under Warren, if I recall?"

"Aye, Lieutenant. Lelaing is the reason I'm alive. She sent me and Yvette running to Boussens with them dispatches. Day of. Ain't sad to have missed that fight."

"No. Me neither."

The building's concierge stood at the top of the steps to greet them. "Might I enquire as to your business such that I may facilitate-"

"We are here to visit the Lelaing residence," Nicole said. People who borrowed importance from their betters tended to give themselves unnecessary airs and graces. Something she always tried to avoid. "My calling card."

"Thank you, Chef."

At least the man could recognise a military rank. He bowed and gestured them inside, indicating a broad sofa with a serving table where they might wait. He snapped his fingers. A boy, clean and eager, ran over with a silver platter.

The card went on the platter. The boy went up the service stairs.

The lobby was grand and decorated well. There was a rustic theme which suited a farming family like the Lelaings. Sad, what happened to her parents but Adelaide never fussed over it and worked well at her business.

A footman served cubes of flavoured jellies dusted in powdered sugar. The tray also contained pâté on sweet biscuits, glasses of infused water, and napkins. A very prestigious building to serve even its visitors such delicacies. Nicole nodded to the fantassin. The girl carefully took one of the jellies and popped it whole into her mouth. Her eyes lit up. She settled into the sofa with a happy little smile before she remembered her place and sat upright, at attention.

"Your first time with fruit delights?" Nicole inquired.

"Sorry, Lieutenant. They's delicious. Well, to me. I'm sure you's sampled them many a time, being under the commandant. He were well rich, weren't he?"

"Indeed." Nicole smiled. "Well rich." She straightened the fantassin's collar.

"What's happenin' with all that money? Now he's dead and ain't got no heirs?"

"There will be a variety of claims upon it. No one has, as yet, discovered a formal will. It is a shame Lelaing didn't accept his marriage proposal or she'd have a claim on it as well."

"If it's anything like that villa outside Foix, near where I grew up, the servants have made off with half the silverware and loose coin already."

"Not if it was under my supervision! However, I was removed rather unceremoniously from my position there. He has few surviving relatives. I suspect the lawyers will spend years arguing over how to carve it up. Those legal vultures will make more money out of it than- Oh now, what is all this?"

The boy hurried back down and spoke urgently to the concierge, who peered up the stairs in distress. Nicole rose.

"A problem, Monsieur?"

"Ah. No answer though the lady has not departed, as far as I am aware, and the boy... There may have been raised voices."

"Has she received any visitors this-?" Nicole glanced up the stairs. A horrible idea cut into her mind. "Emmelot! Haste! Up and break down the door!" The fantassin looked at her in confusion. Nicole had to physically haul the girl from the sofa. "Up! Up! Boy! Show her the door!"

The bellhop ran off. Emmelot started after him slowly then accelerated in confusion as Nicole ran right behind. Her old legs were not going to manage the stairs. Indeed, she had to catch her breath on the third landing along with the concerned concierge. Emmelot knocked loudly on the door above. The boy joined in. Mostly from excitement. When Nicole arrived she turned the handle and shouldered her way straight through. The double-doors were not bolted top or bottom. The lady was expecting company. Only the centre-lock held the doors together. That parted with a single crack and both portals swung wide.

The interior was rich with colours and textures. The walls of the generous reception hall were half-panelled. This allowed a display of some excellent artworks against wine-red, patterned wallpaper. A crash sounded above. Two floors to this corner apartment. An excellent seat, indeed.

"Stairs," she demanded of the concierge who should know the layout of the apartments he serviced.

"Through the cloak," he replied. "Right in the dining room, into the hall. You can't miss them."

Nicole pulled her pistol and hurried through the cloak-room with it's customary hatch. She had an instinct to leave her coat but ignored it. The dining table was unmounted. It rested on one edge against the wall, under a sheet. Ten legs sat stacked beside with chairs backed against the wall, as if the large room was to be used for a private dance. She turned right and exited through a door of glass panels.

The broad stairs climbed at the far end of the passage, again to the right. Nicole hurried along past the drawing room, library and snug.

Up, she climbed, her legs burning with the effort. She drank the air in large draughts. Emmelot was at her heels, bayonet out, the fantassin's only weapon while in the city. Nicole used her hand to heave herself up by the railing for the last flight. On the landing she was confronted with a corridor down to her left with double-doors at the end. Presumably the lounge sat over the dining room.

She paused, feigning caution. Her vision swam back into focus.

An angry voice boomed, shaking the doors, the whole building. "Where is my sister?"

Nicole still felt light-headed. This was too much effort at her age. She was over forty. Older than either of her parents ever reached. Well out of the habit of exercise. Now there was a sister? She edged down the corridor towards the voice. A crash sounded from beyond the door.

"We found nothing in the fire!" That was Adelaide's voice. She was yet living. "No remains! If she wasn't in the cellar, then I don't know what happened to her!"

"Our deaths do not vanish us!"

"Then perhaps she is not dead!"

Nicole burst through the door. The drawing room contained an inordinate scene. The well-appointed, tastefully-decorated space endured complete disarray. Chairs lay overturned, a tea service shattered and scattered across the floor, papers strewn.

Dominating the centre of the room stood a hunched and furious figure. It wore a mask of leaves over its face. Its hands clutched two wooden stakes, body covered in brambles and thorns. Lelaing crouched, pressed against the wood-panelling on one wall. She'd ripped a light-fixture from the surface and waved the end about on what little cord she'd managed to pull through the hole. Clever in her desperation. These things hated the lightning.

Nicole didn't hesitate. She raised her pistol and fired.

Click.

Of course, the first barrel was empty.

The creature snarled at her. The eyes behind that mask bore into Nicole's soul. It leaned towards her, stakes rising. This was death, imminent and inevitable.

Emmelot screamed in desperation and charged at the thing. Nicole reached for the poor girl. No need for someone so young to throw her life away. She failed to grip the fantassin, fumbled the next barrel around.

"Wait!" Lelaing yelled as the creature caught Emmelot's dagger hand. Its other hand grabbed the fantassin by the throat and lifted her off the floor, held close like a shield. Where did the stakes vanish to? Were they just an extension of the thorns? The creature was still tall enough to peer over Emmelot's shoulder. Nicole tried to shift position for a cleaner shot. The creature stepped around and kept the girl dangling as a barrier.

Nicole was tempted to fire anyway and stars burn the end. One should take any chance to rid the world of such a horror.

"Wait," said Lelaing in a calming tone. "All of you. Nicole. Please." She let go of the light fixture and stepped away from the wall, hands outstretched, imploring sanity. The creature did not seem to be in the mood. "Oh, spirit of the woods," said Lelaing. "Kindly One-"

The creature laughed, a rich, throaty sound of grim humour. "We are not kind."

"I am well aware. I bear scars from two encounters." This seemed to pique the creature's interest. "I do not know what happened to your sister but I know that Warren, her captor, is dead. He was trying to provoke her, prodding through the bars of the cage with his sabre." The thing growled at the idea. An actual growl. The reverberations echoed the corners of the room. "And! And... It shorted. The whole thing. He had the cage plugged into the house grid. The whole thing blew, a deafening crack, sparks, sparks everywhere. They set fire to the bedding, then the cage itself. Warren died on the spot. The shock threw me back across the room. By the time I recovered my senses the cage lay broken open. I swear, your sister, the one in the cage, it was gone. She! She was gone!" Lelaing took half a step forward. "I swear by my life."

"My sister would take your life! You put her in lightning! If she lived, she would pull your head off on her way out and feed on your lying tongue!"

"And, with anyone else, that might be true. But I fought that sister of yours. Twice. And managed to fend it off both times. Her. Fend her off. I think she showed me a hint of respect by sparing my life. Or she was too exhausted after her confinement."

"There was fire. Why is the house still standing?"

"It's stone, brick, a properly-designed, new house. We formed a bucket chain. People ran pails of water down into the cellar very quickly, running back and forth. Ask Nicole. She was there. One poor servant-girl fainted from the effort. I had to carry her outside to catch some air. If your sister escaped she is likely still on the other side of the river. Warren starved her. She would need to build up her strength before undertaking a journey."

The creature's head wandered about with indecision. It spat, "Bah!" and threw Emmelot into Nicole. Nicole did her best to catch the fantassin but they both sprawled to the floor.

The thing took one step and was somehow at the open window that led onto the balcony. The lace, inner curtains billowed around it as it turned. "I hunt my sister. I find her not, your life is forfeit."

Nicole fired but the creature saw the pistol aiming and ... something. It seemed to move. But so fast! The bullet flew out the open fenestration and into the city. Nicole hoped it would not strike some poor soul as it fell. More likely to strike a hapless tree in the orchard opposite.

"Have a care!" said Lelaing. She kept looking around the room as if it were not over. "Those things have a trick of slipping up unnoticed and stabbing you in the back!"

A scream sounded from somewhere. Nicole flicked around to the last barrel on her pistol and tried to get to her feet. Emmelot hindered more than she helped.

"Maisy?" Lelaing called.

"Where did that come from?" Nicole demanded.

"The servants' corridor," said Lelaing. "The concealed door, there."

"Where?"

"Ah, yes. It is concealed. Wait a moment." Lelaing hurried over to a wall display and hefted down a fine-looking, two-handed malchus. Once armed, she made her way to a section in the wood-lined wall. Sure enough, Nicole spotted a gap in the panels and a small handle. Emmelot raised her bayonet, rushed past and shoved the door open in her eagerness.

"Wait!" Nicole called. She glimpsed a figure huddled against the wall. "Get out of the way!"

Lelaing gently moved the gun to one side. "That's my new maid," she said. "Are you alright, Maisy?"

"Oh, a terrible thing it was. Slipped under the door like it was made of smoke, then rushed down the stair. Oh, it did give me a start. It left this behind on the boards. Look, Addie."

Adelaide spoke kindly. "You should address me as Mam'selle when we have company, my dear."

"Sorry, m'm."

Emmelot stepped into the servants' passage. Nicole tried to see past her. The corridor was clean. White walls with plain floorboards and a skirting of well-scrubbed wood. This was, indeed, a residence of surpassing accommodations to have its own passages for servants.

"Oh Chef, you must come and look at this!" said Emmelot, crouching to peer at some mark on the floor. A line of dirt. Strange. Perhaps the fey had to carry soil from their homeland.

Nicole stepped into the white corridor. "It came this way?"

"I told you they were tricky," said Lelaing. "It made us think it dove out the window but then snuck down the stairs. Their powers are not so grand as they'd have us believe."

"Oh, look at that!" said Emmelot in amazement, bent over the line of dirt. "Can you see it, Chef?"

Nicole let out a slight grunt of resignation. She made the effort to bend her knees all the way into a crouch, then knelt to peer closely at the fey's droppings. It was about a hand-span in length and a finger wide.

"Look closely," said the maid. "Can you see it? Examine each grain of dirt in detail. Notice the individual shape, size, variation in shade. Then move on to the next piece. You must look at each and every particle with great scrutiny. Do not miss a single one. Give each speck your entire time and devotion."

Nicole could not move. She knelt with one hand on the floor, staring at dirt. Such individually fascinating grains. She tried shifting her hand. The idea melted into her fascination with the tiny variations in the streak of soil.

"I have her," said the maid. "Thank you, Emmie. You can step out."

"Them brambles of yours done scratched up the front of my uniform," said the fantassin.

"I apologise," replied the maid, crouching down to Nicole's right. "It's a new look I'm trying. I will have better control of the thorns, eventually. I should be able to grow berries at will if I need a snack. You did very well, getting up here."

"Ain't hard being the only one available for duty as a runner. It's a shit job nobody wants on a hot day. I didn't even have to do that thing of offering to take the scroll-case, like what you said. She brought me right up. Never a look at the men."

"Might she be sympathetic to our cause?"

"Oh, fuck no!"

"Definitely not," said Lelaing. "She hates the fey with a passion that borders on fanaticism. Her husband, also. She shares that with Warren, at least."

Was the lady of the house involved in this somehow? Nicole realised that the maid was in league with the horrors they'd encountered. She forced herself to speak with great effort. "You ... have bewitched ... Lelaing!"

"Oh no," the maid answered. "Quite the other way around I assure you."

"Stop that," said Lelaing, embarrassed. "Ai, this mess you've made on my floor. Everything turned over."

"You said you didn't like that tea service!" said the witch maid.

"It's not just the cursed tableware, it's..."

The maid stood. Nicole could not see her face but heard the emotion in her voice.

"You helped turn the place over. You are also responsible for this mess."

Lelaing snorted, upset herself. "Fine! I understand this ... arrangement with you will require some upheaval. But if you think for a moment you can appease me with this pro-motion you wrangled-"

"Wrangled! That is very unfair! Everyone I found, every mind I contacted when I walked into that building, they all felt your competence, your suitability for an officer's commission! The only opposition was from people, men, who felt threatened by it. You deserve this."

"And what do you think you deserve? To weasel your way into my life, into my trust? I should never have carried you out of that fire. I cannot allow you to treat all the suffering your slaughter caused with such a cavalier manner! I had to visit each of the families of those soldiers."

"I have attended funerals, too, for people most dear to my heart. You are now the most important thing in my heart. I will bend to your will as much as I can but I am a creature of blood and vengeance."

"I do not wish for any more blood. Our cause cannot be about slaughter."

"I am a hunter. I am not kind to my prey but I do not slaughter. I do not kill on a whim. Ai! You're as bad as my father!"

"Oh, that's what a girl likes to hear."

"Hey, ladies," said Emmelot. "We's doin' a thing here. So, for a whiles, could you just kiss and make up?"

"Do not speak of such things," said Lelaing.

"I thought you liked the kissing?" said Maisy. The servant spoke with a casual salaciousness that might have shocked Nicole had she not just noticed something that might be a grain of sand among the streak of soil. So fascinating!

"Don't! Not in front of ... other people."

"You ain't gotta worry about me," said Emmelot. "I've been snogging girls since I was twelve."

"That's not what I mean!" said Lelaing.

"Aiya. Look," said Emmelot. "You two got issues what needs sorting out but not when you done hypnotised an aspirant-chef in the servant's passage."

"Oh don't worry about her," said Maisy. "She won't remember any of this conversation."

Lelaing sighed and turned away, crunching some piece of crockery under her boot. She kicked it in frustration. "This is such a mess!"

"What do you want me to do about it? I'm not your servant."

Lelaing suddenly laughed, a release of tension. "Yes you are, my dear."

"Yep," agreed Emmelot.

"Oh shush, the pair of you. I'm busy here. Close the door. The less distraction she has the better."

The concealed door swung closed. Nicole was alone with the maid, who crouched beside her. Captivated entirely by the pale speck among the darker motes Nicole almost didn't register that the maid asked her a question.

"Do you recognise me?"

"Recognise..." White. Everything was clean, bright. Light entered through narrow windows facing the courtyard. Nicole still couldn't look away from the line of soil. Her peripheral vision registered the face crouching beside her. "O! You are La Granger's daughter!"

"Ah. That's what I look like in your mind. There. That shape is gone from you. You are aware of me but, like most servants, I am not worth noting. You will never register my face, or anything about me, in any meaningful way. It's like there is a maze between me and your understanding. A maze reinforced by my name."

"...but you are... ...you... ...who are you...?"

"So sorry for the extraordinary level of deception. We anticipated one of the male officers. I wanted to create a plausible scenario whereby my love, Lelaing, could relate the story of the fire. I could then sample the person's mind as it was told. The more heightened the emotion, the deeper I can dig and exonerate any personal doubts you had. Is there anything about her story you do doubt?"

"The fire," Nicole blurted. She could not help herself. "I was there. There was no bucket line. Just individual servants running about. The fire was well advanced. It burned crates. Clothing. Why was there clothing?"

"The fire was well ablaze. You were lucky to catch it in time. The servants had it under control in due course. They could have been quicker, in your opinion. You lost some old storage crates with strange odds and ends in them. The response was fast enough to save the house."

"...yes.." said Nicole. "And she fought off a fey again! With a light socket! Oh, that thing was horrific! A plague on all those warped, evil, twisted things!"

"It was looking for its sister. It was reasonable to question those who visited the cage. It was kind enough to let you live. That is why the survivors of such encounters call those creature the Kindly Ones."

"...yes..." said Nicole.

"Now. What is something that makes you feel an affinity for Adelaide?"

"A dearth of respect. I am more than just a cook. She is more than just a collection of pleasingly arranged features. We are both leaders, capable people..."

The white walls vanished in a blaze of pure light. The dark streak on the floor became her only anchor in the stark emptiness.

Her shoulder hit a wall.

"Oh, ma'am. Are you feeling alright?" asked the maid.

"I... Sorry. A bit light headed. All these exertions."

"Mam'selle!" the maid called. "Mam'selle Adel!"

The door opened and there was such a rush of air and dark shapes after the light, clean corridor. Nicole tried to reach her feet but her head span. How long was she in here? She could not remember any of it. Emmelot and the maid helped her to a seat, a padded armchair of an excellent brocade. It was so embarrassing to be such a victim of her age.

The maid leaned over her. "You should allow yourself some rest before-"

"That's fine, Maisy," said Lelaing. "You're not a surgeon, you know. Forgive my servant. A distant cousin from a small town near Lorda. The family asked me to look after her while she was in the city. I have temporarily employed her as my maid. She's an excellent cook, though she does not seem to understand her other duties very well. Especially when I have company."

"Forgive me Mam'selle," said the maid. "Still a bit in shock at seeing that thing." She stepped back and Nicole dismissed the servant from her mind. Lelaing was far more interesting and someone with whom she had much in common.

"Do you have a lot of company?" Nicole asked.

"I find time to connect to old friends and make new ones," said Lelaing. "I recently met a fascinating surgeon with rooms on the Rue de la Bourse. Fortino d'Peillon. A recommendation from a friend for looking after my arm as it recovers. He trained with the Mountain Monks. Like La Granger's daughter."

"The daughter. I think I might have met the girl. I do not recall."

Nicole recovered her composure. The chair was very comfortable. The maid offered her a drink. Some iced juice in a tall glass. It was superbly refreshing on a warm day such as this and had a beautiful, creamy texture. An old, family recipe. She couldn't quite remember whose family.

"Now," said Lelaing. "Was there something you came here to do?"

"Indeed! Emmelot. The scroll-case."

"Forgive me, Lieutenant, but you left it down stairs. Rushed up here to fight that faery, we did. I'll run down and grab it."

Chatting with Lelaing was so pleasant. Nicole found herself wishing she was not just here to execute her duties. For some reason the details of the conversation eluded her. It felt as though Emmelot took no time to return.

She handed over the official confirmation of Lelaing's promotion. Much to her surprise Lelaing handed her a small, metal-bound lock-box. It was singularly heavy. Inside was the required payment. In gold livres. All of it.

"Where on earth did you come upon such a sum in coin?" Nicole asked.

"There were a few strongboxes scattered about Warr-Ah, my father's residence. Here. For paying bills and the like. I only just discovered it this one. It held a sizeable amount of gold coins. I thought it best if the bulk of them were given over to the army."

"I would feel uncomfortable carrying such a large sum on my person."

"Just tell everyone that it's a thank-you gift in a nice box. A small bottle of my family's brandy. Until you get to the cashier's office in the barracks."

"Very well. I regret that I must bid you good day." She rose, though she was stiff after all the sudden activity. "Oh, my legs. So sorry. I have forgone all custom of exercises and it has caught up with me today."

They made their way down the corridor and back down the stairs.

"You must come here and train," Lelaing offered. "Once my arm has had a few weeks to recover I shall plot a regular schedule to recover my vigour. Maisy is excellent with matters martial. We could do with the company."

"Sounds wonderful. Here. Take my card. I do look forward to including you in my circle of friends."

They parted with pleasantries. Nicole made her way back down the several flights of stairs. Emmelot bounced at her heels.

Outside the sun warmed the streets. The trees in the orchard wafted fragrance over their walls. People strode about in their colourful, summer best. It was such a lovely day in the city.

18

Epilogue: Timeless

A woman leaned on the balcony rail of her high apartment. She looked out over the dusk-obscured, quickened city. The streets were lit by specks of electric blue and fire yellow. Flower boxes in full bloom, tied to the bottom of the railings, masked much of the smell that drifted up from the densely packed business below. A friend brought two glasses of wine. Her bare feet pattered on stone still warm from the blazing heat of a summer's day. She tucked in next to her companion, shoulder to shoulder. They leaned and sipped, and chatted idly about things of monumental importance. They held the fate of the world in their hands like they held their glasses of wine. Precariously, over a great, yawning depth, with no intention of letting them fall.

18

Epilogue: Timeless

David Dawkins was born in the outer suburbs of Sydney, Australia. When he was eight, Dave swapped the suburban scrub-land for the rolling hills of Somerset, England, and became surrounded by the myths and legends of the West Country.

Working mainly as an actor and director Dave has also published half a dozen short stories over the years under the nom de plume D. Harrigon. He has lived in the UK, China and America, travelling the world at every opportunity.

His acting work has engaged with everything from Shakespearean companies, through circus performers, to opera, including working as production assistant for the Women of Asia Theatre Company and movement director for Ragbone Theatre.

The pandemic sent him from London back to Australia, where he currently resides, walking the many trails of the Tasmanian wilderness in his spare time.